The Edelweiss Sisters

BOOKS BY KATE HEWITT

A Mother's Goodbye
Secrets We Keep
Not My Daughter
No Time to Say Goodbye
A Hope for Emily
Into the Darkest Day
When You Were Mine
The Girl from Berlin

The Far Horizons Trilogy
The Heart Goes On
Her Rebel Heart
This Fragile Heart

The Amherst Island Trilogy
The Orphan's Island
Dreams of the Island
Return to the Island

KATE HEWITT

The Edelweiss Sisters

bookouture

Published by Bookouture in 2021

An imprint of Storyfire Ltd.
Carmelite House
50 Victoria Embankment
London EC4Y 0DZ

www.bookouture.com

ISBN: 978-1-80019-300-0
eBook ISBN: 978-1-80019-299-7

Dedicated to Isobel, for dreaming of *The Edelweiss Sisters* first. It's been an amazing year. Thank you for working with me on so many books!

PROLOGUE

Salzburg, Austria, 1945

Spring is bursting like a song through the city, a symphony of beauty and renewal amidst the devastation wreaked by war. In Mirabellgarten, outside the magnificent palace, the flowerbeds are a riot of daisies and wallflowers, pansies and forget-me-nots.

The magnolia trees in Marktplatz Square froth with silken-petaled flowers, and the Salzach River, flowing down from the snow-capped Kitzbühel Alps through meadows studded with the white stars of narcissi, burbles joyfully through the city. The river's blue-green waters are untroubled by the broken bridges that gape above it, shattered reminders of the Allied bombs that destroyed them along with the dome of the cathedral, yet thankfully left much else unscathed.

High above the city, by the ancient ochre buildings of Nonnberg Abbey, a woman skulks in the shadows as the dawn sun creeps over the blue-misted mountains of the Salzkammergut and spreads long, golden fingers of buttery light over the indigo peaks that ring Salzburg like a giant's jagged crown. In her arms a baby stirs and lets out a small, mewling cry, the sound far too weak for a hungry infant.

She draws the blanket up around the child's face, rocking her as she whispers for her to hush. It has taken her nearly a week to arrive at this point, and she is filthy, exhausted, and starving. It would have been far easier to give the child to the relevant authorities that now swarm the cities and towns from here to Hamburg, officious and efficient, or even to leave the creature where it had been born mere weeks ago, in pain and suffering, into a world that seems broken beyond repair.

But she made a promise, and so she is here, her body bruised and aching, her arms cradling this scrap of humanity that has somehow, impossibly, managed to survive.

High above, the clock in the baroque dome that crowns the abbey begins to chime six o'clock. Soon the nuns will be assembling for prime, their voices rising as one as they recite the ancient words in a ritual that has remained unchanged by time, by war.

The baby cries again, and the woman knows she can wait no longer. As reluctantly as she accepted this burden, she is now loath to let it go. This tiny child is the only thing that anchors her to another human being, to a reality other than wandering the world, one of the many lost to war—homeless, nameless, alone.

She cradles the infant to her chest as she remembers the child's mother's fingers clasped in her own, cold and bony, ragged nails digging into skin, eyes lit with the dregs of her strength as it seeped away into the dirty straw.

"*Please… promise me… for the sake of my child…*"

What else could she have done but given her vow?

"*There is a clockmaker on Getreidegasse… a painted sign above it with a sprig of edelweiss… take the baby there… but if no one is there, then take it to the abbey. The nuns are kind there. They will know what to do. Swear to me…*"

And so here she is, with this tiny bundle, who nobody still living wants, clutched in her arms. She went to the shop on Getreidegasse, and it was boarded shut. So she came here, up to the abbey, to give them her offering. There is no way she can provide for the child; she must leave her here. The last chime of the clock fades into the dawn silence, a remnant of the echo reverberating through the narrow courtyard as shreds of mist begin to evaporate under the rising sun. Steeling herself, the woman moves forward, the baby cradled in one arm, an old crate held in the other. She found the crate outside a grocer's in a fetid alleyway off Kaigasse, its damp, half-rotten slats as humble a crib as that for the holy child to whom the nuns raise their voices.

She puts the crate on the doorstep of the abbey, and then gently places the baby inside, tucking the dirty blanket, given to her by a Red Cross worker in Munich, carefully around her tiny, wizened face. She tucks the little knitted flower, the edelweiss, into the blanket; the baby's mother gave it to her, a keepsake she'd managed to hold on to. Perhaps the nuns will know and understand.

She stoops to kiss the baby's pale cheek before she lifts the heavy door knocker and lets it fall once, twice, three times, each reverberation in time to the thud of her heart.

She hears footsteps, quiet and unhurried on the ancient stones, and she retreats to the shadows, hiding behind a pillar, daring to peek around it because she must see this through.

The door opens with a long, protesting creak and a nun steps out, glancing around in untroubled curiosity before, with a start, she notices the crate at her feet. She is young, this nun; her face is a smooth, placid oval underneath her white wimple, and her body is slender, as are the hands that reach for the crate. A look of wonder flashes across her face as she takes the baby into her arms.

The woman watches as the nun cradles the baby against her body; despite her vocation she seems to know how to hold a child, drawing it instinctively towards her, one hand caressing the tiny, fragile head. A smile curves her lips as tenderness suffuses her face.

It is enough. She has made good on her promise; there is nothing more for her here. Silently, her heart and body both aching, the woman slips away as the sun rises high above the city, filling it with its light.

CHAPTER ONE

Salzburg, 1934

Music rose from the tall, narrow house on Getreidegasse, joyous tendrils of sound winding their way through the dim and crowded shop on the first floor, with its glass cabinets of marble mantel clocks. A majestic grandfather clock presided over the premises, along with an intricately carved cuckoo clock, made by the great Johann Baptist Beha, that had chimed every quarter hour for nearly a hundred years.

The music rose up the narrow flight of stairs to the front sitting room with its worn velveteen sofas crowned with hand-stitched antimacassars, the heavy wooden tables and chairs, a mahogany cabinet dark with age—all of it brought from a timbered farmhouse in the Tyrol—and then back to the kitchen, with its square wooden table and blackened range.

Up another flight to the main bedrooms and then further still to the second floor, with its small attic rooms, their small windows overlooking the onion domes of Salzburg Cathedral, the ever-present Alps an indigo fringe beyond.

Music filled every room as three voices joined in sweet melody, alto, soprano and second soprano, the different harmonies mingling together in the popular folk song "Die Lorelei":

"I do not know what it means, to feel so sad;
there is a tale from olden times I cannot get out of my mind.
The air is cool, and twilights falls…"

Then, suddenly, silence.

"Birgit, I think you've gone flat," Lotte said with a kindly laugh, shaking back her blond hair, a shower of wheat-gold about her shoulders. "Or was it me?" She laughed again, smiling at both her sisters with easy joy. "Let's try again."

"There's no time." Birgit turned away quickly, hiding her expression from her younger sister's laughing eyes. "Father's waiting," she added and hurried from the back room of the shop where they'd been practicing to give their father peace from their racket; he had suffered from severe headaches ever since he'd been hit by a Romanian shell in the Battle of Orsova nearly twenty years earlier.

"Birgit…" Lotte began, her voice filling with dismay as she flung one hand out to stay her sister, and the oldest, Johanna, shook her head.

"Let her be. You know how she gets. I'm going to change my apron." Briskly she followed Birgit out of the room and upstairs to the family's living quarters; with a little sigh Lotte followed too, restarting the melody as she mounted the stairs, although this time her sisters did not join her.

Up in the kitchen their mother, Hedwig Eder, was fussing with the cakes she'd made in celebration of the day, her apron tied over her best dress, usually kept for Sundays. Although she had lived in the city for twenty-three years, she had never gone to any of the events of the Salzburg Festival before, save for the free performance of *Jedermann* in the cathedral square that even the peasants came down from the mountains for.

The festival proper was reserved for the wealthy holidaymakers and day trippers who came from as far as Vienna, Berlin, or even further abroad—sophisticated people with sleek motor cars, arch voices, and a sly, knowing manner, or at least they seemed that way to Hedwig. *The elegants,* Salzburgers called them, with either awe or scorn, or perhaps both.

Her husband Manfred appeared in the doorway of the kitchen; like her he was wearing his Sunday clothes, a suit of well-worn wool tweed, smiling at the sight of the sugar-dusted cakes filled with cream and piled neatly on a plate.

"Ah, *Prügeltorte*," he exclaimed in pleasure. "My favorite." He came over to plant a kiss on her cheek; embarrassed, Hedwig twitched away.

"I think I saw a mouse," she told him as she clapped a net dome over the cakes. "We'll have to get the man in again."

He regarded her tenderly for a moment as she bustled around the kitchen, moving the kettle here or a plate there, not meeting his gaze. "Hedwig, there is no mouse," he finally said, his tone gentle.

She shrugged. "I thought I saw something."

Smiling, Manfred put an arm around her waist. "You're nervous."

"Why should I be nervous? I'm not the one singing."

"Even so."

She moved away from him, as she always did, even though she loved him, because his easy affection so often felt beyond her.

"They will be fine," Manfred told her as she continued to bustle around the kitchen. "It is more for the experience than the winning. Besides, it is not as if they will be on stage at the Festspielhaus—they are merely taking part in a competition for amateurs, at a restaurant, no less. Let us enjoy the day."

Hedwig did not reply, because she knew she would not enjoy the day, although she would try. Still, she managed to give her husband a distracted smile, knowing *he* would certainly enjoy it, before she went to the small, cracked mirror by the door and tidied her hair. She might be a simple farmer's daughter, but she would always keep herself neat.

"And here they are!" Manfred announced, beaming as Lotte came into the kitchen with a laughing twirl, followed by Johanna, as brisk as ever, and Birgit, who was trying not to look anxious. They wore full-skirted dirndls with checked aprons; Lotte had laughed that they looked like milkmaids, but as the competition was sponsored by the Association of Austrian National Costumes, the clothes, made with loving determination by Hedwig, seemed more than appropriate.

It had been Lotte's music teacher who had arranged their entry into the competition. Manfred and Hedwig's youngest daughter had been blessed thrice over—of the three Eder girls, she was tacitly acknowledged as the prettiest, the most charming, and the most musical.

Some years ago Manfred and Hedwig had decided she should have singing lessons, something that had not been thought of for either Johanna or Birgit, for there was not really the money. Lotte, however, had such a love of music that to deny their little lark lessons had seemed, to Manfred at least, almost cruel. Hedwig, who managed the household purse strings, had agreed more reluctantly, but nevertheless the silver groschen and gold schillings had gone into the battered tin on the shelf above the range, day by day and week by week.

When the teacher, Herr Gruber, had suggested Lotte sing at one of the competitions for amateurs that ran alongside the famous music festival, Lotte had insisted she not sing alone, but rather with her sisters. They could form a trio; they had sometimes sung in three parts in the evenings, with Lotte's high soprano soaring above her sisters' more cautious voices, although they'd never done such a thing in public.

Herr Gruber had agreed to the trio and duly entered them into a competition for folk singing. Lotte had buoyed her sisters along with her enthusiasm, determined they would all share in this marvelous experience together, because she had never craved the spotlight, even though she seemed as if she were born for it.

"Are we ready?" Manfred asked as Lotte tied a scarf over her golden hair and Birgit fussed with her apron. His daughters, he reflected, were all alike in their blond, blue-eyed looks, and yet they were as different as three people could possibly be: Johanna, so much like his Hedwig, with her strong-boned face and briskly capable manner; Lotte, so playful and pretty and light; and Birgit, sandwiched in the middle, quiet and shy, a bit clumsy, still struggling to find her place in the world.

"How do we look, Papa?" Lotte asked as she twirled again in her skirt.

"Like the most beautiful girls in all of Salzburg. But wait." From his pocket he took the three sprigs of edelweiss he had picked only that morning, on his walk up the Monschsberg. He'd been surprised to find it, growing determinedly from an outcropping of limestone high above the city.

"Edelweiss!" Johanna exclaimed. "Where did you find it?"

"Growing where it always does, on the mountains," Manfred replied with a smile. Carefully he tucked a sprig of the flower with its yellow clustered heads and velvety white leaves into each of the necklines of his daughters' dresses. "Now you are not the Eder Sisters, but the Edelweiss Sisters! Soon to be a sensation."

"What nonsense," Hedwig muttered, but she was smiling, and Lotte laughed, the sound as clear as a crystal bell.

"The Edelweiss Sisters!" Lotte exclaimed. "Yes, indeed."

"We'll be late," Birgit said, and Johanna clucked in impatience.

"Then let us be off." Manfred clapped his hands lightly and they left the kitchen, heading down the stairs and out into the busy street, a steady stream of festivalgoers heading towards the Festspielhaus on Hofstallgasse, just half a mile away, while they were going to the Elektrischer Aufzug restaurant on Monchsberg, where their competition was to be held.

Lotte was prancing ahead, winsome as ever, entranced by the carnival atmosphere. Many of the festivalgoers wore country costumes of leather lederhosen or dirndl dresses—while others wore sleek gowns or dapper suits. The mood was buoyant, carrying them all along with its infectious excitement. As Johanna paused to re-tie her apron, a sleek Daimler nosed out of a narrow side street into the square ahead of them, the pale face of the woman inside eyeing the crowd with sophisticated indifference.

"All right, Birgit?" Manfred asked with a smiling glance for his middle daughter, who as usual lagged a little behind, twisting her hands in her apron.

"Yes, Papa." She gave him a quick smile that lit up her face and made her almost pretty. Manfred patted her arm. He had a special affection for the daughter whose soul was so much like his own.

Ever since Birgit had left the convent school at seventeen they had worked side by side in the shop; of his three children she alone showed interest in the intricate mechanics of a clock, the coils and springs and gears that together were able to mark time. He only wished she could find a way to be truly settled in herself, with a purpose that was perhaps far from their little shop.

Johanna walked alongside Hedwig; save for his wife's graying hair they could have been sisters, so clearly were they cut from the same durable cloth. His hope for Johanna was that she might find something to soften her; love, perhaps, as it had done her mother.

As for Lotte, his laughing, lovely youngest daughter? She was as light on her toes as a ballet dancer, tilting her face to the sky without a care, arms flung out as she reveled in life's simple pleasures. What could Lotte possibly need? Manfred smiled just to look at her.

There was so much to be thankful for, on a day like this—when the air was as crisp and clear as water, and the sky was a deep cerulean blue that hurt your eyes to look at it, and yet still you did, drinking in the color along with the air, as well as the mountains.

Who could fail to gasp or at least murmur a hushed "*wunderbar*" at the beauty of the mountains that ringed Salzburg, the crown of glory that had kept her protected for a thousand years and more?

It was a day for reveling and remembering the good things, for there had been far too much uncertainty across Austria in recent months—the uprising in February between fascists and socialists that had led to hundreds of deaths, and then in May a bomb had exploded in the Festival Theatre right here in Salzburg. In July the chancellor Engelbert Dollfuss had been assassinated by Austrian Nazis in an attempted coup, which had thankfully been suppressed in a matter of hours. Such uncertainty made every day precious.

The family turned onto the Hofstallgasse, joining even more people heading towards Festspielhaus where the festival's major performances would take place—Bruno Walter conducting Mozart's *Don Giovanni* as well as the eminent Arturo Toscanini's debut.

Another few minutes and they finally arrived at the Elektrischer Aufzug, an impressive edifice of timber and stone, with views encompassing the old town as well as Salzburg's ancient fortress perched above the city. Lotte exclaimed over the lift that sent them soaring upwards while Hedwig could not keep from frowning and clutching at the sides.

The restaurant itself was paneled in wood and inset with mirrors, so it seemed much bigger than it was, the tables removed so more chairs could fit, and nearly every one of them was already filled.

"I did not expect so many people," Hedwig murmured in dismay, and Manfred gave her a comforting smile.

"It is good they are here. An audience is important."

She watched helplessly as her daughters were shepherded towards the makeshift stage by someone who seemed important; smiling, Manfred put his arm around her and led her to the seats that had been reserved for them, close to the front.

"Where are they going?"

"Backstage, to get ready. Don't worry. They're excited!" He squeezed her arm, his expression one of fond amusement, while Hedwig looked uneasily about.

The restaurant was filling up, the air buzzing with conversation and laughter as everyone chatted and studied their programs. Hedwig glanced at the sheet Manfred had given her, and the sight of *The Eder Sisters Trio* halfway down the page gave her a sensation like vertigo, a tipping over, as if everything were sliding, and she did not know how to right herself.

Manfred put a hand on her arm. "It's about to begin."

And so it was. They listened in silence to several acts, applauding as necessary, impressed by the voices of even the most obvious amateurs. As the competition was sponsored by the Association for National Costumes, everyone was in traditional dress, singing folk songs, and Hedwig felt herself relax. She knew many of the songs, and the clothes, when not worn by cosmopolitan Viennese, felt familiar and friendly. She began to enjoy herself.

And then their daughters came on the stage—three lovely young women in dirndls and checked aprons, with bright hair and rosy cheeks, and Hedwig felt as if she were looking at them with new eyes. Johanna, so tall and strong, twenty years old and such a hard worker; Birgit, who could look so friendly when she stood up straight and met people's gazes; and Lotte, lovely Lotte, only sixteen, with skin like dew and eyes as blue as the sky above, longing only to please and entertain, seeming almost of another world. Who could fail to love Lotte?

And then their voices—so sweet and lovely, soaring above, the harmonies twining together, the sound of innocence, of purity. Surely everyone was as moved as she was. Hedwig's heart beat painfully with love and she glanced at Manfred with a fierce look of pride and joy. He smiled back so tenderly that her eyes stung.

"Aren't we lucky?" he murmured as he took her hand in his. "Aren't we blessed?"

Hedwig could only nod.

The Eder Sisters did not win; they did not even take a prize, but none of them minded that. It was enough that they had sung at all, and at the end of the competition it seemed all anyone could talk of was the surprise late entry to the event, the von Trapp Family Singers, who had amazed the audience with their complex harmonies, as well as performing as an entire family—not merely three daughters, but nine children, and the mother as well! Even Hedwig had been impressed.

"Maria von Trapp used to be a nun at Nonnberg Abbey," Lotte remarked dreamily as they walked back to the house on Getreidegasse through a violet twilight, the air as soft as silk, a balmy caress on their heated skin. Festivalgoers had returned to their houses and hotels to change into evening dress to spend the rest of the night at the city's finest restaurants or supper clubs, and the streets had, for the moment, emptied out.

"And then she was sent to the von Trapps as a governess to one of the children—there were seven then—who was ill. She ended up marrying their father, who is a baron," Lotte continued. "Isn't that romantic?"

"It is not very sensible," Hedwig replied with her usual bluntness. "What does a nun know of children? And what of her vows?" Hedwig had grown up with a faith as solid and immovable as her husband's; there was not a Sunday in her life where she had missed attending mass, or an evening where she had not said the rosary on her knees before bed.

"She was only a postulant, not a full nun or even a novice," Johanna replied, with a look for Lotte that was both fond and a bit reproving. "Really, it's not such a shocking story. And she has since had two children herself, so she must know something about them. I spoke to her at the intermission. She was actually very interesting, in her own way."

"Well, it is of no consequence to us," Hedwig replied firmly. "We should hurry. The cakes might spoil in this heat."

"Did you like it, Papa?" Lotte asked as she twirled ahead of them, her skirt flying out, her golden hair catching the last of the sun's rays. "Wasn't it wonderful? All that lovely music… it sounded like heaven, to me."

"*You* were wonderful," Manfred replied with a laugh, "as I expect you know very well. I hardly need tell you, but I will, and no doubt more than once. My edelweiss daughters. You must keep those sprigs, as a reminder."

His benevolent smile faltered for a moment, along with his step, as his gaze fell on a rowdy gang of boys across the street, jostling each other and laughing loudly. A few daringly wore swastika armbands, the red and black visible even in the dusky light. One of them was daubing paint onto a brick wall. Manfred could make out *Blut und Ehre*. Blood and Honor.

One of the boys glanced over at the little group and then sent his arm shooting out like a challenge. "Heil Hitler," he called, his tone one of both good humor and veiled threat; the Nazi party had been outlawed in Austria for a year, but it didn't seem to deter its proponents very much.

Manfred dropped his gaze as he put his arm around his wife and continued on without replying. Johanna's glance swept over the boys with their short blond hair and bright eyes with a look of consideration; Birgit's lips twisted as she turned away. One of the boys snared Lotte's gaze with a bold look of his own and she flushed and hurried to catch up with her father.

"Come, girls," Hedwig called sharply, although they'd all already turned away from the scene. "It's getting late."

As the shadows lengthened and the sky grew dark, the little family hurried towards Getreidegasse and the waiting cakes while

Lotte began to sing the last verse of “Die Lorelei,” Birgit and Johanna gamely taking up their parts, their voices rising with melancholy beauty up into the oncoming night.

“The boatman in the small ship is gripped with wild pain,
he does not look at the rocky reefs, he only looks
up into the heights.
I think the waves devour boatmen and boats at the end…”

CHAPTER TWO

JOHANNA

Salzburg, August 1936

The kitchen was stifling. Johanna had rolled up the sleeves of her blouse, but it still stuck to her shoulder blades and perspiration beaded between her breasts. Her mother was baking bread, and Johanna, of course, was helping.

Johanna could not remember exactly when the lines in her family had fallen as they did—Birgit helped her father in the shop, she helped her mother in the house, and Lotte… what did Lotte do? Lotte laughed and sang and made everything brighter, and no one begrudged her for it, because she was Lotte, and she decorated all their lives with grace and cheer.

And, starting in September, she would be a student at the Mozarteum, to study voice and theory and composition, their little lark spreading her wings at last.

"Johanna, the oven," Hedwig commanded, and wordlessly Johanna went to the oven and stoked the fire, shoving a few sticks of wood inside before closing the door. Her mother's kitchen had to be, she sometimes thought, the most old-fashioned in all of Salzburg.

There were no modern conveniences for Hedwig Eder; she based her kitchen on the one of her childhood, and stepping into the large, square room, one might think they'd stepped into a

Tyrolean farmhouse. It was furnished with a wooden table and benches, and an old-fashioned cooking range, while bundles of dried herbs and ropes of onions hung from the ceiling alongside well-used copper pots and pans. She had grudgingly allowed her husband to buy an icebox only a few years ago, for it was hardly practical to keep food in an icehouse or stream as she might have done back at her home in the mountains.

Still, Hedwig insisted on doing everything as she had done it as a girl—whether it was baking bread, or dying cloth, or drying herbs, or bottling jam. Modern methods were to be disdained, and as for buying something in a shop…!

It was bad enough that she had to get her milk from the wagon that came down the street every morning with its rattling cans, just like everyone else did in Salzburg; if she could have managed it, Johanna thought she would have kept a cow in the courtyard. And in all these domestic endeavors, Johanna was her helpmeet.

It was a role she'd taken on with the same determined pragmatism her mother possessed, working alongside her in silent solidarity, finding satisfaction in the small yet significant achievements of a golden loaf of bread, a freshly starched shirt, a polished table. She had never been particularly interested in school learning, despite her father's love of books and music; Johanna preferred the practical and tangible to the obscure or abstract.

But four years on from finishing at the convent school all three girls had attended, unmarried and without any prospects of changing that state, Johanna had started to feel stifled in a way that had nothing to do with the hot kitchen.

"There." Her mother took the round, golden loaves of bread from the oven, a look of almost grim satisfaction on her face. "They are done." She glanced at the clock that hung above the door, and Johanna reached for the small copper pot they always used to make coffee—every afternoon Johanna would bring a tray down to Birgit and her father before sitting down with her mother at the kitchen table to drink their own, usually in fairly companionable silence.

Sometimes Lotte would join them, although more often she would take her coffee to the sitting room with a book, and leave Hedwig and Johanna to their quiet. Their places, Johanna was realizing more and more, were marked and always had been, but today she was determined that it was going to be different.

She waited until the coffee had been made, the tray of cups and saucers, accompanied by glasses of water, delivered to her father and sister, who were bent over their work in the back room, squinting at the bits of metal that Johanna found so tiresome.

"Thank you, *mein schatz*," Manfred said with an affectionate smile and Johanna dipped her head, too nervous now to make a reply. It wasn't like her to be nervous; she was direct to the point of bluntness or even awkwardness, so sometimes her father would laugh that one never had to ask Johanna to "*Rede nicht um den heissen Brei herum*," or "stop talking around the hot mash." "Our Johanna will dump the mash on your head!" Manfred would laugh, his eyes twinkling and Johanna would smile, taking it as a compliment, as a sign of her strength.

And she needed that strength now.

Upstairs her mother was already sat at the table, her normally straight back slightly slumped with fatigue as she sipped her coffee in the afternoon sunlight. She'd eased her shoes off, for her ankles had swollen in the heat, her thick-knit stockings gathering around them in elephantine wrinkles.

As Johanna paused in the doorway, she was suddenly accosted by how *old* her mother looked—her hair, scraped back into its usual tight bun, held far more gray than blond, and there were deep wrinkles etched into her forehead, her ruddy cheeks a spiderweb of broken veins, her body's solid form softened.

She'd never been a beautiful woman, but her husband had been devoted to her all his life. Five years younger and four inches shorter than his wife, Manfred had met her on a walking holiday near Innsbruck. Many times Johanna had heard him tell the story of how he'd seen her mother herding goats across a meadow and fallen straight in love. It seemed to Johanna both romantic and absurd, that someone like her mother, so plain, so *stolid,* could have had a man as gentle and charming as her father fall in love with her on sight, and yet she did not doubt the truth of it; she saw it lived out every day.

"It is a good day's work," Hedwig said as Johanna joined her at the table. It was what she always said, as if a script had been written and her mother was following it, line by painstaking line.

"Yes, a good day's work," Johanna repeated dutifully. She picked up her coffee cup and then put it down again without taking a sip. "Mama—"

Hedwig's eyes narrowed at her meaningful tone, the change of the script. "What is it?"

Johanna took a deep breath and lifted her chin, giving her mother as direct a look as her father praised her for. "I want to go to school."

"What…!" Hedwig expelled the word like a breath. "You've already been to school."

"I know that very well," Johanna replied. "I'll be twenty-three in December. I mean I want to go to secretarial school, Mama. To learn shorthand and how to type and useful things like that." In truth she did not exactly know what she would learn; she had seen the leaflet at the Volksbibliothek, advertising a secretarial course for young women, but the advertisement had only offered vague promises of decent wages and "*respectable office work.*" It had been enough to fire Johanna's soul.

Her mother shook her head slowly, more in confusion than outright refusal, which gave Johanna at least a little hope. "Why would you want to do this?" she asked, sounding genuinely bewildered.

"Because I want to *work.* I would bring in money, you know. It could be useful—"

"We do not need money," Hedwig retorted quickly. "Not like that. You do not need to do this thing on our account, Johanna." She sounded reproving as well as relieved, as if bringing in a few schillings for the tin above the range was all Johanna aspired to.

Johanna took a sip of her coffee as she fought down an entirely expected rising frustration. She'd known her mother, so traditional and set in her ways, would resist the idea. In her mother's world, women did not work in offices with men. They baked bread and stitched shirts and took pride in a polished teapot or a well-swept floor. They stayed at home until they married, and then they moved to their new home, with their husband, and did the same as before there. It was how it had always been and how it always would be, world without end, amen.

Carefully Johanna set her cup back on its saucer, it was part of the dinner set of Hutschenreuther china her parents had received as a wedding present; each precious plate and cup her mother's pride and joy. "I want to *do* something," she said.

"Do something? You aren't busy enough? Shall I give you more of the sewing, the stitching, the cleaning, the baking? There is always more work to do, Johanna. If I had known you were so restless, I would have offered you more." Her mother shook her head and then finished her coffee, the conversation clearly over, needing no more words.

"I mean something *else*, Mama." Johanna strove to keep her tone measured.

"And what else is there?"

"Mama… surely…" She stared at her mother in frustration. "You know I'm not married."

"Pfft. You'll meet someone one day."

How, Johanna wondered. She could not herd goats down the Getreidegasse like her mother had back in the mountains, and there were no longer any eligible men at St. Blasius, where they attended mass every Sunday. In the last few years, the three potential suitors at church had all left—one to Vienna, one to be a priest, and one to become a school teacher. She didn't go anywhere else than home or church, not any more. There was no way to meet anyone.

A few years ago she'd been part of *Naturfreunde*, an Alpine club for young people that had sponsored hikes up the Monschsberg and Untersberg, treks through the Salzkammergut. Once there had even been a skiing trip.

Johanna recalled spending the night in one of the crude mountain huts, its tiny windows heaped with snow drifts; she had cooked sausages over a fire and stayed up late, chatting and laughing with some of the girls in the club. There had been a boy—a man, really, a few years older than her—who had smiled at her when she'd been strapping on her skis. Later, after she'd bumbled down a hill, he'd skied up next to her and offered to carry her skis up for another run. Disconcerted, she had declined, and he hadn't offered again. And yet still the memory had the power to make Johanna's heart beat a little faster.

But *Naturfreunde*, along with all of Austria's other clubs and societies, had been disbanded two years ago, with the inception of the *Ständestaat*, the one-party system of the Federal State of Austria. Her father soberly claimed it had been a necessary step to keep Austria strong enough to resist Nazi aggression, but Johanna missed the treks in the mountains, the hope of something more.

"It isn't just that," she told her mother, determined to persevere despite Hedwig's stony expression. "It is… *life,* Mama! I don't want to spend all of it in your kitchen."

Her mother jerked back, her weathered face crumpling in hurt before she stood up, briskly collecting their cups and saucers, even though Johanna had not yet finished her coffee.

"I did not realize it was such a torment," she said in a voice stiff with affront. The cups and saucers rattled in her hands as she put them in the sink with more force than she would normally use with her precious porcelain.

"It's not a torment," Johanna said, fighting a sense of both despair and anger. "But I want my own home one day, my own kitchen." *My own life*, she thought. "If I have some skills…" She tried for a different tack. "Women will need to work, you know, if there's going to be a war."

"Going to be a war!" Hedwig whirled around, her expression turning thunderous. "Johanna, there is not going to be a war."

Unlike her mother, Johanna read the newspapers, both the *Salzburger Volksblatt* and the *Wiener Neueste Nachrichten* from Vienna. She read about how many Austrians wanted to be part of Deutschland, the Greater Germany; she also read how Germany had marched into the Rhineland unimpeded in March, to begin to make that ill wish a reality. Hitler was rearming unabashedly, even if people pretended not to notice. And the gangs of brown-shirted boys that roamed Salzburg had grown in both size and number, their direct stares far more challenging than they'd been just two years ago.

Johanna had sometimes eyed those young men with covert curiosity; there was something invigorating and even exciting about their brash swaggering, their blond confidence. She knew her father despised Hitler and all his slavish followers, but Johanna thought there was nothing slavish about the way those young men strode down a street as if they owned it.

"Why would you talk of war?" Hedwig grumbled as she began to bang pots about in preparation for their evening meal. "It has not been so long since the last one."

"Almost twenty years."

"And look what happened." Hedwig flung an arm out to encompass the house, the city, the world. "Everything fell apart. Everything!"

Johanna's father often lamented the loss of the world he'd grown up in, when the Austro-Hungarian Empire had stretched from Switzerland to Russia, and had encompassed fifty million people, encouraging freedom of movement, thought, and belief. Now the Federal State of Austria was, according to Manfred Eder, no more than a basket of scraps, the parts of the empire that no one else had wanted cobbled together to form a country, and run with an iron hand to keep it intact.

"Where is our identity as a nation, our culture as a people?" he would sometimes ask, when he gathered his friends in their front sitting room, an informal salon of Christian Social Party members and war veterans who talked of politics and religion, and longed to change the world.

To Johanna they were just a bunch of disillusioned old men, lamenting a world that no longer existed over their brandy and cigars. All she'd known was this—a small country, not an empire, a provincial town that tried to be a cosmopolitan city every summer during the festival. And the kitchen. *Always the kitchen.*

She sighed, knowing she needed to placate her mother if she wanted the smallest hope of achieving her own modest aim. "Even if there isn't a war… the world is changing, Mama, in many ways. I only want to learn useful skills." Hedwig did not reply and Johanna added, unable to keep a belligerent note from her voice, "If Lotte can study music, why can I not learn how to type?"

Hedwig made a dismissive sound, her back to Johanna, rigid and unyielding. From downstairs the bell jangled as someone came into the shop, and she heard her father's cheerful tone as he greeted the prospective customer.

Oh, this life, Johanna thought, *it never changes.* Day in and day out, always the same—cooking, cleaning, stitching, sewing. She would live and die in this kitchen, and nothing would ever happen to her.

"You haven't given me a real reason why not," she declared, and Hedwig whirled around, bringing her hands down hard on the table, the loud sound reverberating through the room.

"What reason must I give? You are needed here, and there is no money for more schooling. *Da Gscheidere gibt noch*!" The smarter one gives in: a command to stop being so stubborn.

Johanna looked away, fighting the urge to snap something back. It would do her no good, and yet she couldn't give up. Not yet. "I could pay the fees back," she finally said, hating that her voice had turned wheedling. Weak. "After I'd found a job."

"A job, a job!" Hedwig threw her hands up in the air. "You have a job. Here." She gestured to the table, and then heaved a heavy sack of dirty potatoes onto it, giving Johanna a pointed look. "They need to be peeled."

Silently Johanna rose from her seat and grabbed a knife. Hedwig turned back to her pots as she began to peel the potatoes, the only sound the angry *scritch scritch* of the knife against the peel that came away in long, dirt-speckled curls. Both women bristled with hostility.

From downstairs came a burst of laughter, then the jangle and clang of the door shutting on another satisfied customer. The air in the kitchen felt thick and heavy with ill feeling. *Scritch scritch.*

Then, after five minutes of interminable silence, a knock sounded, this one on the side door for family visitors that led directly upstairs. Johanna put down her knife.

"I'll get it." She hurried from the room, grateful for a reprieve, no matter how brief, from the oppressive atmosphere. *Would Mother ever relent?* She would have to think of another way. Something, somehow; she would make her change her mind.

"Oh, it's you." Johanna could not keep an unwelcome note from her voice as she stared at Janos Panov, the knife grinder who visited all the houses and shops on Getreidegasse every few weeks with his grinding cart, colorfully painted and decorated with ragged bunting. His dirty cap was jammed onto his greasy hair, and his smile revealed a set of broken, tobacco-stained teeth.

"Hello, Fräulein Eder." His tone was ingratiating, and while Johanna usually felt pity for him, now she only felt irritation as she gritted her teeth.

"We don't need any knives sharpened today," she said, even though she knew her mother would be cross. They always needed knives sharpened, but in her current mood she could not bear to humor the simple-minded knife grinder for even a few minutes. His hangdog expression and ingratiating manner reminded her of all she would miss if her mother wouldn't agree to her scheme—*this* was the only man she ever exchanged pleasantries with.

"Are you certain, Fräulein?" he asked. "It has been two weeks, after all."

"I'm certain," Johanna snapped, and then she closed the door in his face. She took a deep breath and then let it out slowly. For a second, tears threatened, and she blinked them back. She would not cry. She would not show such weakness, even if only to herself.

Hedwig came to the top of the stairs, one hand resting on her lower back, her stolid figure silhouetted by the fading sunlight from the kitchen. "Who was at the door?"

"Just the knife grinder," Johanna answered dismissively, anger and frustration, and worse, a deeper despair, still pulsing through her. She turned from the door as she blinked back the last of her tears. "That idiot Jew."

"Johanna!" Her father's voice, sharp with both hurt and dismay, made her stiffen. "How can you say such a thing?"

Manfred stood in the doorway to his shop, looking stooped and sad, his brown eyes full of sorrow.

"Well, he is," Johanna said defiantly, even as her cheeks began to burn. She knew she shouldn't have said it, she wished she hadn't, but the words had tumbled out along with her frustration. "He spits tobacco and he smells," she declared. "I don't like him."

"He is a fellow human being," Manfred stated quietly. "And our Lord and Savior was a Jew. They are God's chosen people, Johanna. Never forget it."

"It was just the knife grinder," Johanna exclaimed. "Even Mama finds him dirty. Why do you care?"

Manfred was silent for a moment, the corners of his mouth drawn down in a look so sorrowful Johanna squirmed inside as she clenched her hands into fists to keep from twisting them in her apron. Why had her father had to hear her? She hadn't meant it, of course she hadn't; she usually felt sorry for Janos. She'd been speaking thoughtlessly, but what did it even matter? Most people said far worse about the Jews.

"I care because there is much evil in this world," her father finally said quietly, "and I know it can be easy to forget it."

Johanna shook her head, unsure if she didn't understand, or she simply didn't want to.

"Besides," her father continued, "Janos Panov was born into a poor family and orphaned at a young age, driven from Russia by ignorant people who hated him simply for who he was. He had no opportunity to educate or better himself. He has worked hard and found a way to earn his keep. For that alone he deserves our respect." He paused. "If he has done anything to upset you—"

"Oh, he hasn't," Johanna cried impatiently. "But it doesn't matter. None of it matters."

Her father took a step towards her, the look on his face one of utter seriousness. "But it does matter, Johanna, *mein schatz*. It matters very much. And my greatest fear in these troubled times is that it will seem to stop mattering, when it never can. Do you understand?"

Johanna stared at him, the slump of his slight shoulders, the earnest yet serious look in his kindly eyes, the sad smile that curved his mouth. He looked frail, yet he had an inner strength that she realized she had always relied on.

"Johanna?"

She nodded, unable to fully meet his gaze. "I understand."

Manfred regarded her for another moment, the probing look in his eyes making Johanna think of Father Josef when she gave her confession, the glint of the priest's eyes barely visible behind the latticed screen. "Very well," he said softly, sounding accepting but unconvinced.

Unable to bear his scrutiny any longer, Johanna turned away and hurried upstairs. Her mother gave her a grim nod of solidarity as Johanna came into the kitchen and picked up her knife.

CHAPTER THREE

BIRGIT

September 1936

"The trouble with Austria," the wheezy voice of Hans Pichler declared before erupting into a fit of coughing, "is that she is a country without a culture, a nation made of disparate parts, the remnants of an empire."

This pronouncement was followed by another bout of coughing while the handful of other men gathered in the Eders' sitting room nodded sagely in agreement.

Birgit had heard it all before. Once or twice a month her father gathered his compatriots around him—war veterans like himself, as well as men from church or like-minded members of the Christian Social party who had reluctantly accepted Austria's newest government, the fascist Fatherland Front, as the only way to combat the unreserved aggression of the National Socialists.

They talked of books, of art and music, religion and philosophy, and then, inevitably, the discussion turned to politics, or really, pronouncements on Austria's struggles as a country; the ever-present threat of Hitler's goose-stepping Wehrmacht, usually followed by lamenting the many pro-Nazi supporters in Salzburg and, indeed, all of Austria.

"The difficulty," Heinrich Schmidt stated, "is that too many people today confuse our Germanic culture with being German. We are not Germans. We are *Austrians*!"

"Yes, yes!"

"You speak the truth, Herr Schmidt, the truth!"

Several of the men pounded their fists on the table or the arm of their chair as Herr Schmidt sat back, pleased with his pronouncement.

Restlessly Birgit shifted her position on the hard chair in the corner she'd been obliged to take in order to give the men, some of them grieved by old war injuries, the comfortable places on the sofas or armchairs. Lotte was perched on a footstool by her father's knee, listening with a rapt expression to the men with their chesty coughs and trumpeting statements. Birgit didn't know how she did it—how could she possibly be interested in what a bunch of grizzled old men who smelled of tobacco and pine liniment had to say? Especially as they said it every month, year upon year, and even more so since the Fatherland Front had come to power.

Johanna, at least, had escaped to the kitchen, so she could help their mother bring out the coffees and cakes. As soon as they'd served everyone, Hedwig and Johanna had retreated back to the sanctum of their private space, drinking coffee in silent solidarity in the kitchen while Birgit continued to endure, unnoticed, invisible.

She was used to being invisible. As the middle Eder sister, she possessed neither Johanna's strength nor Lotte's beauty. No one had ever told her so, but it was a fact so apparent she acknowledged it every time she looked in the mirror. Like her sisters, her hair was blond and her eyes were blue, but there the resemblance ended.

While Johanna's strong lines and firm jaw made her so striking, and Lotte's porcelain complexion and rosebud mouth made her look delicate and lovely, Birgit had a face like a potato. Sometimes, in her bleaker moods, she thought God must have taken up the leftovers from making Johanna's character and Lotte's loveliness and put her together out of the scraps.

Her hair was the color of dirty snow, her complexion not much better. Although her eyes were blue, they were small, "like raisins in a pudding," as one girl at the convent school had said with gleeful unkindness. Her expression, when she wasn't smiling, looked so dour that strangers in the street had told her "to stop looking so gloomy—you've got a face to sour milk!"

Birgit didn't mean to look gloomy, but she feared when she smiled she looked manic and desperate. There was no winning.

Her talents had not fared much better than her looks. "Birgit is remarkably undistinguished" one of the nuns at school had stated with a sorrowful shake of her head. She'd been competent enough in the necessary bits—reading, writing, arithmetic, history—but nothing had ever fired her imagination and she'd never, ever had cause to stand out. She'd never been picked for running races or playing sport, never been the solo or starring role in the Christmas concerts or Easter plays. Like Johanna, she could carry a tune, but next to Lotte's clear, lark-like voice, her own singing was, as with so much else, merely competent and certainly unremarkable.

Sandwiched between two sisters, both of whom stood out in their own individual ways, Birgit had realized at a young age that she would have to work hard to make her mark in any way at all. And so, when she was eight years old, watching her father repair an ormolu mantel clock, she had decided she would be good at what he was—clockmaking.

The trade did not come easily to her, fiddling with so many tiny, disparate parts was complicated and intricate, and it was only because of her determined interest that her father allowed her to informally apprentice him when she was sixteen. It had taken much study and concentration to understand how the gears and wheels worked together, in perfect balance and exquisite harmony; how the energy in the spring was released to turn the wheels and then with their push of the pendulum, gravity kept its steady swing and the hands of the clock ticked out the time.

Now that clocks were mostly made in factories, much to her father's displeasure, he specialized in the repair of the instruments, especially older ones—taking them apart to replace a wheel or die plate or to repair a rivet. When Birgit had turned eighteen, her father had, with much pride, given her a set of her own tools—a caliper, files, pliers, a piercing saw, a staking tool, and a riveting hammer, all in their own leather case. Birgit had half hoped he might have added *and Daughter* to the painted *Eder Clockmaking* sign outside the little shop, but he had not, and she had not had the confidence to suggest it.

Still, it had been enough that she could work alongside him. She had always enjoyed their hours together, spent mostly in silence, save for the occasional remark about what they were doing. "Look at this mechanism," her father might say, or "do you see how the hand skips? It is the 'clock jitter.'" And she would nod and murmur something back.

And yet, despite those many hours of companionship, Birgit reflected with a small kernel of bitterness she tried not to nourish, it was Lotte who sat on the stool by his knee, Lotte upon whose head he rested his old, gnarled hand, caressing her curls before he turned to Hans Pilcher to ask him about his shoe shop on Linzergasse.

Birgit turned away as Herr Pilcher droned on about the agonies of inflation that had bankrupted so many businesses like his own.

"But people will always need shoes, Herr Pilcher," her father said cheerfully. "Just as they will always need to tell the time."

From the corner of her eye Birgit caught the direction of her father's smile, not at her—his colleague in clockmaking—as it might once have been, but at the newest member of the little salons—Franz Weber.

*

Just looking at Franz Weber made injustice burn white-hot through Birgit. He had arrived in the shop only a week ago. Her father had been deeply involved in the repair of a Biedermeier wall clock, and so Birgit had gone to the front room when the door had jangled, smoothing down her skirt and offering the man she thought was a customer a welcoming smile.

"*Gruss Gott, mein* Herr. May I help you?"

The man before her was tall and rangy, stooping slightly as he came through the doorway before taking off his hat to reveal a head of dark curls. He had been glancing around the little shop with its many clocks with an air of alert and lively interest, but as Birgit spoke he turned to her with an engaging smile.

"I hope you may, Fräulein. I am looking for Herr Eder."

"Herr Eder is deeply involved with his work at the moment, but if you need a repair or are looking to purchase a clock, I am sure I can help you." Birgit was used to customers asking for her father, and often being a bit disgruntled at having to make do with his daughter, but in time many had come to accept her.

"I am afraid I am looking neither to purchase a clock nor have one repaired," the man replied with a winsome smile that Birgit couldn't help but feel was gently mocking her, just a little. "I am here for employment. Herr Eder is taking me on as his apprentice."

"What!" The word had escaped Birgit in a shocked gasp before she could think better of it. She stared at him dumbly, shocked by his pronouncement, given in a tone of such friendly assurance.

Her father was taking on an apprentice, when she, *she* had been his apprentice for these four years and more? And he'd not said one word about it to her?

"I see I have surprised you." The man's smile deepened, revealing a dimple in one lean cheek. He was so *friendly* looking, with eyes the color of chocolate and unruly, curly hair, that Birgit disliked him all the more for it.

"Indeed you have," she said shortly. "My father made no mention of an apprentice to me." *I am his apprentice*, she wanted to cry, but she kept herself from it.

"Then I would say you should ask him. Is he too deeply involved in his work to be consulted?"

Again Birgit had the impression he was teasing her. Again she didn't like it.

"I will speak to him," she replied shortly, and turned away from the man without saying anything further, although she knew her behavior bordered on rudeness.

In the backroom her father was bent over the innards of the Biedermeier, his pince-nez perched on his nose as he frowned down at the broken mechanics of the antique clock. He had noticed neither the bell nor Birgit leaving the room to answer it, such was his concentration.

"Papa, there is a man here to see you," Birgit said, speaking more loudly than usual to gain his attention. "He says he is to be your apprentice."

"Ah, yes, of course! Herr Weber." Manfred looked up from the clock with a beaming smile that made Birgit burn all the more. "He was expected today. I had forgotten."

"You did not tell me about him," she said, and she heard all the hurt in her voice that she could not repress.

"Did I not? Ah, well. I apologize, my dear. It was all arranged rather quickly, you see."

"Quickly? What was the hurry?"

Manfred simply gave her a vague smile. "Oh, you know how these things are. You hear a name, and in the next moment it is done. Well! Let us go greet him. I am sure your mother will have cakes for us."

Birgit followed behind as her father went into the front room and greeted Herr Weber with an unbridled enthusiasm that she was far from feeling. Judging from Herr Weber's sideways laughing look, he knew it.

Duly they all went upstairs to their living quarters and Hedwig, although caught as unawares as Birgit had been, was able to present a sugar-dusted *Gugelhupf* that she had prepared for the afternoon. She made coffee that Johanna brought to the sitting room, giving Franz a frank look of curiosity that he just as frankly returned.

Her older sister, Birgit knew, was not pretty in the sweet, milky way that men often liked, but some might still call her beautiful. Her long blond hair was looped in braids behind her ears, and her blue eyes under strong brows were piercing in their directness. She was nearly as tall as their guest, with a strapping figure, unlike Birgit's own floury softness. She was shaped more like a dumpling, while Johanna looked like an Amazon warrior.

In any case, Birgit hardly cared whether Herr Weber liked her sister or not. She didn't like *him.*

Her father made the introductions, "This is Johanna, my eldest, and such a help to her mother. And Birgit you have met, of course. She has been assisting me in the shop. Lotte, the youngest, is at school. She has been attending the Mozarteum these last few weeks, our little songbird! Daughters, this is Franz Weber, who will be my apprentice."

Birgit watched as her father bestowed Franz with another friendly smile. Anger warred with disbelief as she listened to them exchange pleasantries. Franz was from Vienna, and had only come to Salzburg the day before, to take up the apprenticeship.

Birgit could hardly believe her father had solicited someone all the way from Vienna and what for? There was not so much work that they needed another apprentice. Her mother and Johanna seemed as mystified as she was, although her sister looked pleased by the prospect, especially when it became apparent that Franz would be living with the family, as most apprentices did.

"You can have the little front room in the attic," Manfred declared. "Hot in summer, cold in winter, but we shall make it cozy enough, and it will ensure your privacy, as well as ours." Hedwig had already excused herself to go make up the room. Manfred turned to Franz in smiling expectancy, and he bowed his head in grateful acceptance.

"I am so thankful for your help, Herr Eder."

"It is my pleasure, of course, and you must call me Manfred."

Birgit fumed silently as they continued to chat, and then Franz turned to Johanna and asked her about herself.

To Birgit's amazement, her sister wittered on about how much she enjoyed hiking, and spoke of the Alpine club she'd been a part of years ago. She'd only gone a few times, as far as Birgit could remember, and she'd complained about how cold it was.

"I have had very little opportunity to walk in the mountains, living in Vienna as I did," Franz Weber told Johanna with a smile. "But I look forward to exploring them here."

"We will take you up the Untersberg," Manfred declared, "where Charlemagne is said to sleep. It has the best views of the city."

"I look forward to it," Franz replied, but he was looking at Johanna as he said it.

Birgit, as usual, was invisible.

She wouldn't have minded any of that, indeed she as good as expected it, but when, the next morning, Franz took the bench next to her father's that had been hers since she'd been sixteen she struggled not to snap at him, or worse, break down and cry.

How could this be happening? Why had Father not said a word? The answer, Birgit feared, was that, as with so many other things, she had become invisible.

She moved to a corner of the room where the light was not as good and fumed silently as her father began to teach Franz about clocks. It was clear to Birgit after just a few minutes of listening to Manfred's gentle instruction that Franz Weber knew next to nothing about clockmaking. Her father spoke to him as he'd once spoken to Birgit when she'd been a child of eight, and he pointed to the wheels and gear box, the die plate and pendulum, naming them all, while Franz marveled like one who had never heard such things before. And yet he was her father's apprentice, taking her place as surely as if he'd said so himself.

She kept silent for the rest of the day, and the day after, as her father and Franz worked side by side. Then, one morning when Franz had gone out at her father's request to fetch a delivery of wire, Birgit had been unable to keep quiet any longer.

"I do not understand, Papa," she stated, trying to sound reasonable instead of either hurt or furious, "why you have hired an apprentice who does not seem to have ever seen the inside of a clock."

Her father smiled faintly as he put his tools away before they went upstairs for their midday meal. "Franz has a degree in mathematics from the University of Vienna," he replied mildly. "He is more than qualified to work in my little shop."

"But he has no experience," Birgit protested. "He looked at the gears of the Vienna regulator you showed him as if it was another world."

"Indeed it was. It was my privilege to show him the mechanisms of that miniature universe, and how it is but a shadowy reflection of the complex workings of God's creation." He let out a little laugh. "I have yet to convince him of the latter, but I look forward to the debate."

Birgit knew her father was recalling how he and Franz had debated the philosophy of something called logical positivism that Franz had learned in Vienna that declared, quite emphatically, that the only meaningful philosophical problems were ones that could be resolved by logical analysis.

Birgit had tuned out the discourse, which she hadn't even tried to understand, while her father and Franz had cheerfully gone back and forth, and Lotte had listened, entranced as ever. For once Johanna had ventured from the kitchen to sit and listen, although like Birgit she hadn't spoken.

"I still don't understand," Birgit told her father as he put away his tool case. "There is not so much work that you need an apprentice. *Another* apprentice," she added meaningfully, and a terribly sympathetic understanding suffused her father's face.

"Oh, Birgit, *mein schatz*, is that what this is about?" He rested one hand on her shoulder. "This is not about you, Birgit, not at all. You must not think for a moment I have been in some way dissatisfied by your work, your uncomplaining service." He smiled and squeezed her shoulder. "There are deeper things going on here, things we must trust to the benevolent hand of God. Now, come. Your mother has prepared us lunch, and I believe I can smell *Tafelspitz*."

And so Birgit had followed her father upstairs, and said no more.

*

As Herr Schmidt continued to pontificate—"*The true Germany is not found in the spirit of the hour!*"—Birgit decided she could take no more. For a week she'd watched as Franz Weber had learned the art of clock repair, taking to it with a more natural finesse than she had ever possessed. Whenever he fumbled with the tiny mechanisms or delicate tools, he gave her father a laughing, lopsided smile of apology and Manfred assured him he was doing well, while Birgit remained invisible.

Now she slipped out of the stuffy salon, its windows closed against the night air for the sake of the older guests, and down the stairs to the side door that led out to the courtyard. Johanna, coming from the kitchen, called to her from the top of the stairs as she reached for her coat.

"Where on earth are you going?"

"Just for a walk."

"A *walk?*"

None of them ever went out at night, especially now with the increase in roaming gangs of brown-shirted boys that their father warned them against.

"Just for a moment," Birgit said as she swiftly did up the buttons of her coat. "It's so stuffy in there, and I can't take another second of Herr Pilcher's coughing."

"Birgit—"

"I'll be back soon," she promised, and then slipped out of the door before Johanna could say anything else.

Outside the night air possessed an autumnal chill; the mountains ringing the city were already dusted in snow. Birgit wrapped her arms around herself and tucked her head low as she walked down Getreidegasse. She didn't even know where she was going; there was nowhere, really, for her to go. Shops were closed and she had never before dared to enter a coffeehouse alone. Besides, she had no money.

She headed down the cobbled street as it narrowed and became Judengasse, or Jew's Lane, where the Jews had had their synagogue in the Middle Ages, before they'd been expelled from the city. Birgit knew the brutal basics of the history—how the Jewish community had been blamed for the Black Death, and how they'd been burned alive in the synagogue as a result, but then other Jews had come and settled there until they'd been driven out, and none had returned for three hundred and fifty years.

Even now Salzburg had only a small Jewish community and one synagogue; besides the knife grinder, or, from afar, the founder of the Salzburg Festival, Max Reinhardt, Birgit did not know any Jews herself. But she knew they were hated by many, although she didn't really understand why. It was one of those things that simply *was*, and you shrugged and then got on with life, because what else could you do?

All she could think about was Franz Weber, and she wished he had not come to Salzburg, never mind any Jews.

Birgit's steps slowed as she caught sight of a crowd ahead of her, where Judengasse met up with the Alter Marktplatz, the city's oldest market square, a fountain at its center. Even though the crowd of people was at a distance, Birgit sensed their animosity. It rolled off them with an animalistic heat, a manic fervor. They were up by the marble steps of St. Florian Fountain, and something—or someone—was the object of their malevolent attention.

Instinctively she stepped into the shadow of a doorway as she continued to watch the gang of brown-shirted boys, and a few others besides, harass some unfortunate soul.

"How can we get you clean, you dirty Jew?" one boy jeered, and Birgit drew her breath in sharply as a few of the boys lifted the man above their heads and then hurled him into the fountain. It was, she saw with a lurch, Janos Panov, the knife grinder.

She watched with a transfixed sort of horror as the poor knife grinder cowered in the fountain while the crowd showered him with abuse as well as punches and kicks. Even from where she stood, Birgit could see the blood on his face, his bruised hands as he held up his arms to shield himself from the blows.

If her father were here, he would be furious. He would wade into that crowd of bullies, slight man as he was, and help Janos out of the fountain. He would decry the cowardly, bullying tactics of the crowd, and tell them they should be arrested or even whipped. At least, Birgit thought he would.

But what could she do?

Nothing.

She did not know the knife grinder particularly well, a simple-minded man who was cheerful enough as he sharpened knives on his little cart, harming no one. His treatment now was wrong and, even more, it was evil. *How could these stupid boys not see it?* What could they possibly have against a man like Janos, who pushed his cart and ground people's knives and gave a subservient bob of his head to every person who passed his way?

A choked sound escaped her as the crowd finally left Janos alone. As they headed down Goldgasse, no doubt looking for someone else to torment, Birgit hurried forward. Before she could reach Janos, however, someone else did.

A young woman in a dark coat, her hair hidden under a cap, waded into the fountain, soaking her clothes, and put an arm around him as Birgit came up to the steps.

The woman glanced up and beckoned to Birgit.

"Help me," she commanded, and Birgit rushed up to her. She could hear the gang's laughter still echoing down the street. *What if they came back?* She knew there was no point thinking of it now.

"What shall we do?" she asked as she stared down at Janos, half unconscious, blood blooming in the water around his head in clouds of pink.

"Get him out of the fountain, for a start." The woman's voice was crisp, yet holding a surprising hint of wryness. Birgit could not make out her face in the dark. She reached down and hoisted Janos by his armpits while, fumbling, Birgit took his legs.

Together they half-lifted, half-dragged the knife grinder out of the fountain and propped him against the steps.

He gave them a smile of thanks, blood trickling from a cut on his head, one eye swelling shut and his lip split.

"My thanks, Fräuleins," he mumbled, and then spat out a tooth. "*Proscheniye.*"

"You don't need to ask our pardon," the woman returned fiercely, and Birgit wondered how she knew Russian. She only recognized it as such herself because Janos sometimes spoke a few words when he came by with his cart.

Janos smiled sickly and wiped the blood from his chin. He did not seem very surprised by the treatment he'd received, and somehow that made it seem worse.

"How could they do this!" Birgit exclaimed.

The woman gave her a quick, burning look. "You object?"

"Of course I object. Janos is innocent! It's wrong to hurt someone simply for who they are. It's evil." She was saying no more than what her father said, and yet she realized how much she meant it. The passion in her voice was both surprising to her and real; it fired through her, woke her up from a sleep she hadn't realized she'd been drifting into, consumed by her own problems and little else.

"You are kind, Fräulein Eder," Janos said in a half-mumble. "Just as your father is kind."

"Your father is Herr Eder?" the woman said sharply. "The clockmaker?"

Birgit stared at her in surprise. "Yes… Do you know him?"

She shook her head. "It doesn't matter." She nodded to Janos. "We must get him home. They'll come back, don't doubt it."

With his arms draped around their shoulders, Janos managed to walk to the rented room in Judengasse where he lived, as sorry and squalid a place as Birgit had ever seen.

"I'm sorry," the woman said after they'd left Janos on his bed; she had wiped his face as tenderly as a mother and left a jug of water and a glass on the table nearby. "I believe you've ruined your skirt."

Birgit glanced down at her plain skirt of brown tweed. It was soaking wet and stained with blood. *How on earth would she explain it to Mother?* "It doesn't matter."

The woman gave her a frank look. She had full lips and a strong nose, and her hazel eyes were bright, her gaze direct. Birgit thought she must be about thirty, perhaps a little older. "You were brave."

Birgit shook her head. "No, I wasn't. If I had been, I would have done something before they'd left him in the fountain to drown."

"That would have been stupid, rather than brave," she replied. "There is a difference." She gave Birgit an appraising look that made her want to fidget; no one ever looked so boldly at her, as if taking her measure. Usually their glances skimmed over her, moved on to something more interesting. This woman's did not. "Perhaps you would wish to help again," she said, her tone both challenging and yet also cautious.

"Again? How?" Birgit looked at her in confusion. "Janos is safe now."

"He is but one. There are many more. And many other evils as well that need… resisting." She spoke the word with careful emphasis. "Do you think you would you be interested? Or was this just a one-off to salve your conscience?"

Birgit didn't miss the slightly sneering tone of the woman's voice and something in her burned. Of course, it would be far more prudent to refuse the woman's nameless challenge; she was someone who crackled with energy, radiated danger. Her eyes were bright, her expression fierce, and in response a new reckless courage bloomed in Birgit. She was surely being replaced at her father's shop, by her father's side; here, perhaps, she could still be useful. Important, even.

"Perhaps I would be," she declared, meeting the woman's direct stare with her chin lifted. "What are you proposing?"

A smile flickered across her face. "Here," she said, and from her pocket she withdrew a single sheet of paper with a few printed lines, badly typeset, and handed it to her. "Take this. Show it to no one. And if you are interested, come to Oskar's Coffeehouse in Elisabeth-Vorstadt next Wednesday evening, at seven o'clock. Tell no one else." The woman's eyes flashed. "Or you'll regret it."

A tremor went through Birgit at the implied threat. She had an urge to thrust the sheet back at the woman, no matter what it said, and yet she didn't. "Wednesday," she repeated, and the woman nodded before turning away, her heels clicking on the cobbles as she hurried down the street. Birgit looked down at the typewritten sheet.

Imagining A Greater Germany, she read out loud. *Do Not Let Hitler Lie to You, Comrades! Down with Fascism!* She drew her breath in sharply and glanced up, but the woman was gone, swallowed up by the shadows.

CHAPTER FOUR

LOTTE

October 1936

Lotte sat on a bench in Residenzplatz and watched as a flock of starlings rose in a dark cloud and hovered over the magnificent Residence Fountain with its Triton gazing upward—water jetting out from his conch-shell trumpet—before taking wing to the slate-colored sky. It was the time of year when the *Salzburger Schnürlregen*, or string rain, misted the city in a constant drizzle and turned the whole world to gray, shrouding the mountains behind a thick fog.

Huddling deeper in her coat, Lotte gave a heavy sigh as her cheeks dampened with mist-like tears. She was due at the Mozarteum for her class on composition in just fifteen minutes, and she most certainly should hurry from this bench so she could attend it in a timely fashion.

The trouble was, she did not want to go. At all.

She had been taking classes at the esteemed music academy for over a month, and with each passing day she feared her parents' hard-earned schillings, and worse, their unspoken hope, were both being wasted.

She might have once sung in that silly competition with the von Trapps, who were now musical stars in the making and had already toured Europe, but she had, she realized, a rather ordinary voice. According to the cultured professors as well as the other pupils of the Mozarteum, she was quite an ordinary pupil.

Not that Lotte minded. She didn't particularly want to be anything other than ordinary. She had no delusions of grandeur or illusions of fame, just a hope of happiness, of finding a kind of peace and contentment.

Sometimes she glimpsed it, felt it almost at the tips of her fingers—when she saw the mist rising from the mountains in the morning, or in the hushed breath before the mass was sung, and her whole being rose in delighted sympathy—but then it slipped away again, as she returned with a crash to the weary world with all of its disappointments and dangers, a world that held so much joy, and yet also so much pain.

She did not think she would find the elusive happiness and peace she craved at the Mozarteum.

Attending the prestigious music academy had been her father's idea, after a colleague who had seen Lotte sing in the competition with her sisters suggested she was talented enough to take lessons once she'd finished at school.

Her father had put the idea to her with such a hopeful twinkle in his eye that Lotte had felt she'd had to agree. She couldn't bear to disappoint anyone, especially not her father, and in any case there was nothing else she wanted to do—unlike Birgit she had no affinity for clockmaking, and the kitchen was clearly only her mother and Johanna's domain. Work outside of the home was never spoken about and not to be thought of. Why not study at the Mozarteum if she was accepted into their program? Why not study and learn? Why not please her father if she did not know how to please herself?

And yet she had discovered almost immediately that she loathed the atmosphere of ambition and striving at the academy, the petty gossip and backbiting between its competitive pupils; just as quickly she'd realized she wasn't talented enough to be taken seriously by anyone, teacher or student.

It was a waste of money as well as effort, and she struggled not to feel uncharacteristically despondent as she tried to ignore the sideways sneers of the other pupils, the artistic exasperation of her professors. So here she sat, in the middle of Residenzplatz, dreading to return to her lessons, yet having nowhere else to go.

With a sigh she rose from the bench and started across the wide square towards the footbridge over the Salzach that led to the university's premises on Schwarzstrasse. As she crossed the square Lotte noticed a crowd of people listening to a man standing on the steps of the fountain; he was shouting about something with a look of exultant fury on his face as spittle flew out of his mouth along with angry words.

"Who is responsible for the failure of the banks? The Jews! Who keeps your money and eats your bread? The Jews! Who controls the stocks, the banks, even where you buy your clothes?" He waited, a faint expectant smile curving his mouth.

The crowd, buoyed by his frenzied delivery, chanted, "The Jews!"

"You are right, good people of Salzburg! The Jews are destroying our way of life. They are polluting our pure Germanic blood! We are children and heirs of Deutschland, with a long and noble history going back to Charlemagne himself, and we are now reduced to scrounging for scraps that the Jews deign to give us. This must stop! And it *will* stop, when Hitler unites us with Germany!"

The cheers that went up from the crowd chilled Lotte right through. More and more often she had seen such demonstrations in the city, or read ugly rhetoric in the newspapers—hatred against the Jews as well as the increasing signs of Austrians' affinity with Germany, despite the government's determination to remain independent and outlaw membership in the National Socialist Party.

Last week Lotte had seen Janos, the knife grinder, with his eye blackened and his face bruised. When her mother had demanded to know what had happened to him, he'd shrugged and smiled, revealing several missing teeth. "Some boys decided to teach me a lesson. What can I say, Frau Eder? The world is an unhappy place."

Her mother's mouth had thinned but she had said nothing more. Her father, however, had been greatly distressed by the sight of Janos's poor face, and had insisted on paying him double for the knives he'd sharpened.

"Double!" Hedwig had exclaimed after the knife grinder had gone away with his cart. "There is charity and then there is foolishness."

"Then let me be foolish," Manfred had replied with a sad smile, and Hedwig had harrumphed upstairs.

Lotte knew her father hated the Nazis and all they stood for; she heard enough lambasting of their policies during his monthly salons. She did not, however, know what her mother thought; if Hedwig had any political opinions, she kept them to herself, although Lotte suspected she would agree with her husband, simply out of solidarity.

And what did she herself think of these matters? Lotte had not given them much thought, beyond disliking the shouting and the fury. She preferred life to be peaceful, a gentle stream rather than a rushing river, and everything she did—from listening to the old men during her father's gatherings, or eating her mother's heavy *Gröstl* even though she could barely choke down the pork-fried potatoes, to attending the music classes she didn't even want—was to make people happy.

For Lotte herself, fleeting happiness always seemed to be just out of reach, a shimmer on the horizon that too often disappeared from view, no matter how she tried to discover it, in music or silence, in pleasing others or pleasing herself. She was always,

Lotte reflected, left feeling a bit discontented and restless, chasing after that elusive emotion, that distant glinting.

The man had jumped down from the steps and the crowd began to disperse, Lotte kept well out of the way of them all, doing her best not to meet anyone's gaze. For someone who had commanded such an audience, he seemed a rough-necked sort of person, with a ruddy face and a stained cravat tied loosely around his stubbly throat. He caught her eye and grinned in a way that made Lotte look away quickly.

More and more she had noticed men staring at her like that—with a knowing glint in their eye, a leer to their lips as their eyes wandered up and down her body in a way that felt far too familiar, even crude.

"It's because you're beautiful," Johanna had told her. "Surely you know how lovely you are, Lotte? And men know it as well. They can't help themselves, unfortunately, although they should."

How was she to answer that? Yes, she'd been told often enough that her abundant blond hair, wide blue eyes and rosebud mouth were the ideal of beauty, yet what good did it do her, besides attracting unwanted attention? She would rather be plain, although she never said so, because beauty was a gift, just like a lovely voice or a quick mind. She did not want to be ungrateful, and yet she hated the stares.

Lotte reached the other side of the square and headed across the Mozartsteg, the wrought-iron footbridge that crossed the Salzach, when she realized the man from the fountain had caught up with her and was deliberately dogging her steps on the narrow bridge.

"Well, Fraülein, what did you think about what I said?" he asked in a strong Bavarian accent, his voice filled with what seemed like lewd insinuation.

Lotte ignored him and kept walking, quickening her steps. The man quickened his as well, and then he grabbed her arm, startling her so much that it felt as if her heart was leaping into her throat.

He forced her to turn around as he kept hold of her arm, drawing her body closer to his as his gaze wandered up and down, just as Lotte had dreaded it would. “I saw you watching,” he said in a tone that was caught between a growl and a murmur.

“Only because you were so loud,” Lotte replied as she tried to shake him off, but he kept hold of her, pushing his face close to hers.

“You think you’re too good for me, eh?” he demanded as he shook her arm. “Eh?”

Lotte’s voice bottled in her throat as she stared at him with both fear and loathing; this close to him she could smell the stench of sweat and beer on his body and breath, and it made her stomach churn.

“Let me go,” she demanded, but her voice sounded faint and her head was swimming.

“Too good for the likes of me, eh,” the man stated, giving her arm another shake. “You should be a good daughter of the *Führer*. You know what he says about women? Your only use is your womb.” He laughed, his spittle flying in her face, and once again Lotte tried to jerk her arm away.

“Please…” She hated to beg, but she was too frightened to fight any longer. The man gave her a considering look, and distantly Lotte wondered what on earth he intended to do right here on the bridge, but then, as he caught sight of someone coming across from the other side, he finally, thankfully, let go of her.

“Fraülein, is this man bothering you?” An officious-looking older man in a homburg and heavy overcoat came frowning towards them as Lotte cradled her arm to her chest as if it had been broken. She could still feel where the man’s fingers had dug in.

“He—he was,” she stammered, but the rough man was already loping away from her towards the other side of the river.

“Are you all right?” the gentleman asked, but Lotte could barely see him through the haze of her tears.

"Yes—yes, thank you." She hurried from the bridge, away from the stranger, and away from the Mozarteum as well. She could not bear to follow the odious man, afraid he might leap out at her again. She kept her hurried, frightened pace until she'd reached the far side of Residenzplatz, and was sure she wasn't being followed.

For a few seconds Lotte simply stood there, her heart thudding, her head still spinning. Even now she could picture the man's leering face, the lewd look in his eyes, and she shuddered. She could not go to her class in such a state. Yet if she went home she'd have to explain, and she did not wish to do that either.

Taking a deep breath to steady herself, she glanced up and saw the familiar red dome of Nonnberg Abbey, the oldest nunnery in Austria as well as in Germany, a beacon of faith and hope high above the city.

Slowly, without knowing exactly what she intended, she began to walk up Kaigasse, and then turned onto Nonnbergstiege, the steep set of stairs built between two tall buildings that led to the abbey itself. She was breathing hard by the time she climbed the one hundred and fifty steps and came to the abbey's visitors' entrance, an old wrought-iron gate that led to the courtyard and chapel, the only parts of the abbey open to the public.

Lotte slipped through the gate and into the courtyard, the ancient cloisters leading off it in several directions, the cold, damp air turning hushed, as if she'd come into another world. Indeed, she felt as if she had.

She was utterly alone, and for a few seconds she simply reveled in the quiet she found there, the way the noise and bustle of the city simply fell away, replaced by a perfect stillness that echoed through her like a memory, or maybe a dream.

Here there would never be rough-looking men shouting on steps or grabbing her arm; there would be no supercilious professors or snobbish students. No man would look at her with a leer as he wet his lips. There would be no anger or aggression, no fury or fear. Just this stillness, like the settling of twilight or the rising of dawn.

Lotte released the breath she'd instinctively held in a long, low sigh of contentment as the blessed silence soaked into her bones.

The door to the chapel was open, and she went through it, breathing in the familiar smells of candle wax and incense, letting them comfort her, before she realized with a jolt that the nuns were standing in their stalls, saying their prayers, their voices rising and falling in mellifluous waves, a sound of peace that, for a moment, brought tears to Lotte's eyes. This was even better than the beauty of silence. She stood in the doorway for a few minutes, listening to the ancient prayers, letting them soothe her troubled soul.

She had always liked going to mass at St. Blasius, the simple church carved into the rock of the Monschberg that her family had been attending since before she was born, but this felt like something far more elevated, a devotion given solely and entirely to God.

It caused her a flicker of indefinable yearning, and the opening lines of Rilke's poem from *The Book of Hours* went through her in a shudder:

I am too alone in this world, yet I am not alone enough
to make each moment holy.

This moment felt holy.

The sudden sound of speaking voices from the courtyard startled her, and quickly Lotte left the church, longing to stay, yet feeling vaguely guilty for coming at all, as if she were an interloper into a world that was both sacred and somehow forbidden.

As she came back into the courtyard, she saw a woman and a child standing there—and she realized, with a jolt of shock, that the woman was Maria von Trapp.

Lotte stared at her dumbly, this former postulant who had, in her mind, obtained a certain revered status—married to a baron, mother to nine children, and esteemed leader of the von Trapp Family Singers. Lotte had heard them on the radio several times already.

Maria von Trapp's gaze was friendly but disconcertingly direct as she stared back at Lotte. "Hello," she said. "Do I know you?"

"No—no," Lotte stammered, "that is—we have never met. But we both sung in a competition several years ago, at the Elektrischer Aufzug. Of course you won't remember us—my sisters and I, that is. We sung in a trio, "Die Lorelei…"

Maria's expression clouded for a moment, and then cleared, her whole countenance brightening. "Ah yes, the Edelweiss Sisters!" She laughed, a merry sound, and Lotte gaped at her in surprise.

"But… how did you know?" Only her father had called them that, his teasing term of endearment.

"No, no, I know that is not your name," Maria assured her with another laugh. "It was the Eder Sisters Trio, was it not? But you all wore sprigs of edelweiss in your dirndls, as I recall. So pretty."

"Yes, that is right." Lotte, like her sisters, had kept the sprigs of edelweiss as her father had asked, pressing them between the pages of the family Bible. "I am amazed you remember us, Baroness von Trapp. We were most forgettable, I thought."

"Not at all. You were very charming. I recall talking to you all. I remember that, although I can't actually remember the songs we sung. Those were a blur! But what are you doing up here at the abbey?"

"I just came to visit. It's so quiet and peaceful." Lotte could not keep from giving the chapel a longing glance. "I could stay up here forever, I think."

"Could you?" Maria replied, tilting her head in speculation, her dark eyes as bright as a bird's. She was not a beautiful woman, but there was something alive and vital about her, a bristling, energetic alertness that made her striking. "I once thought the same, but God had other plans for me! And now I am bringing my daughter, my little Lorli, to school here." She glanced down tenderly at the solemn-faced little girl standing silently next to her. "It is a great joy to me to do so."

"I'm sure," Lotte murmured. She smiled at the girl who smiled uncertainly back as she leaned into her mother. "If I could spend all my days here, I surely would," Lotte declared, her tone holding more heartfelt conviction than she'd meant to reveal.

"Perhaps you have a vocation?" Maria suggested, with that same unsettling directness. Lotte thought she meant to joke, but when she saw the seriousness of the other woman's expression she realized she wasn't.

"Oh… I don't…"

"You are Catholic?"

"Yes, my family attends St. Blasius."

"Well then? God's call can be but a whisper, but it is certainly distinct and once heard, impossible to ignore. I heard it when I was about your age, and came here as a postulant. Those were some of the happiest days of my life, although of course I am now happiest settled in my home." She glanced again at her daughter, her expression suffused with love.

"Yes, I had heard of your time here," Lotte replied stiltedly, her mind spinning at the thought of even hearing—never mind heeding—such a call herself.

"It is a great privilege, to dedicate all to the Lord's service. It was all I wanted, you know. I was quite, quite distressed when the Mother Abbess told me it was God's will for me to marry my husband, Captain von Trapp."

"You were?" Somehow this surprised Lotte, when she thought of all Maria had gained—the grand house in Aigen, a life of ease, the love of a good man and her own children. And yet to stay here, wrapped in this solitude and silence…

"Yes, I was," Maria replied seriously. "But one must always heed God's call, whether it takes you into the comfort of the cloister, or the wildness of the world beyond. I hope for your sake, Fraülein Eder, that you listen to whatever it is." She reached out and grasped Lotte's hand, giving her a smile of solidarity, before she ushered her daughter forward and went out into the misting drizzle with her.

The prayers of the nuns had finished, so all was silent as Lotte walked slowly from the courtyard and back down the steep and narrow Nonnbergstiege. As she came down the last of the steps, the clamor and clatter of the city assaulted her senses—the guffaw of a passerby, the squeak and squeal of a tram, the slam of a door, the shout of a peddler. She had an urge to sprint up the steps she'd just come down and hide away in the safety of the chapel forever, removed and protected.

But no. She had enough to answer for already; she had missed an entire afternoon of classes, and she would have to tell her parents of it. The thought of her mother's disapproval, and worse, far worse, her father's gentle disappointment, was enough for the last of that oft-sought contentment to drain away.

"*Once heard, it is impossible to ignore.*" Lotte recalled Maria von Trapp's words and hoped she was right. If she did indeed hear such a call, surely she would have no choice but to follow it.

CHAPTER FIVE

JOHANNA

November 1936

Franz Weber had been living at the house on Getreidegasse for over a month when he suggested the hike up the Untersberg that Manfred had promised right at the beginning of his stay. Although it had been, technically, her father's idea, Johanna recognized at once that it was truly Franz's. In the weeks since he'd been apprenticed to her father, Johanna had often observed him—discreetly, of course—and she'd both seen and felt the force of his personality, laughing charm combined with steely determination. She could not help but find him fascinating.

Franz spent his days down in the shop, but he, Manfred, and Birgit all came upstairs for the midday meal, which Hedwig and Johanna prepared and served. Johanna brought their coffee down in the afternoon, and then Franz spent the evenings with the family—first supper and prayers, and then a few hours in the sitting room, listening to the radio or reading, perhaps playing music.

Only a few days after he'd arrived he'd sat down at their piano and played the first few lilting bars of a Mozart sonata.

"How well you play!" Manfred had exclaimed, pleased, and Franz had laughed and spun around on the stool.

"Everyone in Vienna must play an instrument," he told him with an expansive shrug. "Music and theatre are far more important than politics there."

"Then it must be a happy place indeed," Manfred had replied.

"It *was,*" Franz answered with a disconcertingly dark emphasis, before he gave them all a laughing look. "But I thought Mozart was appropriate, considering this is his city."

"Indeed, his birthplace is only a few doors down from here," Manfred agreed with a smiling nod. "But you have teased us with just a few bars! Play the whole sonata, if you can."

And so Franz had, his long fingers rippling over the keys as the room filled with the mellifluous sound of Mozart. Soon, at her father's bidding, Johanna and her sisters began to sing along to Franz's accompaniment, teaching him some old folk songs.

Despite the dull competency of her voice, Johanna had enjoyed those evenings, standing next to Franz as he played. He had asked her to turn the pages of his music, which she'd been more than happy to do, although Birgit had given her a fulminating look when she'd acquiesced to his request. Although her sister acted as if she despised Franz Weber, Johanna wondered if she secretly admired him.

For surely there was much to admire in such a man, in both his looks and temperament. He had a craggy, expressive face and eyes the color of the mahogany in their sitting room when it was well polished. His body was tall and rangy, his shoulders slightly stooped from a lifetime, no doubt, of ducking under doorways.

But more admirable than his looks, Johanna thought, was his sense of vitality; he crackled with energy, bristled with interest, always looking about himself with an alertness that felt electric—it made her feel alive, simply being near him.

When Franz was in a room, she couldn't help but edge closer, and her gaze continued to stray to his face, roaming over its expressive features, the snapping eyes and slightly crooked nose, as if attempting to memorize them. He fascinated her—like she had never been fascinated by anything or anyone before.

And, she was beginning to dare to think, she interested *him.* She could not imagine she was as fascinating to Franz as he was to her, but she did notice the way he would engage her in conversation over the dinner table, or linger for a few moments in the afternoon when she and her mother were clearing the cups away.

Once, as she'd been leaving for the market, he'd risen from his bench in the shop and asked her if he could accompany her.

"I must buy some notepaper and envelopes to write my family," he'd told her. "Do you mind if I come along?"

"I—no, of course not," Johanna had stammered, already disconcerted by the nearness of his presence, the way he threw his scarf around his neck, his eyes glinting as he smiled at her. He looked as if everything amused and interested him, even her.

Outside the air had possessed a chill, and the sky was the color of slate. Johanna had walked rather primly along, a wicker basket over one arm.

"You look like the goose girl in the fairy tale," he'd told her, and she started in surprise.

"The goose girl!"

"Do you know the story?"

"Yes, a bit." She recalled reading it in a book of fairy tales, how a princess was tricked by her evil servant and forced to become a servant herself. Eventually, Johanna recalled, she was discovered and married the king of a neighboring country.

"She had golden hair like yours," Franz had said, and then he'd dared, laughingly, to touch the coil of braid twisted around her head. "If you combed it out, you'd just be like her."

"I don't know whether I wish to be like the goose girl," Johanna had replied. She was both shaken and thrilled by his gentle forwardness; he was flirting with her, and she did not know how to flirt.

"She is vindicated in the end," Franz had reminded her. "And she marries the king. Wouldn't you like that?"

"To marry a king?" she'd replied with some of her usual spirit. "It depends on what sort of man he was."

"A very good answer," Franz had approved, and she'd looked at him with her eyebrows raised, determined for him not to realize how much she cared for his opinion.

"Oh, do you think so?" she'd said with a touch of sarcasm, and he'd just laughed.

In the market square he'd bought his paper and envelopes, and then he'd insisted on carrying her basket as she went around the Grünmarkt in Universitätsplatz, inspecting potatoes and onions, feeling strangely like a wife, although she'd supposed she could not even begin to know what that felt like.

When they'd returned to the house on Getreidegasse, he'd brushed her fingers with his own. "Thank you for the company," he'd said simply, and Johanna had only been able to nod.

Now, over a month into Franz's apprenticeship, they were all hiking up the Untersberg. He had asked Johanna about the hike one afternoon when she'd brought him coffee as usual, his fingers brushing hers as she'd handed him his cup. But although she dared to think he'd meant the invitation for her alone, her father had taken it up gladly.

"Yes, yes, we must all go, before it gets too cold! Hedwig will pack a picnic. What a splendid idea, Franz. Isn't it, Johanna?"

Franz had given her a wry look that Johanna thought she could interpret, and she'd blushed as she'd answered, her gaze on Franz, rather than her father.

"Yes, Papa, indeed it is."

They set off from the nearby village of Grodig gamely enough, her father using the old, knobbled walking stick he'd had when he'd met his wife herding goats, Birgit walking faithfully alongside him. Lotte had fallen into step with their mother, and had taken the picnic basket before Franz offered, with a funny little bow, to carry it himself.

Johanna let herself fall behind the others, knowing with a feminine intuition she hadn't realized she'd possessed that Franz would fall in step with her, so they lagged a fair distance behind her family.

"A beautiful day, is it not?" Franz asked as he gave her a sideways, smiling glance.

"Indeed it is." Already she felt her cheeks warm. "What do you think to the mountains, Herr Weber?"

"Surely by now you can call me Franz?"

"Franz," Johanna agreed, willing her blush to fade. She felt like a simpering schoolgirl, and yet at the same time an aging spinster. She did not know which she was, and she could not bear the thought that she might be made to look ridiculous.

"I think they take my breath away." But he was looking at her as he said it, and that made Johanna blush even more hotly. Was he teasing her, or did he mean what he'd said? She feared trusting his kindness, the warm admiration she saw so often in his eyes, and yet she longed to do just that.

"Legend says Charlemagne himself is hiding in the caves on Untersberg," she remarked, desperate to think of something clever to say. "Waiting to return to battle the Antichrist."

"Then I hope he makes an appearance soon," Franz returned dryly, "for the Antichrist has surely already arrived."

"You mean Hitler?"

"Of course."

"You know many Salzburgers admire him," Johanna remarked hesitantly. "Many Austrians, even. The papers are full of it." Only last week the headline of the *Salzburger Volksblatt* had been about the "*Pride of Deutschland*," and then of course there was the whole matter of the Jews.

"Yes, I know," Franz said, his tone both heavy and bitter as his gaze rested on the distant peaks. "Vienna was the same, if not worse. Sometimes it feels as if the whole world is going mad."

"Is that why you left?"

He gave her a quick, searching look. "Did your father not tell you?"

She shook her head. "No, he said nothing of why you came."

He paused, as if he would say something more, and then he shrugged. "It doesn't matter."

"Birgit says you don't know the first thing about clocks," Johanna remarked impulsively, and Franz laughed. "Is it true?"

"It *was.* I have learned something about them in the last few weeks, I hope." He turned his smiling glance once more upon her, his good humor fully restored as he gave her a look that felt both teasing and intimate. "But what about you, Johanna? What do you wish to do with your life?"

"Do?"

"You do not wish to repair clocks, I think."

"I haven't the head for it. But no, I never did."

"Then what?"

She shrugged, discomfited by his question, the possibilities it opened inside her. "I had been hoping to take a secretarial course," she said after a moment. "But it wasn't possible."

"A secretarial course!" Franz sounded incredulous.

"Yes, so I could work in an office."

"Typing the dull correspondence of stuffy businessmen? That would be a life wasted, indeed."

"I didn't think so," she replied, a little insulted, and he laughed and reached for her hand.

Johanna let him take it, a frisson of awareness traveling all the way up her arm as Franz swung her arm in his as they walked. Even though both their hands were gloved she could feel the warmth of his skin through the wool, and it electrified her.

"I mean, what do you want to *do*?" Franz said. "Not something pedestrian or pedantic. Something real. What dreams do you have? Do you want to travel? See the world? Go to university? Ride a camel?"

"Ride a camel?" Johanna repeated as laughter bubbled up inside her. "Certainly not."

"What, then?" He turned to her with a look of sudden, burning intensity; he was still holding her hand. Johanna's mouth went dry as her heart beat wildly. She knew then what she wanted, yet she could hardly say it to Franz. *I want you to always look at me like that, to hold my hand, to kiss me…*

"I… I don't know."

"Not allowed," Franz declared with a determined shake of his head and a squeeze of her hand. "You have to think of *something.*"

"I've always wanted to go to Paris," she said finally. "To see the Eiffel Tower. My father has a postcard of it, and it looks so modern. He went there when he was young, before he married Mama."

"Paris," Franz repeated musingly. "Paris it is, then."

She laughed in disbelief at how definitive he sounded. "Are you going to wave your magic wand, then, and have me whisked away?"

"I don't have a magic wand, most unfortunately, but one day we'll go to Paris. I promise."

She shook her head, embarrassed now at his certain tone as well as his use of the word "we."

They'd slowed their steps until they were standing still, at a vantage point overlooking the village now far below them, the world spread out in densely green, undulating waves, the ragged peaks of the snow-capped mountains fringing the bright horizon.

"I must seem very provincial to you," Johanna said after a moment, although it hurt her pride to admit as much. "My father said you had a degree from the University of Vienna, and with all your talk of theatre and music, philosophy and mathematics…"

She bit her lip, feeling compelled to point out what was undoubtedly all too apparent. "I've hardly read any books, and the only play I've seen is *Jedermann* at the festival, and then only because they perform it for free, in the square." She turned to him with a frank, challenging look. "I didn't think much of it, to be honest. So much fuss over a story of an ordinary man."

Franz let out a shout of laughter and tugged her by the hand, pulling her closer towards him. "But that is exactly why I like you, Johanna," he told her as his gaze turned kind, even tender. "The Viennese are such snobs about their music and their theatre. They think they're so cultured, so very sophisticated, but really they're quite, quite dull."

"I fear I must be duller."

"No." He'd nudged her even closer, so their bodies were a breath apart. "You are not at all dull to me."

"Only because my provincial ways are a novelty to you, then," Johanna said, her voice rising as if she wanted to prove something to him, or perhaps just to herself. "Admit it. You must."

"I must?" Franz's eyes glinted. "I think you are fishing for compliments."

"Compliments!"

"Do you want me to tell you how lovely you are, with your golden braids and your flashing eyes?" He touched each of the braids looped over her ears with one finger. "Or perhaps you want me to say how exciting I find you, how when you set a plate before me at supper time I feel as if you are giving me a dare?"

"A dare?" Johanna scoffed, but her voice was breathless.

"Everything you do is so purposeful, Johanna. You make the most mundane action alive and exciting. Your life might be in the kitchen but your mind is not. You are not at all provincial to me, and I think you must know it."

It was true, Johanna realized with a thrill, she *did* know it. Although her pride advised caution, her body flared with feminine knowledge and power. A smile as old as time curved her mouth and Franz laughed softly.

"Yes, you do," he murmured, and he tugged her even closer. He dipped his head, his dark gaze intent on hers.

He's going to kiss me, Johanna realized. It seemed unimaginable, that this handsome, intelligent, interesting man wanted to kiss her—*her*, Johanna Eder, who had spent all her life in the convent and kitchen, whose future had seemed to stretch out unimpeded and uninteresting, for decades. It would be her first kiss, and the prospect filled her with equal measures of terror and wonder.

"Hey, you two," Birgit called, and Johanna sprang away from Franz. "We've found a place to eat. Franz, you have the picnic basket!"

"Coming," Franz called, holding the basket high like a trophy.

Johanna kept her head lowered as she followed him up the slope, her whole body tingling, and he hadn't even touched her, not really. *Does he really find me exciting?* She longed to believe it, and yet pride—and a fear of being humiliated—made her wary. Incredulous, and yet hopeful.

If he was just amusing himself, she would be furious, but far worse, she knew, she'd be heartbroken, even after just a few weeks. She could not bear to be either, ever, yet she feared she would not be able to keep herself from it.

As Johanna crested the hill she saw that everyone had assembled in one of the simple mountain huts that could be found throughout the countryside; her mother was massaging her already swollen ankles and Manfred smiled at them both genially while Birgit merely looked cross. Lotte was standing a few meters away on the brow of the hill, her arms outstretched and her head tilted to the sky. With her blond hair gilded by sunlight, she looked like an angel. An angel in hobnailed boots.

"Lotte, what are you doing?" Johanna called in a mix of exasperation and affection. She sometimes thought her sister was a bit touched, the way she carried on.

"I am praying," Lotte declared, her face still lifted, her eyes closed. "Don't you feel closer to God here? I feel as if I can almost touch heaven."

"Well, we're nearly a thousand meters closer to it," Johanna replied dryly. "But the only way you'll be touching it is you take a tumble!"

Laughing, Lotte lowered her arms and turned to face them all, a look of such joyful serenity on her face that for a disconcerting moment Johanna felt as if her sister was right, and she had, albeit briefly, touched something otherworldly and eternal.

"I'm not going to tumble," she said, her gaze moving beyond Johanna to Franz. "Don't you feel it, Franz? Closer to heaven?"

Franz dug his hands into the pockets of his coat as he rocked back on his heels. "I can't say I do," he told her with a smile, "since I don't believe in heaven."

"What!" Lotte stared at him in surprise.

"What do you mean?" Johanna asked him, a note of uncertainty entering her voice. "Of course you believe in heaven."

Franz shook his head, still smiling. "I'm afraid I don't. Or God, for that matter. At least the verdict is still out on that one. I'm not completely convinced any deity exists, and nothing I've experienced so far has given me cause to think it does."

Vaguely Johanna recalled the heated but good-spirited debates in the evenings between Franz and her father; she didn't feel she possessed the intellect or even the interest to follow the argument, but she recalled Franz talking about all knowledge being based in logic and needing evidence for everything. *But surely God was the most logical thing of all?*

"How can you not believe in God?" Lotte exclaimed, throwing her arms wide again. "Just look all around you!"

Slowly Franz gazed around at the beauty of the mountains, the snow-capped peaks in the distance, the rolling fields still green in autumn, thanks to the *Schnürlregen*. "I admit," he said, "it is easier to believe in God here than in some other places."

Lotte dropped her arms and shook her head. "You miss so much," she said sadly as she walked into the hut.

Franz turned to Johanna. "Are you disappointed?" he asked quietly, and she stared at him, unsure how to answer.

She was more surprised than anything else. She had never met anyone who did not believe in God, who did not attend mass, who didn't mark the year in saints' days and festivals, or spend hours in prayer. It made her realize how different he was. It was as if she were standing on the edge of a precipice and had only just looked down to realize how precarious her position was, and how small.

"I don't know," she admitted.

"Perhaps if you had seen some of the things I've seen you wouldn't believe in God, either," he remarked quietly.

"Johanna, Franz, come eat," Hedwig called, a gruff command, and unable to reply, Johanna turned away from Franz before hurrying into the hut.

CHAPTER SIX

BIRGIT

December 1936

Birgit stood in the doorway of the shabby café, the warm fug of cigarette smoke and coffee enveloping her in a steamy cloud. Outside it was sleeting icy rain and the walk from Getreidegasse to this coffeehouse in the less salubrious district of Elisabeth-Vorstadt, by the train station, had soaked her coat right through.

A waiter by the bar caught her eye and gave a small nod. Birgit nodded back before looking away, a feeling like pride buoying up inside her. This was the third time she'd come to the coffeehouse, and the second that she had been given the knowing nod. She closed the door behind her and wound her way through the tables, her head held high, before she slipped into a small room at the back, its door inlaid with a mirror so it was barely visible.

The room at the back was even stuffier than the main coffeehouse, cluttered with rickety tables and chairs and thick with the smell of sweat, smoke, and schnapps. A few people glanced her way as she came into the room—men in the stained overalls and jackets of railway workers, and a few shop girls and jaded-looking women, some who worked the streets, others who earned a few groschen sewing or cleaning or taking in washing. Since coming to these meetings, Birgit had been exposed to a whole new world, an entirely different universe from the comfortable little shop on Getreidegasse, and she was glad.

Birgit had been terrified the first time she'd ventured across the city to attend the meeting the woman had told her about on the rainy night Janos Panov had been attacked. She'd never even been in this part of Salzburg before, with its shabby tenements and warehouses, except to take the train from the main station, on rare occasions. She'd crept along the sidewalk, afraid of being accosted by one of the many rough-looking people jostling all around her, tempted at every turn to hare back to the old-world comfort of Getreidegasse.

But some stubborn spark inside her that she had not realized she'd possessed had forced her on; at supper that evening, with great ceremony, her father had presented Franz with a set of his own tools, in a leather case just as Birgit's were. He'd been an apprentice then for just over a month. Birgit had not received her own set of tools until she'd been working by her father's side for two years.

The knowledge had burned, just as so much had burned—her father's obvious delight in his pupil, the way Franz engaged him in the evenings with complicated talk of philosophy and logic, in a manner Birgit knew she never could. He was the son her father had never had, the partner he'd clearly wanted. And Manfred was not the only member of the Eder family who had fallen for Franz's charms—it was all too apparent that Johanna was besotted with him.

She'd denied it of course, when Birgit had challenged her, but she knew all the same. Franz had wormed his way into everyone's hearts, and if she did not feel so resentful, she probably would have liked him, as well. All this knowledge had forced her on, until she had entered the coffee house whose address had been on the paper, and, having no idea what to do, she'd gone up to a waiter and asked haltingly,

"Please… is there a meeting here tonight, for those who wish to resist fascism?"

The man had looked at her incredulously and before Birgit even knew what was happening, she was being hustled into little more than a cupboard, her heart beating with hard painful thuds as two rough-looking men demanded to know who she was and how she'd heard about the meeting.

Birgit had barely been able to stammer something about Janos, the fountain, and a woman, before a clear, husky voice she remembered had declared, "Stop pestering her! She's Eder's daughter, and she's with me."

Birgit, brought nearly to tears, had blinked gratefully up at the woman she'd encountered that rainy night in the street. In the light of the café she could see how striking she was, with her dark hair and red lips. She wore a button-down shirt, like a man's, belted into a pair of wide-legged trousers and a kerchief around her throat. Birgit thought she looked like something out of a fairy tale, a female Puss in Boots, perhaps, her stance wide, her hands planted on her hips as she gave Birgit a frank stare.

"I'm sorry they scared you," the woman said, "but we have to be careful. My name is Ingrid." She'd stuck out a hand for Birgit to shake the way a man would and then ushered her into the back room. Over the next hour Birgit had listened, both rapt and uneasy, as a man had pontificated about the evils of fascism, the Nazi threat and the need for socialists, communists, trade unionists and Catholics all to unite to fight the menace not just of Hitler, but of Austria's *Ständestaat*.

"We must unite to stand strong against evil. We must put Hitler and his fascist cronies in Austria and abroad in the dustbin of history! As Marx himself said, let the ruling classes tremble! The proletarians have nothing to lose but their chains, and those chains will be heavy indeed, my comrades and friends, when they are laid upon us by Hitler himself. We must shake them off *now*, before it is too late. Workers of the world, unite!"

Birgit had been a bit taken aback by the furious rhetoric, the man's red face, the claps and shouts and whistles and stomping of feet in response. Ingrid, blowing out a stream of smoke from her cigarette, had given her a knowing and sympathetic smile.

"August can be a bit much to take, but he means well, and more importantly, he is willing to die for the cause."

"The cause against Hitler?" Birgit had asked uncertainly. "He spoke against Schuschnigg, as well."

"Schuschnigg is better than Hitler, it is true, but the Fatherland Front is still fascist and must be fought. Why should our meetings here be illegal? Why should we not all be free to meet and believe as we like?"

Birgit had known the meeting was illegal, of course, yet having Ingrid state it so simply made her insides lurch with alarm. She'd never done anything illegal before. "My father says the *Ständestaat* must endure so we can be strong enough to resist Hitler."

"Your father is a good man," Ingrid had replied, "but he is naïve." She gave Birgit the same sort of direct look she remembered from the night they helped Janos. "Why did you come?"

"Wh—why?" Birgit had stammered. "I was… curious, I suppose." And she'd liked the fact that she'd been invited, wanted. She knew some part of her had longed to do something rebellious, if not actually illegal. Something brave.

"And so? Your curiosity is satisfied now?" A hard note had entered Ingrid's voice. "You go home and that is all?"

"I…" Birgit had trailed off, unsure. She hadn't known what she'd thought about it all, or what she would do. There had been an energy and purpose in the room that she'd found nowhere else, and it had both attracted and alarmed her with its magnetic force. "What can I do?" she'd asked, meaning it, she'd realized afterward, as something of a rhetorical question, but Ingrid had leaned forward, thrusting her face close to hers.

"Plenty," she'd said.

That night, after the meeting had finished, Ingrid gave her a bundle of communist pamphlets and had told her to leave them in public places all over the city. Birgit had stared at her in dismayed shock. If she were to be caught with just one of the pamphlets, never mind five hundred, she would almost certainly be arrested.

Although Birgit had never had much interest in politics, she'd known enough even before coming to Elisabeth-Vorstadt to realize that the Federal State of Austria did not tolerate any political action by other parties, and certainly not by communists or socialists. The pamphlets, with their enraged denunciation of all forms of fascism, its bold call to arms, were dangerous indeed.

And yet, compelled by Ingrid's challenging stare, Birgit had taken them, and hidden them under her bed, wrapped in an old apron. She could have left them there, and indeed she had been tempted to, but that surprising spark of courage and honor had fanned into a flame strong enough to take a few out at a time, and secretly leave them about the city—pinned to a door or on the steps of a fountain, left in the library or in SL Schwarz, the department store on Alter Markt that was run by Jews.

Every time she took out one of the pamphlets, her insides had trembled, and yet the more she had done it, the more she had been emboldened to continue. *This is who I am,* she'd thought in wonder. *This is who I can be.* Someone bold and strong and purposeful, like Ingrid. Someone who believes and acts. And perhaps, after all, it helped to be invisible. No one noticed the potato-faced girl lingering by a doorway or market stall. No one cared, and for once that was a good thing.

Now, two months on from that first meeting, as she settled herself at one of the tables in the back, Birgit felt, if not exactly confident in these surroundings, then at least more comfortable.

She met people's eyes and smiled and nodded, although she did not know their names, she felt known herself. She liked feeling not important, no, not that, but useful. Purposeful. A part of things.

"Our little Catholic has come," Ingrid said in a voice of gentle mockery as she joined Birgit at her table. "Did you distribute all the pamphlets I gave you?"

Birgit nodded, unable to keep a note of pride from her voice as she answered, "Yes. All of them."

"Good girl." Although Ingrid was only thirty or so, she seemed far more worldly and experienced, so Birgit couldn't help but preen a little under the praise like a pupil with her teacher.

"I have never asked how you knew of my father," she remarked as Ingrid lit a cigarette. She could not imagine her father knowing any of the people at a meeting such as this; he despised communism and its anti-Catholic rhetoric.

Ingrid gave her a rather amused look as she flicked out the match and tossed it on the floor. "We assisted each other with a small matter, a few months ago."

"Assisted?" Birgit could not keep from sounding incredulous. "How?"

"Perhaps that is for you to ask him." She cocked her head. "He doesn't know you come to these meetings, I suppose?"

Birgit shook her head. "No, of course not."

"You think he would disapprove?"

"He disagrees with the aims of communism, certainly."

"But perhaps he, like so many others, sees the need for us to unite. Catholics and communists together, working against fascism before it takes over the world like the pestilence it truly is. It could happen, you know." Ingrid leaned forward, an urgency in her eyes. "We *must* unite."

The fierce light in Ingrid's eyes made Birgit experience an unsettling mix of courage and fear. She wanted to share the older woman's sense of purpose, but she didn't know if she did. If she was strong enough. She didn't think she was, like August Gruber had stated so confidently, willing to die for the cause.

"You speak as if the Nazis coming into Austria is a certainty," she remarked finally.

"I believe it is a certainty," Ingrid replied, her voice cool. "They have already taken the Rhineland and made a pact with Italy. Already they are looking to the Sudetenland, and to us. And to their eternal shame, many Austrians long for it. They think their lot will be better under Hitler's iron fist. Of course, it is not all that good under Schuschnigg," she admitted with a grimace, "but Hitler would be far worse. And as if getting rid of all the Jews will somehow help them." She snorted in derision. "How can you think it will not happen?"

Birgit shrugged, feeling both chastised and stupid. She wanted to be brave, but she did not fully understand politics. She could not talk as Ingrid did, with worldly knowledge and confidence.

Ingrid must have sensed something of how she felt, for she lowered her voice, covering her hand with her own. "I forget how young you are," she said. "How innocent. You do not realize how bad things have become, or how bad they will be."

"I distributed those pamphlets," Birgit protested, as if that made that much of a difference.

"One day you may be called on to do more," Ingrid replied. "Much more. And the question you will have to ask yourself is, will you be able to?"

Birgit swallowed hard. She did not know how "*much more*" Ingrid meant, or indeed how much she would be willing to give, but just the thought of doing more than leaving a few leaflets around made her stomach clench in fear, her heart feel as if it were suspended in her chest. And yet… she didn't want to stay safe. She didn't want to lose the sense of purpose these meetings had given her. She wanted to be brave, even if she wasn't sure how.

"Think on it," Ingrid said, and released her hand, leaning back in her chair as the evening's speaker began.

Birgit barely listened, for her mind was racing so much, and in truth she'd heard it all before anyway. Most speakers said the same thing—*Unite! Rally! Dare!* The specifics, however, were left to the imagination, and right then Birgit did not want to imagine them.

She did not want to think about what Ingrid or the group she was part of, a motley crew of communists, socialists, and trade unionists, might ask—or even demand—of her. And why should they not demand it, when she had been coming to their meetings and had learned some of their secrets? And if they did demand it, how would she respond? Could she be brave enough to risk her life like Ingrid or August did?

Ingrid threw her a sharp-eyed glance, and Birgit realized she was fidgeting. Part of her longed to leave, yet she refused to entertain that cowardly notion. She'd found an unexpected welcome in this group, along with a sense of purpose. She was loath to leave either behind, and yet…

"*One day you may be called on to do more… much more.*"

Abruptly Birgit stood up from the table. Ingrid leaned forward, her eyes narrowed.

"The toilet," she murmured. "I must…" She hurried from the room with a trembling sigh of relief. A few people in the coffeehouse glanced at her, mostly in disinterest, and quickly she made her way through the tables and slipped outside into the cold, damp night air.

She was overreacting, she told herself, and Ingrid and all the others most likely were, as well. Sometimes she thought the communists *wanted* to be angry. Schuschnigg had signed an agreement, after all. Austria well might be left alone; it wasn't a certainty that Hitler's Wehrmacht might march across its borders. It couldn't be. It might be that she never had to be that brave. She would never have to make that kind of choice.

A sudden screech of tires had her turning in alarm as she saw a black Mercedes come squealing around the corner, followed by another. As they headed towards the coffeehouse, she realized they must be coming to break up the meeting, and she stumbled back through the door and then ran towards the back room.

She flung herself inside, and heads turned at her noisy arrival.

"Someone's coming," she gasped out. "There were two cars—"

Already she heard the front door of the coffeehouse crashing open, the sound of shouting, tables and chairs being overturned, cries of distress.

At once everyone in the back room began to move—some people running out toward an alleyway in the back, others sweeping up pamphlets and papers. Birgit looked for Ingrid, but she'd gone. Fighting what she knew was an unfair sense of betrayal, she hurried towards the back entrance, her heart pounding as she stumbled through the door into the dark alleyway that ran between the buildings and then fell, hard onto her hands and knees, the cobbles sharp and damp beneath her. She could hardly believe a moment had already come where her courage was being called on. She would have laughed if she hadn't been panting in fear.

Someone who had been running behind her tripped over her and fell heavily beside her with a grunt. Before Birgit could say anything, they'd scrambled up and disappeared down the alley.

Birgit let out a sob of terror as she lurched up to her feet and made her way along the alley, as good as blind in the darkness, her hands stretched out in front of her. From the open doorway behind her she could hear the cries and shouts as those remaining were assaulted—*by whom? The police? The Fatherland Front's paramilitary troops? Nazi bully boys?* Birgit had no idea, but she knew she did not want to encounter whoever it was face to face.

Finally she saw a glimmer of light where the alley led into the street, and she let out another sob, this one of relief.

Then someone else ran up behind her, pushing her aside roughly in their bid for freedom. Birgit's head hit the wall, her cheek scraped by the brick. She bit her lip hard and then, her head swimming, kept walking forward.

Finally, *finally* she emerged onto the street, gasping with relief. Her stockings were torn and dirty; there was blood on her hands and cheek, and her hair had fallen down in tangles about her face. Still, she was free.

"Hey!"

She stiffened with both shock and terror as she realized the angry voice was directed at her. A man was standing in front of the coffeehouse, his rubber truncheon pointed at her. Birgit froze, her heart in her mouth, her legs like water. The man started towards her. He was a policeman, she realized. She could be arrested. Put in *prison.* Still she didn't move, even though her brain was bidding her to run, *run,* as fast as she could.

"*There* you are!"

The voice coming from her right was warm and good-humored, and before Birgit could so much as blink she was swept up into an embrace and kissed soundly on the lips.

"You know her, Oberleutnant?" the police officer asked suspiciously, and her savior, or perhaps her captor, answered easily, his arm around her waist.

"Do I know her? Yes, of course I do. This is my fiancée, I'll have you know. Clearly she was caught up in the violence. I hope you have it under control, *Offizier.*"

The policeman began to bluster, but the man at her side was already guiding her away. They walked in silence for several minutes, Birgit's mind a dazed blur, before he stopped and withdrew his arm from her waist.

"There. We've lost them."

She turned to face this stranger who had rescued her, and saw he wore the peaked cap and gray uniform of the mountain troops of Austria's *Bundesheer*. "Th—thank you," she stammered. "I don't know why you did, but you saved me."

"I could never resist a damsel in distress." He handed her a handkerchief from his pocket. "You have blood on your face. Here." He gestured to her cheek. "And here." To her lip.

"Thank you," Birgit murmured as she dabbed the handkerchief at her scrapes.

"I apologize for being so forward," he continued, "but it seemed necessary at the time."

Birgit had no response to that, and no idea what to think of her very first kiss. Her mind was still spinning.

"Look, you've clearly suffered a shock. How about we get a coffee? My treat, of course. And then I insist on walking you home. Where do you live? Nearby?"

"On Getreidegasse—"

"How lovely. Well, what do you say? A coffee?"

She stared at him in confusion, her thoughts still jumbled. On top of everything else that had happened that evening, she did not know how to respond to this kindly man's offer. And he did seem kind; he looked it as well, with a round, homely face and an easy smile. His eyes were blue, his teeth a bit crooked. He was not handsome, and somehow Birgit liked that. Kindness was better than beauty by far.

"Very well," she finally answered, still shaken although she was desperately trying to recover. "Thank you. A coffee would be most welcome."

CHAPTER SEVEN

LOTTE

December 1936

Snow was falling gently as Lotte once again mounted the steep steps of the Nonnbergstiege. Already, in the late afternoon, the sun was sinking towards the horizon and lengthening shadows as the city became blanketed in white. Lotte drew her coat more tightly around her as she came to the top of the steps; Nonnberg Abbey loomed ahead of her through the snow, seeming as ancient and indestructible as the mountains above.

It had been two months since she'd last climbed these steps, two months since Maria von Trapp had wondered aloud whether she—*she,* Lotte Eder—might have a vocation. Lotte had barely thought of anything else since.

As she went to class, as she practiced her singing, as she ate dinner and sat with her family in the evenings, listening to the radio or Franz playing the piano, the question ran through her mind in a never-ending reel. *Could I possibly have a vocation?*

She'd dared to ask Johanna one morning, as they walked home from church, what she thought.

"Johanna," she'd begun hesitantly, "have you ever thought of becoming a nun?"

Her sister had snorted in amusement. "What! Of course not. Why would I?"

"Because," Lotte had answered, "it would be such a… such a *peaceful* life."

"Dull, more like. And my life is dull enough." Johanna's gaze had wandered to Franz, who was walking with their father. He attended mass with them every week although as a non-Catholic he was forbidden from taking part in Communion.

"So you never even considered it?" she'd asked, uncertain whether she felt relieved or disappointed by Johanna's decisive response.

"Not for a moment," Johanna had responded with a firm shake of her head. "Why are you asking?"

Lotte had shrugged, unwilling to admit the vague yet tempting thoughts that kept circling in her head. "I don't know. You see them sometimes, going to the hospital." Some of the nuns offered their nursing services at the Krankenhaus der Barmherzige Brüder in the old town. Lotte had always thought they looked so serene, with their hands tucked into their wide sleeves, their faces framed by their white wimples and flowing black veils.

"Yes, so?" Johanna had laughed and patted her on the head as if she were a child. "The thoughts you have, Lotte! Although, do you know, I could almost see you as a nun. You seem lost in your own world so much of the time anyway."

Lotte had blushed and said nothing.

Now she approached the abbey, snow dusting her headscarf and coat. The world felt very quiet, the snow softening and muting both sounds and sights. It seemed fitting, this hushed silence. It made the moment more sacred, as if the whole world were her chapel.

"May I help you?" The slightly sour voice of the elderly nun—whose face, framed by her veil, looked like a wrinkled egg—startled Lotte out of her dreamy thoughts.

She was standing in front of the porter's lodge, and a flicker of impatience crossed the nun's face as she waited for Lotte to answer. She did not seem so very serene.

"I—I have an appointment with the Mother Abbess," Lotte stammered.

The nun nodded and withdrew, ushering Lotte into the hall of the abbey, plainly furnished, the whitewashed walls bare save for a wooden crucifix. She sat on the edge of a bench while the nun went to speak to the Mother Abbess. The air was so cold her breath came out in frosty puffs.

"The Mother Abbess will see you now." The sour nun's expression softened slightly as she led Lotte down a narrow, stone-flagged corridor to an ancient wooden door, which she knocked on once.

A voice as serene and mellifluous as Lotte could hope for answered, "Enter."

The nun came in and knelt, while Lotte stood uncertainly. "*Benedicte*," the nun said, her head bowed, and the abbess waved her up with one hand.

"*Dominus*."

The nun rose and nodded towards Lotte. "Fräulein Eder to speak with you, Reverend Mother."

The abbess nodded and the nun retreated, the door closing behind her with a quiet click. Lotte was left alone with the Mother Abbess, and suddenly she felt terrified, her heart beating fast, her mouth dry.

"Please, sit," the abbess said with a smile, and with a slight nod she indicated the one other chair in the room—a plain wooden one, without any adornment. In fact, everything about the room was plain—whitewashed walls, the only decoration a large crucifix.

"Thank you, Reverend Mother." Lotte knotted her fingers together in her lap as she waited for the abbess to begin.

She was an older woman, well into her sixties, and had been the abbess at Nonnberg, Lotte knew, for fifteen years. Her face, framed by her white wimple and black veil, was wrinkled and kindly, her eyes and brows both dark.

"You wished to speak to me of a possible vocation," she prompted gently, and Lotte nodded, biting her lip. Why did she suddenly feel so nervous, as if she were a fraud waiting to be found out?

"Yes, Reverend Mother, I did."

"Very well." The abbess folded her hands, which had been hidden in the wide sleeves of her habit, on top of her desk. "Tell me what you have experienced, child."

And so, haltingly, Lotte told of coming to the abbey two months ago, of feeling a sense of peace descend over her, and how the prayers of the nuns had been the most beautiful thing she'd ever heard. As she spoke, she heard the throb of sincerity in her voice, and she hoped the abbess heard it as well.

"When I am here at the abbey, I feel as if something in me has settled. I'm at peace in a way I am not in the—the real world." The abbess smiled faintly, and Lotte wondered if she'd misspoken. "I mean, you know, down there." She nodded towards the window, indicating the steep Nonnbergstiege down to the old town.

"Yes, I know what you meant." She gave Lotte a kindly smile.

"And so, when Baroness von Trapp spoke to me about having a vocation," she continued stiltedly, "it made me wonder. Perhaps I do have one."

"Baroness von Trapp has often spoken before she has thought," the abbess said with another small smile. "Indeed, her impulsiveness was a continual struggle for her when she was with us here as a postulant."

"Oh." Lotte wondered if the abbess had, in a single stroke, dismissed any possibility of her having a vocation.

"Tell me, child, what draws you to the religious life, other than experiencing this sense of peace?"

Lotte eyed her uncertainly; she had the feeling the abbess was guiding her gently into some sort of trap, and whatever she said would be wrong. "I suppose… a sense of meaning," she answered. "And a desire to dedicate myself fully to God."

The abbess nodded slowly. "One is able to dedicate oneself fully to God, whatever one is called to, whether it be the home, the hospital, the school, or the convent. The religious life is one that is characterized far more by sacrifice than by anything else." Her tone was gentle yet her words felt severe. "It is a sacrifice that is lived out minute by minute and hour by hour. The vows of poverty, chastity, and obedience are not to be taken lightly. Even after many years they can cause great trials and test us sorely."

"I would never, Reverend Mother—" Lotte began, horrified that the abbess would think that. And yet how could she even know what those vows would mean? Her vision of being a nun had not progressed much farther than picturing herself drifting through the ancient cloisters, elegant and serene in a black habit, utterly at peace with her tranquil life. "I would never wish to take any vow lightly," she finished, looking down at her lap. She felt embarrassed and childish, like a little girl playing dress-up, and the Mother Abbess was gently removing her costume and putting it away.

"No, I do not believe you would," the abbess replied. "Whatever your faults may be, Fräulein Eder, I believe you are sincere."

Lotte swallowed and said nothing.

"Tell me," she continued after a moment, "have you spoken to anyone else about this sense of calling you have experienced?"

"No, Reverend Mother. I have not." She thought of her brief conversation with Johanna, when she hadn't dared to say anything of her own deliberations. It had felt too sacred a secret to share with her skeptical sister.

"Your parish priest?" the abbess pressed, and Lotte shook her head. "And what of your family? Would they be supportive of such a decision?"

"I think they would." Although she wanted to appear measured, Lotte could not keep from rushing on impulsively, "But should it matter what they think? If I have a calling from God, I must obey it, regardless of others' wishes… shouldn't I?"

The abbess was silent for a moment, and Lotte struggled not to squirm under her considering, benevolent gaze. "A calling from God must be heeded, it is true, but God does not speak in just one way, like a bolt of lightning, although on occasion that might be the case. But far, far more often, my child, God speaks to us in murmurs and whispers, that still small voice of calm in the midst of the whirlwind."

"Yes—"

"And He shows us His way by giving us spiritual advisers and elders to guide us. If your parish priest or your family did not approve of your vocation, it would give me great hesitation to accept you as a postulant." The abbess smiled to take any sting from her words, but Lotte felt it anyway.

"I see." She realized she'd had some romantic idea of sailing through the abbey gates, leaving the weeping world behind like in the triptych of the last judgment she'd once seen in a church, all wailing and gnashing of teeth, arms outstretched towards a heaven just out of reach. *Of course it wasn't going to be as dramatic as that.* She shouldn't even want it to be.

"If you are truly serious about discerning whether God is calling you to the religious life," the abbess continued kindly but firmly, "then speak to your priest. He will guide you. And talk with your parents, whom I believe to be devout. God has put them on this earth to instruct you."

"And if they all agree that I have a vocation?" Lotte asked, hearing the eagerness in her voice.

"Then we will discuss the next steps at the appropriate time." She paused, and Lotte tensed, sensing something unwelcome. "I should say that most women who have a sense of calling to this life, Fräulein Eder, experience some uncertainty or anxiety, at least at the beginning. They are aware, if only in part, of how much they are being called to relinquish, even if they cannot possibly understand the full depth of the sacrifice God will call them to over the years."

"Yes, Reverend Mother." Lotte knew she did not fear giving up the amusements of the world; she thought she would surrender them gladly.

"For example, Fräulein, you might find it difficult to relinquish seeing your family."

Lotte swallowed. "Would I not be able to see them at all?" It was not something she had considered in all her vague daydreaming.

"If you were accepted as a postulant, you would not see them for the six months of your postulancy, or the following year or two of your novitiate, except at the service when you are clothed as a novice. From then on you would see them only rarely, and only when they came to visit you at the abbey." She smiled in sympathy, and Lotte realized how troubled she must look. "This is to keep you from distraction or temptation, especially early on in your life here, when the world, with all its attachments, may still hold you in its thrall. A sister gives up all her earthly pleasures, Fräulein, even those of relationships, so she can devote herself ever more fully to God."

"I see." Lotte looked down at her lap.

"It would be a cold-hearted woman who did not respond to these conditions with some amount of grief," the abbess told her. "And there are other considerations, as well. For example a sister may not own any personal possessions. She does not look in a mirror, for that feeds her vanity. And, of course, we follow the Benedictine rule of silence—to speak as little as possible, and only when necessary, and never during the Great Silence, between compline in the evening and mass the next morning. These are only a few of the instructions we follow, according to the Rule of

Saint Benedict." She smiled while Lotte suddenly found herself blinking back tears.

Had she known all of that? She thought perhaps she had, in a distant sort of way, but it felt very real now, and yet more out of reach than ever.

"Forgive me if I am speaking out of turn," the abbess continued after a moment, "but some young women approach the idea of the religious life with a sort of romanticism in their minds. They dream of serenity and holiness without realizing those attributes are hard won and come at a high price. The religious life is one of painful sacrifice, costly obedience, deliberate humiliation. Only those who are truly called to it will be able to bear the heavy load that is asked of them."

"Yes," Lotte whispered, because she could think of nothing else to say.

The abbess tilted her head to one side as her kindly yet shrewd gaze swept over Lotte. "If God is indeed calling you to this life, Fräulein, then you will not be able to ignore His voice. What begins as a whisper will start to feel like a shout—and an irresistible beckoning to go deeper in." She paused while a thrill went through Lotte, a delicious expectation, a tremor of both hope and fear at what might still be to come.

"And if He is not calling you," the abbess continued in the same gentle yet firm voice, "then that first whisper will become fainter and fainter, until you cannot hear it at all, and, by God's grace, you will let it go completely, without even feeling a loss."

Lotte's lips trembled as she tried to smile. "Yes, Reverend Mother, I can see how that would be."

"Go well, my child," the abbess said, and Lotte realized she was being dismissed, kindly as the woman's tone was.

"Thank you for your time," she murmured, rising from the chair. The abbess nodded, and Lotte fumbled for the door. As she left the room, the nun from the porter's lodge swooped down on her, reminding her more of a black crow than an angel of mercy.

She inclined her head, saying nothing, and Lotte was reminded of the Mother Abbess's description of unnecessary speech. If she came here, would she get used to saying so little? In some ways it would be a relief. Never have to fill a silence, but simply to let it be.

"Thank you, Sister," she said as she headed outside, and then wondered if she should have said even that.

Outside dusk was falling along with snow, the world as quiet and still as a photograph. Lotte stood once again at the top of the Nonnbergstiege and breathed in the crisp air, snowflakes falling softly onto her cheeks.

The rooftops of the old town were covered in snow as darkness drew in. From up here she couldn't hear the usual sounds of the city—trams and buses, cars and calls of peddlers or newspaper boys. As she started down the steps, the clouds parted and the last of the sun's fading light revealed itself in one perfect shining ray. Lotte caught her breath. *Could this be a sign?*

She closed her eyes, everything in her both straining and still, yearning for that faint yet clear whisper that would tell her the way. Yet as she waited, the cold seeping through her shoes and numbing her fingers, all she heard was the sweep of the wind on the snow as the last of the light left the sky.

CHAPTER EIGHT

JOHANNA

Johanna loved Christmas. She loved the snow that blanketed the city, making everything clean, and she loved how the usually mundane tasks of the household became imbued with a festive and even sacred purpose.

Along with the heavy, dark furniture, her mother had brought many of the old folk traditions from the Tyrol, and when Johanna and her sisters had been children, they had followed them all with great delight—the advent wreath made of fir twigs and adorned with four thick wax candles, hung from the ceiling in the middle of the living room, a candle lit for every Sunday in Advent. They had written letters to the Christ Child, confessing their transgressions and making promises for the new year.

On the sixth of December they had been visited by Saint Nikolaus with his miter and bishop's staff, followed by the terrible Krampus, the black devil with the long red tongue who took away naughty children if Saint Nikolaus let them. They'd been given sweet bags—never switches, which were only for the truly bad children—and they'd never been carried away by the Krampus, usually a neighbor dressed up in a mask and black cloak whom Johanna remembered as being deliciously terrifying.

Although there were no longer any children in the house, there was still much to be celebrated. Johanna and Hedwig had weaved together fir twigs for the advent wreath, and they'd gathered as a family under it every Sunday to read the Gospel and light a candle, to Franz's kindly bemusement, Johanna couldn't help but notice.

Since that day on the Untersberg when he had almost kissed her and then told her he didn't believe in God, Johanna had not known how to act, or even how to feel. While she was as fascinated by Franz as ever, the sheen of his attention had lost of a little of its glinting promise, for she had realized her parents could never countenance her marriage to a non-Catholic. Of course, she'd known he wasn't a Catholic since he'd first arrived in the little house on Getreidegasse, with his talk of philosophy and his declining of Communion. She'd known that, but she hadn't *felt* it, hadn't let herself consider their attachment getting that far.

But when he'd almost kissed her, and he'd given her such a burning look, she'd realized, in a moment of deep dismay, that it could go nowhere. She did not want to merely flirt, as thrilling as that could feel at the time.

And so she'd ended up avoiding Franz when she could, all the while feeling as drawn to him as she'd ever been, so that he'd sometimes give her a puzzled and even hurt look, his eyes asking a silent question: *Why are you doing this?* Johanna never answered it, but merely looked away, her mind a ferment, caught between pride, caution, and desire.

She made sure they were never alone, which was easy enough, and although she still turned the pages of his music—a pleasure she was yet loath to relinquish—she did not stand so close, and her fingers never brushed his, accidentally or otherwise. All in all, it was a most dissatisfying state of affairs.

The weeks before Christmas were busy enough that Johanna did her best not to spare too many unhappy thoughts for Franz Weber. There were *lebkuchen* to bake, and *Spanischer Wind*, and marzipan figures for the tree. There were Christmas clothes to sew and darn, and the house to clean from top to bottom; her mother was a more demanding housekeeper than ever on the high holy days.

And yet still there was Franz. Franz sitting at the table, his knees barely fitting under it, his hair so unruly. Franz giving her that crooked smile, a bemused look in his eyes, or playing the piano so beautifully that Johanna could have wept. Franz settling into bed every night while Johanna lay in her own bed and listened to the creaks of the floorboards above with an ache in her heart.

One evening, as she'd been going up to bed, he'd caught her wrist in the corridor.

"Why are you avoiding me?" he'd asked in a low voice, his look as burning as ever.

"I'm not—"

"You are. Don't dissemble, Johanna. You're too honest for that."

She'd glanced at the doorway of the sitting room, where everyone else was still assembled. "Franz—"

"I like you," he'd said in his easy, open way. "You know I do. And I thought you liked me."

"I do," she'd replied, because he was right, she was too honest.

"Then…?"

She'd stared at him helplessly, knowing he deserved an explanation and yet unable to give one, at least not here in the hall, where anyone could overhear. "I'm sorry. I can't," she'd whispered, and she'd pulled away from him, hurrying up the stairs to her bedroom.

On the twenty-third of December, as was tradition, they decorated the Christmas tree with marzipan figures, gilded nuts, apples and tangerines. They festooned wax candles, nearly a hundred of them, all over its green, spreading boughs, along with chains of ribbon and tinsel, although the candles would not be lit until Christmas Eve.

"Have you ever decorated a Christmas tree before, Franz?" Lotte asked with a little laugh; she had become fascinated with his utter ignorance of such traditions, intent on explaining them to him, as if that would somehow make him believe.

"I have not," Franz replied in his relaxed way, "although I have certainly seen a fair few. Yours is particularly beautiful, I think."

"And you will come with us to mass on Holy Eve?" Lotte asked, and Johanna wished she wouldn't push so much. She made the difference between their family and Franz all the more stark.

"Yes, if you'll have me," Franz replied cheerfully. "Can a heathen go to mass on Holy Eve?"

"That is when a heathen should go to mass most of all," Lotte answered seriously, and Johanna couldn't keep from rolling her eyes.

"Oh, Lotte, enough. You sound as saintly as a nun!"

Lotte remained silent, and Johanna felt guilty for scolding her.

"Well, then, I will go and gladly," Franz replied. "I do find the prayers and singing quite beautiful." He glanced meaningfully at Johanna, as if this level of devotion should impress her, and she made herself look away, because she did not know if it did.

The Holy Eve mass was beautiful, as it always was, the church filled with candles people held to read their hymnals by. As they sang "Tauet Himmel den Gerechten," the music rising to the rafters, Johanna closed her eyes and offered a wordless prayer to God, one that came from the depths of her being and yet she could not articulate.

When she opened her eyes, she saw her father giving her a gently quizzical look, and she tried to smile, although in truth she felt near tears.

She had already said her confession, stammering out her usual sins to their sympathetic priest, when what she knew she should have said was *I have fallen in love with a man whom I know is unsuitable.* What would the priest have said then? How many Hail Marys would she have had to say as penance?

After Holy Mass, the children in the congregation went to the side altar, where a miniature model of the whole town of Bethlehem had been spread out—the shepherds with their flock, Mary and Joseph in their shelter. The manger, of course, was empty, as it would be until that night. As ever, there was a sense of expectation in the air, a hope long deferred but finally approaching. It never failed to lift Johanna's spirits, and yet tonight she struggled to feel that age-old wonder. She felt closer to despair.

Back at the house, after mass, they waited for Manfred to ring the bell to symbolize the start of Christmas. Together they gathered in the sitting room, the tree ablaze with candles, to sing "Silent Night" and exchange greetings and gifts, and through it all Johanna felt closer to sorrow than joy. She could not bear to look at Franz—his dark hair glinting in the candlelight, his ready smile, his easy laugh—and yet she could not keep from looking. Every so often his eyes met hers, and they seemed to ask a gentle question. Johanna always looked away first.

"*Frohe Weihnachten,*" Manfred exclaimed, kissing his daughters' cheeks in turn before he put his arms around Hedwig, who laughed and blushed like a girl. There could be no doubting her father's love for his wife, Johanna thought, not for the first time. Her mother, with her dour ways and steadfast work, was still the golden apple of her father's eye. It gave her a pang of both hope and longing, that one day a man might feel that way about her, for in truth wasn't she like her mother in so many ways—hardworking, sometimes silent, perhaps even a bit dour or at least stern?

As they exchanged gifts, Johanna held her breath as Franz opened the handkerchiefs she'd embroidered for him, with his initials and a little sprig of edelweiss in the corner. As he opened the parcel, so clearly delighted by his gift, Johanna blushed, fearing it was far too personal a present, the kind of thing a woman would give her betrothed.

"I thought you needed some more handkerchiefs," she said, like an excuse. "Yours are forever getting dirty."

As Franz presented the family with a large, extravagant box of chocolates, wrapped with a red silk ribbon, Johanna realized she felt disappointed. She had hoped, and perhaps even expected, despite her recent coolness, a personal gift from him, but there was none. She told herself it was just as well as they ate their evening meal, and then retired to bed, the moon high in the sky, everyone sleepy and satisfied. Everyone but her.

"Why are you so gloomy?" Birgit asked as they were undressing for bed.

There had been, Johanna had noticed, an unaccustomed spring in her sister's step for the last few weeks, a secretiveness to her smile… and yet what secrets could Birgit possibly have?

"Why are you so cheerful?" Johanna returned sourly.

"It's *Christmas*—"

"I sometimes wonder if you have a secret," Johanna continued, determined to deflect her sister's scrutiny. "Or even a beau." Birgit's smile turned smug, almost sly, and Johanna stilled, her hands to her hair as she'd been undoing it. "You don't!" she exclaimed, and for a brief moment ire flashed in Birgit's eyes.

"Why shouldn't I?"

"But who is it?"

Birgit just smiled and Johanna made a sound of impatience as she continued to undo her hair. What did it matter whom Birgit had fallen for? No doubt it was some unsuspecting shop boy who had done nothing more than throw her a smile. Recognizing the unkindness of her thoughts, she unbent a little. "You will have to tell me at some point," she said lightly, "if it is to go anywhere."

"Just you wait," Birgit replied. She was still smiling.

The house settled softly around them as they both got into bed. Johanna lay flat on her back—her hair spread out on the pillow, her hands clasped at her waist like the staidest of matrons—as she stared at the ceiling, sleep impossible, her mind and heart both in an unhappy ferment.

From upstairs she heard the creaks of Franz moving about in his bedroom, and she imagined him taking off his shoes, undoing his waistcoat, unbuttoning his shirt. She banished the images as quickly as they'd come, unbidden, into her mind.

An hour passed, each second seeming to crawl by. The creaks from upstairs had quieted, and Birgit's breathing evened out in sleep. Still Johanna stared at the ceiling, gritty-eyed, heavy-hearted. Moonlight streamed through the crack in the shutters and cast a slender silver beam across the wooden floor.

Finally, after what felt like another age, Johanna swung her legs over the side of the bed and reached for her dressing gown. She inched her way down the darkened hallway to the sitting room, where the Christmas tree stood in all of its glory, the candles now snuffed out, the room holding the spicy smell of oranges as well as the remnant of candle wax. She didn't know why she'd come in here, or what she expected to find, but her hand flew to her chest and a startled "oh!" escaped from her lips when she saw Franz sitting in the corner, gazing at the tree.

"Hello, Johanna." His voice held a hint of humor as well as of sadness, and as he spoke Johanna realized she'd come in hoping he would be here. Knowing he would.

She clutched the folds of her dressing gown together with one hand as she made out his figure in the near darkness—he was still wearing his clothes, his shirt unbuttoned at the throat, his hair even unrulier than usual, making him look wilder and yet more approachable.

"I thought you were asleep," she said.

"No."

"What… what are you doing here?"

"Why are you avoiding me?" he countered. "Will you tell me this time?"

"Franz—"

"Come now, Johanna. You aren't one to play games. Ever since Untersberg, you have been finding a way to keep from being alone with me. Are you going to tell me it isn't true?"

"No," Johanna whispered after a pause. "I'm not."

"It's because I'm not Catholic, isn't it?" he stated. He made it sound like a small thing, something petty, and for a wild moment Johanna wondered if it was. If it could be.

"You must realize," she said after a moment, "how much our faith is a part of our family."

"Yes, I have realized." Franz paused. "And I am moved by it. Logic seems a cold thing when it comes to matters of the heart. I've lived my life by science, but when we sang "Silent Night" tonight, I truly wished I could believe." His smile, lopsided and wry, was barely visible in the darkness. "Does that count for something?"

"I am glad, of course, but…" Johanna hesitated, pride making her not want to presume, and yet she knew she could no longer stay silent. "Franz, you must realize I could never marry someone who wasn't a Catholic." She flushed, grateful for the darkness that hid her scarlet cheeks. "I know I am presuming far too much, even to say such a thing, but I cannot see the point of… forming an attachment, considering."

Franz was silent for a long moment, too long.

"Franz?" she asked, her voice wavering, and he rose from his chair by the window to come to stand next to her.

"I haven't given you your Christmas present yet."

A thrill ran through her. "I didn't think you had one for me."

"Of course I did." He withdrew a small, awkwardly-shaped object from his pocket, wrapped in gold paper. "Here it is."

Johanna took it, her fingers brushing his, making them tingle. He was close enough that she could feel the heat of his body, the softness of his breath. She undid the paper and saw what he'd given her—a miniature model of the Eiffel Tower, perfect in every tiny detail.

"*Oh…*" Tears pricked her eyes as she looked up at him and Franz stepped closer, close enough that his body brushed hers at several exquisite, aching points.

"Johanna…" he murmured, and then his hand cupped her cheek and he was kissing her; her first kiss, like a starburst exploding in her heart.

Her eyes fluttered close and she nearly dropped the little tower until Franz caught it in his hand, clasping hers with his own as the kiss went on and on, her mind doing cartwheels and catapults, sending fireworks fizzing through her whole body. She'd never known it was possible to feel this way. She'd never *realized.*

Finally he stepped back, his breathing uneven, his hair even unrulier. Johanna laughed softly, a tremble on her lips.

"Your hair is mussed."

"So it is." He raked an unsteady hand through it, making it even worse. She laughed again, feeling happier than she'd ever felt before, and light inside, as if she were filled with air, as if she were rising onto her tiptoes without even realizing, and would soon float away on this wonderful, buoyant joy.

That kiss had, amazingly, answered all her unspoken questions. Suddenly it all seemed so dazzlingly simple. It was enough that he *wanted* to believe; it was enough for her, more than enough. None of it mattered at all any more, because she loved him, and he loved her.

"Johanna, I'm a Jew."

She stared at him blankly, blinking slowly, his words like puzzle pieces that would not fit together.

"You're—"

"A Jew. Jewish. That is why I am here. I've come to realize you didn't know. Your father didn't tell you."

"No—"

"Does it make a difference?" There was a slight challenge to his voice, as well as an edge of desperation. Johanna did not know how to reply. She realized some part of her was not surprised, even as another part reeled in shock.

A Jew... that idiot Jew.

Her cruel, careless words about Janos Panov came back to taunt her now. She didn't even know any Jews, not really. They were like characters in a fairy tale, shadows lurking in the corner, at least if the newspapers were to be believed. She opened her mouth and then closed it again, trying to frame a question. "That is why you left Vienna?" she finally asked.

"My professor, Herr Schlick, was killed on the steps of the university. He wasn't even a Jew, but it set off a chain of violence I was caught up in. I admit, I was rash. I... acted out. Caused trouble. The police got involved." He grimaced. "I had to leave."

Caused trouble? Had he been *violent*? "How on earth did my father know about any of this?" Johanna asked, doing her best to absorb what he was telling her.

"I don't really know. Some communists helped to get me out of Vienna. They simply said they'd found a place for me in Salzburg, as an apprentice to a clockmaker." He shrugged. "It was enough for me."

"And my father was involved?" Her mind was spinning. Her father detested communists, or at least what they stood for, their violence-justifying zeal, their determined atheism. How could he have possibly been involved in something like this?

"If it makes a difference," Franz continued, trying to sound wry and not quite succeeding, "I'm only half Jewish. My father. And we were never practicing Jews. I don't even know any Hebrew, or any of the holidays, or anything." He let out a little laugh. "You see, I meant what I said about needing evidence."

She shook her head slowly, not even knowing what to think or how she felt, and Franz caught her hands in his.

"Don't turn away from me now, Johanna."

"What about your family? They are still in Vienna?"

"My mother is safe, because she's Catholic. So really, I'm half Catholic, although she has never practiced the way your family does. And my father has a position at the university, although who knows how long for. We thought of emigrating, but we have friends who went to London—a renowned physicist who is now sweeping streets. It would be a scandal, if anyone cared. No one does." His eyes flashed, his mouth tightening. "Does any of it make a difference?"

"I…" She closed her eyes and he cupped her face in his hands.

"Don't shut me out, please. I love you."

He was pleading with her, and it tore at her heart even as she struggled to believe those wonderful words. "Why me?" she whispered. "Why have you fallen for me?"

"Why you?" He sounded surprised, which almost made her smile. "Why *not* you? You're beautiful and strong and you know your own mind. I think I fell in love with you that first day, when I saw you in the kitchen."

"The kitchen!"

"You were so capable, and yet so serene. I was mesmerized, and I knew from that moment you wouldn't suffer fools gladly."

"Such a quality would hardly make you fall in love with me," Johanna scoffed unevenly.

"But it did." With his hands still cupping her face, he drew her towards him.

"Franz—"

"Please, Johanna," he said softly. "I love you. Truly. I want to be with you." He kissed her again, and just as before her mind reeled and her heart felt as if it were exploding inside her. Her body told the truth of it, no matter what hesitations she might have in her mind. She knew there could be no going back now, no matter what Franz told her. No matter what he was or wasn't. Their kiss had changed everything.

CHAPTER NINE

BIRGIT

January 1937

Birgit had a secret. She'd been keeping it since the night the police had raided the coffeehouse in Elisabeth-Vorstadt, and a strange soldier had rescued her from being arrested.

When he'd asked her to accompany him to a café for a cup of coffee, she'd barely known what she was saying, her mind still dazed from everything that had happened, her lips tingling from when he'd kissed her.

She'd let him lead her down the street as if she were a child, and she'd followed, hardly noticing her surroundings, until they'd entered the warm fug of a coffeehouse on Linzergasse and she'd half-collapsed into a seat across from him.

"Well." The smile he'd given her was easy and open. "That was quite an adventure." He'd raised sandy eyebrows. "What were you doing, getting mixed up with that sort of crowd?"

"My friend brought me along to it," Birgit lied without thinking. "I didn't realize what it was."

"Some friend," he said dryly, and she'd nodded uncomfortably. She hadn't been sure why she'd lied, only that it felt like the right thing to do. She couldn't have him asking questions about the meetings or what she did there.

A waiter had come to the table and with a glance of enquiry he had ordered them both *mélange* coffees, the Viennese specialty of espresso topped with steamed and then foamed milk. The waiter had given Birgit a glance that made her put her hands to her hair, quickly tidying it as best as she could.

"You look a bit windswept," he had told her with a laugh, "but I don't mind."

"I don't even know your name."

"Werner Haas. And yours?"

"Birgit. Birgit Eder."

He'd smiled, and she'd smiled back, suddenly aware that she was sitting at a table with a man who was looking at her with frank admiration, a man who had already kissed her. Without realizing what she was doing, she'd put her fingers to her lips. Werner had smiled.

"Why did you rescue me?" she'd asked as she'd yanked her hand away from her mouth.

"Well, like I said before, I couldn't resist such a lovely lady in distress."

"Don't," Birgit had whispered, looking away. Was he teasing her? He had to be. No one ever said things like that to her.

"I mean it," Werner had replied, and for a second Birgit had thought he was going to reach for her hand, but then he hadn't.

Their coffees had arrived, and she'd spent the next few minutes avoiding Werner's gaze as she'd sipped her coffee. Finally, she'd felt composed enough to say in what she hoped was a normal tone, "Whatever the case, I must thank you for your chivalry. I shudder to think what could have happened."

"So do I."

She'd forced herself to look at him, aiming her gaze at his uniform rather than his face. "You are in the Alpine corps?"

"Yes, sixth division, out of Innsbruck. I was given leave until Christmas and so I came home."

"You're from Salzburg, then?"

"Yes, just outside. I grew up in Aigen. There is only my father and me left." His mouth had pulled down at the corners, and Birgit had felt a rush of sympathy.

"Oh, I am sorry."

He'd shrugged, his mouth still downturned. "My mother and sister both died in 1920, from the flu."

"You must have been quite young."

"Ten, as it happens." He'd smiled. "But what about you? You live here, as well?"

"Yes, on Getreidegasse. My father is a clockmaker."

"Eder Clockmaking?" Werner had guessed, and Birgit had blushed with pleasure. "My father came in a few months ago, to have our clock repaired. It was a wall clock, a Vienna regulator."

"I think I remember it," she'd cried, realizing she was more delighted by this discovery than perhaps was warranted. "It was a Wilhelm Bauer. My father was the one who handled the repair." She paused, ducking her head. "I work with him."

"You are a clockmaker, as well?" Werner had asked in surprise.

"Repairs, but yes, essentially."

"Goodness." He had looked genuinely impressed, which thrilled Birgit, especially after her pride had been so wounded by the arrival of Franz. "You *are* talented," he'd murmured, and she hadn't been able to keep from protesting rather feebly,

"No—"

"But why not admit it? I certainly can't repair a clock."

She'd laughed. "And I can't—I don't know—ski down a mountain!"

He'd laughed back, a loud, clear sound that reminded Birgit of the ringing of a bell. "Have you ever been skiing?"

She'd thought of Johanna and the ski trip she'd gone on; there had been no money for anyone else to go. Not, Birgit acknowledged fairly, that she'd really wanted to. "No, I haven't," she'd told Werner.

"One day, perhaps," he'd said, and as he sipped his coffee there was a look in his eyes that made her lips tingle again.

She didn't remember exactly what else they'd talked about as they slowly sipped their coffees, Birgit trying to make hers last. He asked her about her family, and she'd asked about his Alpine unit; Werner told her how his father had fought in the Alpine corps during the war, and how he'd felt he had to follow. Somehow the conversation had stretched out until she'd realized it was getting late and her parents would be worried.

"I should go." She'd lurched up rather suddenly from the table, and unfazed, Werner had risen as well.

"Let me walk you home. Getreidegasse, yes?"

"Yes, but you don't—"

"Of course I will."

He'd paid for their coffees, while Birgit had murmured her thanks, and then he'd taken her arm as they headed down the street, towards the old town.

"I hope you'll give that friend of yours a wide berth," Werner had remarked as they turned on to Staatsbrücke. "Unless she didn't realize, either?"

"Realize what, exactly?" she'd asked cautiously.

"That the meeting was run by communists." He'd turned to smile at her, eyebrows raised. "You don't want to get involved with that sort."

Birgit had wished then that she hadn't lied about it all, but it was too late now, and in any case, she'd most likely never see him again, a prospect that already caused her a flash of disappointment as well as a flicker of relief. She hadn't wanted to get caught up in lies, had known she wouldn't be able to manage it. "I don't know if she did," she'd said finally.

"They're not the sort of people to get mixed up with," Werner had warned her seriously. "They're coming down hard on those kinds of groups now. They have to."

"Why do they have to?" Birgit had asked, curious as to what he'd thought about it all.

"Well, we can't have a Soviet threat, can we?" he'd answered reasonably.

"You think the Soviets are a threat?"

"The Soviets want to take over the world even more than Germany does. Besides, Hitler is a far better leader than Stalin. Look what he's done for the German economy. They don't have the problem with inflation we still have here in Austria." His mouth had twisted. "My father lost his fortune because of the inflation after the war. Germany has recovered in a way Austria hasn't been able to. And besides, Hitler himself is Austrian." He'd given her a teasing grin, but Birgit hadn't been ready to let it go, even though part of her had known it would be wiser to. She'd never spoken to someone personally who had shown any approval for Hitler, and Werner's easy certainty had disconcerted her.

"And what of the Jews?" she'd asked after a moment.

Werner had taken a packet of cigarettes out of his jacket pocket and offered her one. Birgit had shaken her head, and he'd taken one and lit it, drawing in and exhaling before he'd answered. "What of them?"

"It's—it's not fair, is it," she'd stated slowly. As she'd said the words, she realized how childish they sounded, as if she were talking about cheating at a game of marbles. "The laws and things they have in Germany now. The way the Jews are blamed for everything. The way people treat them. It's not right."

Werner had nodded in agreement, as easy in this as in his approval of the man who had made such laws. "Perhaps, but it's understandable, isn't it, to blame the Jews for at least some of the problems we've had?" He'd shrugged, looking so very reasonable. "They've as good as controlled the banking system for decades. The stock market, as well, not letting anyone else so much as a look in. They keep it all to themselves and get rich off everyone else's hard work. Surely it's their fault at least a little bit if we're all broke?" He'd smiled, flashing his teeth and raising his eyebrows. Birgit realized she didn't know enough to argue or agree with him.

"I saw a Jew being beaten in the street," she'd said quietly, the memory of poor, broken Janos reverberating through her. "The man who grinds our knives. He had nothing. He wasn't to blame for anything."

Werner had nodded sympathetically. "That's unfortunate, of course. But there are bullies and thugs everywhere. It doesn't mean the policies are wrong."

"I suppose," Birgit had said slowly, because she hadn't known what else to say, and her ignorance had shamed her, even as she acknowledged how much more pleasant it would be if she simply let it go. "My friend believes there will be a war," she'd ventured after a moment.

"Of course there'll be a war, but it won't be with us."

"It won't?" Again his certainty had surprised her.

"No. The real question is who will challenge Germany and her right to *Lebensraum*?" He'd shrugged. "Certainly not Austria."

"So if there is a war, you wouldn't fight?" Birgit had asked, and he turned to her with a teasing smile.

"Worried about me?"

"No," she'd cried, blushing, "I mean, not—"

"I'm just teasing, Birgit." They'd reached Getreidegasse, their footsteps instinctively slowing. "How did we end up talking politics for so long?" He'd laughed and shaken his head, and Birgit had smiled.

"I don't know."

"I knew you were smart when you told me you could repair a clock." He'd turned to her, flicking his cigarette into the street before hooking his thumbs into the pockets of his jacket. "Come with me to the cinema next week?"

"The cinema…" Her had mind spun at the thought of an actual date… if that's what it was?

"They're showing *Under Blazing Heavens*, with Austria's very own Lotte Lang."

Birgit had hesitated, wondering what her parents would think of her stepping out with someone they'd never met. Then she'd reminded herself she was twenty years old, and most women her age were stepping out all the time, or at least occasionally. "That would be fun," she'd said firmly, and Werner's face had split into a wide smile that had her smiling back.

"*Wunderbar*! Shall I meet you there at seven on Friday? The cinema on Gislekai. Do you know it?"

"Yes."

They had reached the shop now, its windows shuttered for the night. Werner had taken a step closer to her, and Birgit's heart fluttered. She'd tried to smile but her lips had trembled.

"Goodnight, Birgit. I'm very glad to have met you."

"Yes, as am I…" she'd whispered, and then he'd leaned in to brush his lips against her cheek. She'd breathed in the sharp, citrusy scent of his aftershave, which had startled her with its strangeness.

"See you on Friday," he'd said, and then he was walking down the street, disappearing into the darkness.

*

The next week she met him outside the cinema, and they watched *Under Burning Heavens*, although Birgit could barely follow the story, so aware was she of Werner sitting next to her—the smell of his aftershave, the sprawl of his legs, the way his elbow brushed hers when she dared to put her own on the armrest. Every nerve jangled and she made a great pretense of watching the film as the words washed over her without meaning.

Afterwards, Werner suggested they go out for a drink, but as much as Birgit was tempted to, she made herself decline. She'd told her parents she was going out to the cinema with a friend from school, and that had felt like too much deception already. She supposed she would have to tell them about Werner… if he asked to see her again.

And he did, after he'd walked her home, stepping closer with deliberate intent while Birgit had gone completely still, and then he brushed his lips against hers, smiling faintly as he stepped back.

"Perhaps I can see you after Christmas, before I go back to Innsbruck."

"Ye—yes, that would be nice." She blinked up at him, and he kissed her again.

"Goodnight, Birgit."

She tottered inside in a daze, her head swimming from the kiss as if she'd drunk the finest wine, everything inside her buzzing. Everyone was in the sitting room, listening to the radio, when she came in.

"Ah, Birgit!" As ever, her father looked smilingly pleased to see her. "How was the cinema?"

"It was very good, Papa, thank you."

"What film did you see?" Johanna asked, and Birgit thought she sounded a bit suspicious.

"*Under Burning Heavens.*"

"Was it interesting?"

"It was all right," Birgit said, turning away. "But I'm tired now. I think I'll go to bed."

As she undressed for bed, she considered why she was so reluctant to tell her family about Werner. Surely there was no need to be so secretive—he was from a good family, or at least she thought he must be, since he lived in Aigen, which was one of the best areas of Salzburg. He was a soldier, which was nothing to be ashamed of, and she'd discerned that evening when she'd asked him about Christmas, that he was Catholic. So why wasn't she proudly telling everyone that she had an admirer, a beau?

Then she thought of his easy assurance about Hitler, his casual dismissal of the Jews. She imagined her father's reaction to his seemingly reasonable words, and something in her clenched with both fear and shame. *But he's so nice… and he likes me. He kissed me… he must think I'm pretty, and no one ever has before.*

Birgit gazed at her reflection and she forced herself to examine her face dispassionately—the round cheeks, the smallish eyes, the mousy blond hair. But despite all that… there was a glow to her face, a secretive curve to her lips… Could Werner really find her pretty?

Amazingly, it seemed he did. She thought of the way he'd looked at her, the warmth in his eyes, his gaze so lingering. Yet even so she had an innate fear that he might disappear from her life, like a trick or a dream. And as for his opinions about Hitler? That's all they were—opinions. Ideas. He wasn't a *bad* man.

Still, Birgit knew, it was much better to keep him a secret, at least for now. Perhaps she'd tell her family when she knew Werner a bit more, when he'd made his intentions clear, if he had them. A thrill ran through her at the thought—she pictured herself wearing a white dress, with her hands full of flowers, in the doorway of St. Blasius, haloed by sunlight…

Almost as quickly as she imagined the scene, she forced herself to banish it. There was no need to tempt fate or God with something like that. Something that might never happen, and yet, for the first time in her life, actually *could.*

*

In January, after Christmas, still hugging her precious secret to herself, Birgit met Werner for a walk along the Salzach River, its fast-flowing waters bobbing with jagged chunks of ice. The air was frigid, an icy wind sweeping down from the Salzkammergut, and Birgit had bundled up well to walk alongside with Werner, who looked very smart in his *Bundesheer* uniform, his cap pulled down low on his head, a woolen scarf about his neck.

"I head back to Innsbruck next week," he told her as they walked along, arm in arm. "I'll miss you."

"And I'll miss you," Birgit replied, meaning it more than she thought possible. She'd only seen him a few times, but already she felt transformed. When he looked at her with those admiring eyes, that warm smile, she felt as if she were expanding inside, as if she were *glowing*, and surely everyone would be able to see how radiant she was.

"Will you write?" he asked, and pleasure unfurled inside her like a flower.

"Yes, of course, if you want me to."

"I do." He turned to gaze at her seriously as he held her hands in his. Birgit's heart did a funny little flip. "Perhaps I shouldn't be, but I'm glad the police raided that meeting. Otherwise I never would have met you."

Birgit let out an uneven little laugh. She did not want to talk or even think about that meeting. "I am as well, although I was terrified at the time."

He squeezed her hands, and then he leaned in to kiss her, before they continued walking, Birgit as if she were on air. She felt as if she could twirl down the pavement. He *liked* her. He really liked her. The snowy world shimmered with newfound possibility, ideas that had felt utterly distant now within wonderful reach.

Dusk was gathering by the time he left her at the Mozartsteg, he to walk eastward to Aigen, while Birgit would walk across the bridge into the old town. Werner had wanted to walk her home, but she'd told him it was out of his way.

"I almost think you are keeping me a secret," he said, wagging his finger playfully, and Birgit blushed. He looked at her in surprise, dropping his teasing manner. "Are you?"

"Not a secret, not exactly…" Birgit thought of her boasting to Johanna at Christmas. Her sister had been so disbelieving, it had stung even as it had been satisfying to see Johanna so disconcerted. As for the rest of her family—if Werner made one of his careless remarks about the Jews, she did not like to imagine their reactions.

"The next time I come to Salzburg," he insisted, "I want to meet your family."

"All right." Birgit pictured herself ushering Werner into the house on Getreidegasse, slipping her arm proudly through his while her family watched, amazed, her sisters even a little envious. *And as for his remarks about the Jews… well, he hadn't said anything that bad, had he?* "If you're sure."

"I am."

"Very well, then. The next time."

She practically pranced along the Mozartsteg after they'd said goodbye, her heart overflowing with both wonder and joy at how kind he'd been, how tender and sure. Life looked entirely different than it had just a few weeks ago.

"Birgit!"

The sharp sound of someone calling her name, the way a schoolteacher might scold a pupil, made Birgit freeze in the middle of the pedestrian bridge, one hand resting on its iron balustrade. Slowly she turned around; Ingrid was striding towards her, her face pale, her eyes blazing, her coat flapping out behind her like the wings of a crow.

"Ingrid—" Guilt flooded through Birgit as she saw the anger and judgment on the other woman's face.

"Why have you not come to any of our meetings?"

"I..." Birgit trailed off, ashamed. She'd *meant* to go, but somehow, between meeting Werner and the busyness of Christmas, she'd let it all slip. She'd made herself not think of it, but it came rushing back now—the pamphlets, the police, the importance of it all. She knew that hadn't changed.

"I saw you with that soldier," Ingrid continued, eyes narrowed. "What do you suppose is going to happen to him?"

"Happen?" Birgit stared at her blankly, wondering if Ingrid was somehow threatening Werner. *Had she somehow heard his remarks about the communists? They hadn't been that offensive, surely.*

"When Hitler marches into Austria," Ingrid explained impatiently, "your boyfriend will become part of the Wehrmacht."

"What?" Birgit shook her head, refusing to consider that awful possibility even for a moment. "No."

"I always knew you were naïve, but I didn't think you were stupid." Ingrid took a step closer as she softened her tone. "Don't you see? He's *part* of the problem."

"He's not," Birgit exclaimed. "You talk as if he's a Nazi."

"He will be, one day, if he's not already."

"I don't believe it. Werner wouldn't—" She swallowed as she thought again of him warning her off the communists, his dismissive comments about the Jews. Still, he hadn't been *cruel.* He hadn't justified the kind of attacks like she'd seen on Janos. Besides, her father would have equally warned her off the communists, if he'd known. It certainly didn't make anyone a Nazi.

"I thought you *cared,*" Ingrid stated quietly. "Do you remember the knife grinder? The one you helped?"

"Of course I do."

"And what about others like him? A little boy was beaten half to death on Judengasse last week, for no good reason. Did you know?"

"No, I didn't." She suddenly felt near tears.

"Do you care?" Ingrid demanded. "About any of it? Or were you just amusing yourself?"

"I wasn't," Birgit protested, anger flaring. "I took risks—"

"Who knows if you even distributed those pamphlets? Perhaps you just hid them under your bed."

She'd been tempted to do that just that, but she *hadn't.* Birgit drew herself up. "You have no right to accuse me of such things. I've done everything you've asked of me. And if I haven't come to any meetings, it's because at the last one I was nearly arrested! I would have thought all of you would have wanted to lay low for a while."

"All of you? Or all of us?" Birgit hesitated, and Ingrid nodded slowly. "I see."

"No," she protested, albeit a bit weakly. Guilt twisted her insides. She *hadn't* been amusing herself, no matter what Ingrid had said in anger, and even now she remembered the sense of purpose, of *rightness,* distributing those pamphlets had given her. And yet…

What about Werner?

"Come to the next meeting," Ingrid entreated, putting her hand on Birgit's sleeve. "Don't abandon us now. We need you more than ever."

"Why me?" Birgit asked a bit desperately. She felt herself being pulled in, drawn under, and she was both afraid to let it happen and yet still eager to prove herself to Ingrid.

"Because we still need to unite. Communists. Socialists. Catholics. Your father was willing to work with us—"

"He was?" She hadn't really considered what her father had had to do with the communist group; the knowledge of his involvement had slipped to the back of her mind after the coffeehouse had been raided—and she'd met Werner.

"Only in one instance," Ingrid admitted. "And we helped him as much as he did us. But that is not important. What matters is accepting we need to work together. That is the only way to end fascism. To keep Hitler out of Austria."

"Yet you were speaking just now as if he has already marched across the border!"

"I fear there is no way to stop him now, and yet I still want to try. We must." Ingrid's expression turned fierce as the cold wind blew her hair in dark tangles around her face. "'He who fights can lose. He who doesn't fight has already lost.' That is Bertolt Brecht. The playwright. Do you know him?"

Birgit shook her head.

"Well," Ingrid declared. "I want to fight. The question is, Birgit, do you?"

CHAPTER TEN

LOTTE

February 1937

Lotte also had a secret, one she longed to share, yet she had never been able to find the right moment. Days passed in a flurry of music lessons she barely paid attention to, evenings in front of the radio or by the piano, snow falling and night closing in, and still she never found the time, or really the courage. And yet Easter drew closer, with the day the Mother Abbess had promised, when postulants could enter the order at Nonnberg, shimmering on the horizon.

In late December Lotte had spoken to Father Josef at St. Blasius, her voice faltering at first, and then growing in conviction as she'd stammered about Nonnberg Abbey, and Maria von Trapp, the Mother Abbess, and her own possible vocation.

"Do you think I could be a nun, Father?" she'd finished anxiously, her fingers knotted together as she'd perched on the edge of the hard chair in front of his desk, longing for his seal of approval.

"Speak to your family, child," Father Josef had said. "And pray. I will write to the Mother Abbess at Nonnberg."

"Then—" Lotte's had stomach leapt as she'd leaned forward. Father Josef had nodded, smiling. "Think and pray."

That had been nearly two months ago, and somehow she had never found the time to speak to her parents, although she knew she could have easily enough. It was the courage she lacked, for she feared disappointing them, and worse, hurting them, more than anything.

Then one afternoon in mid-February, when the snow heaped on the sides of the street had turned slushy and gray, and the air still held the damp frigidity of winter without even a breath of spring, her father read her term report from the Mozarteum, a frowning look of surprise on his face.

"Lotte, Professor Paumgartner says here that you do not pay attention in your lessons. That you have some talent, but you do not seem willing to use it." He lowered the letter, his eyebrows drawn together as he looked at her over the rim of his spectacles. "Is that true?" He didn't sound angry, or even disappointed, but rather confused.

The letter had come in the morning post, and Manfred was reading it at the kitchen table, while Hedwig and Johanna had gone out to do the shopping. Birgit and Franz were both working down in the shop, and Lotte was about to head to her first lesson. She stopped in the doorway, her hands fluttering by the buttons of her coat as she gazed at her father unhappily.

"I… I suppose it is, Papa."

"Why is this?" He laid the letter on the table as he gazed at her steadily, without judgment, but wanting to understand. "Do you not enjoy the lessons, *haschen*?" He hadn't used that old endearment—bunny—in years. Tears came to Lotte's eyes.

"I…" She hesitated, knowing there was no other way to answer, and yet how had she not foreseen this moment? She'd been so cowardly, she realized, in continuing with lessons that cost so much money when she didn't enjoy them and she knew she wasn't good enough. She hadn't wanted to disappoint her father, but having him realize she'd been lying to him would be even worse. "It's so competitive, Papa," she confessed in an unsteady rush. "And everyone else is so talented. I know I'm not going for an actual degree, but I just don't have that kind of ambition, or the ability. I'm sorry."

Her father was silent for a long moment. He looked down at the letter on the table, his face drawn into a regretful frown. "It is I who should be sorry," he said at last. "I fear I pushed you into these lessons, Lotte, for the sake of my own pride." He shook his head slowly as he looked up at her with a smile glinting in his eyes. "Who knew that a man could be so foolish at my age?"

"Oh Papa, you're not foolish," Lotte cried. "I should have told you sooner. I just didn't want to disappoint you—"

"Disappoint *me*? Never, Lotte." He smiled and held out his arms. "Come here and embrace your foolish old father."

Lotte rushed into his arms, resting her head against his shoulder. He smelled of pipe tobacco and Pitralon, the pine-scented aftershave he bought from his barber. As she put her arms around him she realized afresh how slight he was, how frail. He patted her on the back and she closed her eyes.

"I never meant to make you do something you didn't want to do, *haschen*," he said softly. "Shall we stop these lessons?"

"Yes, Papa, if you please." Slowly Lotte withdrew from the embrace and stepped back from her father. "But there is something else."

He studied her for a moment, his head tilted to one side. "Something else?"

She had not wanted to say it like this—alone in the kitchen, caught in an unexpected moment, unprepared. She had pictured a grand announcement around the dining room table, hands clutching chests as everyone stared at her in surprise and then dawning admiration.

Again Lotte felt shamed by her own secret pride—what a stupid fairy tale she persisted in weaving! She had delayed the announcement because some part of her knew it would never be like that.

"What is it, Lotte?" Manfred asked gently. "You can tell me."

"I..." She gazed at him, torn between hope and fear. "I believe I have a vocation, Papa," she whispered.

Manfred sat back in his chair, the kindly amusement glinting in his eyes was somehow hurtful. *Little Lotte, having a vocation?* Even she could see the absurdity of it.

"Oh?" he said. "And what is it?"

"I... I want to enter the religious life." Lotte lifted her chin as she met her father's gaze directly. "I wish to be a nun."

"A nun!" Manfred stared at her, his mouth opening and closing soundlessly. Then he let out a huff of laughter that was not unkind. "When did you decide this?"

"I've been praying about it for some time," Lotte answered with dignity. "I spoke with the Reverend Mother at Nonnberg Abbey, and also with Father Josef. He wrote to her, to recommend me as a postulant."

"I see." Her father's expression of good-natured bemusement turned to something more studious and sorrowful, as he regarded her quietly for a few moments. "This is serious, then."

"Yes."

Another moment passed while Lotte waited, everything in her tensed and expectant.

"Nonnberg is Benedictine," he remarked finally. "It would be a cloistered life."

"Yes."

"We would not see you."

Lotte nodded, biting her lip. "No. Save for visits at the abbey, on occasion." She had not let herself think too much about that aspect of her vocation, yet now, looking at her father's troubled face, it slammed into her with a force that could have made her gasp with the shock of it.

"And this is what you want?" he asked slowly. "You are sure? You feel this call on your life, a call from God?"

Lotte hesitated as a kaleidoscope of memories tumbled through her mind—Christmas as a child, lighting the advent wreath, faces haloed by candlelight. Walking along the Salzach, her mittened hand swinging in her father's. All of them gathered around the table while her mother, with quiet triumph, placed a platter of *Prügeltorte* in the middle. Singing around the piano, wandering along the Salzach, curling up in the sunny corner of the sitting room with a volume of Rilke's poetry or the latest novel. All these pleasures would be denied her forever.

"Yes, Papa," she answered quietly. "This is what I want."

Her father's face fell for a second, seeming to collapse on itself, and then he smiled, his slight shoulders squaring. "Then if you're sure," he said. "I can only give my blessing."

Before she could answer there was the sound of the side door opening, and then her mother's heavy footsteps up the stairs.

"You have returned!" her father cried, delighted, as if Hedwig and Johanna had come from a long way—a trek through the Arctic, or down from the Alps.

"The price of butter has almost doubled," Hedwig replied grimly.

"Ah!" Manfred clasped one hand to his chest with deliberate, laughing theatricality. "Did you have to buy margarine?"

Hedwig gave him a look of incredulous disdain, as if the very suggestion, teasing as it had been, insulted her. She, a woman who had churned her own butter from the age of eight, until she'd come to Salzburg, buy such a thing? "Of course not," she replied with dignity, and he laughed and kissed her cheek.

Lotte watched the interaction—like a hundred others her parents had had over the years—with a pang of longing she hadn't expected to feel. This too she would miss—not just witnessing it between her parents, but for herself. Never to know the love of man, the touch of his lips on her cheek, his hand on her waist, his teasing smile, her answering laugh…

She watched as her mother predictably twitched away from her husband's embrace, a smile flitting across Hedwig's lips before disappearing, and Lotte's pang of longing suddenly turned into a welcome wave of relief.

All the complications, all the uncertainties, all the unspoken disappointments and longings. Lotte knew her parents loved each other with a solid strength that was deeper than mere passion, and yet still her mother twisted away, her father's teasing smile dropped for the merest moment. She would miss that confusion for herself, and she did not mind.

"Why the long face?" her mother asked her, although hers was no better.

Lotte shrugged and tried to smile. "I don't know."

Her mother narrowed her eyes as Johanna began to unpack their shopping.

"Lotte has some news," her father said in the manner of a grand announcement. "She will tell us at supper tonight."

So she would have the occasion her vanity had longed for, after all. Now that her father had said it, Lotte felt a tremor of excitement—or was it fear? Johanna had stopped her unpacking and she looked between Lotte and Manfred as she shook her head slowly.

"What do you mean?"

"Lotte will tell us." Her father pressed a finger to his lips as if keeping a secret. "Now I must return to the shop."

With a parting smile for Lotte, he headed downstairs. Hedwig and Johanna turned to look at Lotte expectantly.

"What is this news?" her mother asked in a tone that bordered on suspicious.

"Papa said I was to tell you at supper."

Her mother grunted in reply and Johanna continued to unpack the shopping. After a few seconds, Lotte went into the sitting room, her heart beating unevenly. Tonight she would tell her family. Tonight it would become real.

She pressed one hand to her hard-beating heart as she took a steadying breath. As she gazed out at the February morning, the world washed in gray, Lotte did not know whether she felt excited—or afraid.

CHAPTER ELEVEN

JOHANNA

September 1937

"When are you going to tell your family about us?"

Franz's voice was quiet but intense as Johanna kept her gaze on the blue-green ribbon of river winding through the city; she did not reply. They were walking along the Salzach on a sunny afternoon, the last of the summer's warmth lingering in the air like the remnant of a golden memory. Within a month it would almost certainly snow. The service when Lotte would enter the novitiate was the next day; it had been six months since she'd shocked them all by entering the abbey as a postulant, and Johanna had been surprised by how much grief she felt for the sister that she would only catch glimpses of for the next several years, if not more. She missed Lotte's laughter, her cheerful presence, the way she lit up a room. The house had felt emptier and colder without her.

"Johanna." Franz reached for her hand, tugging on it until she was forced to stop. "Answer me. I have been patient. I am trying to be so still. But when?"

"Franz…" There was no reasonable excuse she could give, Johanna knew. It had been nine months since he'd kissed her by the Christmas tree—nine months of lingering in shadows, and stealing kisses, and keeping secrets. Still she had not spoken of him to her parents, or allowed him to do likewise.

"Is it because I'm a Jew?" he asked, a bleak note entering his voice. "I wouldn't even blame you, with the way things are. It gets more dangerous every day."

Johanna shook her head, caught between guilt and impatience. "You care more about that than I do." Although that wasn't exactly true. She cared less that Franz was half-Jewish and more that he wasn't fully Catholic, yet it was a sentiment she did not know how to explain.

"Do I?" His voice turned hard as he gave her a particularly piercing look, his eyes narrowed against the bright sunlight. "Birgit told me what you said, you know."

"What I said?" Johanna registered his unyielding look with a flicker of unease. "What did I say? When?"

Franz's gaze remained steady on hers; he wasn't angry, and somehow that made it seem worse, whatever it was. She felt guilty as well as panicked, and she didn't even know why yet. "That time you called the knife grinder an idiot Jew."

"The knife grinder… *oh!*" Johanna blew out a breath, the guilt and panic coalescing into a weary resentment; she couldn't summon the strength of anger, either for herself or her sister. "That was before I met you, and in any case I didn't really mean it."

"But you said it."

"About Janos Panov, who happens to be a bit simple-minded!" A blush crept into her cheeks; it felt wrong to try to defend herself. "And I told you, I didn't mean it. We all say things we don't mean in a heated moment. That's all it was, I was angry about something else." She shook her head. "Why did Birgit tell you such a thing?" Johanna realized she *was* angry, and with Birgit. *Why would she tell Franz such a thing, unless to make him dislike her?*

"She was asking me how I came to be here. I told her what I told you, about Professor Schlick."

"And that led to her telling you what I said about Janos Panov, ages ago?" Johanna answered in disbelief. "She's just jealous."

"Jealous?" Franz raised his eyebrows. "She has her own secret in that regard, I think."

"She told you about him?"

"Not in so many words, but why are we talking about Birgit?" He pulled her towards him, and she came into his arms reluctantly, still clinging to the vestiges of her anger even though she didn't really want to. "Johanna, I love you. I want to be with you. When will you tell your family about us?"

She closed her eyes as he nestled her against him. Already he was so familiar to her—the rough wool of his coat, even the smell of him—the spicy tang of his aftershave, the heated scent of his skin. "Soon."

"Your father already knows, I think, or at least guesses. How could he not? He sees us springing apart often enough." He tilted her chin up to face him as he gave her a small smile, his dark eyes still troubled as he scanned her face. "If it's not because I'm a Jew, then what is it?"

Johanna hesitated as she tried to sort through the complicated tumult of her own feelings. "I don't know," she admitted. "I'm…" She paused, hating to admit this vulnerability even to herself, never mind to Franz. "I'm scared."

He caressed her cheek, his smile turning tender as his eyes crinkled with concern. "Scared of what?"

She shook her head, unwilling to say more. She was scared of her parents' possible disapproval or disappointment, because she'd fallen in love with someone who did not practice their faith, never mind whether he was a Jew. But more than that, she was scared of declaring her feelings to the world when she couldn't make herself trust Franz's. Scared of her own feelings, the depth and strength of them, the knowledge that if he left her she wouldn't be merely heartbroken, but completely shattered. She might never be able to put herself together again, and she hated the thought of being so vulnerable. *So weak.*

"Johanna…" His gaze was still tender as he sighed. "If not now, then when? We have been creeping about and hiding for nearly a year now. I want to tell your family how I feel. I want to tell the world."

"Do you?" she answered, before she could think to temper her words, her tone. "Do you really?"

He frowned. "Have I ever given you cause to doubt me?"

Wordlessly, reluctantly, Johanna shook her head. Ever since that Christmas kiss Franz had been nothing but kind, tender, caring. How could she doubt him? And yet she did, and she knew the problem was in her own mind. She really was like her mother—twitching away from a caress, doubting his word, his kiss. And why? Because she couldn't let herself trust in the simplicity of his love. She couldn't let it be easy.

"I'm sorry," she whispered, and then she saw, to her horror, Franz's face harden into unfamiliar lines as he pulled away from her.

"You're always sorry," he said as he walked on, not waiting for her to catch up.

"Franz—" She hurried after him, panic making her heart flutter, her breath come out in a gasp. She'd never seen him look so cold. She hadn't thought he could.

"There are enough people in this city who want to make me feel like a second-class citizen," he told her in a flat voice as he kept walking at such speed that she struggled to match his long strides. "I don't need you, the woman I love, to do it, as well."

"Franz! I don't. I don't mean to—"

"But you do. You want to keep me as some dirty secret." His mouth twisted in a sneer as he looked at her with hard, glittering eyes, his face transformed by his anger into something terrifyingly indifferent. "Your dirty Jew."

"*Franz.*" She gasped as though winded, but he'd already turned away from her again. She knew she'd never wanted him to feel like that, and she'd never heard him talk like this. "It's not like that, I swear."

He shook his head, unmoved. "I've had enough of it, Johanna. I've told you how I felt, many times. I've waited and waited. Well, I don't intend to wait any longer."

"What? No—"

"I won't be anyone's secret," Franz said, and he walked on, leaving her there alone, standing by the river.

The next day Johanna stood in the side chapel of Nonnberg Abbey, numb to everything—the swelling crescendo of the organ, the stark reality of her youngest sister processing down the aisle, dressed as a bride, complete with white veil. The six postulants to be received as novitiates, bringing them one step closer to taking their final vows, were all dressed in the same bridal fashion—long white dresses and matching veils, their hands clasped sedately at their middles. Their families had all been herded to this small, shadowy space, kept behind an iron grille, to watch from afar.

As Johanna peered through the grille, she saw that Lotte looked achingly the same—and yet so very different. She had the same shining hair underneath the veil, the same rosebud mouth and porcelain cheeks and big blue eyes. Yet as Johanna looked at her, she seemed a stranger, her gaze distant, her face tilted upward, as if to a heavenly light only she could see. The small smile curving her lips looked knowing and secretive. She did not glance once to the side chapel where she must have known her family was standing, craning their necks to catch a glimpse of her.

As the postulants approached the chancel steps, they knelt, their white skirts spreading about them, their heads dutifully bowed.

The archbishop of Salzburg came forward and intoned in a stentorian voice, "What do you ask, my daughters?"

"We ask for the blessing of God and the favor to be received in His congregation," the women chanted back. "We offer our Lord our liberty, our memory, and our will, and we ask only for His love and His holy grace."

"Are you firmly resolved," the bishop asked, "to despise the honors, riches, and all the vain pleasures of this world in order to prepare for a closer union with God?"

"We are so resolved, most reverend Father."

Johanna glanced at Birgit, her gaze transfixed on Lotte, who was no more than a white blur against the old stone. She had argued with Birgit last night, had accused her sister of ugly things. She couldn't even be sorry now, although Birgit had been furious and then tearful.

"I'm not *jealous,*" she'd cried, her face red with fury, her eyes glittering with hurt. "And I wasn't trying to cause trouble. It just came out, because Papa arranged for Franz to come *because* he was Jewish. Did you even know that? To help Franz, but also to help us. To make us realize they're *not* idiot Jews, whatever you were stupid enough to say. That's one of the reasons he's his apprentice. Because of you! But I don't suppose you care about that, or what it has meant for me?"

"I don't care about any of it," Johanna had snapped, wishing she meant it, and they'd gone to bed in frigid silence. They hadn't spoken since, and Johanna couldn't even be sorry.

Her gaze moved from Birgit to their mother, whose expression was grimly accepting, her shoulders squared. Her father, she saw, smiled even as he brushed a tear from his eye.

And Franz… Franz stared straight ahead, his mouth in a hard line, his body angled slightly away from her. He had not spoken to her once since he'd left her at the river yesterday afternoon, and Johanna had not tried to approach him. She was angry as well as hurt, and she had her pride. If Franz was going to be so stubborn, well, then, so was she. She knew it was foolish, but she could not keep herself from it.

"Do you make this request of your own free will?" the bishop asked, his voice echoing though the chapel.

"Yes." One by one the postulants answered; Lotte was second to last, her voice ringing out with clear certainty. Johanna looked away, hating that Lotte could feel so certain, so joyous, about her calling, even though it meant she'd likely never see any of them ever again. Did she not love them? Did she not *care?*

"May the Lord who has begun this, bring it to perfection," the archbishop intoned, and everyone said amen.

As the nuns' voices rose in song, the archbishop blessed the white veils the postulants would soon wear, to replace the bridal veils on their heads. Each one held the black habit they would don in their arms like an offering. As each postulant was given the new veil by the Mother Abbess, she kissed the cloth.

Johanna forced herself to watch Lotte—*dear little Lotte*—complete the ritual, and then the postulants filed out of the chapel, to an anteroom where they would put on their new habits, their new lives. None of the Eders would see Lotte again for at least a year, probably more. Johanna had not met her sister's eyes once; it was as if Lotte wasn't even aware of them. As if, for her, they'd ceased to exist.

After the service they walked in silence down the Nonnbergstiege and back to the narrow house on Getreidegasse, Franz lagging a little behind everyone else. Johanna longed to drop back and join him, but she made herself stay where she was. He was still angry; she knew that, but she hoped he might thaw if she gave him enough time. She had already resolved not to beg.

Up in the kitchen she put an apron over her best dress unthinkingly; this was *her* habit, just as Lotte was now wearing the white veil and black robe of a novice.

Her mother gave her a surprisingly sympathetic look as she joined her at the table to prepare the midday meal. With a jolt Johanna wondered if she knew, or at least guessed, about Franz, just as he'd intimated the day before. Why had her mother never said anything, then? Yet why should she have expected her mother, who spoke so rarely anyway, to speak of such intimate matters?

They worked in silence for a few minutes, peeling and chopping, and then suddenly, surprisingly, Hedwig spoke. "Johanna."

The import in her mother's voice made Johanna still, a knife in one hand. "Yes?"

"If you still wish it, if it is still possible… you may go to school." Johanna stared at her blankly and her mother clarified, a touch impatient now, "The secretarial course. You may enroll, if you still wish it."

"I may?" It had been over a year since she'd first asked, and so much had changed. The secretarial course felt like a child's dream, and yet she was as likely to stay in this kitchen now as she ever was.

"Yes, if you still wish it," her mother said, turning back to the potatoes she'd been peeling, her head bowed over the heap of them as she took up her knife and began to peel once more. "You are right. The world is changing. It would be good for you to have skills."

Johanna stared at her mother, shocked by this development. Did she even want to do the course any more? She hadn't thought about it in months, and yet she realized she did still want it, perhaps now more than ever. It meant possibility, opportunity, maybe even hope. "Thank you, Mama."

Hedwig nodded, gruff as always, and Johanna wondered how much it cost her mother to admit as much as she had. The world *was* changing, whether any of them wanted it to or not.

CHAPTER TWELVE

BIRGIT

December 1937

Birgit had seen Werner three more times since he'd left for Innsbruck a year ago, and each visit had been both thrilling and sweet, taken during his all too brief leaves—a walk by the river, or a coffee in a steamy café, snatching a few moments of conversation amidst the clatter of cups. Birgit had not yet summoned the courage to ask him to meet her family.

He had not asked again either, and she'd worried that he might have changed his mind, although he'd continued to write dutifully at least once a month, rather dull epistles, it was true, about army life and the hikes he was taking around Innsbruck, but even so Birgit savored every word. Far more pleasant for him to write of hikes and duties than warn her off the communists or rhapsodize about Hitler. He'd done neither of those, and she'd been able to dismiss the comments he'd once made as if they'd never been spoken at all.

Then in December Werner had written her to say he would be back in Salzburg for the week before Christmas and he wished to meet her family. Her father in particular, he'd written, which had sent a tremulous thrill through Birgit. Surely, *surely* that meant a proposal. Already, and yet at last.

Now that the evening was here, however, and Werner was expected any moment, Birgit felt nervous to the point of near terror. What if her father didn't like him? What if Werner didn't like her family—her mother could be so dour, and Johanna had been in a temper for *months.* Birgit had tried, ages ago, to apologize for telling Franz about the remark she had made, but her sister had refused to listen.

"It doesn't matter now, anyway," she'd said shortly, after Birgit had persisted in explaining how she hadn't meant to cast Johanna in a bad light, although afterwards she wondered if some small, mean part of her actually had, which made her feel even guiltier.

"Leave it," Johanna had said flatly. "It's over."

Since then, her sister had been determinedly busy, having enrolled in a secretarial course. Johanna spent the evenings working at the kitchen table, practicing her typing or stenography, so they'd had little opportunity for any conversation.

Their father had, with typical generosity, procured a second-hand typewriter for her to practice on. It was a monstrous black beast of a machine, and the loud clacking of the keys nearly drove Birgit mad. Still, Johanna was diligent and focused; she hoped to get a secretarial position when she finished the course in June and that seemed to be all she thought or cared about.

As for Franz, when Birgit had tried to apologize when they were alone in the shop, he'd been almost as terse.

"I understand, Birgit, don't worry," he'd said, and turned back to the clock he was repairing, a Schonberger dwarf wall clock made in Vienna. He'd become admirably proficient in the year since he'd started as an apprentice; more of a natural than she was, a fact she acknowledged fairly but with reluctance.

Her parents, at least, had been surprised but pleased when Birgit had told them about Werner.

"Ah ha, I thought there must be someone!" her father had said, wagging his finger at her and smiling. "You have been looking as if you had a secret to keep! So who is this man?"

"His family is from Aigen and he is in an Alpine unit of the *Bundesheer*," Birgit had said; she'd watched as her father's playful smile had faltered. In recent months the whole country had seemed to twang with tension, everyone in a state of uneasy expectation, ears straining to know what might happen next.

Earlier in the year, Mussolini had informed Chancellor Schuschnigg that Italy would no longer defend Austria against a potential invasion by Germany, a far cry from his stance in 1934, when Italian troops had amassed in the Brenner Pass to keep Germany from taking over Austria.

Meanwhile Hitler was become ever more rapacious in his demand for territory; there had been talk of him wanting Austria's iron and Czechoslovakia's coal, although he had yet to make a move on either. Still, Germany continued to rearm at a furious pace. Increasingly its Wehrmacht was becoming a force not just to be reckoned with, but to be feared. And if Germany did invade Austria, there was a question as to whether the Austrian *Bundesheer*, with its many Nazi sympathizers, would bother to defend its borders, although it was being mobilized for just such an occurrence.

Birgit had been able to see all of this in her father's faltering smile before he'd squared his shoulders and given her a briskly cheerful look. "Excellent! I look forward to meeting him."

A knock sounded at the front door; Birgit had forgotten to tell Werner to come to the side door, and so he would have to go through the darkened shop. Nervously she smoothed her hands down the sides of her new dress, made of dark green crepe de chine, bought only last week at SL Schwarz.

Her mother was upstairs at the stove, seeing to their meal; she had made *Speckknödel*, bacon dumplings from the Tyrol, as well as more familiar *Salzburger Nockerln*, a sweet soufflé. Johanna was in the sitting room with their father, having finished laying the table, and Franz had been upstairs in his room for most of the afternoon.

Since Lotte had left, Birgit felt as if they'd all separated into disparate parts, like the gears of a clock that had gone out of sync, catching on and jarring with one another rather than working in harmonious unity for a clear purpose.

The friendly evenings in the sitting room had ceased months ago; without Lotte's soaring soprano, their singing simply hadn't been the same, and so no one had even tried. And now that Johanna and Franz seemed to barely be on speaking terms, the likelihood of companionable evenings had seemed even more remote.

Instead, in the evenings Franz went to his room and her father read the paper, while her mother and Johanna stayed in the kitchen and Birgit read or sewed. Sometimes it felt as if they were all waiting for something, and yet for what?

For Werner, perhaps… and now he was here. But what if it all went terribly wrong? What if he said something amiss? What if her family did? Birgit suppressed a shiver of apprehension as she hurried to answer the door.

"I made it!" Werner doffed his cap as he took Birgit into his arms. He was wearing his uniform, and she wished he wasn't. "Are you pleased to see me?"

"Of course I am," she answered as he kissed her cheek.

"You don't seem it," he told her with a laugh. "Are you nervous?"

"A bit. Are you?"

"Not at all." He grinned. "I'm only pleased to finally be introduced. It's about time!"

"Come upstairs, then," Birgit said as she locked the shop door behind him. Werner took the opportunity to sneak an arm around her waist.

"Werner—"

"Just one kiss," he murmured, and laughing a little, Birgit wound her arms around his neck as he gave her a thorough kiss indeed. She felt herself relax into his easy embrace, glad of his arms around her, their solid strength, the certainty of his affection. It was going to be all right. It had to be.

As they came up the stairs, her father emerged from the sitting room with a wide smile, holding out a hand to Werner.

"*Guten abend!* So pleased to meet you." He gave Werner's hand a hearty shake as Werner doffed his cap. "I would say I have heard so much about you, but I haven't."

"I look forward to enlightening you, *mein* Herr," Werner replied, and her father shook his head, smiling still.

"You must call me Manfred. And look, here is my lovely wife, Hedwig."

Birgit watched as her mother came into the sitting room, looking solid and square in her best dress of shabby brown velvet, her apron worn over it, her hair scraped back into its usual graying bun. Werner gave her a courtly little bow.

Johanna hadn't said a word, merely nodding as their father made introductions, and Franz still hadn't come downstairs. With another panicky flutter, Birgit wondered if this was all going to be a disaster. If only Lotte were here, with her light laugh, her friendly chatter, smoothing everything over, making it easy.

Werner, however, was unfazed by any seeming unfriendliness. As they sipped aperitifs of plum brandy in the sitting room, he chatted about growing up in Aigen, how he had been a member of St. Erhard's since he was but a child, which caused her parents to exchange a brief approving look. After a quarter of an hour Franz came downstairs, wearing his best waistcoat and apologizing for his tardiness.

He shook hands with Werner and seemed like his old, charming self, laughing and tossing back his schnapps while Johanna had a mouth like a prune. Still, Birgit breathed easier. As they sat down to plates of steaming *Speckknödel*, she thought it really might be all right, after all.

And at first it was. Werner asked her father about clockmaking, and he answered easily enough, telling him how his own father had started the little shop on Getreidegasse, how working with time itself felt important, "yes, yes," he laughed, he was a bit of a philosopher, it was true.

That topic of conversation exhausted, Werner turned to Johanna, and she gave somewhat terse replies to questions about her secretarial course while he made noises of admiration and approval. He even had something to say about the Tyrol, having been skiing there several times. When he mentioned having traveled through her mother's home village of Ladis—remarking how charming it was—Hedwig had actually blushed, looking pleased.

And then the talk turned, with alarming predictability, to politics. It seemed impossible not to talk of it, when every day there were new reports of Germany's laws against Jews, the country's rearmament, Hitler's fiery speeches to the Reichstag while other world leaders wrung their hands and waited.

Only that week a new Nazi exhibition had opened in Munich, *The Eternal Jew*, and it was that occasion which threw a stumbling block before them all.

"Have you seen the exhibition?" Werner asked, all interested politeness, as Hedwig rose to clear the plates for the dessert.

"I have not," Manfred replied, after a slight pause. Birgit felt the chilliness steal through the room like an icy fog, although Werner was still smiling. "It is all the way in Munich, after all."

"It is only two hours by train. Not very long at all, really, from here. Closer than Vienna."

Birgit opened her mouth to talk of something else, but Franz spoke first.

"Have *you* seen it?" he asked in a tone that was pointed and barely polite. Werner didn't seem to notice.

"Yes, when it first opened. A few of us in my division went." Werner smiled and shrugged. "It was interesting, if a bit heavy-handed. We don't need to see caricatures of Jews holding whips in one hand and gold coins in the other to know they control the banks, do we?" He let out a laugh, but no one else so much as smiled. Birgit's stomach cramped. She'd seen the cartoon Werner mentioned in the newspaper and had thought it horrible and stupid. But surely that was what Werner meant, even if it didn't quite sound as if he had. *He wasn't saying anything truly terrible, was he?*

Her father had not replied to Werner, and now he glanced up at Hedwig with a smile as she took his plate. "Thank you, my dear. Delicious as always."

The silence stretched on, like something breakable. It would take little more than a breath to shatter it, the single tap of a finger on the glass and all would crack, and then what? Birgit couldn't bear it.

"Oh, who cares about some silly exhibition," she exclaimed. "Everyone knows the Nazis don't know the first thing about art. Why, wasn't it in Munich, as well, that they held the *Great German Art Exhibition*?" The laugh she let out sounded shrill. "And right across the street was an exhibition of what they called degenerate art. Everyone queued for that one and not the other."

"I'm not surprised," Johanna replied tartly. "Where did you hear about it, Birgit?"

"I read about it in the paper, I think." Actually Ingrid had told her all about it, but she could hardly mention that to her family, or to Werner. She had kept the meetings she'd attended a secret from everyone—sometimes even from herself.

It was as if there was one Birgit who wrote letters to Werner and waited for his visits, and another who slipped away to a coffeehouse in Elisabeth-Vorstadt once a month to listen to fiery speakers and crept through the city leaving pamphlets that demanded the end of fascism. Those two Birgits would never meet. She wouldn't let them.

"Well," Werner said after another endless moment, glancing around at everyone with a slight frown as if he couldn't understand their sudden reserve, "it will be coming to Vienna in the new year. Perhaps you will be able to view it then."

"I am sure," her father replied pleasantly, "that the exhibition is quite informative about the views of the National Socialists, especially in regard to Jews and others they have deemed antisocial."

Werner's slight frown deepened. "Indeed," he replied after a pause.

Birgit tried again to divert the conversation. "Let's not talk about politics," she implored, trying for a smile, her voice ringing out with a cringingly false note of gaiety. "It's so very dull. Franz, after supper you could play the—"

"We weren't talking about politics," Franz replied quietly, his even gaze trained on Werner. "We were talking about the Jews."

Another silence descended on the table, this one heavy. Birgit felt as if they must all bow beneath its weight, even though no one moved. Werner looked between her father and Franz, a deeper crease appearing between his brows.

"I have nothing against the Jews," he said after a moment. "Not personally. They have a right to live their lives, after all, but surely you cannot deny their control of our country's finances has been to the detriment of its other citizens."

The silence felt even heavier, unbearably so. Birgit bit her lip. He didn't mean anything by it, she told herself. He couldn't. And yet his words fell like hammer blows.

"Like Birgit said, we should not talk of politics," her father finally said, his tone light, and Johanna, who had said little throughout the whole meal, made a sudden noise of aggravated impatience.

"But you love to talk of politics, Father," she said, her voice rising in strident determination. "At least once or twice a month you have all your old friends here to discuss politics the whole night long!" She glared at Werner, who looked surprised by her sudden, savage tone.

"Johanna," Hedwig said severely, hating any rudeness, and her sister shrugged defiantly.

"What of it? It's true. They talk of how Austria must remain independent and resist the Nazi threat. They all agree on that. They hate Hitler and all he stands for—"

"Austria might not be able to resist the Nazi threat," Werner interjected quietly, and Johanna turned on him, her expression fierce.

"But it should, we all should, and that is the difference. As for that exhibition?" Her lip curled in a sneer. "I would never attend such a thing, *never,* not even out of the merest idle curiosity. I would not spend a single groschen to view the Nazis' horrible propaganda—because that is all it is. Propaganda and lies, to make people like you hate the Jews when you have absolutely no reason to. No reason at all." Out of breath, she sat back in her seat while a stunned silence descended on the table.

Birgit glanced at Werner, and saw he looked shaken but also a bit angry; then she saw Franz, his eyes blazing with both love and pride as he looked at Johanna. He was positively shining with it; a sudden, horrible envy seized her insides. Why should Johanna have the love of a man, and she shouldn't? Why did everything have to be ruined, all because of some foolish, careless talk about an exhibition only Werner had seen? It was so *stupid.* It wasn't as if he'd said anything truly terrible.

And yet the hollowness she felt inside her, as if a cold wind were whistling right through her, told her otherwise.

"Please," she pleaded. "This is all a palaver over nothing."

"Nothing—" Johanna exclaimed, determined to be angry, and Birgit itched to shake her.

"An art exhibition, that is all! Why must you be so… so *indignant?*"

"I fear this is all my fault," Werner interjected, his palms flat on the table. "I apologize for any offense I may have caused without meaning to. I certainly wish no disrespect to such benevolent hosts."

"There is no need to apologize," Manfred replied as amiably as he could, although he looked a bit shaken by the heated conversation. "You are our guest, after all. It is we who should apologize, for not making you feel welcome."

"Papa—" Johanna began, her voice full of outrage, but her father silenced her with a single look.

"Let us adjourn to the sitting room," he said. "Werner, have you ever heard Birgit sing?"

Birgit did not want to sing in the least, but she was desperate to move on from this disaster, and so she duly stood beside the piano as Franz played "The Carriage Horseman," a traditional folk song that could surely offend no one. Johanna sang along somewhat ungraciously, although Birgit thought she seemed at least a little repentant for her outburst.

Still, without Lotte's soaring soprano, it was a poor show indeed, and Birgit didn't think anyone felt anything but relief when it finally ended. Werner took his leave a short while later, and that too seemed to bring relief.

She accompanied him downstairs, battling a wretched misery at how it had all gone, as well as a deepening unease. As much as she longed to, she knew she could not ignore all that Werner had said.

"I don't think I came off as well I had hoped," he remarked with an uneven laugh as they made their way through the darkened shop. "You should have told me your family were Jew-lovers!" He spoke jokingly, but Birgit froze, blinking at him in the darkness.

"Don't say that, please," she told him in a low voice. "You don't mean it. You can't. I know you've said some things, some harmless things, but—"

"Why do you care so much?" He sounded bewildered rather than angry.

"Because…" She stared at him helplessly, unsure how to explain. Why *did* she care? It would be so much easier not to. And yet with every meeting she'd attended at the coffeehouse, with every conversation she'd had with Ingrid, with every pamphlet she'd read or left on a park bench… she knew she *did* care. She had to, because if she didn't then she'd have lost all sense of compassion, of justice.

"Birgit?" Werner prompted, sounding tired now. "I don't understand. You're not Jewish."

"No." *But Franz was. And even Janos.* Did they—did *anyone*—deserve the treatment that was being meted out to them? The answer was obvious. Of course not. And if she could not even say as much to the man she wanted to marry…

She stared at Werner in the dim and dusty shop, the only sound their breathing and the ticking of clocks, marking every moment, and she knew what she had to ask.

"Werner, what do you think of Hitler?" She paused while he simply stared at her. "Really?"

"Hitler?" He shook his head slowly, seeming truly baffled now. "Why are you asking me, Birgit?"

"Because it matters." Each word throbbed painfully through her. She couldn't bear it if he ended things now, and all because of stupid politics. Or perhaps she would end it, if she were strong enough. She didn't know if she was, but she realized she wanted to be, if it came to that.

"Well, it shouldn't matter," Werner said, sounding angry now as he straightened his cuffs, officious in his uniform. "Because I don't particularly think about him one way or another. Birgit, I am an Austrian first. I serve my country, and that is all."

"But the things Hitler has said… the laws they've made… about the Jews," she insisted. "You've said you don't think they're that bad—"

"I haven't said that exactly," Werner huffed. "I'm not… I don't…" He shook his head, angry now as he threw his hands up in the air. "The Jews, the Jews! Why do you care so much about the damned Jews?"

"Do you know any?" she asked quietly. "Jews? Personally, I mean?"

He shrugged, impatient now as well as angry, tossing his head like a horse bothered by a fly. "My father's old tailor, I think. I went to school with his son until they moved away."

That was all? "And yet you can happily go to an exhibition about them, saying how evil and stupid and horrible they are!" She shook her head, incredulous and tearful, struggling to control her emotions, her voice. "You can support laws that deprive them of their belongings, their citizenship, their jobs? Werner, don't you see? Today it is the Jews. Tomorrow it might be the Catholics."

"The Catholics!" He let out a snort of derision. "Never."

"Why not? The Nazis are no supporters of the church. And even if it never is the Catholics… *it doesn't matter.*" The realization throbbed painfully through her. "That shouldn't be the reason, anyway. It's not about just protecting ourselves… if we allow the government to persecute and terrify one group of people, simply for who they are, not anything bad they'd done…" She trailed off, searching his face for some glimmer of understanding, of agreement. "Don't you see how wrong that is, Werner?" she asked desperately. "How evil?"

Werner stared at her for a long moment, his expression unreadable. Had she lost him, Birgit wondered, or had he lost her? In that moment she didn't know which it was.

"I don't care about the Jews, one way or the other," he finally said. "Not really. Maybe I should, maybe I should wring my hands over every poor sod who's had a difficult time of it, but life is hard enough, Birgit, and so I don't." He released a low huff of breath as he stared at her, resigned and weary. "But I don't wish them ill, and I can admit that the laws against them have gone too far. That doesn't make me want to fight for them, though. Perhaps you think I should."

She swallowed hard. "I understand why you feel that way," she managed.

"But it disappoints you."

She didn't answer, and he sighed heavily.

"So here we are." He spread his hands. "I am what I am. A devoted Austrian, a good soldier, a man in love with you. Is that enough?" He spoke tonelessly, yet she sensed his hurt pulsing underneath the simply stated words, and it swamped her with both misery and love. "I don't know what you want from me, Birgit," he continued as she gazed at him in despondent silence. "When I came here tonight, this was the last thing I expected. I thought…" He paused, swallowing, his voice choking a little. "I thought tonight would be something else entirely. For heaven's sake, when I mentioned that exhibition, I was just making small talk! I didn't even think about what I was saying. I wish I'd never said a word."

"If it hadn't been the exhibition, it would have been something else." Her heart felt like a weight too heavy for her to bear. How could she not have realized this reckoning was coming? What on earth would Werner think, if he knew she went to those meetings? If she was fighting against the very thing he said they could not resist?

"So that's it?" Werner's voice rose in a hoarse huff of pained disbelief. "Are we—are we finished? And all because of this… this stupid thing?"

Birgit could not bring herself to reply. Could she really break things off simply because of a few thoughtless remarks? Werner wasn't a Nazi. She was sure of that, at least, even as a dark voice inside her whispered, *at least he's not yet.*

"I love you," he said, the words so simple, so honest, as he held his arms out in helpless appeal. A tear spilled down her cheek and Birgit did not bother to wipe it away. How could she turn away from this man? He hadn't done anything *wrong.*

With a muffled oath, Werner pulled her into his arms, holding her tightly to him, his hand stroking her hair. "Don't let this be the end, Birgit, please. I'm sorry for what I've said. I am. You must believe me. I'll—I'll try to do better. I promise. I need you, to help me."

Birgit put her arms around him as she closed her eyes. How could she resist such a plea? When she was with Werner, she felt like a new person—strong, confident, striding through the world. She felt beautiful and loved and *important.* And he was a good man; she'd known that all along, from the first moment she'd laid eyes on him. How could she throw all they had away, simply because he'd made a remark about a stupid exhibition she'd never even seen?

"This isn't the end," she whispered as she pressed her cheek against the lapel of his jacket. "I don't want it to be. I love you, Werner."

And Werner hugged her even more tightly to him.

CHAPTER THIRTEEN

LOTTE

Nonnberg Abbey, February 1938

"I know I do not need to remind you, daughters, that we answer to a higher call."

The Mother Abbess's careworn face seemed to collapse with weariness as she gazed at each of the nuns of Nonnberg Abbey in turn, all of them assembled in the refectory for their midday meal. She'd just explained to them, quietly and soberly, how in the last few weeks the state of affairs in Austria had suffered several grievous turns.

First Chancellor Schuschnigg had been summoned to a meeting at the Berghof in nearby Berchtesgaden, Hitler's country retreat outside Salzburg, where he had hoped to discuss matters on an equal footing as between two leaders, only to be berated like a naughty schoolboy and then threatened with invasion.

Three days later the chancellor had been forced to appoint two National Socialists to his cabinet, and the week after that Hitler had given a blistering speech to the Reichstag demanding *Lebensraum* for the German people and a restoration of all German colonies, including Austria.

Meanwhile gangs of brown shirts roamed the streets more and more, causing as much trouble as they could, rowdy and jeering in their newfound confidence. Even from their lofty perch above

Salzburg, the nuns had heard shouting, jeers, even the occasional gunshot.

All of Austria waited with held breath, many with hope, others with fear, for what would happen next. The nuns of Nonnberg Abbey were somehow meant to be above it all.

Lotte had been at the convent for a year now, six months as a postulant, and the following six months as a novice. In all that time she had not once left the abbey, seen her family, or even glimpsed her own reflection. Her world had shrunk to a bare room, the daily offices of prayer, the Great Silence, the simple work of tending the abbey's garden or washing dishes, and yet at the same time it felt as if it had expanded to encompass the divine in all of these simple activities.

The beauty of a soap bubble, sunlight catching its fragile, transparent surface… The peaceful quietness of a still night, where stars pricked the sky like a handful of scattered diamonds… The soothing click of the rosary beads between her fingers, the sound ageless, eternal. She felt as if her very self had been finely tuned, as if the strings of her soul could now play the simplest and purest of melodies.

Sitting there on the hard bench, her hands folded at her waist, listening to Mother Abbess speak of the potential destruction of her country without feeling the need to offer so much as a murmur or a frown, Lotte did not regret any of her choices.

When she'd first walked through that door a year ago, leaving the whole world behind her, it had felt exhilarating, like stepping off a precipice and learning how to fly. The firm click of the door closing behind her, sealing her away, had not felt like an imprisonment but a liberation of her soul. Here she could finally be free.

She'd accepted her new name—Sister Maria Josef—joyfully, just as she'd accepted the simple black veil that framed her face, and the regular offices of prayer that rigidly divided her day into minutes and hours. She loved the simplicity of it all, the purity and rightness of steps that had to be followed without question or complaint; for her, submission was easy.

She even appreciated the little notebook that the head of postulants, Sister Hemma, had given her, along with the other postulants, in which to record all her sins. To write her sins out so deliberately and then confess in front of the sisters once a week, spread-eagled on the floor, her forehead pressed into the cold, hard stone, felt like the most obvious and wonderful act of obedience. It *worked.* When she did her penance, she was at peace.

"You seem to have a natural affinity for the religious life, Sister Maria Josef," the Mother Abbess had told her once, when she'd been summoned to her study a few months after she'd started as a postulant. "But even that is something our rebel hearts will try take pride in. We must not take pride in anything, sister, not even our devotion. Humility is our watchword, our means of being."

"Yes, Reverend Mother," Lotte had answered, her gaze lowered. She accepted this gentle rebuke as she'd accepted everything else—with a serenity that had felt otherworldly, given by God rather than summoned from her own strength. She would not chafe against it, against any of it. She was not even tempted.

Even the things that she knew could be seen as tiresome—being woken up before dawn by one of the nuns dragging a stick along the curtains that separated the postulants' cells, making the iron rings rattle, and having to leap out of bed to recite lauds while still half asleep—did not cause her any real frustration.

Walking at a sedate pace along the walls, using hand signals rather than speech, being completely silent from early evening until the next morning—it all served to make her even more tranquil, ironing out those last rebellious ruffles of self-will, causing her to be even more certain of the solace she'd found within the abbey's ancient walls.

Admittedly, after those first few weeks, the balm of silence had, for a short time, started to feel a bit like a sting; she missed singing, or chatting, or simply humming under her breath. Silence started to feel loud, like an incessant ringing in her ears. When Lotte had confessed her feelings about the matter to all the sisters, the Mother Abbess had, with great kindness, ordered her to maintain complete silence for an entire week.

And somehow that week had silenced the silence; it had broken the last bit of resistance in her and the next time she'd spoken, during the dinner hour, the words had felt strange and uncomfortable, like rocks in her mouth. She struggled to shape them, and she realized how unimportant they had become, how unnecessary.

She could let them go freely, and she discovered an even deeper beauty in this simple act of submission and surrender. When she'd become a novice and accepted the constricting white veil that covered her neck and framed her face, her golden plait hacked off at the base of her skull with a pair of scissors and tossed aside like so much rubbish, she had not minded. She had relinquished that last call on her vanity as she had all the others, with gladness.

Before they'd taken their vows as novices, the Mother Abbess had asked every postulant to search their hearts and surrender any last object that tied them to their worldly affections. Lotte had, with no more than a tremor, offered up the dried sprig of edelweiss her father had given her all those years ago, when they'd sung in the competition, the newly christened Edelweiss Sisters. She'd kept it in her prayer book, a poignant reminder of her old life. Once or twice, she'd flipped to the page where it lay pressed and touched the dried blossom with her finger.

She'd felt a flicker of regret, of loss, as she put it in the basket Sister Hemma held out, but no more. That too had to be surrendered.

Now, a year on, Lotte discovered she did not miss that little sprig; she did not miss even her family the way she would have once expected to. In truth, she rarely thought of them. They were no more than ghosts on the fringes of her memory, fleeting and ephemeral, soon turned to vapor.

The hunger for human touch that she'd sometimes craved at the beginning of her time at the abbey, for the nuns of Nonnberg were discouraged from showing any physical affection to one another, now felt alien and strange, far too physical and even embarrassing. The only time she deliberately touched another human being was when she kissed the Mother Abbess's hand.

She did not miss the tall, narrow house on Getreidegasse, or the evenings singing by the piano, or walking in springtime in a city square or underneath the cherry blossoms in Mirabellgarten. She did not miss them because she did not think of them; the discipline of forgetfulness had become second nature to her, as easy as breathing. Finally her life was the placidly moving stream she had once longed for, flowing ever onward undisturbed, untroubled.

And now Hitler threatened it all.

"I am telling you this," the Mother Abbess continued, "so that you may be better prepared to retain your calm and courage throughout. We must go on, sisters, as if nothing has happened, and continue in our prayerful attitude of charity to all." She looked at each of them in turn, her gaze steady and clear, but with a shadow in her eyes, the weight of events heavy on her slight shoulders, which were rounded more than usual. For once the Mother Abbess looked her age. "I do not pretend that it is easy or natural to do so," she continued, "or that the uncertainty of these times cannot give rise to fear. God sends these times to try us, daughters, but we must never doubt His sovereign hand guiding all things, even this."

With a kindly yet tired smile for them all, the Mother Abbess sat down and in silence they began to eat.

It was only later, as Lotte was washing dishes with Sister Kunigunde, named after an early German saint, that she thought more deeply of what the Mother Abbess had said, and then only because the other novice forced her to do so.

"If Hitler invades Austria," Kunigunde asked in a low voice, her hands immersed in the soapy water, "what will change?"

Lotte gave her a look of reproof; surely there was no need to have this conversation. Unnecessary words were forbidden, including these.

"As the Mother Abbess has said, nothing here will change," she replied firmly, and then nodded to the pile of dirty bowls awaiting their attention.

"But you know that can't be true." Sister Kunigunde seemed undeterred by Lotte's stern look. "What of our families?"

"The sisters here are our family."

"You know what I mean." She lifted her chin, a challenge in her bold stare. She was a blunt-faced girl with a snub nose and a sturdy body; the only thing Lotte knew about her was what she confessed every week—usually a tendency to let her mind drift during prayer, and difficulty rising in the morning. "Do you not miss them at all?" she pressed. "Your own mother and father? I remember them, from that first day. Your father looked so kind. He had a twinkle in his eye…"

The words, so simply spoken, caused a sudden shaft of grief to lance through Lotte, leaving her breathless. For a second, no more, she let herself picture her father—his thinning white hair, his red cheeks, that twinkle in his eye.

She could see each detail so clearly, it was as if he were standing right before her, smiling, his arms outstretched. If she lifted her hand, she would be able to touch him. Without realizing she had done so, she let out a gasp and then she bit her lip, shocked by the emotion that she had suppressed for so long, now rushing through her in a turbulent river.

"What will happen to them?" Kunigunde asked quietly. "Or even to us? The Nazis are no friends of the church."

"They have sworn to tolerate…" Lotte began hesitantly but Kunigunde stopped her with a disparaging sound.

"And what good are Nazi promises? Even the Holy Father has spoken of the Nazi aggression to the church. We are Hitler's enemies, whether he says so or not."

Fear clutched at Lotte with icy fingers, which she did her best to push away. "We should not be talking like this," she insisted, her voice caught between severity and desperation. "We are above such things, sister."

"I wonder how long we will be able to take such an elevated position," Kunigunde replied darkly before turning back to the dishes. "When you think of our families suffering…" She shook her head as she scrubbed the pot she held with vicious concentration.

As Lotte looked at the other novice, her head bent over her work, she realized she did not remember Kunigunde's family at all. She had not paid any attention; she had not *cared.* The notion was unsettling, for it smacked of selfishness—or was it simply singular devotion? Lotte didn't know, and her confusion unsettled her all the more. *What—who—was right?*

"Sister Kunigunde," she began, and the other woman glanced at her over the basin of soapy water. "What of your family? Are they in Salzburg?"

"My parents are dead. There is only my sister and her family, in Eugendorf, a nearby village. They don't have very much, and I would have been another mouth to feed, even though I could have helped with the little ones. It didn't seem enough."

"You mean that is why you entered the community here?" Lotte could not keep the shock, and perhaps even the disapproval, from her voice. "You don't—you don't actually have a vocation?"

Kunigunde's mouth twisted. "What is a vocation, after all?"

Lotte shook her head slowly, unable to answer. She had assumed all the novices had had a similar experience to her, a longing for the religious life, its simplicity and purity, a call to higher things, yet obviously Kunigunde did not.

And yet what did it say of her, that she did not remember Kunigunde's family? Who could judge whether a desire for simplicity was a more or less selfish motivation than seeking to ease another's burden? Perhaps Sister Kunigunde's sacrifice was a more fragrant offering to God than Lotte's. Her thoughts jostled for space in a way they hadn't during the year she'd been at the abbey. All her convictions felt as if they could be overturned, never mind Hitler and his army.

Sister Kunigunde had turned back to the dishes once more, and slowly Lotte began to scrub the dirty bowl she held, her mind in more of a disquiet than ever.

*

Just two weeks later the unthinkable, the inevitable, happened. While the sisters gathered again in the refectory, the Mother Abbess addressed them.

"I just received word that German troops entered Austria this morning." She lifted her chin as she looked around at them all. "The Austrian *Bundesheer* was ordered not to resist. Chancellor Schuschnigg has resigned, and I am sure there are many more changes to come. The world around us will look very different, but that is not our concern." She paused, taking a breath to steady herself before continuing, "May I remind you, daughters, that we answer to a higher call. Nothing has changed for anyone here." She looked at each of them in turn, her expression turning uncharacteristically hard. "We will continue to serve our community and those who come to us for aid. Anyone," she emphasized, "who comes to us for aid will never be turned away."

It wasn't until much later that Lotte wondered who she was really referring to.

CHAPTER FOURTEEN

JOHANNA

March 1938

Johanna gazed out the sitting room window at the street below, nearly every building bedecked with swastika banners. Two days on from what was now known as the Anschluss—Hitler's war of flowers—she was still battling a swamping sense of unreality.

It had all happened so *fast*. It seemed as if one moment Austria had been clinging to independence, Schuschnigg doing everything he could to keep his country whole, and then, in a single movement, like a hand sweeping away all the pieces on a chessboard, the world as she'd known it had disappeared completely.

In a matter of mere hours, Schuschnigg had resigned and the Wehrmacht, with its troops, its trucks and tanks, had rolled across the border to the ringing of church bells and the cheering crowds of ecstatic citizens. In Vienna there had been parades; flowers had been strewn across the roads, the thronging crowds wild for Hitler.

In Salzburg the reception had been, if anything, even more enthusiastic. Manfred had ordered everyone to stay inside yesterday when troops marched over the Staatsbrücke and into the old town, to the delight of the crowds. Johanna had heard their swelling chorus of approbation from the kitchen, even with the windows and shutters closed, the curtains drawn. She felt as if they were in mourning while the whole world sang.

The odious "Horst Wessel" song had blared from every radio in every crowded café, its triumphant sound echoing through the streets. When Johanna had turned on the radio to listen to the woman's hour program, "If Women Ask," she heard the program "Women in the National Socialist State" instead.

"How have they done this so quickly?" she'd asked her mother, who merely shook her head, grim-faced and thin-lipped. In a single day the entire country had not just been taken over, but utterly transformed, like a curtain coming up on a play, all the scenery shifted, the costumes changed. A new act had begun, and it was unrecognizable to Johanna.

That day the newspapers had either appeared with blanked-out front pages or had not been published at all, and the banks had closed. Nazis had marched in the streets under their scarlet banners; even the traffic had changed, with many of Salzburg's one-way streets becoming two-way, causing a hopeless snarl of cars. Yet despite all this hassle and uncertainty, still people had celebrated and rejoiced. Johanna could not understand it.

It had been six months since Franz had left her standing by the Salzach. Six months where they had moved around each other carefully, barely speaking, with none of the playful flirtation and easy camaraderie Johanna had come to love and need. There was no longer a teasing glint in his eye, that lovely quirk to his mouth. Johanna thought he seemed as miserable as she surely was.

At first she'd been too hurt and too proud to approach him; she'd focused on her secretarial course, which was far duller than she'd hoped, and getting a job, earning money. Then, when Birgit's Werner had come to supper, Johanna had thought Franz might soften. She'd seen the way he'd looked at her when she'd spoken so sharply to Birgit's Nazi beau, and the next day she'd humbled herself to approach him, while he was alone in the shop.

"Must we go on like this?" she'd asked quietly as she'd stood in the doorway of the shop, her hands twisted together. Franz was bent over a clock; her father had gone upstairs for dinner with Birgit while he'd said he would finish down there first.

"How else are we to go on?" he'd asked, his tone indifferent, offering her no hope at all.

"Franz." She'd stood there uncertainly, her hands bunched in her apron, frustrated by her own hesitation as well as his stubbornness. "I'm sorry for what I said before. Surely you know I didn't mean it?"

"I know."

"And if you want to tell my family—tell anyone—then do it! I don't mind."

He'd looked up then, one eyebrow raised. "You don't *mind*?"

"I want to, I mean!" Johanna had cried. "I *will*. I'm sorry I was reluctant before. It was because I was afraid. Not of you, but of me. Of my own feelings." She'd bitten her lip, hating to have admitted even that, but still Franz did not reply. "Franz, please."

He'd sighed, a sound of resignation. "I'm not sure any of it matters any more, Johanna."

She'd clenched her hands into fists. "Why not?"

He'd looked up at her, his expression weary but resolute. "Because you cannot have a future with me."

He'd sounded so sure that it had taken her a few moments to respond, her mouth opening and closing soundlessly. "What… but—"

"If Hitler marches into Austria," Franz had stated flatly, "which he is surely likely to do very soon, things will look very bleak for me indeed. I doubt I will be able to keep this job, or any other. I won't be able to make money or support myself, much less a—a wife. And that is most likely the best possible outcome. It is almost certainly going to be much worse. I have heard stories of Jews being sent to live in special Jew-houses, like ghettoes, imprisoned, or sent east. They disappear. No one knows where they go exactly, but they never come back."

Johanna's breath hitched. "But you don't know if—"

"Surely you can see how unwise, how unfair, it would be to tie you to me now? I'm a marked man. If you were married to me, you would be as well. You might even receive the same treatment. You could be beaten or thrown into prison or worse. I can't offer you any sort of life, and I won't subject you to any of that."

"You are assuming so much," Johanna had said faintly. "Schuschnigg is determined to keep Austria independent—"

"Schuschnigg has very little power. I fear it is already out of his hands."

She'd been silent, absorbing his words and what they meant—not just for herself, or even for Franz, but for all of Austria. She felt as if the very earth beneath her feet was shifting; she had an urge to reach out and hold on to a chair, to keep her balance as everything around her trembled and shook.

"Is that the only reason?" she'd finally asked quietly. "Because of the way the world is? Or is it just an excuse because you don't really want to be with me?"

Franz had looked up from his wretched clock, anger flaring darkly in his eyes. "I think I've shown you well enough in the past that I want to be with you. I love you, Johanna, and I would be a selfish man indeed if I allowed the woman I love to ruin her life on my account." He had risen from the bench without looking at her. "And now we should go upstairs. They will be waiting for us."

They had not spoken of it again, and now, in March, with the sky a leaden gray and the city full of banners of scarlet and black, it looked as if everything Franz had said was coming horribly true after all. Johanna still didn't think he was right for refusing her, but she'd come to accept it, with a weary sort of despair.

She turned away from the window, restless after two days of waiting for the world to somehow right itself, even though she knew it wouldn't. Her classes at the secretarial school had been canceled, and who knew when or even if they would ever resume? There was not a single certainty in the world, except that Hitler would rule Austria.

Impulsively she went into the hall for her coat, while in the kitchen her mother glanced up from the dough she'd been kneading.

"Has something happened?" she asked, her voice tight with anxiety. Johanna realized yet again just how uncertain everything was, how frightening, that the simple act of her reaching for her coat had her mother worried.

"I'm going out."

"Out!" Hedwig rested her hands on the table. "That could be dangerous, Johanna."

"I don't care."

"*Johanna—*"

"I don't." Johanna turned away from her mother, hurrying down the stairs as she pushed her arms into the sleeves of her coat. Franz glanced up from his work as she unlocked the side door, his brows drawn together in concern, but Johanna turned away, flinging open the door and stepping out into the narrow alleyway that ran along the side of the house towards Getreidegasse.

She hurried to the entrance of the alleyway, only to stop in breathless surprise as the reality of this new world slammed into her yet again. Somehow, seeing it all from the upstairs window had made it feel muted, surreal, like watching a film.

Now she stood at the edge of the street as soldiers in Wehrmacht uniforms marched past her, and businessmen with newly fastened Nazi party pins on their lapels swaggered by. Every building that Johanna could see sported a swastika banner. She took a step into the street, sidling along its side, wanting to stay to the edges of this brave new world.

She passed a shop that sold women's hats and handbags—run by Herr Huber, she recalled, a friend of her father's—and saw, to her shock, even though she knew nothing more should shock her now, a sign that proclaimed in bold black letters: *Für Juden Verboten*—Jews Forbidden. She continued walking, her mind going numb, as she took in sign after sign after sign. What had once been illegal had now become law. Franz had been right, his grim predictions turned to reality in front of her very eyes, and by her own neighbors.

Johanna kept walking all the way to Alter Markt, putting one foot in front of another as a matter of instinct, feeling as if she were wading through treacle or battling through a snowstorm. All around, sinister sights and sounds assailed her so relentlessly it started to feel like some monstrous joke—banners, signs, armbands, jackboots, "*Heil Hitlers!*" that seemed to have replaced the usual "*Gruss Gott.*"

How had this happened so quickly, or even at all? Two days ago—two *days*—Chancellor Schuschnigg had been holding on to his country, proclaiming independence, while people had gone about their business. Austria had been a free country. The Nazi party had been banned. Now its members swarmed the streets, smug and self-important, arrogant and cruel-faced. Johanna met the eye of a tall, thin-lipped man in an SS uniform and looked away quickly, terrified although she couldn't have even said why. He'd barely glanced at her.

She stopped in front of SL Schwarz, the department store where her mother had once bought her dress for First Communion. Signs plastered the window, forbidding Jews and informing passersby that the store was now owned by the Salzburger Sparkasse, a local bank, as were the adjoining properties, including the Neue Galerie, the city's eminent showcase of contemporary art. Johanna saw that its windows were empty, the walls inside bare. All the art had been removed—why? Where?

"They say Herr Schwarz has been arrested," a woman standing next to her murmured, and then gave Johanna a frightened look before hurrying away, as if she'd said too much.

Johanna pulled her coat more tightly around her. Was this what it had come to—this suspicion, this fear, everywhere? *What about Franz?* Her heart lurched. As unbearable as this all seemed, it was far, far worse for him. *How would he succeed in this new world? How would he survive?*

Filled with apprehension and sick with horror at it all, she wheeled around to start back towards home. By the time she left Alter Markt she was almost running, so overwhelming was her sudden terror that everything would have changed in her absence. The police might have already come—they might have arrested Franz just like they did Herr Schwarz and heaven knew who else.

Her breath came out in tearing gasps as she started to run, only to be suddenly stopped by a hard hand on her arm.

"What is your hurry, Fräulein?"

Johanna whirled around, her arm still caught, her heart thudding wildly. The man who had grabbed hold of her arm wore the gray uniform of the SS, the red-and-black swastika on his armband looked like a livid scar. She gaped at him, speechless, as he gave her arm a little shake.

"Well?"

"I'm just going home."

"And for this you needed to run?"

For a half-second, no more, Johanna had the urge to snap at him, *Am I not allowed to run in Hitler's Austria?* "I remembered that I have bread in the oven," she heard herself say, as if the voice were coming from outside herself. "I did not wish it to burn."

The man's gaze narrowed before he finally let go of her arm. "Very well," he said. "But watch where you are going. You almost ran into me."

Johanna nodded, practically bobbing a curtsey, before she continued walking down the street, this time at a slightly more sedate pace. Her heart still thudded, and her legs felt as if they were made of water.

By the time she got back to the shop on Getreidegasse she was weak-kneed and trembling. She had barely begun to open the side door before Franz was there, throwing it wide and then pulling her into his arms.

"I thought something had happened," he said as Johanna clung to him. "I thought I might have lost you."

"I just went for a walk—"

"On today of all days?" His arms tightened around her. "When there are soldiers in the streets and every would-be Nazi's blood is up? Don't you know how dangerous that was?"

"I do now," she whispered.

He pulled back to gaze into her face, his expression both ferocious and frightened. "Did something happen?"

"No—"

"*Johanna.*"

"I was running, and an SS officer stopped me. He let me go. I hadn't done anything wrong."

He pulled her back into his arms. "I can't lose you," he said in a low voice and Johanna pressed her cheek against his shoulder, her eyes tightly closed.

"You won't," she promised. It was as if the six months of silence between them had never happened. In light of all the dangers around them, they melted away to nothing.

And yet now, more than ever, the future—*their* future—felt terrifyingly uncertain.

CHAPTER FIFTEEN

BIRGIT

November 1938

Birgit glanced at the door of the crowded coffeehouse for the third time in as many minutes before turning back to the mélange coffee she'd ordered but could not yet bring herself to drink. Werner had written that he'd meet her here at four o'clock, and it was now fifteen minutes after, shadows already gathering. She tapped her foot as she forced herself not to check the door yet again.

Since the annexation of Austria eight months ago, every day had started to feel like balancing on a tightrope, or perhaps the edge of a precipice. Salzburg had become virtually unrecognizable; swastika banners had turned the city into a sea of red and black, its once well-known streets seeming harsh and unfamiliar.

All the government officials had been replaced by Nazis; the radio was a constant barrage of propaganda and marching music. Shops forbade Jews, and grey-uniformed soldiers swarmed the streets. Worse than any of that were the rumors of arrests, beatings, imprisonments, even executions. Franz had not dared to leave the house since the Anschluss. No one met anyone's eye any more; everyone scurried down the street, head tucked low, trying to be invisible, just as Birgit had always been. At least now that unfortunate quality had some use.

The bell on the door jangled and she looked up, her heart beating fast at the sight of Werner striding into the café, looking jaunty in his uniform—a short-brimmed *Bergmutz*, or mountain cap, and a reversible *Windbluse* worn over his gray field uniform. On the first of April, the Sixth Division of the Austrian *Bundesheer*'s Alpine corps had been incorporated into the First and Second *Gebirsgjäger*, or Mountain Division, of the Wehrmacht, just as Ingrid had once predicted.

"Birgit, *engel*!" He kissed her cheek before he threw himself into the chair opposite, his legs sprawled out as he took off his cap. "I'm sorry I'm late. It's a miracle I managed to get here at all."

"It doesn't matter."

"You've already ordered?" He raised one hand imperiously for the waiter. "Another mélange, and be quick about it!" The waiter gave a short bow before scurrying away, and Werner turned back to Birgit with a smile that felt a little too sure. This swaggering air of brash confidence was something that had emerged since he'd been selected for the First *Gebirsgjäger*, although admittedly he'd always seemed assured. She'd once liked that about him.

Now, however, there was a hard edge to that assurance, a steely arrogance that Birgit did her best to ignore. She fiddled with her napkin as she managed a smile, nervous in his presence, half with fluttery excitement and half with deep apprehension. She didn't know this version of Werner any more, and he didn't know the true Birgit. She did not want him to discover her, either.

It had all started back in April, after Austria had fallen to the Nazis without much of a murmur, never mind a fight. Werner had come to see her after a rally in Residenzplatz where his unit had marched with so many others and, so the newspapers reported, Hitler himself had ridden through the city in an open-topped car, his arm sent straight out, his expression one of hard-eyed nobility, as the crowds cheered themselves hoarse.

Birgit and her family had stayed inside with the curtains drawn, the mood somber. Franz had played the piano, but it had been a melancholy tune that felt like a dirge. No one had spoken.

Immediately after the Anschluss her father had made it clear that no one in his household would be participating in any marches, rallies, parades, or other Nazi events—not that anyone wanted to. No one, he had stated flatly, would assist this new regime in any way, no matter how small. Birgit, who had continued to attend the meetings at the coffeehouse, was in complete agreement—and yet the prospect of outward defiance still terrified her.

Two days after the Wehrmacht had rolled into Austria, her father's edict was put to the test when two gangly boys in Hitler Youth uniforms knocked on the door of the shop in Getreidegasse demanding to know why their home and business did not sport a swastika banner like every other in the street.

"I'm afraid we do not possess one," Manfred had replied, his tone genial although his stare was steely. The HJ boys topped him by well over six inches but he stood straight and met their gazes directly. "And in these hard times, as you must know, schillings are dear—"

"You mean Reichsmarks," one of the teens had corrected him, and Manfred had smiled and nodded.

"Ah, yes, of course. It is so hard to remember all the changes."

"Perhaps you should try harder."

Her father bowed his head and said nothing. Birgit had not thought he was afraid of these spotty teenagers, but he'd certainly recognized their newfound power.

"The next time we come," the other one had told him, poking her father in the chest with his forefinger, "there had better be a banner. Otherwise we'll have to report you."

Her father had not replied, and finally the two boys had left. After he'd closed the door, everyone had stood there in a somber silence that seemed to echo through the rooms.

"What will you do, Papa?" Johanna had finally asked, and their father had not replied for several long seconds. His face had been drawn in thoughtful lines, his hand still resting on the knob of the door.

"I must think on it," he'd said at last. "Think and pray."

"It's just a banner," Hedwig had burst out, sounding angry when Birgit suspected she was only frightened, as they all were. "It doesn't have to *mean* anything."

Franz had looked as if he wanted to say something sharp in return, but he'd simply pressed his lips together. Birgit had known he'd not left the shop once since the day of the Anschluss. Whenever a customer came into the shop, he went upstairs. Several times they had been visited by officials, for various collections or to be given a list of new regulations, and each time Franz had, to Johanna's pleading and his own quiet fury, hidden in the crawl space under the eaves. Birgit wondered how long any of it could go on.

As for the banner… while Manfred had continued to deliberate, Johanna had returned with one rolled up under her arm after school one day, her cheeks flushed and her eyes glittering.

"We are not going to lose our lives for the sake of a symbol," she'd stated, and hung it out of the sitting room window. Their father had not said anything, but neither had he asked her to take it down. Birgit saw how troubled he looked, his eyes drooping as his mouth curved downwards, and she wondered how many situations they would find themselves in when their consciences could neither be contained nor consoled.

And what of Werner? She looked at him covertly as he sipped the coffee that the waiter had hurriedly delivered; a Wehrmacht uniform guaranteed good service, along with a cringing servility. Eight months ago he'd come to the house on Getreidegasse after the rally, and Birgit had hurried outside to meet him, knowing it would be a disaster for her family to see him in his new uniform, never mind if any of them actually talked of politics again.

"You're in the Wehrmacht," she'd said numbly as she gazed at him in his unrelieved gray. She'd known it would happen, had realized it ever since troops had marched jubilantly across the Staatsbrücke over three weeks earlier. She'd told herself it didn't mean Werner was *actually* a Nazi. It was just a uniform, the same as it was just a banner, and yet already she feared she couldn't trust him.

"First *Gebirgsjäger*," Werner had confirmed proudly. "We're still out of Innsbruck, but there's talk of being deployed soon." He'd sounded excited. Birgit had felt only despair. "Aren't you going to tell me I look handsome?" he'd teased.

"You do," she'd admitted reluctantly, but her heart felt like a stone inside her, weighing her down. "Werner… is this… is this really what you want?"

Impatience battled with uncertainty in his face for a mere second before he gave her one of his easy smiles. "I don't have much choice, do I, but even if I did—I want to be on the winning side, Birgit. And it's obvious that's going to be Germany. Did you see the newsreels? When the Wehrmacht came into Austria, they were greeted with cheers and flowers. *Flowers.*" He took a step towards her, his tone turning urgent. Can't you see this isn't just what *I* want, it's what everyone wants? It's good for the country—"

"Not for everyone," Birgit had said quietly, and he'd let out a short, frustrated sigh.

"Not this again. You'd think you were Jewish yourself, the way you go on."

"You don't have to be Jewish to care about what happens to Jews," Birgit had returned. "And in any case, it's not just about the Jews. It's everything. Since it happened, everyone's been frightened. Arrests, imprisonments…" She had stared at him helplessly, knowing he would refuse to understand. "It feels as if anything could happen. No one is safe."

Werner had rolled his eyes. "You're safe if you obey the law."

"Are you? All it takes is for a neighbor to suspect something to report you, and then you could be arrested, without so much as a—"

"And what would there be to suspect?" He had cocked his head as his eyes narrowed in a way that had chilled Birgit right through. She'd realized in that moment she couldn't talk to Werner honestly; she couldn't explain her concerns, her fears—the anxiety gnawed away at her insides until she felt like a hollowed-out shell. She certainly couldn't tell him about her meetings at the coffeehouse, or the fact that Ingrid and the others were urging them to take more action. "*It can't be just rhetoric and pamphlets any more,*" Ingrid had said the last time they'd met, pounding her fist on the table.

No, she couldn't tell Werner any of that because *he* could be that nosy neighbor, that suspicious soldier. He had become a threat, even as she loved him.

For she'd known she still did love him, longed for the future together she'd begun to imagine, no matter that he'd stood there right in front of her in his Wehrmacht uniform and talked of suspicion and law. The realization had swamped her with a despair she did her best to fight, because she longed for it to be simple. Who cared what happened in the world around them, as long as they had each other? Yet as much as she'd told herself that, whispered it like a promise, she had not been able to quite make herself believe it.

"What is it?" Werner asked as he sipped his coffee, startling her out of her thoughts. "You're looking rather dour."

"It's hard not to be," Birgit could not keep from responding. Everything in Salzburg felt either dour or fraught. Salzburg was shrouded in the seasonal *Schnürlregen*, soldiers swarmed every square, and more and more people were disappearing—not just Jews, but communists, socialists, gypsies—anyone who was different.

The meetings at the coffeehouse had stopped months ago, as it was far too dangerous to gather, and Ingrid had told Birgit she would contact her if she were needed. So far she had heard nothing, and Birgit did not know whether she was disappointed or relieved. She wanted to *do* something, but she was so very frightened.

Only last week all Jews with Polish heritage had been rounded up and sent east—where, Birgit didn't know and refused to imagine. All Jews had had to surrender any property, as well as have a J stamped in their passport, for *Juden*. Franz, who continued to spend most of his time in the attic of the house on Getreidegasse, never leaving the house and now venturing only into the shop cautiously, at least had not had to suffer such indignities. For the purposes of the new government, he remained invisible.

Werner's mouth thinned as he put down his coffee cup. "Birgit, everything is so much better now. Why can't you see that? People have jobs. Money. They feel safe—"

"Safe," Birgit repeated with a hollow laugh. "Werner, how can you even say that? You must know it isn't true."

"Like I've said before, if you obey the law, you have nothing to fear."

She leaned forward. "Do you really believe that?" she demanded in a low voice. She didn't want to have to ask, to force another fraught issue, but neither could she keep herself from it. She could not close her eyes and ears to everything, though it cost her.

For a millisecond, no more, something akin to doubt flitted across Werner's face like a shadow. It gave her a wild sense of hope that was quickly extinguished as he sighed and leaned back in his chair.

"Is your father's business doing well?" he asked, as if he already knew the answer.

"Ye-es," Birgit admitted. Since the Anschluss she and her father had had a steady stream of high-ranking Nazi officers eager to repair the clocks in the villas and estates they'd requisitioned from wealthy Jews who had since been either arrested or moved into virtual ghettoes. One such clock had been badly smashed, and her father had regarded it silently, making no comment as he set about the difficult repair.

"Then what is there to complain about?" Werner asked, as if the answer were obvious. *Nothing.*

Birgit didn't reply, merely sipping her coffee as she struggled to keep her expression neutral. Just because her own life was comfortable didn't mean there weren't things worth fighting for. The fact that Werner refused to see that made her both angry and despairing, yet she knew better than to pick an argument with him over it.

"Why don't we go to the cinema?" Werner suggested as he finished his coffee. "*By A Silken Thread* is playing. Have you seen it?"

"No, I haven't." The film, she suspected from what she'd read about it in the papers, was badly disguised Nazi propaganda, highlighting "crooked Jewish capitalists." She had no desire to see it.

"Then let's go." Werner rose from his seat, snapping his fingers for the bill. The waiter hurried over. Werner carelessly tossed a few bills on the table without even looking at the man. Smiling rather shamefacedly at the waiter in apology, Birgit followed Werner outside.

As soon as they stepped out into the damp November evening, it was clear something was happening, although Birgit wasn't sure what. She pulled her coat more tightly around her and stepped instinctively closer to Werner, who put his arm around her as they glanced about in the gathering dusk.

"What's going on?" she asked uncertainly. People were hurrying here and there, heads ducked low, and across the street she could see a gang of brown shirts gathered around a shopfront. Birgit heard jeering and the sound of breaking glass.

She glanced at Werner, whose face had hardened. "Let's just go to the cinema," he said.

"What's going on?" she asked again.

"Do you really want to know?" He reached for her arm, but she pulled away from him and started walking towards the gathering crowd. There were just as many bystanders as brown shirts in the throng, and they were all surrounding a shopfront on the other side of the square, an ugly feeling of menace in the air.

It was a doctor's office, one of the few Jewish-owned businesses that had survived the Anschluss, although only Jews could attend the surgery. The plate-glass window had had a brick thrown through it and a brown shirt had collared the owner, who was trying his best not to cower as the man grabbed him, although his body trembled and his eyes were glassy with fear.

"Let's see what the good doctor has to say!" the brown shirt declared as he shook him like a rat. "Can he make a diagnosis? What's wrong with this dirty Jew?" Without so much as drawing a breath the man backhanded his quarry so hard the man's head whipped around and he fell to his knees on the hard pavement, blood trickling from his nose.

"What do you think is wrong with you, Jew?" the brown shirt demanded, following the backhand with a hard, booted kick to the stomach. The man groaned and rolled on to his side, clutching his middle. A few people jeered, while others laughed. Birgit pressed one hand to her mouth, bile rising in her throat as her stomach churned. *How could people be so wantonly evil?* This man had done nothing, *nothing* to anyone here, and yet she saw expressions of rabid glee on people's faces. They were *enjoying* this disgusting show. She caught the eye of one woman who looked away quickly. Was that the closest she could feel to shame?

"Come on, Birgit." Werner reached for her arm once more. "You don't want to see this. The film is starting soon. We'll miss the newsreel—"

"The *film*?" She whirled on him, incredulous, a sob caught in her chest. "*That's* what you care about now?"

Werner pressed his lips together. "You don't need to see this."

The brown shirts had at last left the poor doctor alone, having moved onto other prey down the street—a father and son who were now surrounded by a jeering crowd, the father's arm around his son's slight shoulders. A sound escaped Birgit, something between a sob and a cry. As she slowly looked around the square, she realized this hadn't been an isolated incident.

It was happening everywhere up and down the street, throughout the whole city perhaps—shops being broken into, people being attacked, brown shirts roaming the pavements, looking for someone to hurt or harass. The air was full of shouts and cries, fury and fear, like the world had gone deliberately mad. It was as if, she realized, it had all been *planned.*

"Werner, what's going on?" she choked out. "Why is this happening now?" An uneasy look of guilt flashed across his face before he shrugged. Birgit stepped closer to him. "Did you *know* about this?"

"I might have heard something," he admitted, "but I didn't know what exactly. I swear, Birgit! And do you think there's anything I could have done? I told you before, I don't hate the Jews." His face settled into truculent lines, so at odds with the terrible violence being enacted all around them. He was like a little boy stomping his feet while the whole world burned. "This isn't my fault," he insisted. "You don't have to blame me."

Birgit just shook her head. The man's wife had hurried over to him, helping him back into the shop. Birgit started forward, wanting to offer her aid, but realizing she might only make matters worse for them. Then she thought of Franz. "I have to get home," she told Werner.

"The cinema—"

"I don't care about the cinema!" she shouted. She looked at him, standing so tall in his Gebirgsjager uniform, and she remembered how he'd first rescued her, how they'd kissed on the bridge, his letters full of dull news and yet she'd still treasured every word… She took a step towards him as her voice gentled, "Werner, can't you see… this isn't…"

He held up his hand to keep her from saying anything more. "Let me at least escort you home," he said stiffly, and she nodded. All around them the world had shattered, and even this, between them, was broken.

They didn't speak all the way back to Getreidegasse, dodging angry crowds and broken glass. As they turned onto the street, Birgit stilled.

"Something is burning—"

"Most likely the synagogue on Judengasse," Werner replied, and she looked at him.

"Did you know—"

He hunched one shoulder. "Isn't it obvious?"

By the time they'd got back to the shop, Birgit was practically twitching with anxiety. Werner caught her sleeve as she hurried to the side door; the front door was locked, the blinds drawn.

"Birgit—what about us?"

She turned back to him, torn between anger, panic, and the deep love she still felt for him, even now, even though she didn't want to feel it. *He isn't a Nazi*, she reminded herself, and yet… with the city in flames around them, he might as well have been.

"I'll write to you," she promised, although she could not imagine what such a letter would contain. "When will you next have leave?"

"I don't know. There is talk of us being needed in the Sudetenland."

Birgit nodded. Hitler had marched into Czechoslovakia two months ago. Of course Werner would be deployed. "I'll write," she said again, and then she hurried to the side door without looking back.

Inside the house everyone was gathered upstairs, huddled in chairs, faces pale and shocked. Hedwig hurried to the door of the sitting room as Birgit came upstairs.

"Birgit," she cried, and to her surprise, her mother began to weep. Birgit couldn't remember when, if ever, she'd seen her cry.

"I'm all right, Mama," she said as Hedwig enfolded her in her solid arms.

"The world has gone mad," her mother proclaimed with a sniff as she stepped away. "*Mad.*"

"What about Franz?" Birgit asked, for he wasn't in the room.

"He's up in the attics," Johanna replied grimly. "He went up as soon as it started. We saw people being beaten in the street right in front of the shop! There was nothing anyone could do." She shook her head slowly as she bit her lips. "Where were you?"

"I was meeting Werner." A cool silence followed that made Birgit flush. "He wasn't part of it, you know." No one replied. She turned away as she took a shuddering breath. She didn't want to talk about Werner. Right then she didn't even want to think about him, much less defend him. "What happens now?" she wondered aloud.

"We fight," her father replied, the hardness in his voice surprising them all, for it was so unlike him. He met each of their shocked gazes with a steely one of his own. "We cannot be part of this regime. Doing nothing is the same as being complicit. We answer to God, not to Hitler." Each statement was spoken with stiff, final-sounding clarity. Each was treason, punishable by death.

No one said anything as they looked around at each other with wide, wary eyes. Finally Johanna spoke.

"But what can we do, Papa?"

"We can start with this," Manfred said, and went to the window and yanked the swastika banner from it with one vicious jerk. They watched in silence as he bundled it up and tossed it on the fire.

"Manfred…" Hedwig whispered, and he looked at her with both defiance and tenderness.

"I love you, and I know this could mean the end of us all, but for the sake of not just my conscience, but all our souls, I must. We all must." He let out a shuddering breath as he squared his shoulders and the remnants of the wretched flag turned to ember and ash.

"Then let us not face our end for simply burning a flag," Johanna said quietly. "For God's sake, as well as our own, let us do far more than that."

Pride gleamed in their father's eyes as he nodded. "Yes," he agreed. "Yes. We will have to think and pray how best to act."

"I might know." Birgit spoke before she'd thought about what she was saying. Everyone turned to look at her in surprise.

"You?" Johanna exclaimed, not even trying to hide the skepticism in her voice. "With your Nazi boyfriend?"

"Werner isn't a Nazi," she retorted, "but in any case, this isn't about him. He's going to be deployed soon. I won't even see him."

Johanna tossed her head while her father gave her a kindly smile. "What did you mean, Birgit?"

"I know someone." Realization bloomed inside her as she turned eagerly to her father. "Papa, you do too! Ingrid. She mentioned you had contacted the group about Franz—"

"You know Ingrid?" Manfred looked shaken. "You've been consorting with communists?"

"As were you! In any case, we all need to work together," Birgit insisted. "That's what Ingrid has always said. Anyone who resists Hitler is a friend, not an enemy, no matter what they believe about anything else."

Johanna looked gobsmacked, her mouth dropping open as she stared at Birgit. "*You…*"

Birgit lifted her chin, filled with sudden pride. "Yes," she told her sister. "Me. I've been going to their meetings and distributing pamphlets, at least I was before the Anschluss. It's gone quiet since then." She turned to her father. "Still, I think I know how to contact Ingrid. I can leave a message at the coffeehouse in Elisabeth-Vorstadt—"

"Wait," her mother cried. "Do you know what you are saying?" She turned to Manfred. "You could be sentencing us all to death."

"I do not fear death," he replied quietly. "Nor should you. I fear facing my Maker and having no answer for Him as to why I did not act when I could have." He turned to Birgit. "Contact Ingrid if you can. And I will speak to Father Josef. Perhaps he knows how to help. He is no Nazi, certainly."

A tremor went through the room, a visceral reaction to his words, and the danger they implied.

Hedwig's lips trembled and she looked as if she wanted to reply, but she said nothing. Birgit felt something inside her swell, an excitement mixed with terror, a desire stronger than fear. *Yes,* she thought. *I want to do this. This is what I've been waiting for.*

"Well?" Her father asked as he looked around at them all. "Are we in agreement, then?"

Slowly each one of them nodded.

CHAPTER SIXTEEN

LOTTE

Nonnberg Abbey, November 1938

The smoke from the fires throughout the city had risen in a ghostly gray smog that shrouded even the abbey high above. On the evening of what became known as Kristallnacht, Lotte had stood at one of the cloisters and watched as Salzburg burned. The synagogue had been set on fire, along with several shops and homes. And while those flames had been doused, the shreds of gray remained like forgotten ghosts, and she feared a greater conflagration raged throughout the place of her birth, all of Austria, the whole world. The world was on fire, and yet here she was meant to be safe.

And yet surely safety shouldn't be her first concern. Ever since her conversation with Sister Kunigunde months ago, Lotte had wrestled with the idea that her choice to enter the religious life had been, at its heart, selfish. An escape rather than a sacrifice. And now that it was threatened—several SS officers had visited the Mother Abbess twice already—she felt the truth of it all the more. She didn't want her life here to be disrupted. She was afraid of change, of upheaval, and at the heart of that fear was a longing for comfort. All of these realizations made her feel sick with shame.

Although the Catholic church had hoped to work with the new Nazi regime, it had become abundantly clear after the Anschluss that the Nazis had no intention of working with the church. They had closed down schools, raided churches, and arrested clerics. Only last month she and a few other nuns had listened on the Mother Abbess's radio to Cardinal Innitzer's rousing speech at Stephansplatz in Vienna, when he had declared to thousands of supporters, "Our *Führer* is Christ—Christ is our *Führer*."

The regime's response to this declaration had been to arrest many of the attendees, some of them only teenagers, and storm the archbishop's palace. No, the Nazis were no friends of the church, and therefore no friends of Nonnberg.

And yet Lotte still longed for nothing to change, even though she knew everything already had.

After that first conversation with Sister Kunigunde, her disquiet had increased when, in late spring, the other novice had, quite suddenly and with no explanation, left her alone in the dormitory to finish scrubbing the floor alone, on her reddened hands and knees with a basin of soapy water going cold and scummy.

Lotte had struggled against the instinctive irritation that had risen up in her—somehow it had become all too easy to succumb to the petty emotions she'd once thought she had put away forever—and finished the task on her own.

When she came across Kunigunde in the refectory later, she'd only just resisted asking her where she had disappeared to in the middle of their labors. Still, she'd raised her eyebrows inquiringly, and Kunigunde had merely looked away, unapologetic, indifferent.

It had happened several more times over the course of the summer—suddenly Kunigunde would slip away from a task or prayers or quiet contemplation, giving no reason for her absence, answering to no one. Lotte had begun, without even realizing she was doing so, to track her movements, watching her creep along the chapel or one of the cloisters with narrowed eyes. *Where on earth could she be going?*

Lotte didn't think she could be the only one who noticed Kunigunde's absences, and yet no one ever remarked upon them, not during their evening council or the public confession once a week. The Benedictine rule of "prompt, ungrudging and absolute obedience to the superior" had been so deeply ingrained during her time at Nonnberg that to raise such an issue herself was unthinkable, and yet her irritation had persisted, like a thorn in her side, or a splinter in her finger. Persistent, aggravating, and eventually consuming her thoughts.

Finally, in November, a week before the night that was to come to be known as Kristallnacht, Lotte had spoken up. At public confession, after Sister Kunigunde had admitted to her mind wandering during lauds, Lotte's hand had shot into the air. It was permissible for sisters to mention sins that the confessing nun had forgotten or not been aware of, yet Lotte had heard an unbecoming note of stridency in her voice after the Mother Abbess had nodded for her to speak.

"Sister Kunigunde has left her chores undone on several occasions," she had announced. "She made no excuse and did not return." Again Lotte had heard the note of accusation in her voice, and she'd blushed. "I fear Sister Kunigunde is breaking St. Benedict's rule of the necessity of manual labor, as well as that of obedience." Another silence had ensued, this one seeming to possess a certain censure, and abruptly she had sat down, staring at her lap, while she'd waited for the Mother Abbess' response.

"Thank you, Sister Maria Josef," the Mother Abbess had said quietly. Then she had given Sister Kunigunde a mere three Hail Marys as penance while Lotte had tried not to fume.

Now, nearly a week later, she turned away from the view from the cloister and tried to temper her disquiet. Life had been so peaceful here for so long, she couldn't bear for anything to change. And yet she knew things already had… and would continue to do so.

A movement caught the corner of her eye, and Lotte turned to see Sister Kunigunde herself walking quickly down the cloister on the other side of the courtyard, towards a rarely used wing of the abbey where garden tools and the like were stored. Interest—along with a determination to discover just what was occupying the other nun—compelled Lotte to cross the courtyard and hurry along the wall after Kunigunde, keeping her distance, staying to the shadows.

It occurred to her that it was far indeed from the rule of St. Benedict to be skulking about as she was, spying on another nun, and yet still she followed Kunigunde past a corridor of storerooms, the air so cold in this unused part of the abbey that Lotte's breath came out in frosty puffs. The only sound was the slap of her sandals on the stone, and the anxious draw and exhale of her own breath. Kunigunde glanced over her shoulder once, but dusk had fallen and, a dozen meters behind her, Lotte was lost in shadows. Still she dropped back a little more, and so when she turned the corner, Kunigunde had gone.

Lotte stood in the middle of the corridor, shivering as she battled frustration. *How had Kunigunde disappeared so suddenly? What on earth was she doing here in this empty part of the abbey?* Lotte knew she must have gone into one of the disused storerooms that lined the corridor, each door made of heavy, aged wood.

She could open each one in turn and discover into which one her fellow nun had gone, yet she was reluctant to do so and reveal herself. What would she say if she came to face to face with her? How on earth could she explain herself? Although how would Kunigunde explain?

She was still considering what to do when the door at the far end of the corridor opened and Kunigunde slipped out, closing it carefully behind her. Without even thinking about what she was doing, Lotte hurried in the opposite direction and ducked into one of the other storerooms so Kunigunde wouldn't see her.

She breathed in the sweet, musty smell of old apples and damp as she listened to Kunigunde's sandaled feet pad softly past. She counted to one hundred, everything in her straining and alert, before she slipped out of the storeroom and headed back to the corridor where Kunigunde had come from.

Lotte could feel the blood pounding in her ears, her heart thudding in her chest, as she walked down the corridor and stood in front of the door Kunigunde had opened and closed just a few moments ago. Night had fallen fully, leaving Lotte blinking in the darkness, and the air was cold and still, the first stars coming out in the sky high above. In just a few minutes the bell would ring for vespers. She put her hand on the icy latch.

As she stood there, her fingers numb with cold, she had a sense of dread that she didn't *want* to know what was in the room that caused Kunigunde to skulk about, and yet at the same time she very much did. Whatever was in there, whatever she discovered, Lotte was suddenly terribly sure that it would change everything—and she didn't want *anything* to change. After another tense pause, she opened the door.

She blinked in the unrelieved gloom of the dark storeroom, unable to see anything, but she heard a few soft gasps, the rustling of clothes, and the stench of unwashed bodies kept in a cramped, closed room rolled over her, making her hold her breath.

Then her eyes adjusted to the darkness and she was able to make out a huddle of people peering at her with dark, frightened eyes.

There was a woman, a man, several children, another woman; Lotte's gaze roamed over them all, taking in their shabby overcoats, their faces grimy and haggard and full of fear. They all stared at her, silent and unmoving, waiting for her to speak or act. After what felt like an age one of the women spoke, "*Bitte…*" she whispered hoarsely.

"What are you doing here?" Lotte demanded, her voice sounding loud and somehow stupid in the stillness, for of course even she already knew. They had to be Jews. Jews that Kunigunde was hiding up here in the abbey, for ever since the Anschluss, Jews had been hounded out of the city, or worse. Lotte had heard the whispers, even up here in the protection of the abbey; the Mother Abbess allowed them to listen to the news on the radio once a week, to inform their prayers. And while Lotte had been happy to pray for those poor unfortunates, she realized she hadn't actually wanted to have anything more to do with them. And yet right here in this musty room, she now stood face to face with the people she'd been happier pretending didn't exist.

The man took a step forward, one hand stretched out, in supplication or threat Lotte didn't know, and she didn't even think. She slammed the door shut and then started running down the corridor, her breath coming out in ragged pants as the bell began to ring for vespers.

Her mind felt frozen as she knelt for prayer, saying the Latin words by rote without even being aware of what was coming out of her mouth. Her glazed gaze moved slowly around the candlelit chapel until it rested on Sister Kunigunde, sitting all the way across the chancel at the other end. Her head was bowed, her expression placid. *How?*

Lotte knew if the Jews were found in that storeroom, it would likely not be just Sister Kunigunde but all the nuns of Nonnberg Abbey who would be in trouble. They might be arrested, imprisoned, even sent to one of the camps she'd heard about on the radio.

A sudden fury burned in her chest at the thought. *How could Kunigunde be so irresponsible, so selfish?* She had disobeyed the Mother Abbess's specific instructions to go on as if nothing had changed. She had deceived her and all the other nuns; she had put them all in terrible danger! And beyond that, she had threatened the stability and security of the abbey itself, which had been running without interruption for thirteen hundred years. Lotte's outrage grew with every moment. She would have to confront Sister Kunigunde… or tell the Mother Abbess.

All through vespers her mind whirred like the gears of one of her father's clocks, thoughts ticking over and over. When the prayers had finally finished, she rose with the other nuns, barely aware of where she was going. Then she caught sight of Sister Kunigunde slipping off to another corridor while everyone else headed towards the refectory. Lotte hurried after her.

"Sister Kunigunde!" Her voice was sharp as she followed her down the freezing passage.

Kunigunde whirled around, stilling when she saw Lotte, a slight sneer twisting her usually placid features. "I should have known it would be you. Trying to get me in trouble again?"

"You were hardly in trouble," Lotte returned. "You only had to say three Hail Marys." She'd had to say four for her own sins.

Kunigunde folded her arms, her hands hidden in the wide sleeves of her habit. Her expression had turned resolute, her round cheeks framed by the wimple, a steely look in her mud-colored eyes. "What is it that you want, sister?"

Lotte shook her head slowly. Everything about this conversation felt wrong, stilted; she had not had one like it since joining the abbey. She took a deep breath and tried to compose herself.

"I know about the Jews," she said quietly.

Kunigunde's expression did not change. "And?"

"How could you do such a thing," Lotte burst out, her self-control of just seconds ago slipping away again, "after what the Reverend Mother said?"

"What the Reverend Mother said?" Kunigunde repeated. "And what was it that she said, Sister Maria Josef? Tell me, do."

Lotte hesitated, for there was a knowing, almost sly cast to the other nun's features that she didn't understand. "That we had to go on as before. That nothing should change."

"And yet so much has changed since then. The Nazis are determined to destroy the church. Surely you can see that."

"Even so..." Lotte trailed off, hating how feeble she sounded.

"She also said anyone who came to the abbey asking for aid would be answered," Kunigunde reminded her. "Do you remember that, sister? Or have you conveniently forgotten it, in your desire to keep your own comforts?"

"I know what she said." Lotte hesitated, new doubts clouding her mind. "You know that's not what she meant," she said at last. It couldn't have been. "And in any case, did the Jews come to the abbey door?" Kunigunde's gaze slid away. "I didn't think so," Lotte stated, unable to keep an unbecoming note of triumph from her voice. "How did you find out about them? What are you involved in?"

Kunigunde sighed impatiently. "It's better if you don't know. Better for you, and certainly better for me, since I don't trust you." Lotte blinked, stung although she realized perhaps she shouldn't be. "There are people in Salzburg who help the Jews as well as others. I learned of them. That is all you need to know."

"What sort of people?"

"Why? Do you want to join us?" Kunigunde taunted.

"How did you learn of them?" Lotte demanded. She wasn't sure why she wanted to know, only that she did.

"There are ways, if you look for them." Kunigunde shook her head slowly. "Are you going to tell the Mother Abbess, then?" she asked in a hard voice. "You realize the Jews would be arrested if you did come forward? They'd most likely be killed. Already they're sending them east to camps. Do you know about those?"

"It is not my business to know," Lotte fired back, feeling now as if she were on more sure ground. "And nor is it yours, whatever you may have been able to find out. We are to obey,

Sister Kunigunde, without asking questions. That is what we have always been called to do."

"I am obeying," Kunigunde replied. "We answer to God, Sister Maria Josef, first and foremost, and *that* is whom I am obeying." And without waiting for her reply, she whirled around and continued down the corridor, leaving Lotte to gape.

It took Lotte three days before she finally resolved to speak to the Mother Abbess about the matter. She'd spent those days in prayer, wrestling with her conscience, with her vows, with the resentment and anger she felt towards Kunigunde for causing so much difficulty and trouble, and the guilt and doubt she experienced herself, for feeling this way at all.

Should she care about the Jews? She was meant to care for all people, to love them better than she loved herself. And yet what of her obedience to the Mother Abbess, to the church, to the government? It was all such a hopeless jumble in her mind, and it left her feeling unbearably restless and anxious. She didn't want to have to wonder. She didn't even want to have to think. She'd come here to the abbey, she realized, at least in part so she wouldn't have to.

Finally, for her own sake, for she needed relief from the misery twisting her insides, she went to see the Mother Abbess in her study.

"Benedicte," she greeted her as she fell on her knees and the Mother Abbess extended her hand to be kissed.

"Dominus."

Lotte rose. The Mother Abbess was smiling at her, her careworn face filled with a patient tenderness that gave Lotte a sense of relief. Surely she would have the answers.

"What is troubling you, my daughter?"

"It is in regard to Sister Kunigunde, Reverend Mother."

"I thought it might be."

She should have known her resentment of her fellow novice had not gone unnoticed. "It is not about her shirking her chores," Lotte said, her head still bowed. "Although I confess that has caused me some resentment. I will do penance for that, of course."

The Mother Abbess brushed such concerns aside with a flick of her fingers. "Then what is it that is troubling you, daughter?"

"Something, I fear, that is far more serious."

"Oh?" The Mother Abbess's voice was as gentle as ever, and yet even so Lotte thought she detected a faint note of reserve.

"She is sheltering Jews," Lotte blurted as she looked up. "Hiding them here at the abbey. Involving herself in political matters which is forbidden. If the Jews were discovered, we could all be arrested or even killed—"

"Do you hold your life in such high regard, daughter?"

The question, so gently asked, left Lotte speechless for several seconds. "I… no… but…" she finally stammered, before she gathered her wits about her. "But you said yourself things were not to change. We were to act as if nothing had happened. We must obey—"

"Obey God. What are the first two commandments, Sister Maria Josef, according to our Savior?"

"To—to love God and love our neighbor as ourselves." Lotte felt like a child learning her catechism as she recited the commandment.

The Mother Abbess inclined her head. "Indeed."

Lotte stared at her, the silence stretching between them, spooling into realization. "You knew," she said slowly, still disbelieving. "You knew about the Jews."

The Mother Abbess did not reply. Lotte stared at her helplessly. "Why?" she asked. "When the church forbids it? When it is surely an act of disobedience to—"

"Does God forbid it?" she interjected gently, and after an endless moment, trying not to show her reluctance, Lotte shook her head. No, God would not forbid it. Of course He wouldn't. To help those in need—the poor, the persecuted, the suffering? Of course it could be nothing but one's sacred Christian duty, one's privilege and joy, and yet the realization brought no comfort, for she felt as if all her careful assumptions, all her placid practices, everything on which she'd founded her faith, had been upended and scattered. She *had* been selfish. All along she had been selfish, not pious or pure—and now she was afraid. She looked away, unable to meet the Mother Abbess's shrewd gaze.

"We are now in the unusual position," she told Lotte after a moment, "of you having a certain amount of power over me." She smiled faintly while Lotte turned back to her and simply stared.

"Power—"

"It is within your power to tell the relevant authorities about what is happening here. If you did so, you would undoubtedly save yourself, and perhaps others, as well. If you did so, I would take full responsibility, of course." The Mother Abbess gazed at her unflinchingly while Lotte gaped.

"Reverend Mother, I—I would never. I—I couldn't—"

"You could," she corrected gently. "I fear for many it would be all too easy. The question is, will you?"

The words seemed to hang in the still air as she continued to hold her gaze and Lotte realized what she was really saying. If she didn't report her, then she would be complicit. If the Jews were discovered here, she, along with many others, would be arrested or worse. It was her choice.

"I wish I'd never found out," she confessed in a choked voice.

"Curiosity so rarely becomes us," the Mother Abbess told her with a small smile, before she fixed her with a steely stare. "But you did find out, and so the question now, Sister Maria Josef, is will you help us?"

CHAPTER SEVENTEEN

JOHANNA

March 1939

Johanna studied the window display in SL Schwarz, now renamed after the bank that had taken it over after Kristallnacht. Two female mannequins dressed in dirndls and sporting blond braids stood in the window, offering fixed smiles to the passersby who barely gave them a glance.

They were meant to represent the epitome of Germanic womanhood, the desired model of *kinder, küche, kirche*—children, kitchen, church—that the Nazis so espoused. Johanna had thought that she already managed two of those quite well; she was two-thirds the way to becoming the ideal National Socialist woman, never mind that she was in love with a Jew.

With a sigh she turned away from the window and headed back to the house in Getreidegasse. Home felt so dark these days, and yet it was the only beacon of light she knew of in the whole city. Since Kristallnacht, when her father had become determined to resist the Nazis, they'd been in a state of high tension as well as terror, anticipation, and anxiety twined together, as they waited for the knock on the door, the end to everything, yet so far their acts of resistance had gone undetected.

No one came to question why the house did not sport a swastika banner; Johanna supposed the Nazis had bigger things to concern themselves with now. Birgit had done as she'd said and left a message for the mysterious Ingrid at a coffeehouse in Elisabeth-Vorstadt, and her father had spoken to Father Josef.

At first, nothing had happened. Johanna had felt as if their inquiries had been stones skipped across a pond, only to sink without a trace. And then, a month after the inquiries, suddenly, silently, things began to change. A pile of pamphlets—communist propaganda, Johanna had thought, a bit scornfully—had been shoved under their side door. Birgit had taken them without a word.

"If you are caught with one of those pamphlets," Johanna had not been able to keep from telling her, "you will most likely be executed."

Birgit had looked remarkably unfazed. "I know."

"You're not even a communist, are you?"

"I am against Hitler, and they are, as well. That is all that matters."

Johanna had felt a sudden surge of admiration for her sister's surprising courage. "What about Werner?" she'd asked, not unkindly. "He doesn't know, I suppose?"

"No."

"And I suppose it wouldn't be good for you if he found out?"

"I…" Birgit had bitten her lip. "Probably not."

Johanna had shaken her head. "We're both playing with fire, then. I'm in love with a Jew, and you with a Nazi. And here we are, flirting with the resistance!" She'd thrown up her hands and Birgit had let out a sudden laugh, and Johanna had joined her, because surely it was better to laugh than to cry. They'd put their arms around each other, laughing until their sides had ached and they'd had to wipe the tears that streamed from their eyes. By the time they'd regained their composure, Johanna could not have said if they'd been truly laughing at all.

The next week there was another bundle of pamphlets under the door, and a few days later two furtive-looking factory workers had come into the shop, their grimy caps in their hands, and asked if the repair on the Johann Baptist Beha had been finished. Johanna had been bringing a tray of coffees down to the shop, and she'd stared at them in disbelief.

There was only one Johann Baptist Beha in the shop, the one-hundred-year-old cuckoo clock that had pride of place by the counter. It was not for sale, and it did not need repair.

Yet as soon as her father had heard the request he'd risen from his bench and replied in a friendly, easy way, "Yes, of course! It has just been finished. Come this way and I will show you."

Johanna had watched him lead the two men upstairs, before she'd turned to Birgit and Franz, a question in her eyes.

"It's a code, of course," Birgit had said under her breath, although there was no one about to overhear. "They must have been sent by Father Josef."

"Not Ingrid?"

"She's said nothing to me."

"Who are they?" Johanna had asked, and Birgit had shrugged.

"Christian socialists perhaps? People who need to hide."

When Johanna had gone upstairs, the men had been wolfing down the meal Hedwig had set before them, before Manfred took them upstairs to the attic. Johanna had glanced at her mother, who had looked tight-lipped and troubled, but she'd cut extra thick slices of bread, and she'd given the men two bowls of soup each, even though it meant they'd have less for their own meal that evening.

Since then there had been more pamphlets for Birgit to distribute, and more people coming into the shop asking if the Johanna Baptist Beha had been repaired. The people Father Josef sent to them only stayed for a night or two before moving on, but even so Johanna knew how dangerous it all was—so many knocks on the door, so many shadows creeping away. Surely their neighbors would notice.

She'd managed to come to terms with that ever-present danger over the months; she'd learned to live in a state of high tension, just as Franz had to. Since Kristallnacht he'd never left the house, and she knew the enforced seclusion was making him restless. She'd tried to make the best of it, urging him to play the piano again, and singing along with Birgit even though they dearly needed Lotte's soaring soprano, but it wasn't the same. Even the snatched moments they took together, lingering in the sitting room by the dying embers of the fire after everyone else had gone to bed, didn't feel like enough.

"I want to live with you as my wife in our own house," Franz would say, and Johanna never had any response, for she wanted that too, more than anything, and yet it felt farther away than ever. She knew she would marry Franz tomorrow, if he would but ask, but he'd already told her he would not tie her to him until he was a free and respected citizen. When that day would be, or if it would ever come, Johanna had no idea.

Now as she stepped into the house on Getreidegasse, the mood was somber and wary, as it was so often now. Her father looked up from his bench, his expression clearing when he saw her. He looked a decade older than he had just a year ago; he suffered from headaches far more frequently now, although he still managed to keep his good humor as well as his determination to resist.

"All right, *mein schatz*?" he called.

"Yes, Papa."

Her gaze moved, as it ever did, to Franz, who was at the bench next to her father as usual, although he would go upstairs if someone came to the shop door. She smiled at him, and he winked back, as determined as her father to keep his good humor, even though every day it felt harder to do so.

But today, at least, they were safe, and the sun was shining, and spring was a whisper in the air. Eventually the madness that gripped the world would end. She had to believe that.

Johanna had just put her foot on the first stair to head up to the kitchen when a sudden knock at the door of the shop, a hard *rap rap rap*, had her stilling, her blood freezing. There was something officious about the sound, something demanding.

In one fluid movement Franz rose from his bench and hurried past her upstairs, his hand brushing hers, fingers squeezing, before he quickly moved on. Hedwig was already waiting at the top to bolt the attic door after him. Birgit had swept her own tools away and taken Franz's place as Manfred went to the door, all of them operating in a swift, soundless ballet of subterfuge.

Two SS officers of the Gestapo stood at the door in their gray uniforms, swastika armbands like splashes of blood on their sleeves.

"Officers." Manfred bowed his head respectfully, his voice betraying not a tremor.

"We have reason to believe there are treasonous activities taking place here," one of the officers stated coldly, and Manfred looked up at them in surprise.

"Treasonous? I assure you—"

"We will search the premises."

After a second's pause, Manfred bowed his head again and stood aside. Johanna watched from the bottom of the stairs as the two men strode into the house, looking, she thought, both elegant and cruel. Their leather boots gleamed and their uniforms were well-pressed and spotless. They exhaled arrogance and evil with every breath.

"You repair clocks?" one of them asked politely as he glanced down at the Biedermeier her father had been working on.

"Indeed, yes."

"What a beautiful clock," the man remarked.

"It is a lovely specimen." Manfred smiled, and the man smiled back before, with one leather-gloved finger, he nudged the clock so it tipped over the side of the bench and smashed onto the floor.

Birgit drew her breath in sharply but no one said a word as the broken sound reverberated through the taut stillness. A cog or gear—some mechanism of the clock Johanna didn't recognize—rolled across the floor and then came to a stop by the other officer's foot.

No one moved; time felt suspended, as if they'd all been frozen in their places, transfixed by the sheer horror of the situation. Johanna realized she was biting her knuckles hard enough to draw blood. The officer walked across the shop, the shattered glass crunching beneath his boots, towards her.

"There have been reports of meetings held at this house," he announced in a clear voice, his tone jarringly offhand. "Reports of treasonous meetings discussing the possibility of an independent Osterreich, separate from Germany."

Osterreich, not Austria, even though the country had had its new name for barely a year. Johanna swallowed and pressed her body against the wall as the man eyed her with cold-eyed interest.

"You are Fräulein Eder?"

She nodded. He looked her up and down and then away. Johanna exhaled as quietly as she could.

"We did once have such meetings," her father stated calmly from his place by the door, "but they ceased as soon as Austria—Osterreich—was annexed. We have not held any since."

The man swiveled to face him. "Even so, your loyalty to the Reich is suspect."

Her father did not reply, and Johanna felt as if her heart were leaping into her throat, a silent scream bottling in her chest. If the Gestapo had only heard about those old meetings, and not the other activities, surely they couldn't be in too much trouble? And yet she knew her father would not lie, even to the SS, even to save his life. If the man asked him if he was loyal to the Reich, Manfred Eder would tell the truth, God help them all.

The silence stretched on for nearly a minute. Johanna stood completely still, each beat of her heart a slow, painful thud, anchoring her to the floor, rooting her to reality when all she wanted was to escape.

"We will search the house," the man announced, and walked past Johanna up the stairs, the other following him. Johanna threw her father and Birgit a quick, panicked look. If they searched the house, they would almost certainly find Franz. He was under the eaves, just behind a door. It wasn't even *hidden,* not really. Stupidly, they hadn't thought it necessary, as long as he wasn't seen. They hadn't, Johanna realized, ever actually believed it would come to this, as much as they'd thought they'd been waiting for it.

His face set, her father followed the officers up the stairs. Johanna and Birgit hurried after him; Hedwig let out a cry of surprise as the SS officers came into the kitchen, followed by a crash and clatter.

Johanna stopped in the doorway of the kitchen to see a tray of her mother's cherished Hutschenreuther porcelain in broken pieces on the floor—cups, saucers, teapot. The officer eyed an aghast Hedwig with a curled lip.

"How clumsy of me," he drawled.

Rage filled Johanna, like a red mist sluicing over her. There had been no need for the man to break the clock, the china. He just did it because he could. He *enjoyed* it. They all did.

Her father came into the kitchen, pressing his lips together at the sight of the broken tea things. "We are a simple, God-fearing family," he stated quietly, and the other officer gave him a silent, scornful look.

Johanna remained in the kitchen, huddled with her family, as the men worked systematically through the house, heedless of their furniture or possessions. The glass-fronted cupboard in the sitting room was tipped on its side, its front smashed, its contents of curios and porcelain figurines crushed beneath their boots. Books were flung onto the floor, their spines cracked as pages fluttered to the ground like white flags of surrender. No one made so much as a murmur of protest; they knew there was no point.

"They are only things," Manfred said softly, his arm around his wife. "Just things."

"But…" Johanna could not keep the word from slipping from her lips, and her father gave her a quelling look. She did not want to say anything that could reveal Franz, and yet it could surely be only moments until they found him.

A whimper escaped her, like the mewl of a hungry infant.

"Have faith, Johanna," her father said quietly. "Have faith."

Faith? In what? The SS officers suddenly becoming blind, or Franz turning invisible, like a miracle out of the Bible? Johanna had always taken those at face value, but she couldn't believe in one here, now, actually making a difference. They would find Franz. They would have to. Her fingernails bit deep crescents into her palms as she closed her eyes and helpless, offered a silent prayer.

Please, please don't let them find him. Somehow… please.

After what felt like an age the men returned downstairs. The first officer, the one who had broken the clock, stared coldly at her father.

"You will come with us to answer some questions."

Hedwig opened her mouth, but Manfred silenced her with a look. "Of course."

They watched in appalled silence as Manfred, with quiet dignity, went to retrieve his coat. Her father, her poor, frail father, looking so slight in his shabby black overcoat, to go to the Gestapo headquarters on Holfgasse? To be *interrogated*?

And yet did this mean that by some holy miracle they hadn't found Franz? Johanna glanced at Birgit and her mother, but they were staring at the scene unfolding in front of them; the officers waited with an impatience that felt dangerous, her father putting his old black felt bowler on his head.

He turned to them all. "God go with you," he said, and then he was heading downstairs with the Gestapo. Johanna heard the shop door open and close. In the ensuing silence the three of them simply stood there as an emptiness blew through the room. Then Hedwig let out a sob, and Johanna turned towards the hall.

"Franz," she said, and ran upstairs. With her heart thudding, she ducked into the last narrow room along the corridor and unbolted and wrenched open the little door to the eaves, crouching down to peer into the shadowy space.

"Franz!"

He wasn't there.

"*Franz!*"

She stood up, her breath coming in panicked gasps, as she looked wildly around the room for him. Had he somehow managed to leave the house without any of them knowing? Impossible, surely, and yet she pictured him tiptoeing down the stairs, ducking in and out of rooms to avoid the Gestapo, and then running out into the street. The thought of his freedom terrified her almost as much as that of his arrest. *What if he never dared to come back?*

Swallowing hard, she turned around and went through the rooms again, looking behind trunks and under the one narrow bed, as if he would still be hiding in such an improbable space.

Where was he?

Then she saw that the window looking out over the peaked roof was open a fraction of an inch. She ran to it and yanked it up, poking her head and then letting out a soft cry as she saw Franz perched precariously on the roof, clinging to the side of the house by his fingertips as the March wind buffeted him. He looked both resolute and half frozen.

"Have they gone?" he asked, and she nodded, extending a hand to help him inside. As soon as he had clambered through the window, he fell onto his knees, and she realized how cramped he must have become, huddled out there in such a precarious position.

"Who was it?" he asked as he rose unsteadily to his feet, his face gray in the pale afternoon light. "I knew they were searching."

"The Gestapo. I think they'd heard about Papa's meetings. They didn't mention anything else." He nodded, and a sickening memory rushed through her. In her panic about Franz, she'd almost forgotten about her father. "Franz, they've taken him! They've taken Papa." Her voice was lost on a sob and she pressed her fist to her mouth. "They took him in to be questioned."

"What?" Franz's eyes widened to dark pools, his face going even grayer. "Oh, poor Manfred." His voice was a groan as he shook his head, and then he turned from her. "I have to leave."

"Leave?" Johanna exclaimed. "You can't! We need you. *I* need you—"

"Johanna, he'll tell them I'm here."

She drew back, taking refuge in anger rather than fear. "He won't! He never would do such a thing!"

Franz turned around to take her by the shoulders, his tone gentling. "Johanna, they'll *make* him say."

Realization slammed into her and she doubled over, Franz's arms still around her as she choked on her sobs. Her father, her *papa.* "They can't…" she managed, even though she knew the words were useless. "Why would they? They don't even know anything."

"You know that doesn't matter." Franz's arms tightened around her. "This is my fault."

"No—"

"I never should have stayed after the Anschluss, and especially not after Kristallnacht. I knew this was coming. I put you all in danger."

She straightened, wiping her cheeks as Franz dropped his arms from around her. "Don't say that. We wanted you here. You *belong* here—"

"If I turn myself in—"

"Franz, *no.*" With strength she hadn't realized she possessed, Johanna grabbed him by the shoulders, anchoring him in place. "If you turn yourself in, you'll make his sacrifice worthless. You know they'll… interrogate him anyway." She could barely make herself say the words. Her stomach churned and she had to take several breaths to steady herself. "They will imprison him or… or worse." A howl rose within her and she bit her lips to keep from allowing it to escape. "Turning yourself in won't change that. But you're right. You can't stay here, for your sake, not ours. We need to find you somewhere safe."

A bleakness stole over his features and clouded his eyes. He shrugged his shoulders so she was forced to drop her hands. "Where?"

"Somewhere—"

"There's nowhere."

"There has to be. Birgit can ask Ingrid, or I'll speak to Father Josef—"

"Father Josef has been sending people to *us.* And all the communists care about is their pamphlets, their propaganda. They're more concerned about the rights of workers than those of Jews."

"We're on the same side—" Johanna protested, although she knew there was some truth in his words. People hated Hitler for all sorts of reasons.

"For now, perhaps. And in any case they're rounding up communists just as they're rounding up Jews. Why should this Ingrid help me?"

"Still," Johanna insisted, her voice growing stronger, "we have to try. It's not going to end like this, Franz, I promise you."

For a second his expression softened and he reached for her hand, lacing her fingers through his. "I love you," he said simply, and a terror seized her, because the words sounded so final, like a farewell. "I've always loved you, I think from the first moment I saw you, standing in the kitchen, looking like you owned the world."

"I didn't," she replied unsteadily, and he squeezed her fingers.

"You did. You owned my heart, at least, from that moment."

She drew a shuddering breath. "Franz, don't talk as if—as if this is goodbye—"

"I just want you to know."

"I do know. And you know I love you." Her voice grew stronger with the force of her conviction. "One day when this is over—"

"It won't ever be over."

"It *will.* Madness cannot last forever." She clasped his hand with both of her own. "Franz, promise me you won't do something stupid. You won't turn yourself in, thinking yourself noble or something ridiculous like that." Improbably, a smile twitched his mouth. "Promise me," Johanna insisted.

"Very well," he said, rolling his eyes, that lovely little smile still quirking his mouth. "I promise I will not be stupid."

"Good." She put her arms around him, savoring the solidness of him, the fact that at least in this moment, he was here and she was touching him and they were both safe. "Then we'll find Ingrid, or Father Josef, and one of them will tell us what to do."

"It won't be that easy," Franz warned her as his arms came around her.

"It will," Johanna said, and her voice came out sure. She felt, quite suddenly, strong, determined. This was something to fight for. To live for. "It has to be."

CHAPTER EIGHTEEN

BIRGIT

As the door of the shop closed behind the men and Manfred, Hedwig fell to her knees, a sound emerging from deep inside her, like the moan of a wounded animal.

"Mama." Birgit hurried to her, dropping to her knees to put her arms around her. Her mother's head was lowered as she rocked back and forth, and tears stung Birgit's eyes. She'd never seen her mother look so lost, so broken. "He'll be back," she said. "They just want to ask him questions."

Except she knew it didn't work like that. She'd heard enough horror stories of people who had been taken in for questioning, only to return a shadow of themselves, a shell, with bandaged fingers or broken hands, bruises and cuts and burns all over their bodies. Her stomach cramped and she struggled to breathe. That couldn't happen to her father, her dear papa.

"Mama, it's going to be all right," she said, but she heard how weak her voice sounded and she knew her mother didn't believe her. She didn't believe herself.

Somehow she managed to help her mother up and then to the table, where she sank into a chair, her head in her arms. Birgit went to make coffee, fumbling with the pot because she never made the coffee, but she didn't know what else to do.

The water had only just begun to boil when Johanna rushed into the room. "You need to find Ingrid," she told Birgit, her voice strident, even angry. Her gaze moved to their mother, still sitting slumped at the table, and then flitted away again.

"I don't know how to find her." Since she'd started receiving and distributing the pamphlets again, she had never actually seen Ingrid, although she'd had messages from her, with the pamphlets. She'd supposed it was better for them never to meet. Safer.

"What about the coffeehouse?" Johanna demanded. "You said you could reach her there. We need her help. Hers or Father Josef's, and I'll speak to him today."

"Father Josef will not be able to help," Hedwig interjected dully. "Your father was the only one he knew who resisted. The men he sent here were parishioners who had got into trouble. They had nowhere else to go."

Birgit and Johanna exchanged an uncertain look before Johanna stated, "Then it will have to be Ingrid. Franz has to be moved as soon as possible. They'll come back, once—" She stopped abruptly, glancing again at Birgit.

"Once what?" Their mother demanded, lifting her tear-stained face to look at them both.

Johanna's expression softened, her lips trembling before she pressed them together. "Once Papa tells them," she said quietly, and her mother glared at her.

"He will not do that," she stated with dignity.

"Mama, he might have no choice—"

"*Johanna.*" Birgit gave her sister a quelling look. The last thing their mother needed was to hear how her husband was going to be interrogated. Thinking about it herself made her stomach heave and she pressed one hand to her middle, determined to be strong, for all their sakes. For her father's, and for her own.

"You think I don't know?" Hedwig demanded as she let out a hollow, humorless laugh. "They will beat him. Torture him. I *know* that."

"Mama…" Johanna looked at her helplessly while Birgit turned back to the coffee pot, to hide the tears that threatened.

"He still won't tell," Hedwig continued. "Your father is strong. Far stronger than I am. I've always understood that."

Birgit glanced at Johanna and knew she must look as dubious as her sister did. Her father wasn't strong; he suffered from severe headaches, as well as other aches and pains from his war injuries, and sometimes he went to bed right after supper, or fell asleep in his chair by the fire. He was funny and intelligent and gentle and wry, but *strong?*

"He is," Hedwig insisted, as if Birgit had spoken her thoughts aloud. "But go find this Ingrid if you can."

"I'll go right now," Birgit said as she headed for the stairs. She felt a new sense of purpose fire through her, driving her forward. "I'll find Ingrid, Mama, I promise." She'd left a message for her at the coffeehouse once before; there was no reason why she could not do it again.

Outside Birgit hurried down the street, her coat drawn tightly around her, her head tucked low so she wouldn't inadvertently meet anyone's eye. It took nearly half an hour to reach the coffeehouse, and as she slipped inside, the warmth of the room and the smell of coffee and schnapps giving her a sudden yearning for normalcy, everyone fell silent for a second before the conversation started up again. She glanced at the man behind the bar; he was the same one she'd left the message with before. Back then he'd given her a blank look, but somehow the message had been passed on, and she had to trust the same would happen again.

"I'm looking for Ingrid," she said in a low voice as she stood in front of the bar, her palms placed flat on the polished wood. "She knows who I am. I've helped… with things."

The man continued polishing a glass, his face expressionless as he stayed silent. Of course she knew she couldn't expect him to say anything revealing, but what if he was an informer? Or someone else here was? She couldn't let herself think about that. "I need her help now," she said, her tone turning insistent. "Urgently. Do you know where she is?" Still nothing. "Please," Birgit begged as quietly as she could. "I've been helping for months now—and I alerted everyone to the police when they were about to raid. Don't you remember?"

"Be *quiet.*" The man had finally spoken, his voice an angry hiss although his face remained expressionless. "No one talks like that any more. Are you stupid?"

Birgit bit her lip, chastened. "I need to find Ingrid," she whispered after a moment. "There is someone I need to help. I'm hoping she can tell me how." He stared at her, his expression still giving nothing away. "It's a matter of life or death!" Birgit cried, and if anything, the man looked even more annoyed.

"Everything is a matter of life or death these days. Do you think you're the only one who's in trouble?" He put down the glass he'd been polishing and then nodded towards the door. "Come back in an hour."

"What—"

"Come back in an hour."

Knowing she had no choice, Birgit left the coffee house. She spent the hour wandering the streets of Elisabeth-Vorstadt, her mind in a ferment. Once the insalubrious neighborhood had been bustling with people—workmen and day laborers, shopgirls and seamstresses, as well as raggedy children darting in and out of the streets. Now the streets were practically empty; everyone was hiding indoors or had already gone—emigrated, arrested, or worse.

Finally an hour had crawled past and Birgit returned to the coffeehouse, relieved beyond measure to see Ingrid seated at a table in the back, smoking a cigarette, a glass of schnapps in front of her.

Birgit hadn't seen her in over a year but she looked the same, with her dark hair and red lips, her strong face drawn, improbably, in lines of good humor, although there was a certain cynical cast to her features, a weariness in her eyes.

"My little Catholic," she greeted her. "What's the rush, *mausi*?"

Birgit flushed at the mocking diminutive. "My father has been arrested by the Gestapo," she said in a low voice as she sat opposite Ingrid. "And his apprentice, Franz, you helped him before, a few years ago. You know he's a Jew. It's not safe to have him with us any longer. He needs to be moved. Hidden."

"Oh?" Ingrid raised her dark, arched eyebrows. "And what does any of that have to do with me?"

The hint of indifference in her voice shocked Birgit. She'd thought somehow that Ingrid would care. "I… I thought you might know of somewhere," Birgit stammered after a moment. "Or someone who can help. You must have connections."

"Someone who will risk their life for you, you mean?" Ingrid corrected coolly. "Why should I, for the sake of a single man?" She blew out a stream of smoke as she stared at Birgit with hard eyes. "It works both ways, you know, *liebste*. You can't just come running to us when it suits."

"I'm…" Birgit opened and closed her mouth as she fought a sudden fury. "I've been *helping* you," she hissed, leaning forward, her gaze burning into Ingrid's. "All this time, I've been helping you. I've distributed every single pamphlet that has ever been shoved under my door—"

"Oh, *well,* then," Ingrid drawled, her eyes flashing a challenge. "Aren't you brave."

Birgit sat back, more exasperated than angry now. "What is it you want from me?"

"More," Ingrid replied immediately. "Much more. Austria will not be freed by paper, but by action. Are you willing?"

"Action?" Birgit felt a stirring in her soul, something like excitement, twined with terror. "What do you mean?"

Ingrid reached for her glass of schnapps and tossed it back in one swallow. "What do you think I mean?"

"I think you mean violence." Communists were known to deal in blood rather than words. Sabotage, assassination, guerrilla warfare. Birgit swallowed and met Ingrid's bold stare. "Am I right?"

"Call it violence if you want," Ingrid replied with a shrug. "I call it defense. The Nazis have already invaded the Czech Republic, and soon it will be Poland. After that, who knows? No one is brave enough to stop them. It's up to us, the workers, as it always is."

Birgit reached for the bottle of schnapps and sloshed a measure into the glass on the table. The other woman watched, amused, as she tossed it back just as she had done—and then erupted in coughing.

"My little Catholic," Ingrid said with a smile. "You do like to pretend, don't you?"

"I'm not pretending." Birgit pushed the glass away, her throat on fire. It had been an act of foolish bravado, but at least it had given her courage. "What do you want me to do?"

Ingrid was silent for a moment, her head cocked. "Are you still seeing that soldier?" she finally asked, and Birgit started in surprise, saying nothing. "The one in the *Bundesheer*? Of course he's not now, is he?"

"He's in the First *Gebirgsjäger*," Birgit admitted. "And I suppose I am. He's been deployed, so I haven't seen him since November."

"But he writes you? And he sees you when he can?"

Birgit shrugged, uncomfortable with the other woman's questions. As much as she loved Werner—and she knew she still did, sometimes to her own shame—she didn't like talking about him, especially to a leader of the communist resistance. "I suppose."

"Good. Then here's how you can help us, at least for now. There will be other ways, I'm sure. When you see him, find out what he's doing. What his unit's plans are. Whatever he knows about troop movements, military plans, anything like that."

Birgit did her best not to gape. "You want me to spy?"

"Call it what you will. The more information we have, the better we can plan. His letters will be censored, so there's no point trying to dig for information that way. In fact, it's better to keep your letters light, breezy, just a silly girl to her sweetheart." Ingrid's mouth twisted as she jabbed her cigarette towards Birgit. "But when you see him, you need to gain some information. Do it in a way where he won't suspect. I think you can probably manage that, can't you?"

"I—" Birgit could not imagine herself asking Werner any such thing, and yet she knew she would.

"Do that, and we'll help you."

"But I may not see him for months!" she exclaimed. "And Franz needs to be moved *now.*"

"Fine." Ingrid shrugged as she stubbed out her cigarette. "We'll take it on good faith. But if you fail us or betray us, you'll regret it, and so will your family." Her tone was perfectly pleasant and yet Birgit was chilled to the bone. She believed Ingrid meant it, utterly.

"All this time, I've been on your side," she said. "I've done what you asked. I'm… I'm one of you."

"Then we don't have a problem, do we?" Ingrid said, her tone as pleasant as before. "As for Franz, go to Nonnberg Abbey and ask for Sister Kunigunde."

"Nonnberg!" That was the last thing Birgit was expecting. "My sister Lotte is a novice there."

"Oh, really?" Ingrid sounded unimpressed. "Well, it's Kunigunde you want. She'll tell you what to do, and in the meantime we'll arrange for identity papers. He'll have to leave the country, of course. He can only stay at Nonnberg for a few days at most."

"Leave the country?" Birgit thought of Johanna. "Couldn't he just… hide?"

"And keep everyone involved in danger? No, it's best to move people on quickly." Ingrid rose from the table, the conversation clearly over. "When you have something to report, leave a message with Hans." She nodded towards the bartender. "And don't be stupid."

On impulse Birgit decided to go to Nonnberg Abbey before returning home. Better to have a plan in place to tell Johanna and Franz than simply the prospect of one. There was, she realized shamefully, a small, proud part of her that wanted to be the one to sort it all out, to return home with a *fait accompli*. It was ridiculous to have such petty aspirations in the midst of a crisis, and yet she knew she did.

By the time she reached the top of the Nonnbergstiege, she was hot, tired, and out of breath. She had not been up here since Lotte's novitiate service a year and a half ago. Surely Lotte should be taking her final vows soon, and yet they'd had no word. *Had it happened?* Or had that, like so much else in life, been postponed or forgotten?

The nun who came to the porter's desk when Birgit rang the bell gave her a frowning look. "Yes?"

"I'm here to see…" Suddenly Birgit hesitated. She didn't know anything about this Kunigunde, and Kunigunde didn't know her. And what if this nun, looking so sour, was suspicious? Every conversation, every *word,* seemed fraught with danger. "Lotte Eder." It would be good to see her sister, and, she realized, she needed to tell her all that had happened.

"You mean Sister Maria Josef?" the nun asked with a sniff, and Birgit nodded.

"Yes, I am her sister. There is… bad news from home."

The nun nodded in understanding. "Very well."

A few minutes later Birgit was ushered into the small, bare sitting room where Lotte had said goodbye to them nearly two years ago. It felt like a lifetime—one that had ended when the troops had rolled across the border. Everything had changed, and yet Lotte had remained here the whole time, seemingly undisturbed, untroubled.

Had her sister been anxious about them, Birgit wondered. *Afraid?* Or had she not even been aware of the dangers they'd faced? She had no idea.

The door opened, and a woman came through it—a woman whose pale, smooth oval of a face was framed by the white wimple that hid her hair and covered her neck right up to the chin. Her black habit rustled as she walked, and her hands were hidden in her sleeves.

It took Birgit several stunned seconds to realize the woman was her sister.

"Lotte," she whispered, and her sister inclined her head.

"I am Sister Maria Josef now."

For some reason this made Birgit angry, and she had to choke back an instinctive retort. "How have you been?"

"I am well." Lotte stood in front of her, arms folded at her waist, looking at Birgit as if she were a stranger who was taking up her time. She had a patient air, but it seemed forced, like a costume one might put on and then take off again. "Sister Agnes said you had news of the family."

"Yes…" Birgit gestured to a pair of hard armchairs. "Why don't we sit down?"

Lotte hesitated, and for a moment Birgit thought she would refuse. Then she moved to one of the chairs and perched on the edge, as if at any moment she might get up to leave. She waited, saying nothing, and Birgit started to feel resentful. After all this time, her sister had nothing more to say, to give?

"Papa has been arrested," she stated, and was gratified to finally see a reaction from her sister—Lotte's eyes widened, her lips parting soundlessly. "The Gestapo came to the house because they said they heard reports of treasonous activity." Birgit's voice trembled as she spoke; it was only now, hours later, that the shock of what had happened was starting to truly sink in. "They searched the house—they broke Mama's good china and lots of other things, besides. And they took Papa, Lotte!" She leaned forward, as if she could somehow make her sister understand the terrible reality of such a thing. "They *took* him."

Lotte flinched and then looked away. "And Franz?" she asked after a moment.

Birgit shook her head. "They didn't find him. I don't even know why not. I left right away to find help." She stopped abruptly, unsure if she should tell her sister about what Ingrid had said. What if Lotte didn't know about the Jews being hidden here? Yet surely even if she didn't know, her sister would never be an informer.

"Help?" Lotte repeated neutrally, her expression revealing nothing.

"Franz has to leave the house," Birgit explained after a pause. "It's not safe there any more—for him or for us. I know someone whom I thought could help."

"And did they?"

Birgit took a breath. "They said to come here," she admitted. Lotte did not look surprised. "They said to ask for someone named Kunigunde."

Lotte nodded slowly. "Yes," she said, her voice sounding heavy. "I know about Sister Kunigunde."

"You do?" Relief flooded through Birgit. "Is it safe? What should I do? Can Franz come here?"

Lotte shook her head. "I don't know any details. I just know what she does."

Birgit wasn't sure, but she thought her sister sounded vaguely disapproving. "Do you help?" she asked. Lotte did not reply. "Surely you must help?"

"I… I only just discovered what was happening." Lotte bit her lip. "I didn't know what to think or do about it. I still don't. It's all so confusing, Birgit!" For a moment she sounded like a little girl, as if she'd fallen down and wanted her big sister to pick her up again, brush her off.

"It's not *confusing*," Birgit answered, and was surprised at how hard her voice sounded. She leaned forward, her gaze burning into her sister's. "It's not confusing at all. It's very clear and simple, Lotte. We are fighting evil. Evil people who want to destroy everything that is good and right in the world. That is how simple it is. There is no choice to be made here." She gestured to the wimple that hid so much of her sister's face, her golden hair. "By the nature of your vows, you have already made that choice."

"The Mother Abbess said something similar," Lotte whispered. "But—"

"But what?"

Lotte shook her head, her voice coming out in something close to a whimper, "I don't know how to be brave."

As Birgit looked at her, she was reminded again of Lotte as a girl—light, laughing Lotte, who had only wanted peace and fun, singing and joy. "I don't either," she told her. "It's not about being brave, Lotte. It's about *doing,* even when you don't feel brave."

Lotte drew a shuddering breath. "But what can I do?"

"You can help hide Franz here," Birgit said. "You remember Franz, Lotte? Franz, who plays the piano so beautifully, who always joked and teased and made you laugh?"

"Of course I remember Franz," she whispered.

"If he stays at the house, he will almost certainly be arrested. We all will." The prospect of those men, with their leather gloves and their cruel smiles, returning, made a cold sweat break over her body, everything prickling. "Please, Lotte. I'm not even sure how to speak to Kunigunde, or whom I can trust here. Please, you're my sister. Won't you help me? Help Franz?"

CHAPTER NINETEEN

LOTTE

Birgit stared fixedly at her sister, waiting for her answer, and yet still Lotte struggled to find the words. She'd spoken the truth when she said she didn't know how to be brave. She didn't even know how to *begin.* Right now all she wanted to do was run away and pretend Birgit had never come, had never asked…

It had been several weeks since Lotte had confronted the Mother Abbess about what, or really who, she'd discovered in the storeroom. She'd given no answer then, either. She was in a torment of indecision, a true crisis of faith—and of fear.

What was obedience? The Mother Abbess seemed to think it was to a higher call, to God Himself, and yet everything Lotte had been taught since coming to the convent, everything she had learned and believed and trusted, was to submit to the authorities God had placed over her. To humble herself, to surrender any thought of self-will or determination, to obey without any question or doubt. There was safety in that, as well as comfort, and it was *right.* It was meant to be right.

"Lotte…" Birgit said helplessly, spreading her hands wide. "Say something, please."

"You don't realize what you're asking—"

"I don't realize?" Birgit looked incredulous. "*I'm* the one who saw the Gestapo storm into the house only this afternoon! I saw them take Papa. He is most likely being interrogated as we speak."

Her voice wavered before she continued on more strongly, "How can you think I don't know what this means for all of us?"

Lotte swallowed, longing to look away yet unable to. "I could be putting all the other nuns in danger," she protested in a whisper. "Is that even my right—"

"Putting yourself in danger, is what you really mean," Birgit replied, and Lotte heard the derision in her voice and she flushed. "It's already going on, isn't it? This Kunigunde is involved, so it must be. So if you're already in danger, why won't you help?"

Lotte stared down at her hands, folded neatly in her lap. She thought of the days and months and even years—almost two—that she'd spent behind these abbey walls, savoring the simplicity, the serenity, the silence. Never having to worry. Never having to fear. And at the first call on her comforts, such as they were, the first possibility of risking them—for the sake of her own family—she balked.

Had she learned *anything* during her postulancy, her novitiate? Or had she just become more selfish, all the while thinking she was learning humility, obedience, sacrifice? She blinked back tears of shame at the thought. How could she hesitate even for a moment, for a second? And yet still she struggled to speak.

"It's so strange to be here again," Birgit remarked after a moment as she looked around the room. Lotte looked up and saw how exhausted she looked—her face pale, her hair falling out of its usual knot. "Are you taking your final vows soon? I though the novitiate was only a year."

"It is at least one year, often two. The Mother Abbess has not spoken of any of the novitiates taking their final vows yet."

"I suppose everything is uncertain now, even that." Birgit sighed, the sound like a gust of wind leaving her body, making her sag. Then she straightened, turning practical. "Can you at least summon Kunigunde, so I may talk to her, if you will not help?"

Lotte stiffened, jolted to realize Birgit had given up on her already. Of course, she'd given her no reason to hope.

"I didn't say I wouldn't help," she protested feebly, and Birgit looked at her in weary resignation.

"I thought you just did."

"It's just…" Lotte swallowed. "It's hard."

"I know it is." Impulsively Birgit reached over and grasped her hand, tucked in her lap. Lotte stiffened in surprise; she couldn't remember the last time she'd been touched. Birgit's skin was warm and soft, although there were calluses on her fingertips from her work. "Half the time, or even more, I'm so frightened, Lotte. I'm terrified. For the last few months I've been waiting for the knock on the door. Everyone has. And then it came…" Her voice choked and almost of their own accord, Lotte's fingers clasped her sister's.

"I'm sorry I wasn't there," she whispered, and realized she'd meant it.

"We miss you." Birgit squeezed her hand. "The house isn't the same without you, Lotte. It's so quiet. We don't even sing anymore." She gave her a sorrowful smile. "How can we be the Edelweiss Sisters without you?"

Lotte let out an uneven huff of laughter. "That seems so long ago, that we were all singing at the Elektrischer Aufzug."

"It was. It was nearly five years ago now."

She shook her head slowly, both nostalgic and yet reluctant to think of it, any of it. She'd put her old life behind her, had made herself not remember, not long for what once had been. It had been so much easier then, yet now that Birgit had cracked the door open to her memories, they came flooding back, and she found herself yearning for what once was.

"So much has changed," Birgit told her in a hollow voice. "If you went out in the city now, Lotte, you wouldn't believe it. Swastika banners everywhere. Nazis in the streets. People being arrested or beaten at a moment's notice. Everyone's either arrogant or afraid." She glanced at her, a flicker of curiosity in her eyes. "Have you ever left Nonnberg since you first came here?" Lotte shook her head and Birgit released a long, low breath. "How strange. How little you must know about any of it."

"I'm not meant to know," Lotte replied a bit stiffly. "I've left that life behind."

"Must be quite comfortable for you, then." Birgit sounded weary rather than bitter. "I wouldn't mind becoming a nun, considering the way the world is now."

"It's not just about escaping the world," Lotte began, and then stopped. She was repeating what both Father Josef and the Mother Abbess had told her, and yet it felt like a lie in her mouth. She had escaped the world—and she'd been glad.

"So you will help?" Birgit leaned forward, their hands still clasped.

Lotte stared down at their twined fingers. Everything about this exchange—the intimacy, the emotion—chafed at her. It felt like too much, nerves suddenly twanging to the painful realities of life, old yearnings long buried rising to the surface, along with all the doubts and fears.

"Yes," she whispered, her gaze still on their hands. "I will."

Birgit released a long sigh as she sat back, removing her hand from Lotte's. "Thank you. You'll speak to this Kunigunde?"

Lotte let out a hollow laugh. "Yes, but she doesn't like me."

"Nuns don't like each other?" Birgit raised her eyebrows. "I thought you were all meant to get along."

"We are, but…" Lotte thought of how she'd spoken about Kunigunde in public confession. How she'd followed her, confronted her. She saw it all as so petty now, and her shame bit even deeper. "I'll talk to her," she promised.

"We need to move Franz as soon as possible. Today, if we can."

"Today…" Lotte glanced out the window. Dusk was already falling. "I don't know if it will be possible."

"This is a matter of life and death, Lotte."

Life and death. Franz's life and death, perhaps even her whole family's. Her stomach clenched as she nodded. "I'll go find her now," she said.

"I'll wait."

Lotte felt as if she were walking through a fog, or perhaps in a dream, as she headed down the corridor. She had a heightened sense of everything—the slap of her sandals on stone, the cool air brushing her cheeks. Outside, light was being leached from the sky in streaks of vivid orange and red as a violet twilight crept like a cloak over the mountains.

The air was so sharp and cold, Lotte had an urge to take it in big lungfuls, to feel it travel and expand through her body, the very breath of life. *I'm alive,* she thought. *Right now I'm alive.*

Was this what courage felt like? This excruciating awareness, the sense of time being both fleeting and precious, running through her hands like water, constantly ticking like one of her father's clocks? How much more would she have? She'd thought she'd put to death her earthly, fleshly desires, yet now she felt them keenly. *I'm only twenty,* her mind cried. *I want to live. I may have put so much to death already, but this? This breath in my body, this heart beating so steadily? I cannot put those to death. I won't.*

She felt as if in the last two years she had learned nothing at all.

Lotte knew Sister Kunigunde had been assigned to clean the dormitory that afternoon, although soon it would be vespers. She walked quickly down another corridor, conscious of each moment passing, time seeming to go faster and faster. In the dormitory Sister Kunigunde was on her hands and knees, scrubbing the stones. She looked up as Lotte entered.

"Sister Maria Josef." Her voice was cool as she sat back on her heels.

"There is someone here to see you." Lotte spoke stiltedly, more aware than ever of the ill feeling between them. "It is my sister."

Kunigunde raised her eyebrows in silent inquiry. "She has come on behalf of my father's apprentice, Franz Weber." A pause as Kunigunde kept her gaze. "He is a Jew."

"Ah." She nodded slowly. "You want my help."

"My sister…" Lotte began, then stopped. "Yes."

For the first time a look of something close to respect flashed in Kunigunde's eyes. She rose from the floor, brushing the dust off her habit. "Is your sister here?"

"Yes, in the visitor's room."

"I'll go now." Kunigunde started towards the door, and then glanced over her shoulder. "Are you coming?"

Surprised, Lotte hurried after her. "Yes—yes, I'll come."

Birgit whirled around as soon Kunigunde opened the door. "You are Kunigunde?" she asked.

"Sister Kunigunde, yes." Kunigunde came into the room and Lotte followed, closing the door after them. "You need help," she stated quietly.

"Yes, as soon as possible. You have… space?"

"Yes, we have space." She glanced at Lotte, a spark of defiance in her eyes. "We always have space."

"So what shall I do?"

"Come to the side door this evening, during vespers."

"But it's almost vespers now—" Lotte began, before she was silenced by another look from Kunigunde.

"Wait by the side gate," Kunigunde instructed. "Do not knock. Someone will meet you."

"Not you?" Birgit asked with some alarm, and Kunigunde gave a swift shake of her head.

"Perhaps, perhaps not. I can't be sure. If the person who opens the gate seems surprised, walk away quickly."

Birgit's eyes flared with fear. "You mean someone might come to the gate who doesn't—"

"It is unlikely, but you never know. The man who delivers wood uses that gate on occasion, as well as a few others."

Birgit gulped. Nodded. "And then?"

"Then he will stay here until he can be safely moved. It's better for everyone if it happens as quickly as possible. Of course, he'll need papers first. We don't have any capacity to provide those."

"Yes, I know someone who can arrange for them. But what happens then—where will he go?"

"That is not my concern," Kunigunde replied swiftly. "Or yours, for that matter. The less anyone knows, the better. Then if they ask you, you cannot say."

"Well, they're hardly likely to *ask,* are they," Birgit said soberly.

"They will demand," Kunigunde agreed, and for a moment all three women were silent, contemplating the terrible risks they faced.

Finally Birgit spoke. "Our father was arrested this afternoon. They took him in for questioning."

Compassion flashed across Kunigunde's face and then was replaced with resolve. "All the more reason to get this apprentice out of your house. Go now, quickly. And come back as soon as you can, when it's dark."

Birgit nodded, and then glanced at Lotte. "Will…" She swallowed. "Will I see you again?"

Lotte stared at her, shocked by how much had changed in so short a time. Already she felt as if her past had come rushing up to meet her, and she could not imagine returning to the life she'd cultivated with such careful deliberation. To go back to saying the rosary, sweeping the floor, sitting in silence. It seemed absurd. It seemed *awful*, and yet she realized she craved it now more than ever. The simplicity of it, the safety…

And yet she didn't think she'd ever be able to go back.

"I'll see you tonight," she told Birgit, and she felt Kunigunde's surprise like a ripple in the air. "I will be at the side gate," she promised, and Birgit smiled.

The next hour seemed to pass with terrible slowness, and yet with the ticking of each minute, each second, Lotte felt both her terror and her determination grow. She was going to do this, despite Kunigunde's skepticism as well as her own fear. She wanted to, even though she was still so afraid. Perhaps *that* was courage.

"We shouldn't both go during vespers," Kunigunde told her after Birgit had gone. "It might arouse suspicion."

"Who would suspect?" Lotte asked. "Who doesn't know?"

"Several, at least," the other nun replied grimly. "And they would see it as their God-given duty to report us." She gave Lotte a pointed look, and she lifted her chin.

"I never reported you."

"You spoke to the Mother Abbess."

The Mother Abbess must have told her that, Lotte realized, and experienced an inward curdling of guilt. What had the Mother Abbess thought of her sanctimonious tattling? She looked back on her former self and cringed, and yet she knew she still wasn't much better.

"I wasn't trying to get you in trouble," she insisted. "At least, not that kind of trouble."

"You wanted me to say a few more Hail Marys?" A surprising glint of humor sparkled in Kunigunde's eyes.

"I don't know what I wanted," Lotte admitted. "For things to go back to the way they were, but they can't, can they?"

"No," she agreed. "They can't."

Lotte bowed her head humbly. "I'm sorry for reporting you to the Mother Abbess. And I'm on your side now, Sister Kunigunde. We are in this together."

*

The bell for vespers had just started to ring, its chimes pealing out into the still, cold night, as Lotte made her way to the side gate of the abbey. She had slipped away as the sisters had started to gather, and she'd caught Kunigunde's eye as she'd stolen down the corridor, away from the chapel, and seen her give a tiny, encouraging smile.

When she came to the side gate, all was quiet. She shivered in the cold air; although it was March it still felt like winter, and the peaks of the Salzkammergut were covered in deep snow.

When would they come? What if they'd been stopped, arrested? They would tell everything, just as Kunigunde had said, and the Gestapo would soon be at the door of the abbey.

Then, Lotte told herself, *they tell everything, and you are arrested, and in faith you will be brave. That is all you will be able to do.*

It felt like small comfort indeed, and yet it was enough. She squared her shoulders, everything in her tensing when she heard footsteps on the alley.

She peered out into the darkness, wishing she'd brought a light yet knowing she couldn't have. Then Birgit's pale moon-like face loomed out of the darkness, followed by Franz and Johanna.

Lotte could not keep from gasping at the sight of both her sisters together. "You came—"

"It wasn't easy," Birgit whispered. "We hardly ever go out at night anymore."

"And there are curfews for Jews," Johanna added. She smiled at Lotte. "It's good to see you. Although I almost didn't recognize you!"

"I suppose it is strange," Lotte admitted with an uneven laugh. She had not seen her own reflection in a year and a half; she had no idea what she looked like now. She turned to Franz. "It is good to see you, as well."

His eyes seemed to glow in the darkness, and his teeth flashed white as he gave her a smile. "How are you, Lotte?"

"She's Sister Maria Josef now," Birgit reminded him, shooting Lotte an uncertain smile. Heartened, Lotte returned it as she stepped aside so they could come through the gate.

"You can still call me Lotte," she told Franz. "Quickly now. I will show you the way." She turned back to Birgit and Johanna. "It's best if you go now. The fewer people about, the fewer questions there will be."

Birgit nodded and then turned slightly away from Franz and Johanna. Confused, Lotte turned to her, but not before she saw her sister embrace Franz tightly, her face pressed against his shoulder.

"I will come back," Franz promised as he stroked Johanna's hair. "I will return to you, Johanna, I promise."

Johanna nodded, sniffing, and then stepped back. "Go," she said. "And Godspeed."

Franz turned to Birgit, embracing her quickly. "Thank you for being so patient with me. You are a far better apprentice than I ever was."

"Don't say that," Birgit told him unsteadily. "You have far more natural ability than I ever did."

"Take care of the shop," Franz said, and he glanced once more at Johanna, a look so full of love and yearning that something in Lotte ached. "Goodbye," he said, and as they turned to leave Lotte darted forward to hug both her sisters in turn. The feel of their bodies against hers was both surprising and welcome, their arms embracing her tightly. She'd missed this, she realized. She'd missed the physical affection she'd once taken for granted.

"God go with you," she whispered, and then she hurried back into the abbey garden, closing the gate behind her. The sound of her sisters' footsteps echoed in the silence and then disappeared altogether. Franz turned to Lotte with the approximation of a cheerful smile.

"Where to now?"

"A storeroom that isn't used. It's not the most comfortable accommodation, I'm afraid, but it will have to do."

"I don't mind."

Lotte locked the gate before leading Franz along the shadowy cloister to the storeroom whose door she'd flung open only weeks ago, to her own shock and dismay. It was empty now; Kunigunde had shown her it after they'd met Birgit, swept clean and looking innocuous. "I'll bring in a fresh blanket," Kunigunde had said. "And some food. We can't spare much without someone noticing—it has to be able to be cleared away at a moment's notice."

Now, as Lotte opened the door of the storeroom, she felt she had to apologize for its sparseness—the room held nothing but a blanket, a loaf of bread, half a sausage wrapped in wax paper and a jug of water. "I'm sorry, it really isn't much."

Franz laid a hand on her arm. "It's perfect. I'm so grateful to you, and to the other nuns here. To everyone who has helped me."

The warmth and sincerity in his voice both shamed and moved her. "How can you be so kind?" she whispered. "Why aren't you angry?"

Franz was silent for a moment. "I am angry," he said finally, but she heard sorrow, not fury, in his voice. "I'm filled with rage at what the world has become, what madmen are allowed to do. But I recognize that being bitter serves me no purpose, and helps no one else, either. There is too little kindness in this world already."

"Yes, you are right," she answered. "And it is our task—our duty—to bring more kindness into this world, even if it costs us."

His eyes and teeth gleamed in the darkness. "Are you afraid, Lotte? That it will cost you?"

"No," she answered, with at least some truth. "Not any more."

CHAPTER TWENTY

JOHANNA

September 1941

Johanna glanced quickly up and down the empty street, lit up with the last of the sun's rays, before darting into the narrow alley that ran alongside the abbey. Although there was no one in sight, she kept her head tucked low, a scarf over her hair. Even after two and a half years of visiting the abbey once or twice a month, she knew she could never be too careful.

Lotte had left the gate off the latch so she was able to slip inside easily and then hurry along the empty cloister to the little brick shed at the back of the garden used for storing broken tools, empty sacks, and the like. A quick, light knock—two taps, a pause, and then another, their signal—and then the door was unlocked and opened. Johanna hurried inside, to be enfolded by a pair of wiry yet strong arms.

"Hello, *liebling*," Franz murmured against her hair.

Johanna pressed her cheek against his collar and closed her eyes, overwhelmed by emotion just as she was every time she visited him. These visits were so fleeting, so precious, and at every one she wondered if it would be the last. It seemed incredible that they'd been living this way for two and a half years.

When Franz had first come to the abbey, he and Johanna had both expected him to be moved on within a matter of days. Birgit had said that as soon as he received his new identity papers he would be spirited across the border to Switzerland, to freedom. Johanna had said goodbye to him, thinking she might never see him again, despite Franz's promises that he would survive the war and come back for her. She couldn't help but feel it was dangerous, to want something so much.

In any case, it hadn't worked out like that at all. Only two days after Franz had left for the abbey, Birgit returned to the house on Getreidegasse, her face pale, her eyes wide with alarm.

"I've just had a message from Ingrid," she'd said in a low voice, although there was no one to overhear. "The man who forges the identity papers—he's been arrested."

Johanna had pressed one hand to her throat as her mind had raced with the potential implications, the certain dangers. "What does that mean for Franz?"

"He's safe, at least," Birgit had replied. "The man didn't know any details of anything. Kunigunde told me it was better that way, and now I believe her."

"But what about Franz? How will he get away?"

"He won't," Birgit had told her bluntly. "Not until they can find another forger."

They hadn't found another forger for several months, for it had no longer been a priority. The resistance group had moved relentlessly, resolutely on, once Hitler had declared war on the Allies, targeting supply trains and railway lines, making homemade bombs out of brown glass bottles and acid, sawn-off pipes and gunpowder. Johanna heard about their activities from Birgit, and she suspected her sister was involved in some of them, judging from the nights she'd heard her slip out of bed when she thought Johanna was asleep, only to return just before morning. Johanna didn't ask Birgit about her involvement; she knew it was better not to know, even as she quaked with fear at the danger her sister was putting herself, and indeed all of them, in.

In any case, by the time another forger had been found, Franz had decided to stay at the abbey, with the blessing of the Mother Abbess.

"It's more dangerous to attempt to get to Switzerland now than stay in Salzburg," he'd told Johanna one evening when she'd come to visit, slipping along the streets and alleyways like a shadow. "Most of the nuns here are on my side, and the few questionable ones can be kept in the dark. To them I'm just the man who comes in to do the gardening, and I've got the papers to prove it now."

"But what if they suspect and inform on you?" Johanna had asked, torn between relief that Franz would be staying and worry for the danger he might still be in.

"It's a risk I have to be willing to take. I want to stay." He'd held her hand, twining his fingers with hers. "I don't want to leave you."

And so he'd moved to a shed at the back of the abbey garden, away from any prying eyes. The nuns had kitted it out with a bed roll, blankets, some books and dishes. He'd made himself useful by repairing things in the abbey, tools and the like, as well as helping with the garden. If anyone were to ask, he was Heinrich Müller from Grodig, a simple farmer's son whom the abbey employed to do the work the nuns could not.

And yet still they lived in fear, and had been for so long Johanna couldn't remember what it felt like not to have a knot of anxiety gnawing away at the pit of her stomach, or to feel her heart start pounding at a sudden footstep or knock on the door.

She gave Franz one last squeeze before she stepped away. "You smell nice," she told him.

Franz let out a laugh. "Better than a sewer, you mean," he said. "I had a wash at the pump last night. The water was freezing but it felt good."

"You need to be careful," she admonished, as she always did, and Franz gave her a look that was half tender, half exasperated.

"I am, Johanna. I never go out when there are visitors."

"It can't be too much longer," Johanna told him, unconvincingly.

Franz let out another laugh, this one hard. "Oh, I think it can."

Johanna often brought him a newspaper, even though they contained nothing but propaganda and outright lies. They usually put Franz in a dark mood, yet she brought them anyway because she knew he was desperate for news, for anything other than the four walls of this shed, the confines of the abbey garden.

"Surely it will change soon," Johanna insisted. "Things haven't been going quite as well lately, if you read between the lines of the newspapers."

"Hitler's still high on his success." In June the Wehrmacht had mounted a massive invasion of the Soviet Union, with thousands and thousands of troops, including, Johanna knew, Werner's First *Gebirgsjäger*, deployed to the Ukraine to march towards Moscow, racking up easy victories along the way.

Yet only a few days ago Soviet troops had killed a thousand German soldiers through booby traps in Kiev, and Hitler had promised a swift and vicious reprisal. He had already proclaimed that Leningrad would be starved into submission.

Franz had insisted that the Soviet Union's vast resources of both weapons and men—cannon fodder, he'd called them bitterly—would be more than a match for Hitler, but it would take time. Time no one knew if they had.

"You must keep hope," Johanna told him staunchly. "We are nothing without it."

"I know." But he didn't sound convinced, and Johanna could hardly blame him. He'd been living in what was essentially a cupboard for a long time, with brief forays into the garden, and on little more than starvation rations. The nuns were as generous as they could be, but food was scarce for everyone, and their diet was simple enough as it was.

And, Johanna knew, the few nuns who were not aware of who he really was might notice if food went missing. They couldn't be too careful.

As Franz moved away from her to pace the shed, she saw how pale he was, despite the three months of summer sunshine they'd just had. He was thinner too, his naturally rangy form bordering on gaunt even though there was still strength in his arms, his force of personality as compelling as ever. She'd loved him for five years, yet a future together seemed as far away as it had ever been, if not more.

"How is your father?" Franz asked, as he always did, and as usual Johanna didn't want to give an honest answer.

Ever since her father had returned from the Gestapo headquarters on Holfgasse, he had been a broken man. He'd only been gone a single night, returning the following morning looking haggard and dazed, but without a mark on him.

Hedwig had fallen upon him, weeping, and Manfred had patted her arm a bit clumsily without saying a word, while Birgit and Johanna had both watched, overcome with a cautious joy. Then a cold, creeping feeling of dread had stolen over Johanna as she'd registered the vacant look on her father's face.

"Papa," she'd asked, "what happened? Are you all right? Did they…" She couldn't make herself finish that question.

Her father had nodded, an almost mechanical up and down, as he'd continued to pat his wife's arm. "I'm back," he'd said, over and over again. "I'm back."

He had refused to say anything about his ordeal at Holfgasse, whether because he didn't want to or he simply couldn't, Johanna didn't know. What she did know was that her father had changed; some necessary, vibrant part of him had been irretrievably lost. Whether it was the old war injury to his head coming back with a vengeance, or the unseen torture that could have been inflicted on him, no one knew, and her father wouldn't—or couldn't—say, but he had been irrevocably changed.

What remained was a shell—pleasant, congenial, with hints of the wry humor she'd so loved, but no more than that. His headaches came with more frequency and severity, as well as his episodes of confusion, which alarmed Johanna more than anything. He stopped work almost entirely, without even discussing it; he rose late, went to bed early, and spent hours in front of the sitting room window, staring into space. Sometimes he'd read, but usually the book lay forgotten in his lap after just a few pages.

Her mother, Johanna soon saw, had become fiercely protective of her husband, swooping down on anyone who dared disturb his peace, not that anyone did. Occasionally Birgit had asked their father for advice on something to do with the shop, as she continued to toil in it alone, but mostly they let him be, hoping with time and space and sunshine, he'd improve.

And perhaps, Johanna had to acknowledge, he had improved, at least a little. The day war was declared on Germany—and therefore on Osterreich, as well—he concentrated on the report on the radio as September sunshine had flooded the sitting room.

"We knew this would come," he'd said sorrowfully, looking around them all, after it had ended. "We knew."

Johanna had just been glad he'd said anything at all.

"He's the same," she told Franz as he continued to pace the little shed. "I don't think he's ever going to get better, not really."

"At least he hasn't gotten worse."

"Yes." Perhaps that was all they could hope for these days, for things not to get worse. At this point, Johanna realized, that would be enough for her. As long as they could have this…

"Come, sit on the blanket," she invited. "I've brought coffee."

"You mean chicory?" Franz returned, but he was smiling.

"Well, yes." Johanna gave a little laugh as she set up a picnic on the blanket—a carafe of coffee, as well as some cakes her mother had made, albeit with margarine and powdered egg, much to Hedwig's disgust. More than once she had muttered under her breath that if they'd stayed in the Tyrol, they would still have eggs and butter, fresh, creamy milk by the pail. "I'm not a magician, after all," Johanna told him with a smile, for there had not been real coffee for months.

"You're better than that," Franz replied. His face turned serious in a way Johanna didn't like, because it meant he was becoming melancholy and she couldn't bear that. "What would I do without you, Johanna?"

"Good thing you don't have to find out," she answered breezily, but he refused to be dissuaded.

"If I were a better man, I would have let you go. I should have."

They'd had this conversation too many times before. "Then I'm glad you're not a better man."

"Still." Franz's normally laughing face fell into discontented, and worse, despairing, lines. "I'm selfish, to allow you to keep risking your life, coming here to visit me. If I'd set you free, you might have met someone else, perhaps at work."

Since graduating from her secretarial course over a year ago, Johanna had secured a position as a secretary at an accountant's, typing letters and taking shorthand. It was terribly dull, and it made her wonder why she'd wanted to learn to type so badly, but at least it brought in some money.

"Then I'm glad you're selfish," Johanna stated, thrusting her face close to his. "And what is this about allowing me anything, Franz Weber? I'm my own woman, you know."

"I know you are." He smiled again, catching her up in his arms as they lay back on the blanket and he kissed her, tenderly at first and then with a passion that fired Johanna's body and soul.

"I'm never letting you go," she murmured against his mouth, and felt his smile in return.

"Good."

A little while later, as they ate the cake and drank the coffee, they played a game they'd started when Franz had first come to Nonnberg, a game of make-believe that sustained Johanna with its fairy-tale hope.

"Let's talk about our house," she said dreamily as she leaned against his chest and he wrapped his arms around her. "Our little farmhouse in Galtur," she continued, although sometimes it was a flat in Vienna, a villa in Aigen, or an estate near Linz. The one place they never picked was Paris, because that felt too sacred. "Will we have a garden?"

"Oh, I think so," Franz replied as his arms tightened around her. "I've always wanted to grow roses."

"Roses! Do you suppose roses grow in the mountains?"

"Why shouldn't they? Or if they don't, I'll build a glasshouse. Then you can have roses *and* tomatoes."

"And we'll swim every morning in the river that runs by the house," Johanna said. She had only been to Galtur, a village high in the mountains of the Tyrol, once, as a child, but she remembered a joyfully burbling river. "And there will be a bedroom upstairs for the children, and one downstairs for us."

"Only one bedroom for the children?"

"It's a small house. Cozy."

"Very well." When it was Franz's turn to embroider their dreams, he chose, not the plain cloth of a Tyrolean farmhouse, but the jeweled threads and fine fabrics of a stately apartment in Vienna or Budapest, with its high ceilings and walls of mirrors and paneled wood. "And what about the kitchen?"

"There will be an icebox," Johanna said firmly. "And the newest range. And a table that you'll make yourself."

"I'm a woodworker now!"

"You will be." Anything was possible when they were spinning their dreams. "And you'll teach our son."

Franz was silent for a moment, his arms still around her. "I'd like that," he finally said, and his voice held a throb of both sincerity and sorrow. "I'd like that very much."

They were silent for a moment, and Johanna closed her eyes, doing her best to imagine it all—the farmhouse, the table, the children upstairs tucked in bed. It could happen. They could have it all. Then the bell for compline rang, and she jumped up. "I'm late," she cried. "My parents will be worried."

"Go now." Franz reached for her coat and helped her into it. "Quickly. Stay out of sight as much as you can."

"I know." It was never wise to wander the street after dark, a woman alone. She embraced him, and he held her tightly for a second before he gave her a push towards the door. "Go."

Johanna did, slipping along the cloister and then the alleyway, down to the Nonnbergstiege, keeping to the shadows, in case anyone might see her and become suspicious. She hurried along Kaigasse to the magnificent Residenzplatz, now nearly empty under the moonlight. On to Alter Markt where the once Jewish-opened shops had all been reopened under new Aryan names, and then to Getreidegasse and home. She slipped inside the side door with a sigh of relief. Safe.

"Where were you?" Birgit asked as she came upstairs. Their parents had already gone to bed, and her sister was sitting at the kitchen table, smoking. It was a habit she'd taken up since she'd got involved with the resistance, and Johanna thought it made her look jaded.

"I was with Franz."

"You stayed out awfully late."

"I know." Johanna tucked her hair back into its bun and glanced at her sister with a frown. "What's wrong?" she asked, because clearly something was.

Birgit didn't answer for a moment, her gaze distant and unseeing as she drew on her cigarette. "Werner is on leave," she finally said.

"That's not a good thing?" Johanna was never quite sure how her sister felt about her sweetheart. She knew she spied on him, and passed any tidbits of information she gleaned onto Ingrid, but she also knew, or at least suspected, that she still loved him, no matter that he was a proud soldier in the First *Gebirsgjäger*, and an enthusiast of Hitler, or at least he seemed enough of one to Johanna.

"It *would* be, perhaps…" Birgit let out a long, low breath as she stubbed out her cigarette in the saucer on the table. "His commanding officer has been awarded the Knight's Cross. Apparently Hitler is very taken with him." She pursed his lips. "He's invited the entire division to a reception at Berchtesgaden, along with their wives and girlfriends."

Johanna's mouth dropped open. "Berchtesgaden… you mean the Berghof?" Birgit nodded. It was Hitler's mountain retreat, just thirty kilometers outside of Salzburg, and yet thankfully a world away. "You're going to meet *Hitler*," she said incredulously, and Birgit gave her a grim look.

"If I go."

"But of course you must go," Johanna exclaimed. "Think of the opportunity, Birgit. What you might learn that you can pass onto Ingrid! Who knows what any of those officers or even the man himself might say in your presence?"

"Do you actually think they're going to discuss military plans in front of a bunch of strange women?" Birgit retorted in disgust. "You know what Hitler thinks of our sex."

"Still—"

"I don't want to go." Birgit shivered, and then reached for her pack of cigarettes again. "It feels as good as a death sentence."

"It will be a party—"

"With *Hitler*."

Johanna was silent for a moment. She knew she wouldn't want to go, of course she wouldn't. "It will be worse if you don't attend," she said at last. "Werner might suspect something, never mind our great *Führer*." Bitter sarcasm corroded the words.

"I think he might suspect something already."

"How? He hasn't been home in months." The First *Gebirsgjäger* had been given leave last Christmas, and then again in the summer before they'd set off for the Ukraine. Both times Birgit had gone out with Werner, seeming tense and brittle when she returned.

"And whenever he is home, I keep asking him questions," Birgit reminded her. "Questions about what he's doing, where he's been, where he's going. It sounds suspicious, even to me."

"Then don't ask any questions this time. Just listen."

Birgit shook her head as she lit her second cigarette. "I don't know if I can do this any more. I feel as if I'm selling my soul."

"Because you're lying to *Werner*?" Johanna couldn't keep the scorn from her voice.

"I still love him, you know," Birgit said quietly. She drew in deeply on her cigarette and exhaled. "He's not a bad man, no matter what you think. I still love him."

"Even though he doesn't know about what you do?" Johanna said quietly. "The nights you slip out?"

Birgit gave her a fathomless look through a haze of cigarette smoke. "Best not to talk about that."

"What do you think he would do if he found out, Birgit?"

Her sister simply shook her head.

In the last two and a half years, Johanna knew, Werner had been involved in the invasion of Poland, the Battle of France, the invasion of Yugoslavia, and more recently, the invasion of the Soviet Union. Birgit had gleaned a few details about each of those operations—even if it was just a thoughtless lament about the lack of equipment, or the fact that they would be joining the Second *Gebirgsjager* when they crossed the Stalin Line. Any and all information could be useful, and Ingrid seemed to be glad of it all, always eager for more.

Johanna could see how anxious the duplicity made her sister, and yet she struggled to summon sympathy. Werner *was* a Nazi, whether Birgit wanted to believe it or not.

"So will you go or not?" she asked, and Birgit blew out a stream of smoke as she stared at the night sky, looking far older and wearier than her twenty-five years.

"I'll go," she said.

CHAPTER TWENTY-ONE

BIRGIT

September 1941

Birgit lay flat on her stomach as she strained to see in the darkness, waiting to hear the sound of the coming train. The autumn air was chilly, the damp from the ground seeping through her clothes as she watched Ingrid creep slowly towards the railroad tracks.

They were a mile outside of Salzburg, on the edge of a forest, and they were about to derail a train.

In the two and a half years since Birgit had officially joined the resistance, she'd participated in a dozen or so of these missions; they'd blown up several railway lines, raided two depots for weapons, and once they'd rescued several patients from a nearby psychiatric hospital, spiriting them away into the woods, before they could be systematically killed by the new regime. Every time Birgit wondered at the morality of what she was doing, she reminded herself of what the Nazis were capable of. Ingrid was right. Violence was the only way to fight. To win.

Ingrid had reached the tracks and Birgit tensed instinctively. She knew the other woman was experienced, far more than she was, at placing a bomb, but it was still a dangerous thing to do—and that was without accounting for the possibility of being discovered. Once the train was derailed, they would melt back into the woods, using the valuable few minutes it would take for any soldiers on the train to mount an attack. So far those minutes had been enough.

Birgit's ears pricked as she heard a rumble, distant and faint. She whistled once as a signal, a quick, high trill, and saw Ingrid start to scuttle back. The rumble grew louder and Birgit came into a crouch, ready to run. Ingrid continued to edge backwards as the train came into sight, a dark hulk against the night sky.

If Ingrid didn't move faster, she'd be blown up by the bomb she'd just placed. Birgit rose, her heart thudding. She glanced to her right at Elsa, another woman in their group, standing a dozen meters away. They had chosen not to involve men in any of their nighttime endeavors, because the punishment was much harsher for what was classed as military activity. Women attracted less attention, and yet Birgit knew they would most likely be hung, the same as a man would, if they were caught.

The train was seconds away from running over the bomb, and Ingrid wasn't far away enough. As she peered through the darkness, Birgit realized Ingrid had to be stuck; she looked as if she were trying to yank her foot free from something.

The train rolled on, and in the next second the sky was full of light, the air full of flying debris. Birgit saw Ingrid being flung backwards by the explosion as she turned away to protect herself from the blast.

"Run," Elsa said, already turning towards the woods.

"Ingrid—"

"It's too late for her."

It was a rule, Birgit knew, that you never risked the whole group for the sake of an individual. Ingrid would be left to die, she would expect it, and yet, for an agonizing second, Birgit hesitated. What were they fighting for, if they left a fallen comrade to suffer torture and death?

The front of the train had exploded into fragments, and the rest had run off the tracks. Already soldiers were coming from the back to investigate, rifles drawn.

Birgit ran towards Ingrid. She was bloodied and unconscious, but breathing and whole. Birgit grabbed her by her arms, hauling her over her shoulder with a strength she hadn't realized she possessed. As she reached the edge of the woods, she heard a gunshot, and something whistled by her ear.

"*Halt! Halt!*"

She half ran, half stumbled, her breath coming in tearing gasps, as another shot rang out. They would shoot them both. They would die here in the woods, and that was if they were lucky. It was impossible to get away in time.

Then someone fell into step beside her, and Elsa hoisted Ingrid's arm over her shoulder, to help carry the weight. "Come on," she whispered as they ran through the woods as best as they could, Ingrid between them. "The car is waiting. We can make it."

The next few minutes felt endless. Birgit's body was screaming with pain and fatigue as she forced one foot in front of the other, stumbling over the uneven ground. She could hear the soldiers in pursuit, thrashing their way through the undergrowth, but they did not know the woods as she and Elsa did, with its secret, narrow, winding paths.

They ducked and weaved between the trees, finally—thankfully—emerging on a dirt road where the car waited; Eva, another woman in their group, was at the wheel. They flung themselves into the back seat, Ingrid lying prone between them as Eva pushed hard on the accelerator and they roared off in a gust of fumes.

Ingrid's eyes flickered open as they left the forest behind. "You should have left me there," she murmured, but she was smiling.

*

Just six hours later, with Ingrid safely recuperating, Birgit was waiting by the front door for Werner to pick her up for their trip to the Berghof. Her body ached with tension and fatigue, and she'd dusted her face with powder to hide the circles under her eyes. When Werner pulled up to the house in a little two-seater, she couldn't keep from gaping in surprise.

"How on earth did you get a car?"

"It belongs to a friend, and he had petrol," Werner replied grandly. "It's not every day we go to the Eagle's Nest, is it?"

No, indeed it wasn't. Birgit's smile felt fixed as she kissed Werner's cheek and then got into the car.

"I thought we'd be taking the train," she managed with a little laugh as they sped out of Salzburg, the sky a hard, bright blue above, the mountains glittering beneath it like jagged diamonds, some of them dusted in snow.

"Not today." Werner kept one hand on the wheel as he put his other around Birgit so she had to scoot closer to him. "I'm so happy to see you, *engel*," he told her. "And you do look like an angel in that white dress."

"Oh, this old thing," Birgit replied with a toss of her head, even though it had taken several clothing coupons and hours at the sewing machine to produce the simple dress of white eyelet cotton, with puffed sleeves and a nipped-in waist. She'd wanted to look the part, after all. She glanced down at her hands and saw she had dirt under her nails from last night. Quickly she hid them in her skirt.

"I really am," he said, sounding as if he meant it, even more than he usually did. Birgit slid him a sideways glance, noting how much leaner he looked since she'd last seen him, just a few months ago. There was a certain grim hardness to his features that even his easy smiles and laughing eyes could not soften. She'd asked him, when she'd first seen him, how he had been, and he'd shrugged off the question with an impatient jerk of his shoulders and said nothing.

Birgit knew she should try asking again, but she couldn't make herself. It was hard enough to think about spending the day at the Berghof, in Hitler's presence, along with who knew how many other Nazi officers and officials. She felt as if the truth of who she was, what she did, would be written on her face, plain for all to see. And what about finding some information to pass on? She could not imagine how she would manage it. For now, as they sped down the lane, the mountains rising up before them, everything bright and glittering, she simply wanted to enjoy the time with Werner, or at least try to.

"I'm glad to see you," she told him as she squeezed his arm. "I only wish we didn't have to spend the whole day with other people." Especially these sorts of people.

"You aren't looking forward to getting a glimpse of the Berghof?" He slid her a smiling glance, although his face still looked hard, and Birgit thought she detected an uncharacteristically sardonic note to his voice. "Not many people get a look into the *Führer*'s private residence."

"I know. I'm rather nervous, to tell you the truth." She had discovered that it was best to be as honest as she could with Werner; it made navigating the web of lies that little bit easier, even though she still hated the deception.

"So am I, actually. I've never actually seen him in person before. Even when he came to Salzburg, my division didn't get so much as a glimpse. We were too busy marching."

"Now you might even talk to him," Birgit remarked, suppressing a shudder at the thought. She had absolutely no interest in saying so much as a word to Hitler; in fact, the prospect filled her with both terror and revulsion. She knew many women were half in love with their *Führer*, kissing his photograph or even baring their breasts when he rode by in his motorcade. Birgit could not fathom any of it.

"The likelihood is he won't even notice us. He'll be paying attention to General Schörner, not to me."

Birgit thought Werner almost sounded relieved by that notion. She knew she was.

Half an hour later they were driving up a winding road, the gatehouse to the estate in front of them flanked by two SS guards. Birgit knew that the pretty tourist area had been completely taken over by the Reich in recent years, with the surrounding area's hoteliers and homeowners alike bought or forced out by the government. Besides Hitler's Eagle's Nest, several other high-ranking officials, including Goebbels and Göring, had holiday residences there. There were also constant patrols of SS guards and anti-aircraft guns to keep the whole compound secure. Werner turned into the road and stopped at the gatehouse to show his identification along with Birgit's.

Her heart was drumming in her chest as the guard examined them both, giving their faces a hard, probing glance before turning to the papers.

"The First Mountain Division, eh?" he said as he handed the papers back, satisfied. "You saw some action in the summer, didn't you? Captured Lviv?"

"That's right," Werner replied. Birgit noticed how his fingers had tensed around the wheel.

"I heard those communist bastards went crazy over there. Killed half their population."

"Just the Jews and Bolsheviks," Werner replied with a dismissive shrug, but Birgit saw that his knuckles were white.

"They're practically doing your job for you," the guard replied with a laugh as he waved them through.

Birgit glanced at Werner as he drove up the lane that led to the Berghof. Perched on a mountaintop, the enormous chalet had several wide terraces overlooking the panorama of snow-capped mountains. She didn't ask about what he'd meant when he'd spoken to the guard, but Werner gave his head a little warning shake anyway. They were both silent as he drove towards the chalet, and another guard waved him through to park in front of it.

Birgit's legs felt watery as she got out of the car, fixing her hair nervously, her fingers trembling as she took off her headscarf and replaced it with a straw hat adorned with a sprig of edelweiss; she'd chosen it to match her dress. As edelweiss was the insignia of the mountain divisions, she'd thought it appropriate, but as she glanced at a few of the other women accompanying their soldiers, her whole ensemble seemed a bit too childish.

They were all wearing either belted jackets and narrow skirts or dirndl dresses, which Birgit knew Hitler preferred as the epitome of Germanic womanhood. She feared she looked like an overgrown girl in her cotton eyelet, and yet she'd wanted to look innocent. She just hoped she hadn't gone too far.

"Come on, then," Werner said. He looked even more tense and unhappy than he had before, his mouth set in a grim line, his body taut as they walked towards Hitler's holiday home. The day was meant to be a festive celebration, but it didn't feel like one at all.

As they passed through the front doors, Birgit experienced an unexpected flicker of curiosity. Here was the home, the beating heart even, of the man who controlled nearly all of Europe and longed for the world. The man who had ordered the deaths of thousands, if not millions, of people. Who approved the arrest, torture, and execution of innocents. *What would his home look like?*

Birgit didn't know if she had been expecting some spartan and utilitarian place, or chambers of marble and gilt and excess, but the interior of the Berghof was, in its own way, both.

The wide entrance hall was filled with cacti in pots of tin-glazed pottery; they walked through it to a large lobby boasting an enormous mantel of red marble and several pieces of Teutonic furniture, all built on a grand scale.

Birgit barely had time to take in a wood-paneled dining room and a large library with walls lined with bookshelves before she and Werner, along with all the other guests, were ushered out to a wide terrace overlooking the mountains, with tables adorned with colorful canvas umbrellas scattered about.

Although the view was stunning, the air was brisk, and Birgit shivered in her cotton dress. It was far colder up here than it had been down in Salzburg, where a hint of summer had still lingered in the air.

"Shall you introduce me to some of your fellow soldiers?" she asked, trying for a light tone but knowing she sounded strained. Still, she had to make an effort to chat, to socialize. To learn any information she could.

Waiters were handing out glasses of lemonade—Hitler never allowed alcohol to be served in his presence—and Birgit took a glass, clutching it like a lifeline. Even though most of the other men present were members of the First Mountain Division like Werner, there were, she saw, a few SS officers in their black dress uniform, as well as some other high-ranking Nazi officers she didn't recognize, circulating about. Every single one of them terrified her.

She had a horrible fear she might blurt out something inappropriate without even realizing, although in truth she couldn't imagine being able to say so much as a syllable. Her lips were drawn up like the strings of a purse, as she glanced around with what she hoped was an expression of friendly interest rather than fearful furtiveness.

"I'll introduce you if you like," Werner replied, sounding unenthused, and he walked up to several men and their wives.

The introductions washed over Birgit without her taking in any names or details; she felt as if her body were on hyper-alert, waiting for the arrival of the man himself, a buzzing in her brain that drowned out all noise so she could barely pay attention to the innocuous chitchat about the view and the weather and the latest films; Hitler was, Birgit knew, a great fan of Hollywood cinema.

Everyone was nervous, she realized with surprise. She saw it in their tense smiles, their strained voices, the way they clutched their glasses of lemonade and darted glances all around just as she was doing. Everyone was afraid of Hitler, of what he might say, of what he might do. And why shouldn't they be? This was a man who was engineering the systematic persecution of an entire religion. Just as she'd once told Werner, why shouldn't any of them be next?

She wondered then about the adulation of Hitler she saw so often—the women she'd read about in the papers who kissed his photograph or even bared their breasts—was that motivated by fear, as well? Was adoration the other side of terror?

She had no more time to consider the matter for a ripple of awareness was moving through the room like an electric current; people were standing taller, straightening shoulders and craning their necks, caught between curiosity and alarm. Hitler was about to enter.

Birgit instinctively took a step back as he came into the room at a brisk stride, dressed in uniform. Her first thought was how surprisingly small he was. He was only a little taller than her father, and almost as slight. Yet he had an energy, a vitality, that made him seem to fill up the space, as he stood in the center of the room and everyone sent their right arms shooting out in the required *Hitlergruss*.

Birgit hesitated, for in the three years and a half years since the Anschluss she had managed never to perform the odious salute. In the street she'd always made sure to carry something so she couldn't lift her arm, and she'd never attended any rallies or parades. In the shop, when a customer entered, she kept her focus on the clocks and merely nodded in reply. Yet here, at the Berghof? With Hitler himself in the room?

Her arm trembled as she raised it. "*Heil Hitler*," she whispered, a beat later than everyone else, so it fell into the silence like a pebble into a pond. Werner gave her a quelling look, but thankfully no one else heard or noticed her. Birgit lowered her arm with a feeling of both relief and shame that she'd made the salutation at all.

Hitler began to work his way around the room in a clockwise direction, greeting all the men and shaking their hands as they clicked their heels in response, looking both attentive and somber. Werner continued to move around the room too though, drawing Birgit along with him, so he was always ahead of Hitler, and it took her a few minutes of hurrying after him before she realized he was doing it deliberately. He didn't want to meet him, a thought that made her glad but also curious and even hopeful. Was Werner no longer the admirer of Hitler that he'd once been?

The rest of the afternoon passed with agonizing slowness—another hour of socializing, and then an interminable hour in the dining room, picking at a selection of cakes, and then a speech by Hitler that grew in volume and angry insistence.

"Ahead of us lies a winter of work. What remains to be improved will be done. The German Army is now the strongest military instrument in our history. No power and no support coming from any part of the world can change the outcome of this battle in any respect. England will fall. The everlasting Providence will not give victory to him who, merely with the object of ruling through his gold, is willing to spill the blood of men!"

A chorus of "*Heil Hitlers*" followed every dramatic pronouncement, with Hitler pausing deliberately for the wave of adulation that inevitably followed. Birgit merely mouthed the words, her heart leaden. She thought Werner was mouthing them, as well. And then, with a round of applause and yet more "*Sieg Heils*," it was finally, thankfully finished.

Although Birgit had tried not to listen to any of it, she'd found herself bizarrely compelled to keep sneaking glances at Hitler, taking in the bright blue of his eyes, the neat trim of his moustache, his pride-bearing shoulders ramrod straight, as if someone had put a poker down his back. He was charismatic, she'd acknowledged reluctantly, even as he remained utterly dreadful.

As they were filing out of the room, she realized this was her last opportunity to gain any information. Before she could think better of it, she walked towards Hitler, flanked by his guard, sending her arm out.

"Thank you, *mein Führer*, for your inspiring words," she said, amazed at how confident she sounded. How sincere. "It has been such an honor to listen to you speak."

Hitler's gaze narrowed as he gazed at her, his chest puffing out a little. "The truth always inspires, Fräulein."

"Indeed it does," Birgit replied, bowing her head humbly as she slipped her arm through Werner's. He stood stiffly next to her, practically vibrating with tension. "I am so proud of *Hauptmann* Haas and the entire First *Gebirgsjäger*," she said, allowing for a tiny pause. "And all they have overcome and achieved, considering the challenges they have faced and will no doubt continue to face." She let a questioning lilt into her voice, but if she thought Adolf Hitler was going to volunteer any information, she was, of course, wrong.

"Indeed."

Birgit looked up from beneath her lashes, but Hitler's gaze gave nothing away. She got the sense that any opportunity she might have had to discover something significant had already slipped away. What had she expected him to say? To announce his military plans to a wittering woman he'd never met before?

"Thank you, *mein Führer*," Werner murmured, and then ushered her away, his arm like a band of iron beneath Birgit's.

"What were you thinking?" he hissed once they'd gone outside, and Birgit bit her lip.

"I just wanted to meet him."

"Why?" Werner demanded. He gave the SS guards a tight-lipped smile as he headed to the car. Neither of them spoke again until they'd driven through the gates and had left the Berghof behind.

"I thought you didn't even like Hitler," Werner remarked tensely, his eyes on the winding road.

"I don't." Birgit gazed unseeingly out at the country road. She felt weak and shuddery all of a sudden, the tension draining out of her, making her tremble. She closed her eyes briefly and then opened them again. "You've changed," she told Werner. He did not reply. "Do you not admire him any more?" she pressed, needing to know. "Hitler?"

"I know who you meant."

She stared at him, waiting for more, but he stayed silent. "Werner?" she finally asked hesitantly.

He flexed his hands on the steering wheel, continuing to stare straight ahead, his jaw tight.

"What's happened?" Birgit asked softly. "You've changed since I saw you last. You're… harder now. Since the summer… when you were in Russia… Did something… something must have… What happened?" she finished helplessly.

Werner clenched his jaw even tighter. "You don't want to know."

"I do," Birgit insisted. She wasn't thinking about Ingrid now, or information, anything like that. She was thinking about this man in front of her, whom she loved, had loved since she'd first met him, even when she hadn't wanted to, and how tormented he looked now. "Werner, please." She laid a hand on his sleeve. "Tell me."

To her shock, Werner jerked the wheel of the car hard, sending them careening off the road, pebbles flying up as the car skidded and Birgit let out a scream. She clutched at the door to keep her balance as the world blurred by and she wondered if Werner would catapult them right off the cliffside.

He kept his grip on the wheel, bringing the car to rest on a grassy bank on the side of the road. Birgit's heart was pounding and her whole body felt weak as she collapsed against the seat. If he'd pulled the wheel in the other direction, they would have gone straight down the side of the mountain.

Her breath came out in a frightened rush as she pressed her hand against her chest. "Werner—"

"You don't know the things I've seen," he stated. He still had his hands on the wheel as he stared straight ahead; his skin had taken on a grayish cast, beaded with sweat. "You cannot even imagine."

"Tell me, then," she answered in a thready voice. Her body was trembling.

He hit the steering wheel hard with the palm of his hand. "I told you, you don't want to know! You *couldn't* know. You wouldn't believe me. You wouldn't want to believe."

"But I think you need to tell me, whether I want to know or not."

He shook his head, and then he let out a low moan as he put his hands up to his face and he rocked back and forth, like an animal in pain. Birgit stared at him in both dread and shock; where was the breezy, confident man with the easy smile and the light laugh? What had happened to him? What had he seen or even done, to be reduced to this whimpering wreck?

"*Werner…*"

"They kill them, Birgit. They kill them by the thousands." He spoke through his fingers. "Hundreds of thousands. In cold blood. Systematically, like… like slaughtering animals.

Without… without so much as a thought. *Enjoying* it, even, in a… in a bored sort of way."

"What?" She stared at him with a confusion she longed to cling to, because she knew understanding would be worse.

"Jews. Mainly Jews. But Bolsheviks too, gypsies, Poles, anyone they don't like the look of. We made them dig pits, huge pits…" He let out another moan, the keening sound raising the hairs on the back of her neck. "Pits they lay down in. *Alive.* On *top* of one another. I saw a man with his son; the boy couldn't have been more than ten years old. The father, he tried to comfort him, to help him to lie down on top of other bodies because he didn't want to, he was afraid. My God, Birgit!" For a second he dropped his hands from his face as he stared sightlessly in front of him, an invisible horror unfolding before his eyes. "You can't even… they had to lie down in their own graves while we watched. And then they were all shot." He dropped his head back into his hands as his shoulders shook silently.

"No…" Bile rose in her throat as she imagined a scene of such horror. She didn't want to; she shied away from it, and yet some resolute part of her insisted on picturing the grim, grisly scene, the man and his son, despairing, afraid, trying to be brave. *This is what Hitler does. This is who he is. And you must always, always fight it and fight him, no matter what it costs.*

"When I close my eyes," Werner said in a choked voice, "I still see them, lying there, staring up at me. A woman caught my eye, right before she was made to lie down, on top of the others. She mouthed some words. '*I'm only twenty-three*,' I think she said. She was so young, so alive, and then…" He released a shudder, the sound guttural and full of desperation. "When I close my eyes I see rivers of blood. Swamps filled with rotting bodies. Sometimes they shot as many as fifty thousand in a single day and just *left* them there. They weren't even buried."

Birgit shook her head, the movement instinctive, necessary. "No," she said again, woodenly. She still couldn't imagine such a thing, and yet at the same time she could, and that made it even more horrible.

Werner dropped his hands and leaned back against the seat. "After that…" he shook his head slowly, his gaze unfocused. "I don't care what Hitler has done for the damned economy, or how many battles he wins. I don't *care.* There's no justification. There *can't* be." He turned to look at her, his expression suddenly turning fierce as he grabbed her by the shoulders. "There can't be, because if there is, if we ever believe there is, we've lost our humanity. We're no better than savages, monsters. Do you see, Birgit? Do you see?"

"Yes," she whispered. "I see."

He let out another shudder as he released her. "I don't want to go back. I've thought of killing myself, but I'm not brave enough. I still want to live." He gave a hollow laugh. "And they say suicide is for cowards."

"Oh, Werner." She reached for his hand, clinging to it, her heart full of both sorrow and love. She'd *known* he was a good man, and now he'd shown her. "We could run away—"

"To where?" Werner shook his head. "Hitler controls almost of Europe. And you know what happens to deserters? They're shot on sight, no questions asked."

"Yes, but…" Her mind spun. *What if Ingrid could get Werner new identity papers?* She might balk at providing them for someone she saw as a Nazi, but after last night Ingrid owed her. She'd saved her life, after all, and Werner had shown he wasn't really a Nazi. The possibility shimmered in front of her. Freedom… freedom for them both! They could run away, be married. Live the way they'd dreamed of, in Switzerland or even England. A little house, a quiet life, *children.* "I might know a way," she said.

Werner stilled and then turned slowly to look at her, his eyes narrowing. "What do you mean?"

"I know someone who can arrange for false papers." In her excitement she spoke in a rush. "She's done it before, for… well, for Jews. But I think she could do it for you, especially since she owes me a favor."

"Birgit," Werner demanded, gripping her hand hard, "what are you talking about?"

"Do you remember when we first met? I was at a meeting for communists? I met her there. Well, I met her before, but—"

"You said you went to that meeting because your friend took you," he interjected.

"Well, yes, but I went again." Birgit started speaking faster and faster, as if that would somehow help him to understand. "I've been helping her, along with some others. Not very much, it's true, but I do what I can." She wouldn't tell him about the nighttime escapades, not now.

"*Helping—*"

"You know what they're like now, Werner! You've seen for yourself how evil they are. I had to do something. And besides, Franz—"

"Franz? You mean your father's apprentice?"

"Yes. He's a Jew. I helped to hide him."

"Where?"

Birgit hesitated, aware suddenly that this could all go horribly wrong. What if Werner had simply been venting his frustration and no more? What if he felt beholden to turn her in? Turn Franz in? But no, he wouldn't. She trusted him. She loved him.

"Nonnberg Abbey. There's a nun there who helps us. Kunigunde," she said, just in case he thought it was Lotte. Her heart was beating furiously now and her stomach was in knots. What if she'd made a horrible mistake? What if she'd ruined everything? Werner might tell someone about her, about Kunigunde, about all the secrets she'd been keeping. "You understand, don't you?"

she pleaded. "You must. You know now, Werner, there's no going back once you know—"

"Do I understand?" With something between a moan and a sob Werner dropped his head back into his hands while she regarded him with both uncertainty and terror. "Birgit," he groaned, his voice muffled, "how could you? Don't you know how dangerous this all is? If they find out, you'll be sent to a camp, and that's at *best.*"

"I know."

"Do you have any idea what the camps are like? No, of course you don't. You can't imagine." He lifted his head, shaking it grimly before he reached into his jacket pocket for his pack of cigarettes. Birgit watched him uneasily as he lit it and inhaled deeply; she couldn't tell what he was thinking.

"You don't… you don't disapprove?" she ventured after a miserable silence. "You wouldn't—"

"Of course I disapprove! Not because I'm any lover of Hitler or hater of Jews, no matter what your family thinks of me, but because of *you.* I don't want you to be put in danger, Birgit. I love you."

"I know the dangers," she assured him quietly. "Trust me on that. I'm not saying it's easy—"

"So you're willing to sacrifice your life for your father's apprentice?" He sounded despairing rather than scornful.

"I'm willing to sacrifice my life for the good of humanity," Birgit replied. It was that knowledge that had emboldened her to creep out into the night, to keep watch while Ingrid laid bombs or stole guns or whatever else to fight back. She was terrified by it all, but still she knew she had to. "It's just as you were saying, Werner. We can't lose our humanity. This is how I am able to keep mine."

He was silent for a long time, smoking. "This is why you've been asking me about where I've been, what I've been doing," he remarked finally, his tone weary. "To pass on the information to these communists?"

Birgit stayed silent.

"You would most certainly be killed for that. Shot as a traitor. Most likely I would, as well. Almost certainly, in fact."

"I never…" She paused, struggling to know what to say. "I'm sorry," she said at last. "You know I had to?"

He didn't reply.

"You aren't going to—" She swallowed, unable to continue. Werner gave her a look full of hurt.

"Turn you in? Do you actually think I would do that, Birgit?"

"I think you're a good man," Birgit told him, a throb of sincerity in her voice. "A good man who has been caught in a terrible, evil situation. Don't go back, Werner. You could hide at the abbey too, with Franz—"

"Hide for the rest of the war?" He looked at her in disbelief. "And what about after? Hitler's determined to win, you know, no matter what the cost. Even now I think he'll probably do it."

"It will be different then, surely. This—this carnage can't go on forever."

"Either way it will be worse." He flicked his cigarette out onto the ground as he stared grimly ahead. "I can't see a future for anyone, Birgit, no matter what happens. Win or lose, we're all still on the road to hell."

"Then we must do as much good as we can along the way," Birgit replied staunchly. Werner just shook his head. After another few moments of uneasy silence, he started the car and maneuvered back onto the road. They didn't speak for the rest of the journey back to Salzburg.

CHAPTER TWENTY-TWO

LOTTE

January 1942

The war was turning. It had to be. Although the nuns of Nonberg were meant to be above such worldly affairs, Lotte and several of the other nuns continued to listen to the radio in the Mother Abbess's study most evenings, trying to discern the propaganda from the truth.

Last month the Americans had finally entered the war, to the relief and of joy of many, although no one admitted as much. Surely, *surely* with the Americans on the side of the Allies, it could only be a matter of time. Germany was still embroiled in a never-ending war in the Soviet Union, and meanwhile Allied bombers were apparently strafing the skies, though none had come as far as Salzburg. Lotte had heard on the radio, along with the other nuns, of bombs dropping on France, sometimes on Germany. Soon the United States' Flying Fortresses would dominate the skies, or so they hoped.

In the meantime they waited. Lotte went about her duties, her acts of resistance and obedience, and came to accept that they both sprung from the same root. Franz continued to live at the abbey, while others had come and gone. Lotte did not fool herself that she was either as brave or daring as Kunigunde, but she was glad that she was at least involved.

When someone crept to the side gate, sometimes she was the one who answered it and ushered them in. Communists, Catholics, those seeking to elude arrest—whoever they were, Lotte never even knew their names, but she sheltered and fed them, and when they slipped away again, she prayed for them.

In September it was several patients from a nearby hospital run by the Sisters of Charity; they'd been scheduled to be killed for their supposed inferiority. Then in October they sheltered deserters from the Wehrmacht, and after Christmas it was several Poles who had fled from conscripted work that was little more than slavery. They were all different, and yet they were all in need; like the Mother Abbess, Lotte had come to see them all as children of God. She learned to live with the fear she always felt, and even to find a certain peace within it.

And then, at the end of January, the Gestapo came. Lotte was in the library, shelving books, enjoying the quiet, when she heard a thunderous knocking at the door. The book she'd been holding slipped from her fingers, falling to the floor with a flurry of pages. She remained motionless as she listened to the sounds of commotion—the bolt being drawn, the raised voice of Sister Winifred, the shouting, the stomping of boots. A minute passed, perhaps two, when she simply stood there, frozen.

Then—a scream, followed by silence. Lotte tiptoed to the doorway of the library and peeked out, just in time to see Kunigunde being marched between two Gestapo; they were moving so quickly that her feet barely touched the floor. Her wimple had been knocked askew, but her face remained calm, her gaze defiant. Her eye caught Lotte's and she mouthed a single word, "Franz."

Franz. They would come for Franz. Others might be searching for him even now, and if they weren't, they would be soon. As soon as they had left the abbey with Kunigunde, Lotte raced out of the library. She heard the slamming of car doors and the revving of an engine before she practically threw herself into the Mother Abbess's study.

The Mother Abbess was, to Lotte's surprise, calmly packing a bag. She watched for a few stunned seconds, breathing hard, as the Mother Abbess put a loaf of bread and a jug of water on top of what looked like some blankets and clothes.

"We will need to move him immediately," she said briskly, as if answering a question. "I think it best if he returns to your parents' house for the moment, until we can think what to do."

"But they're already suspicious of—"

"Only for a short time, while preparations are made. We'll need a car, a driver. The fewer people who know, the better."

"A car…" Lotte stared at her blankly. She felt stupid, for she had no idea what the Mother Abbess was talking about. *Move Franz, yes, but how? Where?*

"To take him to the border," she explained as she counted out some Swiss francs. "It is the only way."

"But that's hundreds of kilometers."

"Yes, you will have to travel on back roads and by night, I should think. You can rest during the day."

Lotte stared at her for a moment before her words sank in. "I will?"

"I think it best. You know Franz, and if you're stopped, a nun is less likely to be questioned. Your sister Birgit should go, as well, since she has the necessary contacts. Does she drive?"

"I don't think so." Lotte's mind spun. To take Franz all the way to Switzerland—it was a journey that could last days, every second fraught with danger. "Why me?" she asked, her voice coming out in something close a whimper.

The Mother Abbess's lined face softened with compassion, "Why not you, Sister Maria Josef? What were Isaiah's words in response to our Lord's calling—'here am I, send me'. And so we must be just as obedient, no matter the danger or the cost."

"Yes, I know." She forced the words out, knowing they were true and yet wishing desperately that they weren't. Wishing there was someone else, anyone else.

"You are more likely to be arrested here than on the road to Switzerland," the Mother Abbess told her gently. "So it is a mercy, really. You can say you are visiting your mother's family. She's from the Tyrol, is she not?"

"Yes, Ladis, past Innsbruck."

"Which is as good as on the Swiss border! That is perfect." The Mother Abbess nodded in satisfaction as she closed the bag. "Hurry now. Go directly to Getreidegasse."

"And what of Franz?"

"He will go with you."

"But he might be stopped—"

"God willing his papers will pass if he is. He can act as your porter. Have him carry something heavy—a sack of coal or potatoes, perhaps. They are less likely to ask questions then."

"But…" Lotte stared at her, feeling faint and sick. If she was stopped by the SS, the Gestapo, anyone, they could very well be arrested. Franz's papers were forged, and Lotte suspected they looked it. They might both be imprisoned. *Tortured…* "Couldn't we wait until night?"

"There is no time, Sister Maria Josef. As our Lord Himself said, 'anyone who walks in the day does not stumble, because he sees the light of this world.'" She pushed the bag into Lotte's arms. "Go well and Godspeed, my daughter."

Lotte felt as if she were walking within a dream, as if everything was happening to someone else and she was merely watching, uninterested and uninvolved. She found Franz in the shed in the back of the garden, and with a strange, sudden sense of calm explained to him what had happened.

Franz's face paled as she spoke but he did as she said, putting on an old workman's jacket and a flat cap, and hauling a sack of potatoes over his shoulder. Lotte took out her winter cloak and walking boots; she had not left the safety of the abbey in nearly three years.

They met no one on the Nonnbergstiege, the city cold and quiet all around them. It was only a fifteen-minute walk to Getreidegasse, Lotte reminded herself. Fifteen minutes was no time at all. And, as the Mother Abbess had said, the Gestapo were unlikely to stop and question a nun.

Except for the fact that they'd just arrested one.

"Let's walk a bit faster," she told Franz, who was walking as quickly as he could with his heavy load, his head lowered.

"It looks suspicious if we go too quickly," he muttered as they headed down Kaigasse. "You're a nun, remember. You're supposed to *glide.*"

Lotte had never felt less like gliding. She struggled not to break into a sprint. All around her the city blurred into a formless haze of color and noise, everything about it accosting her senses and overwhelming her with even more terror. Had Salzburg always been this loud, people this brash? Her heart was thudding and she'd soaked through her habit with icy sweat. She caught the eye of a man in uniform and she looked away quickly.

Lord of mercy, help us. Save us…

Down Kaigasse, then across Mozartplatz, to Judengasse, every step painstaking, and then finally, *finally,* the little shop with its clockmaker's sign and the sprig of edelweiss was in sight. *Home.* Even now, after her years at Nonnberg, it was home.

She entered the shop with her head held high like any other customer even though everything in her was trembling. Birgit came into the front room as the bells jangled, her mouth dropping open at the sight of them both.

"What on earth—"

Quickly Lotte explained.

"A car," Birgit repeated dazedly. "A *driver*."

"You can drive, can't you," Lotte said a bit desperately.

"A bit," Birgit said after a moment. "But not much. And in any case, you know women don't drive very often. It would look strange."

"I can drive," Franz said. They turned to look at him. "I can be your chauffeur. It will look less suspicious that way—two women in the back, a man at the wheel. If you're visiting your aunt in Ladis, then you hired me to drive you."

Birgit and Lotte exchanged glances. "It might work," Birgit said.

"But who has a car?" Franz asked. "As well as the petrol to run it?"

"I know someone who owes me a favor," Birgit told them. Lotte and Franz both looked at her questioningly. "Ingrid," she explained, although neither Lotte nor Franz had ever met her, they both knew her name. "I've… helped her a bit."

"Helped," Franz repeated, his eyes narrowing. "Johanna has told me something of it. You've done more than help, Birgit."

"I am only doing my part. But it's true, after everything, the least she can give me is a car and petrol." She turned to Franz. "Stay out of sight for now. I'll have to find her. I might be a while."

"There isn't time," Lotte warned, thinking of Kunigunde. Already she would be back at Holfgasse, perhaps already being questioned or worse. How long would it be before she told them everything? Lotte's stomach felt hollow as she realized she would certainly be indicted. Never mind going to Switzerland, coming back to Salzburg would be the danger.

Her mind remained in a ferment as Birgit left and she and Franz went upstairs. As they came into the kitchen, Hedwig let out a cry and flung her arms around Lotte first, and then Franz. Manfred wandered in from the sitting room, his tired face breaking into a smile at the sight of them both.

"How lovely to see you again," he exclaimed, shaking Franz's hand over and over again. Lotte gazed at him, shocked by his seeming confusion. She knew from Johanna that he had not been his old self, but he was acting as if Franz had returned from a holiday.

"Your papa is tired," Hedwig said quietly. "He has been very… tired since his arrest."

Lotte swallowed down her distress as her father turned to her. "Lotte," he said wonderingly. "Lotte. Why are you dressed so?"

"It's my habit, Papa," Lotte replied. "I am a nun now, do you remember?"

He shook his head, tapping his temple with a smile. "I'm not as clever as I once was," he told her, before he drifted back into the sitting room. Lotte bit her lip to keep from crying. She hadn't realized he was quite that bad.

"He has good days and bad days," her mother said swiftly, defensively. "Today has not been a good day." She glanced searchingly between the two of them. "But now you must go upstairs. Quickly, in case they come." Her face turned grim. "If they do, they'll find you only over my dead body."

In return Franz grinned and kissed her cheek, which made Hedwig blush and Lotte laugh. It amazed her, that in the midst of all this fear, they could find something to smile about.

The next few hours passed with agonizing slowness as well as a strange, sweet poignancy. Who knew how long either of them had left? This time tomorrow they could both be arrested, imprisoned, or dead. And what of Birgit? She too was in danger. Everyone was.

Franz paced the attic room while Lotte sat, her hands folded in her lap, trying to summon a prayer, both of them ready to duck deep under the eaves if the knock at the door came.

"Where will you go once you get to Switzerland?" she wondered aloud, and Franz shrugged.

"If I get to Switzerland." He rubbed his hands over his face. "I suppose I'll try to make it to a city. Find a way to live. There are organizations for refugees there. At least I think there are." He shook his head slowly. "I can't imagine any of it, to tell you the truth."

"Nor can I." Lotte could not even imagine getting into the car that Birgit would, God willing, soon procure. What if she never saw the Mother Abbess again? Or her own parents? She thought she'd made her peace with such things when she'd said her vows, but now she realized she hadn't. She still longed for so much—the sun on her face, the embrace of her father, the sound of bells calling her to prayer…

From downstairs they heard a door open and shut, and she and Franz exchanged a silent, wary look. Footsteps hurrying up the stairs, and then Johanna burst into the room and flung herself into Franz's arms.

"My mother told me—I'll go with you," she sobbed against his neck while he held her and patted her back. "I won't let you go alone—"

"Nonsense, you know it's dangerous. I need to know you're safe, Johanna, so I have something to live for." He eased back, smiling down into her tear-stained face. "Besides, if you go missing from your job, they will notice. And what of your parents? They need you more than I do, especially now. You know as well as I do Birgit is better placed to take the risk."

"I don't care," Johanna insisted, but Lotte could see she agreed with Franz. She wiped her cheeks as she turned away from him.

"I saw Birgit in the street," she told them. "She said Ingrid is getting a car."

A look of relief passed over Franz's face, but Lotte could only feel dread. If Birgit hadn't been able to get a car, they wouldn't be able to go. *What then?* There was no way out, she realized. Whether they went or stayed, they were putting their very lives at risk.

The next few hours passed in a blur. Birgit returned with a beat-up "people's car" made by Ford nearly ten years earlier, its fenders dented and one of the windows without glass.

"We'll freeze," Lotte exclaimed, but besides covering it with wax paper, there was nothing they could do about it.

They dressed as warmly as they could and Hedwig packed them baskets of food, nearly a week's rations and surely more than they could eat, but Lotte knew it was her mother's way of showing her love. Then they embraced Manfred, Hedwig, and Johanna in turn, staring into each other's faces as if to memorize their features, before they finally walked out into the night.

They sat in silence as Franz drove down the narrow, darkened streets towards the main road to Innsbruck, which he would turn off as soon as possible, to make their way through the tiny hamlets and villages between the two cities, while avoiding the higher roads through the mountains because of the snow.

Within minutes, the temperature in the car was well below freezing. Lotte and Birgit were both bundled right up to their noses and they clung to each other for warmth as they shivered in the icy wind coming from the broken window.

Their story, should they be stopped, was that they were sisters visiting a poorly aunt in Ladis; Lotte was both a nun and a nurse. They were traveling by night because she was deathly ill and they wanted to get there as soon as possible. In fact, they did have an aunt in Ladis, although they had not seen her since they were children. Hedwig had given them all the details they could remember to make the tale sound more believable. She had also written a letter to her sister, asking her to take them in once Franz had got safely across. They would stay in Ladis for as long as they needed to, a prospect that Lotte couldn't imagine. She couldn't even remember her aunt, or the village where she lived.

The first few hours passed uneventfully enough, and after a while Lotte fell into an uneasy doze, awaking stiff-limbed and groggy to find they were still driving, on and on through the darkness. It felt, she thought, as if the whole world had turned to endless night, as if the sun would never rise again.

When dawn broke with pale gray light spreading over the horizon, they ate some of the food Hedwig had provided and tried to sleep, despite the cold.

"Why don't we also travel by daylight?" Lotte asked as the sun rose higher in the sky and the whole world shimmered, sunlight on snow. "Surely it would look less suspicious, and it will take ages to get there going only by night."

"It's too dangerous," Birgit protested, but then Franz shook his head.

"Lotte's right. The longer we take, the more likely it is that word will get out. Sister Kunigunde might have already told them all she knows. They might already be looking for us." No one said anything to that and he continued more stridently, "The faster we get across, the better."

Birgit hesitated, looking between them both, and then she nodded. "All right," she said. "So be it."

Franz started the car and then pulled out onto the road. The hours passed with painstaking slowness. Sometimes Lotte tried to relieve the tedium, as well as the terror, by asking questions, but Birgit was not very forthcoming.

"Where did Ingrid get the car from?"

"I don't know."

"And the petrol?"

"I don't know."

"How do you suppose they found out about Kunigunde?"

Something flickered across Birgit's face as she looked away. "I don't know."

"Where did you meet Ingrid, anyway?"

"I met her a long time ago, in a coffeehouse."

"She's a communist?"

"So she says."

"And what have you done? How have you helped her?"

"It's better for you not to know," Birgit said, and turned to look out the window.

Eventually Lotte lapsed into silence and they continued on, past Lofer, Waidering, St. John in Tyrol. There were only a few cars on the road, but they were never stopped.

"God is watching over us," Lotte proclaimed when they were only fifty kilometers from Ladis. They had been traveling for nearly two days, and she was exhausted and clinging to hope.

"If we get there in one piece," Franz told her, "I'll believe in your God."

"And if we don't?" Lotte challenged. "God is God no matter what happens to us."

"That's what I'm afraid of," Franz replied grimly.

Another twenty kilometers crawled past. Although no one spoke, the tension in the car felt thick, palpable. They were so close. *So close…*

Then, finally, Franz was turning off onto a narrow track that led to the tiny village of Ladis, its wooden farmhouses blanketed in snow like drifts of icing, everything seeming impossibly peaceful.

"My aunt's house is the second to last on the main street," Birgit told him in a low voice. They had agreed to visit her first, for they knew they needed help. Although they were very near the Swiss border, they could not go by the main road, and attempting to cross by foot in January alone—without local knowledge—was surely a death sentence.

"Can we really trust her?" Franz asked, and Birgit shrugged.

"We have to. My mother said she is a good woman. We must throw ourselves on her mercy."

They found the house easily enough, its front window lit as darkness fell. They parked the car in front and then glanced at each other. Everyone around would have noticed the car, the only one in the village; if there were any Nazi sympathizers among them, they would have very little time indeed.

Silently Franz climbed out of the car, followed by Birgit and Lotte. They walked along the cleared path, the snowbanks nearly reaching their waists, to the front door, and then knocked.

The woman who answered the door was tall and stout, with graying blond hair scraped back into a knot, just like their mother's. Her expression was a mixture of fear and suspicion.

"*Tante* Elfriede," Birgit said. "It is your nieces, Birgit and Lotte. Hedwig's daughters."

"What on earth…" Elfriede stared at them in shock before she ushered them in, glancing nervously out at the darkened street before closing the door. "Is Hedwig all right?"

"Yes, she is well, and our father, too," Birgit said. "But we need your help, *Tante* Elfriede." Her gaze moved to Franz, and her aunt's gaze widened in alarmed understanding. "Urgently."

Less than an hour later they were driving onward, along the road that led to the Swiss border, just a few kilometers away. Elfriede's husband, a man named Karl whom Lotte didn't remember at all, had agreed, with deep reluctance, to help them. They were to drive to about a kilometer from the frontier, and from there Franz would hike through the mountains on foot. There was, Karl had told them, a mountain hut about a mile up where he could shelter for the night, but he should be careful because frontier guards were all about, looking for smugglers or refugees, armed with rifles and Alsatian dogs who were trained to kill.

"We are so close," Birgit told her, squeezing her hand. "So close. Only a few more minutes."

Minutes. That's all that was left. Lotte nodded and tried to smile, but her lips trembled.

They drove in silence, and then Karl pulled the car off the road, the hood nosing a snowbank. As Lotte stepped out of the car, she was amazed at how still and silent it was—moonlight glittered on the hardened crust of snow, a sheet of white spreading endlessly upwards into darkness. *How on earth could Franz climb all that and survive?*

He must have been thinking the same thing, for he tilted his head to look up the mountain above him with an expression of mingled determination and despair.

"Godspeed, Franz," Birgit said in a whisper. "You will write when you can?"

"Yes, when I can."

He embraced them in turn while Karl waited, his hands tucked into his armpits, one foot tapping impatiently. No doubt he wanted to be rid of them all as soon as he could.

Heaving his rucksack on his shoulder Franz started towards the mountain looming in front of them, his boots crunching through the crust into the deep snow. The knot in Lotte's stomach began to loosen. They'd done it. They'd actually *done* it.

Then they heard the sound of a motor breaking the stillness. Franz threw a startled look behind him and then started running as best as he could through the deep snow while Lotte and Birgit stood as if frozen. Karl shielded his eyes against the sudden glare of headlights that swept across the snow.

Lotte heard the slam of a car door, the barking of dogs, and then the bright light of a torch caught her in its beam, making her blink and cringe. The breath rushed out of her lungs as she heard a voice call out in strident, sure demand, "*Halt!*"

CHAPTER TWENTY-THREE

JOHANNA

Salzburg, January 1942

It had been five days with no word. Johanna told herself not to panic. It would have taken them several days to get to Ladis, and in any case the post was unreliable at the best of times. Franz might be safely settled in Switzerland—she pictured him sipping a coffee at a café in Geneva or Zurich, overlooking a lake or a mountain—and her sisters might be staying with her aunt at the wooden farmhouse high in the mountains. They could all be safe, and she just didn't know it. The letter would come. It had to.

Meanwhile she went every day to work, typing letters and taking shorthand and trying to seem calm. She returned home, trudging through the dark evenings, the air bitter with cold, to the house on Getreidegasse that now seemed so empty. She'd closed the shop, for her father certainly couldn't go back to his repairs, and shuttered the windows. The sight of the shop so empty and dusty made sorrow sweep through her. It felt like a different kind of death, the life they'd all once known and shared gone, perhaps forever.

The evenings had become terribly quiet as well; she and her mother rarely spoke as they made supper and then sat down to it, working and eating in silent, grim solidarity. At night they listened to the radio, but they turned it off when it came to the news, for the reports had begun to distress her father, and he would flap his hands and make little noises that tore at Johanna's heart.

Sometimes he would ask a question that made her despair all the more—"*What happened to Franz?*" or "*I haven't seen Birgit in a while.*" She answered as best as she could, keeping her voice gentle, explaining that Franz and Birgit had both gone away.

"Gone?" Manfred's forehead would crinkle as he scanned her face in confusion. "Gone where?"

"Somewhere safe, Papa. You don't need to worry."

"It's better this way," her mother said once, in a low voice, while her father stared at the pages of a book without taking anything in. "You know it is."

Johanna nodded without replying. Yes, it was better that her father wasn't aware of the dangers they all faced—or were, perhaps, already in. The possibility that Lotte and Birgit, Franz as well—*no, they had to be safe*. They simply had to be.

*

Another week passed with no word, and Johanna, unable to bear the awful unknowing any longer, decided to go in search of some answers herself.

On Saturday she walked through falling snow to Nonnberg Abbey, her head lowered against the cold flakes drifting down, hoping she was not walking into some sort of trap. She had no idea what had happened to the nuns after Kunigunde's arrest; she'd heard nothing. Perhaps nothing had happened, or perhaps they'd all been arrested. Either possibility seemed just as likely.

The woman who came to the porter's lodge when Johanna rang the bell looked both sour and suspicious.

"I would like to see the Mother Abbess," Johanna stated firmly. "It is in regard to my sister, Lotte Eder. Sister Maria Josef," she corrected quickly.

"I shall see if she is available," the nun replied, leaving Johanna to wait in the cold.

A few minutes later she was ushered into the Mother Abbess's spartan study. She smiled as Johanna came into the room.

"Fräulein Eder."

"I haven't had any news from my sister," Johanna said bluntly, too worried and too tired to bother with the usual niceties or prevarications. "Nothing from either of them, or Franz. Do you know where they are? Do you know what happened to them?"

The Mother Abbess's expression remained irritatingly serene as she answered quietly, "I know as little as you do, Fräulein Eder. But they are in God's hands."

"God…!" Johanna repeated derisively. Right then she had as little faith in God as Franz ever had.

"Yes, God. It is in times such as these that we must rest on faith."

"Times such as these?" Johanna's lip curled, almost of its own accord. "You all seem quite cozy here." She knew she was being rude but she couldn't keep herself from it. She felt as if she might explode with her anger and fear; she might scream or claw at her skin, something, anything, to relieve the terrible tension inside her. "It doesn't seem as if Sister Kunigunde's arrest affected you overmuch, from what I can see."

A shadow passed across the Mother Abbess's face. "Three days ago Sister Kunigunde was executed for her involvement in the resistance movement," she replied, so quietly that Johanna strained to hear her. "But she did not break under questioning. She revealed nothing, as far as I am aware."

"Executed…" Suddenly her legs felt watery and she sank into the chair in front of the Mother Abbess's desk, dropping her head into her hands as her vision blurred and her breath came out in shallow, uneven pants.

"Breathe," the Mother Abbess advised gently as she put her hand on Johanna's shoulder. "I'm sorry. It was a shock to us, as well. I should not have told you so abruptly."

"I didn't even know her very well." Johanna raised her head as she impatiently brushed the tears from her eyes.

"She was a good woman. A faithful servant of Christ."

"If they killed her…" Johanna whispered as her mind began to whirr, the gears clicking over just like in one of her father's wretched clocks, marking time, making sense. "They would certainly kill Lotte and Birgit, and Franz too. If they've been found, then…" She doubled over, her arms wrapped around her waist as her body shook with the force of her sobs, realization thudding into her. *They were dead. They were almost certainly dead.*

"They are in God's hands," the Mother Abbess repeated. "Alive or dead, they have been commended to His care."

"But I don't want them to be dead!" Johanna half screamed before she burst into sobs again. She, who never cried, who thought herself stronger than tears, was now weeping like a child and she could not keep herself from it.

"And you do not know if they are," the Mother Abbess replied evenly. "Is there no way to get news?"

"I suppose I could ask Ingrid," Johanna said doubtfully as she wiped her streaming eyes and then her nose. Silently the Mother Abbess handed her a handkerchief; Johanna took it with a mumbled thanks.

She'd never met Ingrid; all she knew was what Birgit had told her, that she could be reached through a coffeehouse in Elisabeth-Vorstadt. It was not much to go on at all.

"That is perhaps best," the Mother Abbess told her. "From what I know, which is not very much, she is the most likely to know something. And in the meantime…" She paused. "It is probably best for both of us if you do not visit here again."

*

Johanna walked to Elisabeth-Vorstadt that afternoon, even though dusk was already falling. The neighborhood was shabby, a collection of warehouses, factories, and crumbling apartment blocks, the streets empty save for a few people who hurried along, making sure to meet no one's eye.

Johanna went into three different coffeehouses, stammering about needing to speak to Ingrid, before she finally saw a flicker of recognition from the man behind the bar at the fourth.

"I don't know anyone of that name," he answered smoothly, not meeting her eyes, but Johanna had already seen the glimmer of recognition and she thrust her face close to his, dropping her voice to a hiss.

"I know you do. Don't bother to deny it. Ingrid helped us, and if she wants her car back, she'd better be in touch with me."

"I don't know anything about a car," the man replied, as impassive as ever.

"She does." Although Johanna doubted very much if she'd ever be able to get it back.

The man met her gaze with unveiled hostility. "I don't know anything," he said. "Now either order a drink or get the hell out."

By the time Johanna got back home, her feet and heart were both aching, her coat was wet through with snow, and she felt frozen to the bone. Her mother lifted her weary gaze to hers as she came up the stairs, but at the sight of Johanna's despondent face she did not even bother asking her how she had fared.

Johanna sank into a chair and rested her elbows on the kitchen table. "What if we never find out?" she asked into the stillness.

Her mother turned back to the soup she'd been stirring—an unappetizing mix of pork fat and potatoes floating in a watery broth, all that was to be had. "Then we never find out," she replied starkly.

"I can't…" Johanna began, only to trail off as she realized it wasn't about whether she could or not. She would have to, that was all. That was always all.

Her mother had accepted this dark turn of Providence in her grimly stolid way; she was a woman, Johanna knew, who had already seen much hardship—two little brothers dead in their cradle; a childhood of scraping what living she could from her father's peasant farm; years of near-starvation and poverty following the first war. Hedwig Eder was a woman who had learned never to expect good things; what good things had come, she'd regarded with fearful suspicion.

Johanna did not want to be the same, and yet now, sitting alone, having no recourse at all, she feared she would not have a choice.

Several hours later, as she was about to go up to bed, her parents having already retired, she heard a sound at the side door—not quite a knock, but something. Her heart leaped into her throat as she hurried down the stairs, pulling the curtain away from the door, but she saw no one through the glass, and she was not willing to open it this late at night. Then she caught sight of the slip of folded paper someone must have slid under the door.

With fingers that weren't quite steady she took and unfolded it. It held a mere five words: *Your sisters are at Schanzlalm.*

The next morning Johanna went directly to Schanzlalm, the name locals used for Salzburg Prison, a large, square building in the old town, next to the courthouse. She hadn't even told her mother where she was going; she wanted to be certain of the facts before she alarmed either of her parents. Ingrid might have got it wrong. Johanna had assumed the hastily scrawled note was from Ingrid, although in truth she didn't know. She didn't know anything.

The note had, she'd acknowledged painfully, made no mention of Franz. *What did that mean? Did Ingrid not know what had happened to him—was he dead?* But if he was dead, surely she would have said as much. The not knowing made Johanna feel as if something was clawing at her brain, eating her from the inside out. She'd bitten her lips to near shreds in her anxiety, and her nails down to the quick.

A cold, determined resolve settled inside her as she mounted the steps of the Schanzlalm and a porter let her into the cramped outer office. She rang the bell for the sergeant to come to the desk.

"I am looking for Birgit and Lotte Eder," she said, her voice sharp to hide her fear, as a man in the khaki-green uniform of the German *Ordnungspolizei*, or *Orpo*, came to the desk. Ever since the Anschluss, the *Federal Gendarmerie* had been incorporated into the *Orpo*, with many of the Austrian *gendarmes* dismissed or imprisoned.

"Are they in trouble?" he asked politely, making Johanna regret her aggressive tone.

"I believe they are being held here," she replied.

The man's demeanor changed at once. "Prisoners are not allowed to receive visitors, Fräulein."

She swallowed. "Please… I just want to know if they're here. They've been missing for two weeks now and my younger sister, Lotte, she's only twenty-two."

The man softened slightly, giving a small sigh. "What makes you think they're here? Were they arrested?"

"I don't know. Someone told me they might be here." Realizing she was skirting dangerous territory indeed, Johanna gave the approximation of a helpless shrug. "Please… I don't know what happened, but my mother is beside herself with worry, and my father isn't well. We just want to *know*."

The man hesitated, looking reluctant but not without some compassion. "Very well," he said finally, and he reached under the counter for a heavy leather-bound ledger. As he opened it, Johanna saw a list of names written in the elegant *Fraktur* calligraphy so beloved by the Nazi regime. He trailed one finger down a page, and then another, while Johanna held her breath.

Then his expression tightened, his mouth pursing almost primly, and her heart sank. "Yes, they're here. They were transferred from Innsbruck three days ago." He looked up, his eyes now narrowed, his mouth thinned in disapproval. "For aiding and abetting in the escape of a Jew."

"Oh." Johanna spoke faintly, too overwhelmed even to try to dissemble. "I didn't… that is… what happened to him?"

"I never said the Jew was a man."

"Oh, I… I just assumed. It doesn't matter." It cost her everything to force the words out of her mouth.

"He'll have been dealt with," the man told her shortly, closing the ledger, and she did not want to think about what he meant. She couldn't, not without breaking down completely, right here in the entrance of the prison.

"Please… my sisters. Is there no way I can see them? Or at least send them a parcel?"

"You can send them a parcel," he told her with some reluctance. "Although I don't know how long they will be held here."

"What will happen to them? Will there be a trial?" The sergeant shrugged, and panic took hold of her, digging its claws in so deeply that for a few seconds she could not breathe. "Please," she practically gasped, leaning over the desk towards him, although she didn't even know what exactly she was asking him for.

"I can't tell you anything more," he said shortly, his sympathy gone. "Good day, Fräulein."

Johanna walked slowly out of the prison, down the steps into Rudolfsplatz, unsure where to go, what to do. She couldn't go back home, not without any real news to give her parents, and yet she had no idea how to find out anything more. She was spinning, lost, her insides hollowed out by fear and grief.

She started walking without even knowing where she was going, blindly putting one foot in front of the other, as an icy wind funneled down the street and a damp, freezing snow began to fall. After fifteen minutes she realized she'd walked towards Elisabeth-Vorstadt without even meaning to. Ingrid, she realized, was the only person who might know anything.

The same man was behind the bar as she entered the coffeehouse, and he scowled as she came in before looking away.

Johanna shivered, shaking the snow from her coat before she let a waiter guide her to a table. She was too weary, frozen and grief-stricken to confront the man now. She ordered a café mélange and took off her wet things, hanging her scarf and coat on the chair. She couldn't remember the last time she'd sat in a restaurant on her own, if she ever had. Lunch was a sandwich made of rye bread and a thin smear of meat paste eaten at her desk at work, although the other secretaries sometimes went out for a meal together, so they could gossip and smoke.

The coffee came and for a few seconds Johanna simply stared at it, as if it were a foreign object. Although she knew it was most likely ersatz, made from chicory or acorns, the milk on top looked foamy and rich. Still she could not bring herself to drink it.

She did not realize she was weeping until the tears dripped off her face and splashed onto the table. Even then she was unable to stop; she simply sat there, half frozen, and stared at the cup of coffee while she silently wept.

She might never see her sisters again. As for Franz… it was more than likely that he was dead, and even if he wasn't, he was far beyond her help now. She couldn't bear to think what might have happened to him, where he might be now. Had they shot him where they'd found him, in a field perhaps, or running away from the car? She pictured his body crumpling, his blood staining the snow scarlet.

Or perhaps they'd arrested and interrogated him in some dank hole; she couldn't bear to think of him afraid, screaming out in pain, his body broken beyond repair.

A shudder escaped and she pushed the coffee away, her stomach churning. She had no appetite for it now.

"Did you find them?"

The low voice, and the sense of movement across the table, made her jerk her head up to blink in surprise at the woman who slid into the seat opposite her. Although she looked only to be in her mid-thirties, with dark hair and red lips, there was a worldliness to her that Johanna knew she lacked herself. She possessed a certain sophisticated glamor, despite her stained shirt and man's trousers.

"Ingrid," Johanna said slowly.

"The very one." Ingrid tapped a cigarette out of a pocket before offering it to Johanna.

"No thank you," Johanna began, only to then thrust her hand out. "Oh, why not?" She'd never smoked in her life, but now seemed as good a time to start as any.

Ingrid gave a throaty chuckle as she lit both their cigarettes and then flung her head back as she drew deeply on hers. "So?" she asked as she exhaled. "Did you find them?"

"You were right. They're at Schanzlalm." Johanna took an experimental drag on her cigarette, and only just kept herself from coughing as the smoke flooded through her, making her feel surprisingly dreamy. She relaxed against the seat as Ingrid cocked her head sympathetically.

"I'm sorry."

"I'm allowed to send them parcels." Johanna's voice wobbled and she pulled on her cigarette again, drawing the smoke deep into her lungs. "How long do you suppose they'll be in there?"

A look of something like pity flashed across Ingrid's face before she veiled it, glancing away as if in thought.

"What is it?" Johanna asked. "What is it you don't want to tell me?"

"I don't know how long they'll be at Schanzlalm," Ingrid said slowly, her gaze still on some distant point. "But I doubt they'll be released."

"Ever?" Even though she'd suspected that would be the case, it still held the power to surprise her.

"Helping a Jew to escape? The best they'll get is a labor camp until the end of the war."

"A labor camp," Johanna repeated. Perhaps that would not be so bad.

"That's what they call them, anyway." A note of bitterness entered Ingrid's voice as she flicked a bit of ash off the end of her cigarette. "The truth is, they work them to death. Literally."

Johanna gripped the edge of the table with both hands. "How do you know that?"

Ingrid turned to look at her, her lips twisting. "Because my husband died in one." She stubbed her cigarette out in the ashtray on the table.

"Your husband?" Johanna repeated in surprise. "When?"

"1934. He was sent to Dachau for being a communist." She sat back and folded her arms.

"I'm sorry." Ingrid made no reply. "And Franz?" Johanna asked after a moment. "Do you know… that is… what do you think happened to him?"

"He's either dead or has been sent to a camp." Johanna recoiled from the harshness in her tone. "I don't believe in giving false hope," she continued. "The truth is, I doubt you'll ever see him again. He'll likely die in one of those camps. Most people do. I've heard talk that they are killing them systematically. Mass executions. And also in gas chambers."

Johanna let out a little cry before pressing her fist to her mouth.

Ingrid leaned forward, her eyes burning with a fierce passion that frightened Johanna as much as it moved her. "It's easier when you have nothing more to lose," she said softly. "No one left to lose. They can't hurt you then. They have nothing over you. You can be powerful."

"I don't feel powerful."

"But not caring *is* power."

"My father said we had to care. When we stopped caring, we lost our humanity."

Ingrid tutted under her breath. "Then care about the defeat of evil, and good prevailing. Care about that, Fräulein, and you will be far more useful."

Johanna stared at her blankly. "Useful?"

Ingrid's eyes glittered as she gazed back steadily at her. "For the cause." Johanna's gaze remained blank as she tried to make sense of her words. "So now," Ingrid continued, "the question is, will you join us?"

CHAPTER TWENTY-FOUR

BIRGIT

Schanzlalm Prison, Salzburg, May 1942

Birgit had lost count of the days, weeks, even, and most likely months. They all blurred together, an endless landscape of gray, punctuated by the arrival of her guard with her paltry meal—once in the morning, and again in the evening. The rest of the time she paced the confines of her small concrete cell and tried to keep herself from going mad.

There was one window, high above her, and through it she could see a small square of sky. Nothing else—no trees or buildings—nothing but sky, like a blank canvas, sometimes blue, sometimes gray, sometimes orange or violet, at the beginning or end of the day. She didn't know what she would have done without that slice of sky. The sight of it—the world outside, still there, still existing—kept her anchored to reality, if only just.

How long had she been in the Schanzlalm? At first she'd tried to keep track of the days, making a mark on the wall with a piece of straw. The arrest on that snowy slope had been in late January—a blur of pain and fear as the dogs had raced towards them and Franz had turned around, a wild look on his face, his hands held up in the air. She could tell he'd thought of making a run for it, but he'd realized he wouldn't have got very far. Better to be captured than shot in the back. Maybe.

That was the last time she'd seen him.

She and Lotte had been taken to a prison in Innsbruck, they'd given their names, been stripped of their belongings, and then, for a few weeks, judging by the marks she had made, it had seemed as if they had simply been forgotten. No one visited them, or charged them, or spoke to them at all. They were given food and left alone, in adjacent cells, so at least they'd been able to whisper encouragement to one another. Birgit had been soothed by Lotte's prayers, her lovely voice rising like an offering as she'd gone through the daily offices, only falling silent when a guard began to shout.

But then, about a week after they'd been arrested, guards had hauled them both to their feet and marched them into the covered back of a truck. They'd clutched each other, too dazed to do anything but offer reassurances that they were, so far, unharmed.

"I've spoken to no one," Lotte had whispered as Birgit had put her arms around her.

"Nor have I." Her sister looked so young without her habit, her blond hair having been shorn for her novitiate, but now it bloomed around her face in a ragged halo. Like Birgit she was wearing a shapeless dress of coarse gray cloth. The guards had taken everything from them.

When the truck had stopped outside the prison in Salzburg, both she and Lotte had stared at each other in surprise. They were only a stone's throw from the house on Getreidegasse, yet it felt like a world away. It was.

In they went to the Schanzlalm, asked again to give their names, address, and date of birth before they were herded into separate cells, this time not near enough to hear each other. Birgit had never felt so abandoned, so alone.

Days, weeks, and months had passed, an agony of slowness and unknowing. Twice Birgit had received precious parcels from her older sister, which had grounded her in the same way that sliver of sky did. Both times they'd been opened and carelessly rewrapped by the guards, but Birgit had hardly minded that.

She'd undone the string and unwrapped the brown paper—saving both—and marveled at the treasures inside: a bottle of jam, another of beef broth, a set of embroidered handkerchiefs, and an old sweater she'd used to wear that was heavy and warm. The sight of all that bounty had made her weep, both for missing her family and with incredulous gratitude for the guards who had been willing to pass it all on. Was this what she had been reduced to—feeling grateful not to be cheated or robbed?

Johanna had included a letter in the parcel, that had been necessarily brief, in order to be allowed through: *Dearest Birgit, We are all well, as are all our friends. We pray for you every day.*

A few weeks after, another parcel had come, with the same message. Who, Birgit wondered, did her sister mean by friends? The nuns of Nonnberg Abbey? Ingrid and her group? *Werner*?

She found herself thinking often about Werner, wondering if he had learned of her fate, if he was safe on the Russian Front, or at least as safe as a soldier could be. Was he continuing to fight, to kill, or had he found some way to resist, even if quietly, secretly, in the privacy of his own mind? She thought of him, she prayed for him; she knew she still loved him. She thought she always would, imperfect as he was. Weren't they all? Perhaps it had to take the witnessing of great evil to realize what you truly wanted to be, and whether you were capable of achieving it.

As the weeks passed, winter had melted into spring, marked by the fetid warmth in the dank air and the sound of the birdsong, and still Birgit had spoken to no one, save for a few words to the guard who brought her food—a bowl of watery gray porridge in the morning, and another of thin barley soup in the evening, sometimes with bread, often not. She did not know where Lotte was; she had no idea what was happening to anyone anywhere, and the ignorance was enough to make her want to scream or claw at the concrete walls of her cell, eight feet by eight feet of bare cement and a bit of dirty straw—her home for what she suspected had been at least three months, and might as well be forever.

Then, in what Birgit thought had to be May, something finally happened. A guard opened the door to her cell and summoned her with a stern look and a brisk beckoning of his hand. Birgit followed him, stepping out of the cell, her heart hammering, her legs trembling. She had not stepped out of her cell in months. The liberation was overwhelming, but it also filled her with fear. Where was the guard taking her?

Not far, as it happened; they walked down a couple of corridors and then into a room that felt as if it came from another world. There was a carpet on the floor, an intricate Turkish design in blues and reds, and a table of polished wood with several cushioned chairs. All of it made Birgit gape. She'd gone without such luxuries for so long she'd almost forgotten they existed.

"Please, sit down." The guard had left, closing the door behind him, and the one man in the room, seated in one of the chairs, smiled at her with what seemed like genuine friendliness. Birgit stared back, bewildered and suspicious, for on his collar she saw the silver gleam of the *Totenkopf*. Yet his face looked both intelligent and kind, hazel eyes glinting with interest and humor behind a pair of spectacles. He crossed one leg neatly over the other and laced his fingers across his knee.

"You must be thirsty," he remarked. "I have had tea brought."

Tea? Birgit simply stared. This had to be a trick.

"Please." The man gestured to the chair opposite him. "Sit down."

Slowly, unsure if she even had a choice, Birgit walked to the chair and sat down gingerly on it. The cushion felt ludicrously soft beneath the rough weave of her shapeless prison dress. The officer smiled at her.

"My name is *Oberleutnant* Wolf." Birgit nodded jerkily. "And you are Birgit Eder." Another nod, and then a guard came in with a tea tray that he put, rather clumsily, on the table between them. "Shall I pour?" *Oberleutnant* Wolf asked, and Birgit fought a sudden, ridiculous urge to laugh.

"I don't know why you are being so kind to me," she remarked, her voice sounding rusty, as he poured them fragrant, steaming cups of tea.

He glanced at her, his eyebrows raised. "Because I wish to help you."

"Help me?" She let out a disbelieving laugh. "I have been kept in a concrete cell for the last three months, Oberleutnant. How exactly do you want to help me?"

"If you tell me everything you know, it will go easier for you. I can make sure it does."

"Ah, of course." Birgit nodded slowly as she folded her arms. At least he wasn't threatening her with torture, she supposed. *Yet.* "What is it you wish to know, exactly?"

"Why were you traveling so far from Salzburg?" His voice was pleasant, his expression almost gentle. In a strange way, he reminded her of her father—that slightly quizzical, whimsical look, the tilt of his head, the kindness in his eyes. A lump formed in Birgit's throat.

"To visit my aunt in Ladis. It is a small village. Do you know it?"

"Someone has already spoken to your aunt and uncle," *Oberleutnant* Wolf told her. "They said you had come unexpectedly."

Birgit remained silent. She supposed she could not blame her relatives, whom she barely knew, for trying to save themselves. It jolted her that the Gestapo had been so thorough. Was that why they'd left her for so long, so they could amass evidence against her? Perhaps this *oberleutnant* had spoken to her family here, just a few blocks away. Surely he must have. "I know you were trying to get the Jew to Switzerland," he told her in a patient voice. "Why are you lying to me?"

"If you already know, why are you asking?"

"How many others were there? That you helped to get across?"

"None," she replied. "He was the first." She could only hope he did not know about her other activities. If he did, she would surely be executed.

"And where did you get the car?"

"From my boyfriend," Birgit lied instinctively. She would not betray Ingrid. "Werner Haas. He is in the First Mountain Division, and has been commended by the *Führer* himself. He let me borrow the car to visit my aunt, but he didn't know of anything else, of course. He is loyal to the *Führer*." She met the man's gaze without flinching, but she saw knowledge in his eyes and it frightened her. Why had she mentioned Werner?

"Ah yes, *Hauptmann* Haas." His mouth twisted in what looked like sympathy, or perhaps a parody of it. He may have looked kind, but she knew she could not trust him. She had not touched her tea.

"What do you mean by that?" *How could he know about Werner?* And yet how could she be surprised? These men, they knew everything.

The man let out a heavy sigh, as if the question—and its answer—burdened or even saddened him. Birgit knotted her hands together in her lap. "*Oberleutnant* Haas was arrested several months ago," he told her.

Her mouth dropped open. "What? Why?"

"For treasonous activity against the Reich. He failed to obey orders." He met her gaze coolly, and Birgit realized that he knew far more than she did. *Had Werner refused to murder more Russians?* She was glad if he had, fiercely so, and yet… *arrested.*

"It was he," he added, his head cocked as his gaze scanned her face, "who told us about Sister Kunigunde. Not willingly, I must admit. Sadly it took some time."

Birgit stared at him for a moment, his words, so pleasantly spoken, taking a few seconds to penetrate her dazed mind. Then she lowered her head so he wouldn't be able to see the torment in her eyes and concentrated on taking deep breaths. "Did you kill him?" she asked eventually, when she trusted herself to speak.

"He has been sent to a camp. As was your Jew." He made a little moue of sympathy that she caught out of the corner of her eye. "I thought you'd want to know."

Birgit forced herself to lift her head. "I did. Thank you," she said, although what she really wanted to do was fly at him, rail at him and pummel him until he was insensible and bloody as Werner must have been… but, no. She could not let herself think about that. Not now, when she had to be in control, on her guard. "What of my family?" she asked, since he seemed so inclined to impart news.

"What of them?"

"Did you speak to them?"

"Yes." He recrossed his legs as he took a sip of tea. "Your father is completely witless."

"He was taken in by the Gestapo for no reason at all and has never been the same since," Birgit returned sharply. "But perhaps you already know that."

Oberleutnant Wolf inclined his head in acknowledgement. "Your sister and mother had nothing of interest to tell us." He spread his hands wide. "We are not unreasonable people, Fräulein. We do not arrest without cause. We do not wish to punish or even annoy innocent people who do their best to serve the Reich."

She said nothing.

"What of the car?" he pressed. "It did not belong to the *hauptmann.*"

"How do you know?"

He shrugged. "I know." She stayed silent, and he sighed. "Fräulein Eder, it really would be better if you simply told me. Whose car was it? We will find them eventually, you know. It only hurts you to keep the information to yourself."

"I don't know whose car it was," she said, truthfully. Ingrid had never told her. "There was a woman in a bookshop in Aigen." She lifted her chin and met his gaze directly. She could be bold now; what did she have to lose, after all? The worst had already happened. If she was tortured and killed, so be it. She could accept such a fate now far more than she'd been able to when she'd been free. "I never knew her name. She arranged it for me."

The *oberleutnant*'s eyes narrowed. "A bookshop in Aigen? What was the name of it?"

"I don't remember."

He shook his head. "You're lying."

"I can't tell you what I don't know. They make it that way, so you can't be forced to give away secrets."

"How did you know about her?" She hesitated, and he continued tiredly, "I will find out one way or the other. You may be sure of that."

She *couldn't* give up Ingrid to them, and possibly the whole resistance cell. And yet Birgit feared she was not strong enough to hold out.

"Fräulein…"

"Werner told me about her." Surely that was believable, and they would not punish him further, if he was already in one of their wretched camps. Even so guilt curdled Birgit's stomach. What if she'd made it worse for him? She could not bear the thought, yet she could not indict anyone else who might still go free.

"How did you know how to contact this woman?"

"I was to go to the bookshop and ask for a book of poetry. *Vott lieben Gott und Anderes*"—Rilke's *Stories of God*—one of the volumes her father had loved. She met the oberleutnant's gaze unblinkingly, amazed at how calmly she could lie, the words bubbling to her lips before she'd even thought of them, spoken in such a sure voice she almost believed herself.

He pressed his lips together. "And then?"

"And then this woman would contact me, usually by a written message. And I would write back."

"So you never saw her?"

Birgit hesitated, then said, "Once." She thought it might strain credibility to insist she'd never even seen the woman's face.

"And what did she look like?"

"Blond hair, blue eyes, medium height." The opposite of Ingrid. "As far as I can recall."

"So you sent her a message, asking for a car, and you saw her only the one time." Birgit nodded, and he raised his eyebrows. "And based on this rather flimsy acquaintance, she gave you a car plus the petrol, which as you know is severely rationed, to drive it hundreds of kilometers?"

"She wanted to help."

He was silent for a few moments, and then, slowly, deliberately, he shook his head. With a sinking feeling Birgit realized he hadn't believed any of her lies. She'd been stupid to think he had, to think she'd been that clever. She looked away, struggling not to give in to despair, or worse, tears. She knew they wouldn't do her any good now.

"You know, Fräulein," he said after a moment, his voice strangely soft and sad, "I am familiar with Rilke, as well." He paused, and then quoted:

"Let all things happen to you—beauty and fear.
Just keep going. Nothing is final."

He paused again, cocking his head. "Do you know that verse?"

"It's from the *Book of Hours*," Birgit answered, and he smiled.

"Yes. You know your Rilke, as well."

"My father read him."

"I often think of that phrase—beauty and fear, both together. It holds so much, doesn't it?"

Birgit stared at him, utterly unsure what point he was trying to make yet knowing she still needed to be on her guard. "I suppose."

"And we have to let each happen to us," he continued musingly. "We have no choice in the matter. We must simply let it flow over us, beauty and fear, both or either, and pray we don't drown."

"I have no choice," Birgit couldn't keep from replying a bit sharply. "You seem to have many choices, *Oberleutnant*."

He gave her a small, sad smile. "Ah, but that is where you are wrong. In many ways, I have as little liberty as you do. You may not see my chains, but they are there."

Birgit frowned, searching his face as if looking for clues. What was he trying to tell her?

"I wanted to be able to help you, Fräulein," he said quietly, his gaze boring intently into hers. "But you have lied to me and I cannot pass on such flimsy untruths to my superiors. Surely you see that? I am as trapped as you are in this manner."

Birgit opened her mouth and then closed it. She realized she believed him; in his own way, he'd wanted to make her burden a little easier. Even so, she would not tell him any truth, no matter what it cost. "What will happen to me?" she asked finally. "And my sister?"

He sighed, seeming disappointed by her refusal, and then he pushed away from the table to press a button on the wall. "Please," she said. "You must know. What will happen to us?"

"It is out of my hands," the *oberleutnant* told her regretfully, and then the guard came to take her back to her cell. She had not taken even one sip of her tea.

CHAPTER TWENTY-FIVE

LOTTE

July 1942

The heat was stifling in the small cell, but Lotte didn't mind. She rested her head against the concrete wall and closed her eyes as she silently mouthed the words of the Office of the Blessed Virgin Mary. "*Aperi Domine, os meum ad benedicendum nomen sanctum…*" Open thou, O Lord, my mouth, to bless thy holy name…

It was strange and wonderful how, over the course of these months, these words had come to her as the greatest comfort. They were like old friends—soothing, emboldening, strengthening, enlivening. She had said these prayers for years at the abbey, but they had never meant as much as they did now, when they were all she had.

Already, just after dawn, the sun was sending bright fingers of light through the tiny window at the top of the cell. By noon it would be utterly airless, and Lotte would be desperate for the water she would not be given until evening. Something more to go without. She did not mind.

How strange, she had mused more than once during these long, empty days, *that the thing I feared the most has come to pass, and all I feel is freedom.*

Yes, freedom, even in this cell, this isolation; by her reckoning she had not spoken to another soul save the guard, who responded only in grunts, for several months. Early on after being transferred to the Schanzlalm she had been questioned by a man called *Oberleutnant* Wolf. He had been, in his own way, kindly but purposeful; Lotte had told him all she knew, which had amounted to next to nothing.

"The only person I knew who was involved in any activity you have already arrested," she'd said simply.

"You mean Sister Kunigunde." She had nodded and he had told her rather sharply, "She is dead. She was executed for treason."

Lotte had simply bowed her head. "She is free now."

"If you wish to be actually free, Fräulein, you will tell me more. I want to help you."

She had looked up at him and spread her hands wide. "I have nothing more to tell."

He must have believed her, for he sent her away and never asked for her again. Weeks passed, and then months, and she would have thought she'd been forgotten, save for the food and water that was delivered every day, and two precious parcels sent by Johanna.

She was at peace, aside for her concern for Birgit; *was she safe? Well?* Lotte had not seen or heard her since arriving in Salzburg back in February.

Then, finally, change. The guard rapped on the door of her cell. "Get your things! Move! *Schnell, schnell!*"

Lotte gathered her few possessions—a sweater Johanna had sent her, her rosary, which had, by some miracle, not been taken from her, and a comb. She had nothing else. She wrapped the rosary and the comb in her sweater, making a bundle of it. Then she waited by the door for what was to be several hours before the guard finally came.

It was clear that there were many people on the move, for the guards were milling about, shouting at everyone to get in lines of five. Startled, Lotte glanced at the others emerging from cells, blinking in the light. As they gathered in the prison courtyard, she thought there had to be twenty or thirty people there—some women, mostly men. She looked for Birgit, and saw her at the far end of the courtyard, looking weary but alert. Lotte tried to wave, but a guard shouted for her to put her hand down. There would, Lotte hoped, be opportunity to reach her sister later.

Outside Schanzlalm there was a bus parked by the curb with blacked-out windows and the seats removed. The guards prodded the prisoners hard between their shoulder blades, demanding they get on the bus. Lotte let out a cry of joy when she saw Birgit standing in the back, and she hurried towards her, pushing her way through the crowds.

"You're here!" Birgit exclaimed, smiling even though she looked exhausted, a grayish cast to her face. "Thank God." They embraced clumsily, weak as they were. "You are safe, Lotte? Well?"

"Yes, well. Very well." As the other prisoners crowded onto the bus, Lotte inched closer to Birgit to give them more room. "Where do you think we are going?"

"A camp, I should think." Birgit folded her arms across her middle as her face set in grim lines. "Where else?"

A camp. Lotte knew of the camps, of course, but that was not the same as knowing what they were like, or actually being in one. "Are you afraid?" she asked, and her sister shrugged.

"I'm just tired," she said, her voice wavering a little. "I'm so very tired." Lotte put her arm around her, and Birgit gave her a grateful smile. "I'm sorry, Lotte, for involving you in all this."

"You have nothing to be sorry for."

"You only wanted to stay at the abbey. Live peacefully—"

Lotte shook her head. "I was wrong to want that. I know that now."

"Is it so very wrong to want to serve God?"

"I was serving my own comfort, really." She glanced around at the crowded bus, sweltering and airless in the midday heat. "Perhaps I can serve God better here."

Birgit gave her a look full of doubt, but for once Lotte felt certain. She understood so much more now what the Mother Abbess had been talking about. Obedience and sacrifice were to be acted out in the prison cell, the crowded bus, even the camp, not just in the peaceful solitude of the abbey. That was easy; this would be hard. She understood it; she felt the rightness of it. *Here I can truly serve God.*

"Look at all these people, Birgit," she whispered. "They are broken and desperate, so much in need of love." She caught the eye of a man whose face had taken a battering, his skin livid with violet bruises. She smiled at him and he looked away.

Birgit let out a huff of disbelief. "It's not love these people need, Lotte, but food and water, safety and freedom."

"Love is freedom," Lotte replied firmly.

Birgit just shook her head.

Lotte's determined optimism did not dim as they waited for several hours in the stifling heat, exhausted and aching with thirst, before the bus finally lumbered off. It was a short journey, only to the Hauptbanhof, where a train made up of wooden, windowless freight cars was already waiting on the platform.

As they left the bus, they were separated into men and women; there was only a handful of women, and the guards prodded them towards a waiting car, its open door looking to Lotte like a yawning black mouth.

Birgit stepped inside first, reeling back with one hand covering her mouth and nose. "Dear heaven."

Lotte came in after her and struggled not to retch at the smell of dirt, sweat, feces, and death that was like a miasma in the air. The car was empty save for a pile of flat black loaves in one corner.

Lotte's stomach swooped at the sight. How long would they be on the train, to leave that much bread?

Only a few other women shuffled in after them, everyone giving each other uneasy looks.

"More will come," one woman, old and withered and resigned, said flatly. "Enjoy the space while you can."

As the door was rolled shut, the car was plunged into near darkness, sun filtering through the wooden slats and creating thin bars of light across the floor. Lotte took a deep breath and then wished she hadn't. With the door closed, the smell was more overpowering than ever. She and Birgit sat against the side of the car, their legs drawn up, both of them clutching their paltry possessions. No one spoke, but after a few moments Birgit let out a sudden choked sob before shaking her head and pressing a fist to her mouth.

"I'm sorry," she said.

"Don't be sorry."

"I am." She leaned her head back against the wall and closed her eyes. "Do you know Werner is at one of the camps?"

"He is?" Lotte had heard about Werner from Johanna; she had referred to him with derision as Birgit's "*Nazi boyfriend*."

Birgit let out a ragged laugh. "Yes, they arrested him when he refused to obey orders. He was brave, no matter what anyone else thinks, and I would have married him." She turned her head away from Lotte. "He was the one who told them Kunigunde's name. They had to torture him to get it. And he only knew it because I told it to him, and I didn't even have to." She let out another sob as she shook her head. "It's all my fault."

"You cannot blame yourself for others' evil," Lotte said softly. "And Kunigunde is truly free now. Do not mourn her, Birgit. She is better off than we are."

"I shouldn't have been so foolish," Birgit insisted as she wiped her face. "I was chasing a stupid dream. It will never come to pass now." She shook her head again and then turned her face to the wall, away from Lotte.

The train did not leave the station for hours, and by the time it did the women inside the freight car were raging with thirst. At least the sun had set, which provided a little cool relief. Yet as the train moved off through the endless dark, Lotte wondered where they were going. *A camp, yes, but where?* There were camps all over Germany and Poland, and even farther east than that. They might be traveling days, even weeks. Would they survive? Would they be given more to eat, something to drink?

She glanced at the elderly woman who was half-sprawled against the side of the car, her scrawny, withered limbs jerking with every jolting movement of the train even as she slept, her eyes closed, her mouth slack.

They traveled throughout the night, often stopping for no apparent reason, sometimes for hours at a time, before juddering onwards.

Sometime in the mid-morning of the next day, when Lotte's mouth was so dry, her tongue so swollen, that she could barely speak, the door opened. After a few anxious minutes when no one came, one woman stuck her head out before jerking it back in.

"Guards everywhere," she whispered. "And women too. We're at a station… it's busy. I think we might be in Vienna."

After an endless hour, more women boarded their car—a dozen, two dozen, and then Lotte lost count. It was so crowded no one could sit down, bodies pressed intimately against each other as women angled their heads to avoid hitting the women next to them. The stench of sweat and fear was overpowering. A guard shoved a bucket of water into the car, spilling nearly half of it. Birgit let out a strangled cry as she watched the water slop onto the floor.

"Please," Lotte forced out through dry, stiff lips. "My sister is thirsty. We have been traveling all night."

It was, she knew, only God's mercy that allowed both her and Birgit, as well as the other women who had been with them, to have a few sips of water each. The door clanged shut and the women moved around, trying to find some way to get comfortable. Lotte swayed on her feet, exhausted by it all, and yet how much longer would it go on? When she met someone's gaze, she tried to smile, to offer them hope, but everyone seemed to be in too much of a daze to receive it. *I want to do something good,* she thought, but all she could do was wait.

They traveled for three days, often stopping for hours at a time, subsisting on no more than the flat black bread that had been left in the freight car. Halfway through their journey, they were given another bucket of water, but only the women by the door drank any; by the time the bucket reached Lotte and Birgit, it was empty.

"We're going north," one woman announced, as she peered through a knothole in the wood one evening, gazing up at the stars. No one replied. North meant, of course, toward Germany, where none of them wanted to go.

On the morning of the third day the train finally came to a halt. Lotte felt the finality of it in the long, low hiss of the engine, the judder of the freight cars rocking back once and then going still. They would not be traveling on.

The women, some of them in a stupor, others as good as unconscious, shifted uneasily, their expressions glazed and unseeing. Lotte looked around for the old woman who had traveled with them from Salzburg, wanting to help her out of the train; she saw with a frisson of shock that she was very clearly dead, and had been for some time. She grabbed Birgit's arm, not wanting her to see, but her sister's gaze skated over the dead woman with weary indifference.

"We'll all end up like that. It's just a matter of time, and most likely not much."

"Don't, Birgit." Lotte gave her arm a gentle shake. "Have faith."

"Faith? In what?"

"In God. In His love and mercy, even now. Especially now." Lotte studied her sister's face, gray with exhaustion, smeared with dirt. "Do you not still have your faith?"

"I don't know," Birgit replied starkly. "I've seen and experienced too much to know anything any more."

The sliding door to the freight car was pulled open; bright, hard sunlight poured in. The women reeled instinctively back; they'd become used to the dark in the last few days, along with the stench, the exhaustion, the hunger and thirst.

"Out, out," the guards began to shout as they pulled women off the train none too gently. "Out! *Schnell! Schnell!*"

Lotte linked arms with Birgit as they were herded off the train with the others. The sight that greeted her as she stepped into the clear summer's day shocked her with its simple beauty—a lake, deep and blue, fringed by sycamore trees; in the distance, a white church steeple pointing to the achingly blue sky. To Lotte it felt like a sign.

"Water," Birgit murmured longingly, and Lotte urged her on. "Come. We'll drink. Wash."

Women were milling around, looking dazed; a few young guards, no more than a handful, watched with lazy, bored indifference. Lotte urged Birgit towards the lake, crouching down to cup the crystalline water between her hands. She drank, marveling at the taste of it, so clean, so pure, and then she sluiced water over her face and hair, scrubbing her cheeks to get at the worst of the grime. Birgit did the same, but only half-heartedly; she seemed too tired, her heart too weary, to do much more.

"Doesn't it feel good to be clean, Birgit?" Lotte exclaimed. She let the water trickle between her fingers, the crystal droplets catching the sunlight.

"We're hardly clean," Birgit protested. "Look at us." She held out now-scrawny arms as she regarded her wasted, filthy body.

"Even so." Lotte would not be deterred, but her sister gave her an irritated look.

"You don't need to try so hard," she told her with an acid edge to her voice. "God won't think you more holy, you know, for being thankful for a simple drink."

"I'm not trying," Lotte exclaimed. "Birgit, do you know, I've been trying all my life—trying so hard to do the right thing, to find some sense of satisfaction, of peace and… and belonging, and I've never truly found it, not until now."

Birgit stared at her incredulously, not even bothering to reply.

"I mean it," Lotte insisted. "It's horrible, what they're doing, what they've done. It's wrong and evil, of course it is. All of it. I do not deny that in the least. But God is here, Birgit. He is here with us." She lifted her head to glance around at the women still milling about. Some were drinking from the lake, others simply sat on the grass and stared dazedly in front of them while the guards loitered about. "We can do good here," she said softly. "I feel it. I don't know how, but… we're here for a reason."

"Maybe you're here for a reason," Birgit snapped, "but I'm not. I'm here because our aunt's nosy neighbor ratted us out." She clambered up from the lake with effort as one of the guards blew a whistle, and another shouted for them to form into lines.

Neither sister spoke as they organized themselves into a line with three others and, with the guards urging them on, began a slow, weary march around the edge of the lake, for a mile or more, their feet and bodies both aching.

Lotte drank in the beauty of the day—the sky such a brilliant bright blue above them, the sun pouring over the countryside like butter, turning everything golden. As they walked, a few children ran up to them, smiling cautiously, curiosity in their innocent eyes.

Lotte smiled back but Birgit just looked away. What must these children think of these tattered lines of women coming off trains, skeletons dressed in rags, only to disappear behind barbed-wire walls? Already the camp was coming into view—a sea of gray barracks surrounded by wire, a wooden watchtower at each corner.

Her heart fluttering with fear for the first time in this whole miserably arduous journey, Lotte swallowed hard. Once she and Birgit went through those looming gates, would either of them ever come out?

She didn't have time to think about it, for the guards were prodding them onwards, angry now, pushing them through the gates and then into a massive tent without any walls, the ground covered in dirty straw that Lotte saw, to her horror, was crawling with lice.

"Never mind," she told Birgit. "At least we're out of the sun."

After being hurried by the guards into the camp, Lotte thought they would be seen to directly, but she realized she should have expected them to make the prisoners wait—again. They sat for hours under that tent, eventually sitting down on the straw, heedless of the lice.

"We'll get lice anyway," Birgit had told her with a shrug. "It might as well be now."

It was early evening before they were finally summoned to stand before a woman with a face like stone and arms like slabs of meat on a butcher's hook. She gazed at them all with cold disdain, impatient as they hurried to form yet more lines, as if they were wasting her very precious time.

Lotte tried not to sway where she stood; she had not eaten anything but the black bread on the train, and then only a little, for several days; she'd had nothing that day save for the cup of water at the lake. Her body felt like no more than a collection of bones held together by a bit of sinew and skin.

Soon they were marched past the woman and into a room resembling a concrete shed or a milking barn; at a table sat several bored-looking officers who asked for their names and ages, and then pointed to a pile of belongings—battered suitcases and carpet bags, leather handbags and worn pillowcases crammed with precious belongings—all now lying in a jumbled heap.

"Put your belongings there," one of the guards barked.

Briefly Lotte thought about when she'd surrendered her pressed edelweiss to the Mother Abbess, feeling so magnanimous, so *holy*, for sacrificing that precious object. Now she threw her bundled sweater with its comb and rosary onto the pile with barely a flicker of remorse. She would miss the rosary, yes, she would, but they could not take away her prayers.

After they'd been marched through another line, they were taken into a shower room and forced to undress under the leering eye of another guard, this time a young man with dark hair and heavy eyebrows. Lotte's fingers trembled as she stripped off her prison garment, appallingly conscious of her nakedness. No man had ever seen her unclothed before.

As she hurried past the man to the spigot offering no more than a trickle of icy water, he slapped her bottom the way a farmer might slap the flank of a mare. Lotte jumped, and he laughed.

"You're a pretty one," he told her, and Lotte's stomach roiled. She turned away from him, shielding herself as best as she could, as the cold water dripped over her.

CHAPTER TWENTY-SIX

JOHANNA

Sankt Georgen an der Gusen, Upper Austria, January 1943

"Papers, please."

Without so much as a tremor Johanna handed her papers to the guard standing by the door of the innocuous-looking, red-roofed building that housed the Granitwerke Mauthausen, the company that managed the quarries worked by the Mauthausen concentration camp.

He flicked through them before handing them back without a word. With her head held high, Johanna proceeded into the building to start her first day as one of the women who worked in the typing pool at the company, a position that Ingrid had arranged for her.

When Ingrid had asked her, a year ago now, whether she was willing to work with the resistance, Johanna's answer had been instant and unequivocal. "*Yes.*" Of course, always, yes. Ingrid had been right; she had nothing left to lose. Her sisters and Franz were all out of reach, perhaps forever; her father was a shell of a man and her mother lived only for her father. There was nothing she wanted to do but fight back; anger and certainty blazed through her like a flame, burning any doubt and fear away.

"You have learned the hard way," Ingrid had said simply. "You can do much good for our cause."

But the next six months had passed with dreary sameness, and Johanna hadn't done any good at all. She'd continued her dull work at the accountant's, coming home every night to eat dinner and listen to the radio with her parents before going to bed. When she'd sought out Ingrid to ask her what could be done, the other woman had pursed her lips and shaken her head.

"Lie low for now, until the danger passes. Until they forget about your sisters and the Jew."

"*Franz*," Johanna had said through gritted teeth. "His name is Franz."

A look of mingled sympathy and irritation had flickered across Ingrid's face. "You need to stop caring so much about people," she'd told her. "There is a greater cause."

"A cause that is *for* the people," Johanna had flashed back. "There is no cause without individuals, and there is no victory without their effort. I will continue to care because that makes me human. The danger is when I *stop* caring."

To her surprise, Ingrid had laughed. "Yes, yes, as your good father said. Very well. Look, perhaps I can find out what has happened to your Franz."

"And my sisters," Johanna had returned quickly. "I need to know where they are."

True to her word, Ingrid had, after a few months, found out where they all were—Birgit and Lotte in Ravensbrück, north of Berlin, while Franz was only a little more than a hundred kilometers away, at Mauthausen, a camp reserved for political prisoners and members of the intelligentsia.

"It is considered one of the worst camps," Ingrid had warned her. "The SS have nicknamed it '*Knochenmühle*.'" The Bone-Grinder. "I'm sorry," she had added, briefly covering Johanna's hand with her own, "but it is unlikely he will survive. He is probably already dead. They treat the Jews the worst, and the journey down to the quarry is called the Stairway of Death. They work them—"

"I understand," Johanna had interjected sharply. "You don't need to say any more."

Yet Ingrid had said enough, for the images she'd brought to mind—bones ground to dust and staircases leading down to hell—tormented Johanna in her weaker moments, when she let herself think about it. What if Ingrid was right and Franz was already dead? She thought she'd know if he'd died, but then she dismissed that as a fanciful, fairy-tale sort of notion. Of course she wouldn't know.

Then, after six months, Ingrid had contacted her, at last. "We are arranging for you to have a position in the typing pool at Granitwerke Mauthausen."

"Mauthausen." Johanna had stared at her in surprise and alarm. "But that is where Franz is."

"This is the company that is in control of the quarry. It is located in Sankt Georgen an der Gusen, about ten kilometers from the camp." Ingrid had smoked silently for several moments, her face drawn, the lines from nose to mouth cut deeply into her skin. She was starting to look old, Johanna had thought, her body thin and angular, her suffering written on her face.

"How did you arrange such a thing?" she'd asked.

Ingrid had shaken her head. "Better not to know. We have people in place, that is all."

"But Mauthausen is over a hundred kilometers from Salzburg," Johanna had said slowly. "How can I work there?"

"You will have to board in the village. It's a very pretty place, with the mountains and the lake. Most of the villagers pretend the camp doesn't exist." Her mouth had twisted and she stubbed out her cigarette in one vicious movement.

"And what will I do? How will this help?" Johanna's mind had been whirling with all this new information.

"For now, simply work there and show what a capable, loyal, devoted servant of the Reich you are. Your time will come."

Johanna had swallowed and nodded. To be working in the office associated with a concentration camp, under the very men who orchestrated the deaths of so many—and to have it be the camp where Franz was. It seemed both a wonderful and terrible thing.

"Will I be able to see him?" she'd asked, her voice wobbling with hope and desperation; Ingrid had grimaced.

"I don't know. It is doubtful, but perhaps, in time. If he's still alive. For now, do nothing but your work. Like I said, you have to be *devoted*." She'd given Johanna a fierce look, and she'd nodded in understanding.

And now Johanna was here, standing in respectful silence, her head bowed, as Frau West, the stern-looking woman in charge of the typing pool, indicated her place. Johanna put her coat on her chair as she sat down and began to type the first of a long list of tools that had been ordered. The work was as mind-numbing as that at the accountant's, yet at the same time every moment in this place frayed her nerves. The men who emerged suddenly from offices, with slicked-back hair and smelling of cigarette smoke, were murderers.

Granitwerke Mauthausen was a subsidiary of the massive Deutsche Erd- und Steinwerke, the building works owned and managed by the SS as part of its vast commercial empire. They controlled quarries, mines, armament and munitions factories, and like Ingrid had said, they worked their laborers to death.

Despite the fear that kept every sense on high alert, Johanna's first day of work was uneventful, even dull, and so were the following weeks and months—every day she typed up lists and letters, none of them offering any relevant information that she could pass on, and then went back to the house in the village where she rented a small, shabby room. She ate a stodgy supper of stew filled out with old potatoes, and then usually went to bed right after. She was merely marking the days, waiting for something to happen.

Then, a year after she'd started, something finally did. A man, blank-faced, not even looking at her, dropped a file on her desk.

"To be typed immediately," he said, and then kept walking.

Johanna looked up in surprise, but the man had already disappeared. She glanced at the file, which looked like any other she might come across, made of yellow card, and yet… strange men did not drop files onto her desk. They all went into the wooden tray and then Frau West divvied out the jobs.

Cautiously, glancing around to make sure she was not being noticed, Johanna opened the file. It held only one page, with a few lines quickly scrawled onto it, clearly in some sort of code. It looked, Johanna realized, like poetry. She stared at it in stupefaction, having no idea what it could mean.

"Fräulein Eder?" Frau West's voice cut sharply across the clacking and clatter of the typewriters, and quickly Johanna closed the file and replaced it on her desk. Her heart was thudding as Frau West came toward her.

"Do you need more work?" she demanded, and Johanna shook her head.

"No, Frau West. *Danke.*" She reached for a clean sheet of paper and fed it through the typewriter, the incriminating file lying only inches from her supervisor. She willed herself not to look at it, not to give anything away. Finally, after what felt like an age, Frau West moved on.

Johanna worked for the rest of the afternoon, doing her best to keep her expression composed as her mind raced. What was the meaning of the lines of poetry? And what was she to do with the information? She supposed the answer to the first question didn't matter; as for the second, the only thing she could think of was to tell Ingrid. She memorized the lines of poetry and destroyed the file; when she returned home, as she did once a month, she went to the café in Elisabeth-Vorstadt and left the strange message of poetry with the man behind the bar, having no idea if what she'd done was useful at all.

Still, the whole bizarre episode had given her an idea; the man who had left the file most likely had come from the camp, to pass messages from there to the outside world. What if she visited Mauthausen herself and was somehow able to find Franz? Surely it was possible. Dangerous, yes, foolish, certainly, but possible.

Some of her superiors at Granitwerke moved regularly between the office and the camp: foremen, their clothes covered in a thin, gray film of granite dust, came to give reports, and SS officers went to inspect prisoners to see if they were able to work. Ten kilometers was a fair distance, but if she had to, she could walk it. She just needed a pretext to get into the camp itself.

She began to fantasize about a reunion with Franz; in her mind she brushed away all the obstacles—the barbed wire, the watchtowers, the guards and the guns—and she pictured only her and Franz running towards each other under a wide blue sky. He'd sweep her up into his arms and kiss her tenderly; the whole world would melt away.

*

A few days later, another file landed on her desk. Johanna bolted upright as she saw the man walk quickly away.

"Fräulein Eder—" Frau West began in remonstration but Johanna gabbled something about needing to use the toilet. She hurried after the man, catching up with him in the corridor.

"*Mein* Herr, please," she whispered breathlessly. "I need to know—" Johanna caught his sleeve, and he jerked his arm away, giving her a quelling look. He was wearing the uniform of a functionary, a civilian who worked under the SS in camp administration.

"Please," she whispered. "You come from the camp. I need to go there. I need to find someone." The man looked at her incredulously; his face was filled with fury rather than fear. Johanna realized how foolhardy she was being, and for what? It wasn't as if she could rescue Franz, or even help him. And by confronting this man, her fellow worker in the resistance, she could be jeopardizing the whole operation and endangering both their lives. Even so, now that she'd got this far, she felt compelled to persist. "Franz Weber," she whispered. "A Jew from Vienna, then Salzburg. Can you tell me what block he is in?"

Tight-lipped, the man simply shook his head and walked away. Johanna watched in despair, and then, a few days later, another file dropped on her desk. This one had another incomprehensible message, but it was followed by two hastily scrawled words: *Block 13.*

The next day, after work, Johanna put a typed list of tools in a file folder and then took the bus to Mauthausen, a small town on the Danube, and then walked the rest of the way to the camp. It was easy enough to find, a sprawling scene of barbed wire and barracks, watchtowers pointing to the sky, the stench of suffering and death heavy in the air. She clutched the file to her chest, keeping her head high and her gaze haughtily officious as she approached the camp's gate.

"I am here to see Kommandant Stuber," Johanna announced sharply; she'd looked up the name of one of the commandants of camp administration in the staff book at the office. "I have to deliver classified information from the Granitwerke immediately." She waved the file with its Granitwerke stamp on the front, but the guard barely glanced at it.

"Papers," he said, holding out his hand, and she gave them over. "And the file?"

"I told you, it is classified. Ask Kommandant Stuber if you wish to know what it contains." She met his gaze coolly, almost believing her own story, and with a shrug he waved her through.

Johanna walked into the camp on wobbly legs, doing her best to look as if she knew where she was going. It was already early evening, darkness falling swiftly; she hoped the quarry workers would have returned.

The guard had already forgotten about her, not even checking to see if she was going to the block of administrative buildings at one end of the vast compound. Quickly she walked the other way, towards the barracks. The sight of a man shuffling toward one of the blocks had her faltering in her step. He looked… he looked… like a *skeleton.* She gazed in stupefied horror at his arms and legs, skin stretched over bone. She could even see the outlines of his shin bones, like two twigs twined together. He barely looked human, and yet he, like all the others, was surely being sent to work in the quarry for ten hours or more a day.

A sudden rage, fiercer than ever before, burned in her chest. It was more than monstrous, what they were doing here and everywhere. It was beyond what anyone could even comprehend as evil. To grasp the whole horror of it was impossible; her mind shied away as she clutched the file to her chest and walked blindly on, searching for Block 13, determined now more than ever to find Franz. Would he look like that man? Worse? *Dear God, let him still be alive.*

Finally she came to the right block; she stood in front of the wooden hut, like dozens of others, her heart thudding, her hands clammy. She could hardly walk inside, and yet she longed to.

"*Johanna?* Johanna Eder?"

She whirled around, blinking at the sight of a man she only vaguely recognized. He was not quite as emaciated as the other man she'd seen shuffling along, but he looked sinewy and pale, a haunted look in his eyes, his head shaven, as he stared at her in disbelief.

"I—"

"Don't you remember me?" He let out a huff of something almost like laughter. "God knows I look different. I'm Werner Haas. Birgit's Werner."

Her mouth dropped open. "What on earth are you doing here?"

"What are you…?" He glanced around and then took her arm, ushering her over to the side of the barracks where they were more hidden from view. "Birgit? Is she all right? I heard she was arrested."

Johanna stared at him, still too shocked to formulate a reply. He was wearing, she realized, the striped uniform of a prisoner. "You're… you're an inmate here?" she said stupidly, for it was surely obvious.

Werner's mouth twisted. "Yes, I've been here for two years."

"But why? I mean, you're a—" She stopped abruptly as he gave a bitter laugh.

"A Nazi? I tried to be one, it's true, but I found I didn't have the stomach for it." He shook his head. "I'm ashamed of myself. Please tell me Birgit is all right. After they arrested me… I had to tell them—"

"It was you?" Johanna's mind was spinning so fast she felt dizzy. "You told them about us? About Franz?" His name came out in a cry.

"About you? No. Your name never crossed my lips. I told them about Sister Kunigunde at the abbey. She was the only name I knew. I never said anything about Birgit. They didn't get that from me."

"Kunigunde was executed," Johanna told him coldly. "Did you know that?"

Werner stared down at the ground. "I thought she must have been," he said quietly.

"How could you—"

Werner nodded, accepting her anger as his due. "I'm not as brave as I thought I was." He held his hand out to her and Johanna let out a gasp. It was a mangled, useless, dead-looking thing, the fingers twisted beyond recognition. It looked like a waxwork.

"I'm sorry about Kunigunde," he said. "Truly. But Birgit—"

"She and Lotte were taken to Ravensbrück."

"Oh, God." Werner turned away, hunching his shoulders. Johanna glanced around, and saw two SS officers walking near them.

"Werner, I'm trying to find Franz Weber. My father's apprentice—do you remember? He's a Jew, and I believe he's in this barracks. Have you seen him?"

"Franz? Yes." He turned back to her, his forehead furrowed, as the officers walked past.

"He's alive?" Relief flooded through her, turning her weak. She reached one hand out to the wall of the barracks to steady herself. "Can you get him for me? Please? I need to talk to him, see him—"

He frowned, shaking his head. "How did you even get in here, Johanna—"

"I work in the office nearby. I told them I had a file to deliver."

"Johanna, that's dangerous—"

"I know it's dangerous," she snapped. "I wanted to take the risk. Please, *please* fetch Franz for me."

Werner stared at her for a moment, and then, resigned, he nodded. "I'll see if I can find him. But Johanna… when you're back in Salzburg… can you take a message to my father? Georg Haas. He lives in Aigen, on Traunstrasse, number 22. Tell him… tell him perhaps now he can finally be proud of me."

Johanna gazed at him silently as he swallowed hard, and then she nodded. "I'll try."

"Thank you."

Werner slipped back into the barracks while Johanna waited, her eyes closed, everything in her racing, straining.

She heard the slap of the door opening and closing again, and then footsteps. She opened her eyes. Stared. *That man isn't Franz* was her first wild thought. *It can't be.* Why, the man standing in front of her—he looked old! He looked as if he were at least fifty or more, not under thirty. His head was shaven, his scalp gleaming white, the bones of his face so sharply drawn she could see his skull plainly, his body like a stick underneath the shapeless uniform. She opened her mouth. Closed it.

"Johanna." The voice, little more than a rasp, was recognizable. Johanna let out a cry and then covered her mouth with her hand. "Why did you come here?" Franz demanded; he sounded angry.

Johanna rushed to him, flinging her arms around him, his bones pressing sharply into her, his body so painfully thin she feared she might snap him right in half. He smelled terrible, he felt strange, but he was Franz. *Franz.* "I had to see you," she whispered.

Franz's arms came around her as he shook his head. "I never wanted you to see me like this," he choked out, and then, to her horror, he began to cry.

"Franz… *Franz.*"

"I never wanted you to see me like this," he said again as tears trickled down his wrinkled, withered cheeks. "Or this place. Oh God, this place…" He shook his head again. "This terrible, terrible place."

"It can't go on forever," she whispered. "It *can't.*"

"What happened to Birgit and Lotte?"

"They're at Ravensbrück."

"Your father?"

"He's still the same," she told him, even though he was worse.

"And you? How on earth did you get here?" Quickly she told him about her job, and he drew back. "You *work* for them?"

"It's—it's not like that," she said quickly. She wouldn't burden him with the knowledge of details, information that could be tortured out of him if anyone ever suspected.

He stared at her for a moment, and then he lowered his voice to a whisper she strained to hear. "You mean you are doing… other work? Risking your life?"

"Why shouldn't I, after everything that has happened? If we don't risk our lives, nothing will change."

"But your *life,* Johanna—"

"It's just one life." She thought of Ingrid, talking about serving the cause rather than saving individuals. She understood the sentiment more now, and yet *this* was what she was fighting for—her and Franz together, two beating hearts, a life shared still to dream of. "If you promise to stay alive," she told him, "then I will too."

Franz smiled sadly, his lips sticking over his gums, his face so painfully narrow. "I don't know if I can make that promise."

"You must." She held him by the shoulders, staring into his face, longing to imbue him with her strength. "Remember our apartment in Vienna? It's there, waiting for us. The mirrors, the paintings on the wall, the view of Stephansplatz. It's there. I swear to you it is."

For a second, no more, she saw the old wry gleam in his eyes. "What about the farmhouse in the Tyrol?"

"That too," she said fiercely. "All of it—and Paris! You still have to take me to Paris." He let out a laugh that sounded more like a sob. "I'll hold you to it," she told him. "I swear. You won't believe how cross I will be if you don't take me. I still want to see the Eiffel Tower, Franz."

"I couldn't bear to make you cross," he told her with the ghost of a smile, his eyes bright with tears.

Somewhere a whistle blew and a dog barked. Franz threw a fearful glance behind him. "This is so dangerous, for both of us. You're lucky Werner is in charge of this barracks. He's a reasonable man, unlike some others."

"He's a kapo?" Johanna exclaimed, recoiling at the knowledge. Even in the office she had heard about the prisoners who were chosen by the SS to act as guards; they were disdained and reviled, often doling out harm on their fellow inmates to obtain little luxuries for themselves, or even just because they could.

"He's one of the good ones. He does what he can—he finds extra food, sends us to the infirmary if we're ill. Don't judge him for it. Now, go." He gave her a gentle push. "If we mean to keep those promises, you must leave. Now. Don't take such a risk again, Johanna. It's not worth it."

Johanna nodded, even though she wanted to cry out, to scream, to sob. She forced a smile as she embraced Franz one more time, memorizing the feel of him, so different, and then she watched him go back into the barracks, his shoulders slumped, an old man.

After the door had closed behind him she walked blindly back through the camp, through the gate, and out into the night. She'd only gone a few meters towards the town before she sank to her knees by the side of the road and began to sob.

CHAPTER TWENTY-SEVEN

BIRGIT

Ravensbrück, Germany, August 1944

A whisper was running through the camp, as dangerous as wildfire. *The Allies have invaded.* No one knew for sure, although the skies were often filled with fighter planes, the growl and swoop of them causing the prisoners to silently cheer and rejoice, even though they did not betray so much as a flicker of what they were feeling as they went about their work—hauling stones, shoveling dirt, making—and sabotaging—the rockets that Germany was desperate to send westward.

The guards who prowled around them seemed more short-tempered than usual, snapping or slapping at every imagined provocation, flinging their food—a barrel of porridge or stew, and another of coffee or water—into the barracks at night with so much force that much of it spilled. They whipped a prisoner for merely a look, more often than they usually did, and many mornings they made them stand for hours at roll call as the sun rose and then beat down high above, for absolutely no reason at all.

No one actually seemed to mind. "If they're angry, they're scared," one woman said, her eyes gleaming in her gaunt face. "They're losing. Finally, they're losing. It won't be long now. It can't be."

Birgit wasn't so sure. She wanted to hope, God knew, but time and suffering had beaten it out of her. She could no longer imagine a world where Nazis did not exult in their reign of terror, as much as she wished she could. She had forgotten what freedom felt like—to lie in a soft bed and stretch, to stroll down a street, or simply to wash her face. Even as the whispers of defeat and retreat traveled around the camp, she struggled to believe in them, or to feel anything but resentment or despair.

Surely the Nazis would fight to the very last man, and even if they *did* lose, would they allow their prisoners to survive, or kill them all beforehand, either out of spite or to hide the evidence of their evil? Either way, Birgit could not see a future where she and Lotte—and Werner and Franz—strolled out of the camps, whole and healthy and free.

Lotte, nearly two years on from their arrival at Ravensbrück, had somehow continued to maintain her indefatigable good spirits, despite the starvation rations, the back-breaking work, the endless abuse. She prayed every morning and night, lauds and compline, whispering the words so as not to attract the attention of the guards. Over the course of the months and years, women had begun to join her, a huddled little group of devotees, the faith they clung to shining in their eyes, their faces: Catholic Poles and Orthodox Russians, women who had only a little German or even none at all, who found joy even in the midst of their terrible brokenness, heads bent together as they fervently whispered their prayers to God and trusted that He heard and would one day answer.

Birgit never joined her sister at these times. She couldn't bring herself to, even though she thought it seemed to help Lotte and some of the others, because she was too angry at a God who, in the midst of such grievous suffering, had made himself so terribly absent.

"God is here, Birgit," Lotte would insist, her lovely face, now so painfully thin, wreathed in smiles. She looked even more ethereal now, her eyes alight, her body so slender, her hair grown long, in wild blond tangles about her lovely face. Unlike the Jews and Poles, Germanic women had not been forced to have their heads shaved, although it meant they often lived with a head of matted, dirty, lice-ridden hair. "He is working here, in so many ways. You simply need to believe."

"I need to *see*," Birgit had snapped. "And I don't." She felt mean to speak to her sister so, but her anger—even if it was aimed at God—sometimes felt like the only thing that sustained her. Without its strength she would give in to despair, and then she feared her fighting would be over. She would no longer have the will to keep living—day in and day out, breath after breath, fighting starvation and cold, beatings and cruelty, and most of all, a swamping sense of futility.

When they'd first arrived at the camp, struggling to acclimatize to a world even more brutal than what they'd experienced before, Birgit had expected to be killed right away. She'd *wanted* to die, because the prospect of existing in this living hell for any length of time had sickened and terrified her. Death was surely preferable, as long as it was quick.

A bullet in the head would be quick, and plenty of women were shot for no reason at all, dragged out of line during roll call and put against a wall, their lives ended in a single moment. After just a few months, Birgit stopped so much as blinking an eye when it happened. Sometimes she just felt tired, even irritated, by the wait, for they had to stand the whole while.

Then there were the gas chambers, constructed during her first few months at the camp, and used with horrifying regularity, mostly for the Jews and gypsies. Even so, she'd thought more than once that it was only a matter of time before she was taken to them, and the thought brought mostly relief.

She'd seen piles of dead bodies thrown into carts, legs and arms dangling. Just as she'd seen the children who roamed the camp like desperate, feral dogs, until they wasted away to nothing, dying of starvation, if they weren't first targeted by a vicious guard, just for their amusement. Some of the SS *Aufserherinnen,* Birgit had found, were even crueler than the male guards. The prisoners called one such woman, a stony-faced guard who delighted in tormenting prisoners in sick and novel ways, the "Beast of Ravensbrück."

As the months had passed, Birgit had watched as Jewish women were lined up and taken away, never to return. Polish women were singled out; some of them returned, eyes glazed with horror, barely able to walk, while others never did. Birgit had heard whispers of medical experiments being performed on the women; they'd become known as "*Die Kaninchen*," the rabbits. She couldn't bear to think of such horrifying possibilities, even as she supposed nothing could surprise or horrify her any more. She felt flattened and hardened by it all, as if the very humanity was being leached out of her, day by day and drip by drip, and she could not keep it from happening.

Now, nearly two years on, she had nothing left to feel but a weary numbness, and still she didn't die. Early on she and Lotte had been sent out each day with hundreds of others to shovel dirt; it seemed a useless task, moving a pile from here to there, and Birgit was sure it would be the death of them both—back-breaking work with little food or rest; the women who fell during their work were either beaten or shot.

But then someone in authority at the camp had discovered she'd once been a clockmaker, and had sent her to the Siemens factory to make electrical components for V-2 rockets. Lotte had been sent to another factory, to haul metal plates, and so they only saw each other in the evening, to eat a hasty meal before Birgit fell into bed, and Lotte went to pray.

The days at the factory were easier than the shoveling, and yet they were, in their own way, terrible. Birgit knew the rockets would be used against innocent people, as well as the Allies she was praying would save her, and everyone she loved, even as she struggled to pray or believe at all.

The mood in the factory was desperate and unrelenting; the work they were doing was far more important to Germany's war effort than shoveling dirt, and so they were constantly patrolled by grim-faced guards, who were all too quick to pull someone from her workstation if they thought she was being too slow. Somehow the guards thought a beating made you work faster, but Birgit knew nothing did.

A month after she'd started in the factory, Birgit looked down at the pile of her components on her work station and realized it would take no more than a simple twist of her fingers to render one of them useless. No one would know until it was too late—until the rocket was fired and shown to be faulty.

It only took her a second of indecision before she picked up a component and gave it a little wrench. Then she continued on with her work, her fingers not even trembling as she put the rest of the components together and then into the basket.

Punishment for sabotage was death—either by hanging or a bullet to the head, and that was if you were lucky. If you weren't, the guards might use you for their amusement; an agonizingly leisurely target practice, or perhaps as prey for their dogs—huge, slavering Alsatians that strained at their chains.

And yet I always expected to die here, she thought as she reached for another component, gave another twist. *Why shouldn't I risk this?*

Even though the guards patrolling them wouldn't be able to tell what she was doing, Birgit knew she could still be found out. Every V-2 rocket was numbered, and that number was associated with the prisoner who had worked on it. If one were rendered useless, they would, with a small amount of effort, be able to trace it back to her.

But by that time the war might be over… or I might be dead. The knowledge had been, in a strange way, comforting. When the guard had gone back down the aisle, Birgit had done the same again. This time the woman working next to her, Frieda, saw what she did and let out a soft gasp. Birgit met her stricken gaze with a silent plea of her own; the guard was coming back up the aisle. Frieda could give her up, to save her own skin.

"*Schau weg,*" she whispered. Look away.

Frieda turned away and Birgit took a steadying breath. Would she inform on her? These might be her last moments on earth. So be it.

The guard paused by them, and Birgit's body prickled with a cold sweat. She was both unafraid and completely terrified at the same time, her mind cold and clear as her body trembled. Then he continued on, and Birgit glanced again at Frieda. The other woman gave a small nod and then a twist of her fingers. Filled with an exultant relief, Birgit smiled and kept working.

*

And so the months passed as planes flew overhead and bombs fell on Berlin, only seventy-five kilometers away. Sometimes they could hear the crackle and thuds, and once the town nearby was bombed, the sky lit with a strange, otherworldly orange.

"I'd rather a bomb got me than a Nazi," Birgit told Lotte one night as they lay together on the wooden board that was their bed, a woman on either side of them, and nothing but a thin blanket to cover them all, even though it was September, and in the mornings there was frost on the ground. They could hear the distant crackle of the bombs, the growling of the planes.

Lotte put her arms around her and said nothing; she'd learned, at least, not to offer the platitudes of faith that only annoyed Birgit.

"It will be over soon," she whispered. "It has to be. We must hold on, Birgit, for just a little longer."

Over the months, hopeful whispers had continued to run through the camp, the wildfire burning higher. The Allies had liberated Paris, prisoners said under their breath; Parisians were dancing in the streets. Belgium, too, in September, and soon, they hoped, the Netherlands. They were coming! The Americans and British were finally coming.

But then so were the Soviets, and the guards loved to tell them, with deliberate relish, what the Soviets would do to anyone they found, prisoner or not. Birgit tried to close her ears to their poisonous words about murder and rape, but she still felt hopeless. The Soviets would get to Berlin, to Ravensbrück, before the Americans or British did.

"You don't know that," Lotte insisted, but somehow Birgit did. Nothing had gone right for them so far—both of them here, Werner and Franz most likely dead or in a camp like this one, her father insensible if he hadn't already died. And what about her mother and Johanna? Birgit had no idea where they were, what they were doing, or even if they were alive.

Why shouldn't more bad things happen, even the worst? God didn't care. Birgit didn't say as much to Lotte, for she knew how much it would hurt her, but she felt it all the same, a burning resentment in her heart, her gut.

In late September, as summer faded and a chill entered the air, Birgit developed a cough in her chest. At first it was no more than a tickle, a sense of never quite being able to catch her breath. Then one morning she woke up and felt as if her throat were on fire, or covered in razor blades. Every swallow hurt.

The guards had little time for ill prisoners, Birgit knew. No one was sent to the infirmary, such as it was, unless they had a fever of over one hundred and two, and even then they were usually sent away again, to stumble back to their barracks and shiver under a thin blanket.

Those who became too ill to be useful disappeared, loaded onto stretchers and then into trucks that never want farther than the gas chamber, the crematorium. As much as she'd once wanted to die, Birgit realized that she did not want to die like that.

"You must hold on," Lotte urged her, gladly giving her sister her own blanket, her bowl of soup, even though it meant she went without. "They'll be here soon, Birgit. I swear it."

"Will they? The Americans or the Soviets?" This grim question was followed by a hacking cough that tore at Birgit's chest until she felt as if she were being stabbed with fiery knives. She was drenched in a cold sweat, shivering uncontrollably, barely able to stand at roll call every morning in the chill morning air, and yet still she went on, because the alternative was worse. It infuriated her, that after surviving two winters in the camp, she was falling ill now, so near the end, when a hint of summer still lingered in the air like a taunt of what had once been.

"It's just that you're so weak," Lotte explained gently as she bathed her forehead and fed her soup at night. "Your body can't fight any longer."

"But I have to fight." The despair she'd felt for so long was replaced by a burning desire not to succumb. Not now, when victory was—maybe—so close, if she could just let herself believe in it.

And so she continued—getting up, stumbling outside, going to work. At the factory she fumbled with the electrical components, her fingers feeling thick, her mind so fuzzy she could barely concentrate, her pace far slower than it had ever been before. Frieda quietly made up the difference, saying nothing. Birgit could barely mumble her thanks.

"You won't last unless you get some treatment," Frieda told her under her breath as they filed out one evening, and Birgit stumbled. She would have fallen if Frieda hadn't grabbed her elbow.

"Treatment?" Birgit rasped, trying to laugh. Everything ached. Her head throbbed, her vision blurred, and her chest was on fire.

Death almost—almost—seemed preferable. "Shall I go ask them for medicine, then? A warm compress? A—"

"Even a day's rest in the infirmary would do you a world of good," Frieda replied, a hint of worry in her dark eyes. She was a Pole and a Jew, Birgit knew, and it was amazing she was still alive, still here. Most Jews had been already marked for transport or sent to the gas chamber.

"You're a good worker," Frieda continued, "and they're desperate now more than ever to complete these damnable rockets. They won't want to lose you."

Yet it seemed they did, or at least they didn't mind, for when Birgit took herself to the infirmary that evening, on Lotte's urging, she was sent away without so much as a word, after having waited in the yawning anteroom with several dozen other women who, despite their hacking coughs and flushed faces, received the same indifference.

"Please," Birgit told a nurse before she shut the door. "I'm sure I have a fever—"

"The beds are full," the nurse told her firmly, but not without a flicker of sympathy. Her eyes were troubled, and dazedly Birgit wondered how much it cost her to nurse these poor, pathetic women, beset by illness, starvation and worse, knowing most of them would die or be killed outright.

"Please…" Birgit whispered again, clinging to the doorframe to keep herself upright. She suddenly couldn't bear the thought of going back to the barracks—to the hard wooden plank she had to call a bed, the ragged blankets that offered the barest modicum of warmth. The roll call, sometimes as early as four o'clock in the morning, the eleven hours of work… she couldn't do it. She *couldn't.* "I don't need a bed. Even a chair would do…" The infirmary was warm, at least, and the prospect of sitting in a chair and being able to sleep, to feel warm, seemed right then like the greatest treasure to Birgit.

"Please," she said for a third time, and foolishly she reached a claw-like hand out to the nurse, who backed away. Her kindness extended only so far.

"I'm sorry," she said again, firmly this time, and then closed the door in Birgit's face.

Birgit stood there for a moment, swaying, her legs watery. The other women had already gone; she was alone, with no one to help her. The ten-minute walk back to her barracks might as well have been ten kilometers. She didn't think she could do it. She was sure she couldn't.

Lotte had wanted to come with her, but Birgit had refused, not wanting to get her in trouble for being out at night without permission; even when the *Aufseherin* agreed to let someone out, another guard happening by might decide otherwise. Now she wished her sister was here, because if she collapsed on the way back, there would be no one to help her. If a guard found her, it would be worse for her still.

Slowly Birgit turned around and faced the rest of the camp. The barracks were cloaked in darkness, their humped uniformity reminding her suddenly of loaves of bread in a baker's window. *Bread…* warm, white bread, steaming from the oven, with the golden crust her mother made so beautifully, butter melting into the delicious softness… When had she last eaten something like that?

With painstaking slowness Birgit put one foot in front of the other; it took the utmost focus to manage each step. She had only gone a dozen before she faltered and nearly fell. Somehow she kept herself upright, thinking of her mother's bread.

And then she thought of her father's kindly smile… the case of soft, supple leather she'd had for her tools, her initials engraved on the top… Franz playing the piano while they all sang in harmony… Memories tumbled through her mind, a kaleidoscope of color and warmth and love. The first time Werner had kissed her, when she'd been so surprised, and he'd smiled at her as if he really, truly *liked* her. The sun rising over the Salzkammergut, the pealing of bells in the morning, her mother's *Prügeltorte*, puffed golden and filled with cream… the elevator at the Elektrischer Aufzug, sending them soaring upwards as they'd giggled and grinned… they'd been so *young,* then! So young and innocent, fresh-faced girls who had looked at the world with delight. Everything had been before them… *everything…*

Another step, but her legs were wobbling, her knees weak. Her vision blurred and then blackened. *I can't die now,* she thought, with a sudden, dazed franticness. *Lotte's right. It could be over so soon—months, maybe, or even weeks. I could see my family again… Werner… I can't die now. I won't…*

The words blazed through her mind even as her body rebelled. She took another step and stumbled, and then, as weakness flooded through her, she fell to her knees.

I can't, I can't…

Her hands hit the ground hard as her head swam. Somewhere in the distance she heard a dog bark, one of the terrible, growling Alsatians that loved to rip prisoners to bloody shreds.

I must get up, Birgit thought. *I must. Before the dog finds me…*

But her body would not obey, no matter how urgent her commands to her recalcitrant limbs. Her arms trembled and she managed to heave herself up once, only to fall back down again, her cheek hitting the hard-packed dirt. Her head spun and then stilled.

The dog barked again as her body relaxed into the ground, the fight finally leaving her. It was so peaceful, really, the sky so lovely and dark, the air turning sharp with cold…It would be October soon, if she could just turn her head, she would be able to see the stars…

As her eyes fluttered closed, the dog barked once more.

CHAPTER TWENTY-EIGHT

LOTTE

September 1944

It took Lotte an hour before she decided to go after her sister. She'd wanted to accompany her to the infirmary at the start, had in fact insisted, but Birgit's will had been stronger.

"I won't have you getting into trouble," she'd said between coughs that wracked her whole frame as she'd doubled over, wheezing. "They'll just send me away again, in any case. You know how it is."

"They *can't*," Lotte had exclaimed. She didn't think her sister realized how ill she truly was—she was pale except for her cheeks which possessed a hectic flush, and when Lotte had put her hand on her forehead, she'd had to draw it away quickly, it had been that hot.

"They can and they will," Birgit had replied grimly, and with a surly nod from the *Aufserherin* who had granted her permission to go, she'd headed out into the night.

Lotte had gathered with the others to pray, but for once the words of compline seemed to slide over her, meaningless. "O God, come to our aid. O Lord, make haste to help us…"

She'd never meant the words more, and yet they seemed to bounce off her brain. What if they turned Birgit away? Magda, a Ukrainian Catholic whose entire village had been ruthlessly murdered while she'd been saved for her nursing skills, put her hand on her arm.

"It will be all right," she said in her broken German. "She will get help." Lotte nodded and tried to smile.

But as the minutes passed, and the words of the prayers slipped from her lips, her worry grew. How could she have let Birgit go alone? *She was ill, so ill.* Rising from where she'd been kneeling at the back of the barracks, Lotte slipped past the *Aufseherin* and headed outside.

It was never a good idea for a prisoner to be seen wandering around the camp alone, not without a very good reason. The guards were restless and grew more so every day. They were looking for a reason to make an example of someone, or perhaps just have some sport. Anything to alleviate their boredom—and their fear.

Lotte hurried toward the infirmary, keeping to the shadows. Even though it was only late September, the night air held a chill, and it made her worry for Birgit all the more. Then, as she came within sight of the infirmary, she saw a sprawled body on the ground just a few feet in front of it. *Birgit.*

She ran towards her sister, dropping onto her knees as she cradled Birgit's inert form. "Birgit… Birgit…" Her sister's face was burning, but her body was cold, her limbs seeming boneless, flimsy. Her eyes fluttered open and then rolled back. Lotte bit her lip to keep from crying out.

"I'll get you help," she promised. She looked up, but no one was in sight. And who would help, even if they came? Then, in the distance, one of the SS guards, looking menacing in his great coat, leading an Alsatian held by a length of chain, emerged from the shadows like a monster from her nightmares. Even so, Lotte rose from where she'd been kneeling, flinging one hand out in desperate supplication.

"Please, please, can you help? My sister is ill. She works in the Siemens factory… she is a good worker, she was once a clockmaker."

She fell silent as the guard came forward, the dog straining at its chain, as his dark eyes swept over her. Beneath his peaked cap his hair was as dark as his eyes, his cheeks ruddy, his gaze shrewd and assessing. Lotte met the man's gaze, even though it cost her. She had no idea what he might do—take out his pistol, set the dog on her sister, or, please God, agree to help. *O Lord, make haste to help us…*

To her shock, the guard tied the dog up and then knelt down, scooping Birgit up in his arms. She must have weighed no more than a handful of twigs, the way he carried her so easily—but to where? Lotte made a sound, whether it was a protest or a plea, she didn't know, and he glanced up at her, his dark eyes intent on hers.

"I'll take her to the infirmary."

"Thank you," Lotte whispered, only to have the man continue to stare at her with an unsettling intensity.

"She'll have a bed, medicine, time to rest."

"Thank you, thank you…" Lotte could hardly believe what she was hearing. *Thank you, God…*

"But I expect something in return."

The finality in his tone reverberated through Lotte as her gaze remained locked on his. She knew, of course, what he meant. There were other prisoners who had made such arrangements; they were looked down on by their fellow inmates, scorned, and sometimes even beaten for what was seen as their collaboration. She swallowed, nodded.

"Yes. All right."

The man smiled, and with a jolt Lotte realized she remembered him. He was the man who had told her she was pretty, two endless years ago. He had slapped her bottom as she'd raced toward the shower.

Wordlessly she stepped back as he took Birgit to the infirmary. A chill breeze blew and she wrapped her arms around herself as she waited for the guard, wondering what to do, how it worked. Would he want her to come with him right now? She couldn't let herself think about what would actually happen.

He emerged from the infirmary only a few minutes later. "It's all settled."

"Thank you," Lotte said yet again. She wondered if she should even trust him. It would be just the kind of sheer cruelty the guards delighted in, to promise to help, only to have tossed Birgit into a cart and have her trundled off to the crematorium. Lotte pushed the thought out of her mind. She had to believe.

The guard jerked his head towards the part of the camp where prisoners never went—the SS guards' barracks, a separate enclave. "Come."

Silently she followed him, everything in her feeling surreal and numb; it was the same feeling she'd had when she'd walked from Nonnberg to Getreidegasse, an otherworldly sensation, as if she watching herself, wondering, with a distant, mild curiosity, what would happen next.

The guards' quarters, she saw, were even more comfortable and homely than she might have expected. Besides their sleeping quarters, there was a little shop, a meeting hall, even a cinema. It was almost like a pleasant little town, in the midst of such devastation and evil, a haven for their persecutors. A few guards were milling about, both men and women, but no one bothered to look at her. Lotte supposed they were used to it; guards took prisoners for themselves often enough, and she'd heard rumors of affairs between the male and female guards themselves. Here in this enclave, life possessed a certain kind of normalcy she'd forgotten existed.

The guard ushered her into his barracks and then a single room; Lotte saw a bed, a chair, a washstand, a few hooks for clothes. He closed the door behind her, his coat brushing her arm.

"Wash first," he told her, with a slight curl to his lip. Lotte realized she must reek. The bed creaked as he sat down on it and she understood that he was going to watch her.

Cautiously she went to the washstand. There was a pitcher of water on it, a bar of soap, a rough cloth.

"Should I—" she began, because for a prisoner to use the same water and soap as a guard was the sort of thing that could surely be punishable by death.

"Yes." He sounded impatient as he nodded towards the soap.

Lotte hesitated for a fraction of a second; she thought of resisting, for the sake of her own honor and pride, and realized the pointlessness of it. If she resisted, she might anger him, and that could hurt Birgit. Besides, she had agreed; this was a bargain struck, a deal made, and she would honor it. She would not fight; she would be obedient even in this.

A sudden memory pierced her like a shaft of light. The Mother Abbess's kindly face as she'd spoken to her, "*The religious life is one of painful sacrifice, costly obedience, deliberate humiliation.*"

Lotte had thought she'd understood what she'd meant years ago, when she'd said her penances and cut her hair and donned the habit. Now, however, the words hit her afresh. *Here* was her obedience, her sacrifice, her humiliation, and all for the good of another. The *life* of another. How was it that she could feel more like a nun when she was acting like a whore? Yet she knew it was true.

Quickly she poured some water on the soap and began to scrub her face and arms.

"The dress," the guard commanded, and this time she didn't hesitate. She shrugged the filthy garment off and washed her whole body, running the cloth under her arms and across her belly, between her legs.

"Your hair," he told her, and she poured some of the water from the jug over her hair, soaping it and rinsing it as best as she could. She supposed she should be thankful for the opportunity to wash, and then decided she was. She would be.

"Good," the guard said when she was finished, shivering and dripping naked before him. "Come here."

Lotte walked towards him, willing herself to make every step, for now she trembled from fear as well as cold. She knew so little of what went on between a man and a woman, although she realized this would not be anything like what it was supposed to be, the sacred, loving union of a husband and wife.

"It's a shame how thin you've become," he remarked as he ran a callused hand down her body, from her shoulder to her hip. "You were so pretty before."

Lotte, having no idea how to answer, did not reply.

He curled his other hand around the back of her neck and then drew her to him for a kiss. His lips were both fleshy and hard as he kissed her, his tongue probing her mouth in a way that had her struggling not to choke. After a few seconds he pushed her away, a look of irritation on his face.

"Haven't you ever kissed a man before?"

"No," Lotte said simply, thoughtlessly. The guard stared at her for a moment before he swore and then he stood up, his back to her as he fumbled for his cigarettes.

Lotte stared at him uncertainly, sensing she'd displeased him. Did he disdain her inexperience? Had he wanted a courtesan, here in the camp? She knew there were brothels for guards in the other camps, and the women came from Ravensbrück.

The guard lit his cigarette and smoked silently while Lotte shivered, still wet and dripping. Finally he turned around, eyeing her coldly.

"You're lying to me. How can you never have kissed a man before? You must be well over twenty." He spoke with accusation; Lotte hesitated, not wanting to make him angrier.

"I… I was a nun before this," she said. "I entered the abbey when I was eighteen."

"A *nun*?" The guard stared at her in disbelief, and then he swore again. He kept smoking as he glared at her and she waited, unsure what would happen next. Then, in a savage movement, he threw his cigarette onto the floor and ground it under his boot before striding towards her, grabbing her by the shoulders as he kissed her hard enough to make her want to cry out, his hips thrusting purposefully against her.

Lotte closed her eyes as he flung her onto the bed. She heard him fumbling with his belt buckle, and then, thankfully, wonderfully, she felt as if she were floating above the room. This wasn't happening to her. It *wasn't.* She was high, high above it, floating, floating, mindless of the heaviness of his body on top of her, his ragged breathing, the stabbing pain…

Eventually, although surely only a few minutes later, he rolled off her onto the bed. Lotte felt as if she were coming back into her body, her soul occupying this broken flesh once more. She was conscious of tenderness, stickiness, pain. She didn't move, because she did not know if he wanted her to.

He let out a shuddering breath as he stared at the ceiling. "I wasn't a bad man, you know, before this," he said. He turned to look at her, and after a second's pause, Lotte turned her head so she could see the bleakness in his eyes. "I wasn't," he said again.

She hesitated, having no idea how to reply. "What is your name?" she finally asked, and his mouth opened and closed silently for a few seconds.

"Oskar," he said finally, his voice a throb of surprise and sorrow. His eyes glittered and Lotte thought he might actually cry. Then she saw anger enter his eyes, like iron into the soul, and he rolled up from the bed, reached for her ragged prison dress, and hurled it at her. "Get out," he told her, and his voice was cold.

When Lotte slipped into the barracks just a short while later, several of the women gave her narrowed looks.

"Why is your hair wet?" one of them demanded, and she had no answer.

"Is Birgit all right?" Magda asked, hurrying up to her, and Lotte nodded. "Yes, they've agreed to take her into the infirmary."

The woman who had asked her about her wet hair pursed her lips.

The next day Lotte managed to slip out to the infirmary after the evening meal. At the front door, she was turned away as she knew she would be, but what she really wanted was information.

"Please… is my sister here? Prisoner 66482? She was brought here last night, by one of the guards. He said she would receive medicine—"

The nurse frowned at her, one hand already starting to close the door. "Yes, I think I know who you mean. She's here."

"Has her fever broken?" Lotte asked eagerly, relief flooding through her. Birgit was safe; she would get better. It was going to be all right.

"How should I know?" the nurse demanded in a surly tone, and closed the door.

That evening, while Lotte was praying with the others, the *Aufseherin* shouted her name and jerked a thumb towards the door.

"You're wanted," she said, and it felt as if every woman in the room froze, understanding trickling icily through them as they all stared at her. Lotte rose from where she'd been kneeling and walked on unsteady legs to the front of the room. A few women hissed as she went by.

Again? Already? she thought numbly as she made her way to the guards' enclave, wondering if she would be stopped, beaten, maybe even shot. She wasn't allowed here, yet new rules existed now for women like her. A few of the guards loitering about glanced at her but said nothing.

Oskar—could she even think of him as Oskar, like a person, someone she *knew*?—was waiting outside his barracks, his arms folded, already looking impatient. Lotte stood in front of him, unsure how to greet him. She wanted to ask him how long he would summon her for, but she knew it was a question she didn't dare ask. Besides, she realized she already knew the answer. As long as he wanted.

He remained silent as he turned to go inside, and she followed, longing for the sense of surreality she'd felt the night before, cloaking her in its comforting numbness. She didn't feel it now; she was all too aware of her hard-beating heart, the soreness still between her legs, the sense of inevitability, the terror lurking at the fringes of her mind, the resolve that stole through her bones.

The moment she crossed the threshold of his room he grabbed her, slamming the door shut and then pushing her against it so her cheek hit the wood hard and her ears rang. She opened her mouth to say something—she knew not what—but he was already yanking at her dress, tearing the thin cloth, his body against her back as she closed her eyes. She could feel his hot breath on her cheek.

Afterwards he fell onto the bed as if exhausted, one arm thrown over his eyes. Lotte pulled her dress down, her legs trembling so much she feared she would not be able to stay upright.

Lord, give me strength to stand. She put one hand against the door to steady herself.

"I've told them your sister has to stay in the infirmary for at least two weeks," he told her, his arm still over his eyes. "And when she's released, she'll be put on knitting duty. So will you."

Lotte opened her mouth, closed it. Knitting duty—knitting socks for soldiers—was the easiest of duties in the entire camp, reserved for women who had been singled out for favor or who were too ill to do anything else. Some women were even able to use the leftover wool to knit themselves sweaters. The room was barely supervised, and the women had more freedom than any of the other prisoners.

"Thank you," she whispered.

Oskar lowered his arm from his eyes to give her a fathomless look. "I was a bookkeeper before the war," he said. He seemed to be waiting for a response.

"Do you miss it?" she asked after a moment, and he let out a choked laugh as he lay his arm back over his eyes, as if he couldn't bear the sight of her.

"Yes," he said, his voice muffled. "I do." He turned away from her, his shoulder hunched. "You can go."

Lotte stared at him for a moment, having a strange yet strong urge to comfort him—*him,* her attacker, a man capable of evil that she'd experienced and more she didn't even know of—for heaven only knew what he'd done, what he was guilty of—and yet, a man. A man who could, perhaps, be forgiven.

"God loves you," she said impulsively, wondering if she was mad to say such a thing in a moment like this.

Oskar was silent for a moment, and then he let out a huff of weary laughter. "No, he doesn't. He can't." He flung an arm out towards the door, his back still to her, his voice hardening. "Now, go."

CHAPTER TWENTY-NINE

JOHANNA

Mauthausen Granitwerke, January 1945

Johanna had been passing on messages to Ingrid for a year, written in a code she didn't understand but knew must be important. Almost every month she dutifully went home and passed the messages on; she could no longer visit Salzburg so often, thanks to longer hours and fewer buses.

Some months back Ingrid had told her to stop going to the coffeehouse for it had become too obvious; she'd arranged for Johanna to leave messages folded and pushed under the slats of a bench in Mirabellgarten, always at three o'clock on a Saturday afternoon.

Johanna refused to think about what it meant—that it had become obvious—although that in turn was obvious enough. They were being watched, or at least Ingrid suspected they were being watched. Every time the unnamed administrator dropped a file on her desk, Johanna wondered if it would be his last—and hers. If they were discovered, they would both be shot. And as the days bled into months, she thought it likely they would be discovered. Surely it was only a matter of time.

Still she continued to type the letters and lists, and pass on the information as regularly as she could. She longed to return to the camp to see Franz, but she knew she couldn't take such a risk again, and in truth a small, shameful part of her didn't want to see him like that again, or in an even worse state, just as she knew he wouldn't want to be seen. It saddened her, that knowledge, but it also filled her with determination. Somehow they would survive all this. *Somehow…*

By the new year, the mood at Granitwerke and indeed throughout the whole Reich had become even more dangerously desperate. Day by day, as Johanna continued to type, doors slammed and footsteps sounded in halls, and she heard urgent whispers and sudden shouts. Supervisors were short-tempered. Everyone was tense, silent, alert to danger. The other secretaries had stopped taking lunches to gossip and smoke, and stayed at their desks, hunched over their typewriters, meeting no one's eye.

It all spoke to Johanna of a horrible futility; Germany was losing the war, of that there could be no question. The American and British Allies had already liberated France, the Netherlands, Belgium. The Soviets were approaching the borders of Germany itself. Planes strafed the skies on an almost nightly basis, and the photographs of their devastation—"the Allied atrocities"—showed just how effective they were. No matter how the newspapers liked to couch the German Army's "strategic withdrawals," the fact remained that the Wehrmacht was in near-constant retreat.

Johanna and her landlady had listened to Hitler's broadcast on the thirtieth of January; she had tried to keep her expression neutral as he had railed against Bolshevism and Jews with a shrill, manic desperation. When he had spoken of the sacrifice everyone would be called to make, her gaze had flitted to the landlady's, who had quickly looked away, neither of them saying a word, yet both of them knowing Hitler's cry for victory was really an admission of defeat.

Meanwhile the smoke stacks above the camp belched thick black smoke into the sky more than ever before, filling Johanna with both bitterness and fear. Even now, when the Nazis were surely on the cusp of surrender, they continued their reign of terror. It was so incredibly unfair, so utterly evil, that she felt as if she were constantly screaming inside, even as she typed so sedately. *Sehr geehrte herren…* Dear Sirs.

And then, on the second of February, everything changed. Johanna sensed the weirdly heightened mood as she walked into Granitwerke on the Friday, the tension and more bizarrely, the exultation, that seemed to tauten the air as she went to her desk. She heard a burst of hard laughter, and as one of the SS guards left his office, he tossed a joke over his shoulder about "joining the hare hunt." Something about his tone, the callous cruelty of it underscored by unmistakable relish, made her tense even as she strove to seem natural.

"What are they talking about?" she asked one of the other typists in a low voice, doing her best to sound casual. She sat at her desk and pulled her typewriter toward her, as if she didn't much care about the answer.

"Didn't you hear the sirens last night?" The typist, Anna, raised her eyebrows. "There was a breakout from the camp."

"A breakout?" Johanna couldn't keep the sharpness from her voice. "You mean, prisoners escaped?"

Anna rolled her eyes. "Who else? About five hundred of them, apparently."

"But how?" *Had Franz…?*

Anna shrugged, already bored. "How should I know?"

Over the course of the morning Johanna gleaned the details: five hundred prisoners, armed with nothing more than paving stones, fire extinguishers, or even just pieces of coal, had rushed the watchtowers and thrown wet blankets over the electric fences to short-circuit them.

"They were desperate, of course," another of the typists, Else, told her in a low voice. "They were from Block 20, Soviets and political prisoners. No one gets out of there alive." She looked away quickly, as if she'd said too much.

"All of them were from Block 20?" Johanna asked, hearing an urgency in her voice that she knew she shouldn't reveal. Else nodded.

"And did they… did they escape? I mean—"

"No, they were too weak, of course. Most of them were rounded up right away. The rest…" She swallowed, looking around furtively. "Didn't you hear the shots?"

Johanna shook her head. She'd become so used to noises at night—noises she didn't want to think about—that she'd trained herself to sleep through them.

"They're still hunting them down," Else said, lowering her voice even further. "Some of the men in town have joined in, to look for them. The Hitler Youth and the old men. They all want their turn." Else's mouth twisted as Johanna vaguely recalled doors slamming, a shout in the street, before she'd rolled over and gone back to sleep. She had long ago reconciled herself to the fact that if they came for her, there would be nothing she could do about it. "They're calling it the 'Mühlviertel Hare Hunt,'" Else finished with a grimace. "They've told everyone involved not to bring back anyone alive."

Johanna's stomach cramped and she nodded quickly, looking away. It shouldn't surprise her, not after everything she'd seen and heard, and yet it did. It always did.

She spent the rest of the day trying to focus on work, but her mind was spinning uselessly. Franz wouldn't have been involved, she felt sure of that, and yet she also knew such acts of rebellion led to reprisals. Severe reprisals for everyone, even those who had not been involved.

It might not matter. He is most likely dead. You haven't seen him for nearly a year, and those smoke stacks are working nearly every day…

She bit her lip, hard enough to taste blood, so she would not cry out.

Her mind was still spinning, her heart heavy, as she left for the day. Already the sky had grown dark, and a bitter wind, metallic with the promise of snow, blew down from the mountains. Were the men still out there somewhere in the woods, hiding, hoping, fighting for their lives, or were they already dead, rounded up and shot in the head? She'd just crossed the street to head back to her boarding house when someone bumped into her, hard enough to make her cry out.

"They know." The voice was low and urgent in her ear. "Don't go back to your lodgings. You must leave at once."

For a second the words didn't penetrate. Johanna was still rubbing her shoulder, feeling ridiculously aggrieved, as the person who had bumped into her—a man in uniform, someone she didn't recognize—walked past her.

They know. She stilled, her arms dropping to her sides. Was it a trick? Were they waiting to see if she ran, so they could indict her? Or did they really know? Had this attempted breakout exposed a weak link in the chains of resistance?

Her heart felt as if it were being squeezed in her chest. She thought she had reconciled herself to the possibility of discovery, but in that moment she knew she hadn't. She took several breaths to calm herself, scanning the street, relieved to see that no one was paying her attention… for now. The man who had whispered to her had already disappeared.

Slowly, so as not to attract notice, she turned around and began walking towards the train station. She had no idea when the next train to Salzburg would be, or if there would even be one that day. Trains had become notoriously infrequent and unreliable. Even if she did get on a train, she would almost certainly be asked for her papers at some point. If they really did know she was involved in the resistance, it could be as good as a death sentence. What could she do? Where she could go?

Johanna kept walking as she tried to think, her mind racing down blind alleys and finding only dead ends. She could not go back to her boarding house. She could not get on the train. If it was a trick, so be it, but she could not take the risk that it wasn't. But where could she go? Salzburg—home—was nearly one hundred and fifty kilometers away. Linz was only fifteen kilometers, but it was still a long way to walk as night was coming on, when the weather was below freezing and she had no food or shelter.

Johanna's steps slowed as the impossibility of her situation slammed into her. This wasn't a puzzle where she simply had to find the missing piece, or a game where she just needed to know the rules. This was her life, and she could see no way ahead.

She jumped as she heard a car coming up behind her, and as she pressed herself against a building, a Jeep roared by. She glimpsed several SS, rifles resting against their shoulders. *They were going on their hare hunt.*

She took a deep breath and then she kept walking. Somehow she would have to get to Salzburg, or at least to Linz, where she might be able to find a place to hide. But until when? What if the war wasn't over for weeks or even months?

She couldn't go home, Johanna realized, because she did not dare implicate her parents. Nor could she go to Ingrid, because she might already be implicated. *But where?* There had to be somewhere, some safe place.

Then an address fell into her head; she had not gone to 22 Traunstrasse in Aigen since Werner had asked her to, nearly a year ago. She should have, Johanna knew, but caring for her parents and delivering messages to Ingrid had taken up all of her mind, all of her time. But she would go there now. At least she would try.

As she left the town, Johanna veered onto a dirt track that ran alongside a snowy field. Night was falling, which gave her some protection, but she was all too aware that they must still be looking for prisoners, and they would undoubtedly shoot at anything that moved.

Oh God, what if she was being stupid? What if that man had been teasing her, or maybe he'd just been wrong? Wandering out here in the woods on a winter's night was a suicide mission, and that wasn't even taking into account the SS patrolling the area, and who knew who else.

She walked west for an hour, aligning herself by the hills that ringed the horizon, her fingers numb in her thin gloves, her coat little protection against the arctic winds, the temperature dropping steadily as night drew in.

Finally, *finally*, she stumbled upon a farmhouse—and a barn. Johanna skirted the farmhouse, making sure to give it and any barking dogs or nosy people a wide berth. Then she crept into the barn, blinking in the gloom. Slowly she made out a pile of hay, several cows snuffling in their stalls—and two men half-collapsed on the floor.

She let out a soft gasp, and one of them looked up, his eyes seeming to blaze into hers.

"*Bitte*," he said, but he sounded angry rather than pleading.

"I'm a friend," Johanna said quietly. She closed the door behind her. One of the cows lowed, making her jump. She was not used to animals. The men, she saw, were filthy and gaunt, their striped prisoner uniforms ragged and stained. Here were two rabbits that had escaped that damnable hunt, she thought with a savage sort of satisfaction. If it was at all within her power, she would not let them be caught. "You are safe with me," she told them, hoping they understood, for they were undoubtedly Russian.

Slowly the one who had spoken nodded.

"The SS are still out there, looking," Johanna said as she came towards them. She wished she had some food or water to offer, but she had nothing. "You should stay here until it is safe."

"*Da*," the man said gruffly. "*Spasiba*."

Johanna nodded and eased herself down on the pile of hay, pulling her knees up to her chest. It was warmer in the barn, but only a little, and the rustling of the cows was an unfamiliar sound. Her stomach growled; she hadn't eaten since lunch, a sandwich of black bread and meat paste. She did not know when she would eat again. And how would she get all the way back to Aigen?

But then she thought of what these men had endured, how much they were willing to risk for their freedom, and any flicker of fear or self-pity vanished. If they had been brave enough to break out of a camp guarded by armed men and electric fences, she could get herself back to safety.

With this thought foremost in her mind, she let her head fall onto her knees, and the tension that had been banding her body began to ease as she was lulled to sleep by the cows' rustling, the very sound that had first alarmed her.

It took Johanna nearly a week to get to Aigen. She walked for much of it, having left the Soviets a little while after their night in the barn, all of them acknowledging it was safer if they did not travel together.

She subsisted on potatoes scavenged secretly from people's barns, melted snow, and hope. One night a widow came out to the barn where she was sleeping with a bowl of soup and a hunk of bread. Johanna fell on it ravenously, while the woman watched, grim-faced rather than sympathetic.

"When the Allies come," she said, "remember I helped you."

On the other side of Linz a farmer gave her a ride in his wagon for nearly fifty kilometers. He asked no questions, and he clearly didn't want to hear any answers. Johanna was too exhausted to care. She was filthy, hungry, and scared, and she didn't feel quite human anymore. By the time she reached Aigen, she thought she must look feral or mad, even though she'd done her best to tidy her hair and brush off her coat.

But she was here, on Traunstrasse, half-staggering down the street as she looked for number 22. As she passed number 34, she paused; she knew the elegant yellow villa with its private park and wrought-iron railings had been the von Trapps' family home, and was now the summer residence of Heinrich Himmler.

She recalled meeting Maria von Trapp all those years ago, how simple and happy those days had seemed. Remembering the girl she'd been, so anxious to make something of her life, angry at her mother's refusal to let her attend secretarial school… Johanna didn't know whether she wanted to laugh at herself or give herself a good shake. *You were a fool,* she thought, *but at least you had the luxury of being so.* She walked on.

Number 22 was a far more modest house but still elegant in its proportions, although the paint was peeling and one of the shutters was askew. Johanna hesitated only a moment before knocking.

The man who shuffled to the door looked old and weary; his thinning hair was white and his shoulders were stooped. Still, Johanna saw something of Werner in his face, the hazel eyes, the look of amiability that had been whittled away by suffering and fear.

"*Ja?*" he said warily, holding the door only half open.

"Are you Georg Haas?" she asked, and his eyes narrowed with suspicion.

"*Ja—*"

"You don't know me," Johanna said quickly, "but I have a message from your son, Werner."

He stiffened, his hand tightening on the doorknob. "How could you possibly have a message from my son?"

"He's in Mauthausen. I was there. I was working for Granitwerke, the company that manages the quarry." She was still speaking quickly, glancing around the empty street as she did so. "Please, may I come in?"

Georg Haas looked caught between shock and suspicion, but after a second's pause he nodded wordlessly and stepped inside.

The house was as shabby inside as it was outside, with bare patches on the wall where paintings once must have hung. The only furniture in the narrow, high-ceilinged sitting room was a moth-eaten velveteen chaise and a few armchairs, the silk shiny with wear.

Johanna perched on the edge of one of the chairs while Georg Haas stood, his arms crossed as he frowned down at her. He was a frail man, the energy and interest sapped out of him, leaving him looking little more than a shell, his face heavily lined, his hair wispy.

"Well?" he asked.

Haltingly, overcome suddenly by exhaustion now that she was actually, possibly safe, Johanna explained how she'd spoken to Werner, and what he'd said.

"He is helping in the camp," she said carefully, for she realized suddenly that she did not actually know where this man's sympathies lay, although she had hoped, based on what Werner had intimated, that they would not be with the current regime. God help her if that was not the case. She'd taken a risk, coming here, but she'd had no other choice. "He was helping the prisoners, limiting their suffering as much as he could. He said he hoped you were proud of him now."

Georg's lips trembled and he wiped a tear that had leaked from his eye as he shook his head. "Poor boy. My poor boy." He drew in a shuddering breath. "Did they hurt him… the Gestapo? I know he was arrested. Tortured."

"His hand," Johanna said quietly. "It is mangled."

He nodded slowly, accepting. "And this was a year ago that you saw him?"

"Yes, about."

Georg sank onto a chair opposite, his head in his hands. "God be praised. He might still be alive."

"I pray so, Herr Haas."

He lifted his head and looked at her critically. "You need food. Clothes. You have nowhere to go?"

She shook her head, then bit her lip. "The SS… I have reason to believe they might be looking for me. I could be a danger to you. I'm sorry."

He shrugged her words aside. "You will stay here." It was a command. "The war will be over soon," he said firmly, a new light in his tired eyes. "You will be safe here until it ends."

CHAPTER THIRTY

BIRGIT

Ravensbrück, Germany, February 1945

It had been four months since Birgit had been released from the infirmary and sent to knit socks for soldiers. Even here they were able to practice a form of sabotage, making the wool thinner in the heel and toe so the socks would wear out faster. It was a small act of defiance that felt necessary to life; a way to keep the fighting spirit now the end was so close. Still, Birgit could not help but feel a tiny, reluctant twinge of sympathy for the unsuspecting soldiers who would freeze in their faulty socks.

This new sense of compassion had both surprised and displeased her, coming upon her unawares when she'd first been in the infirmary. For the first days she'd simply slept, grateful for the unimaginable luxury of a bed, such as it was, and time to sleep. Her fever had raged and her body had lain wasted, but with time, sleep, and a few paltry doses of medicine, she'd begun to recover.

The woman lying next to her, Birgit couldn't help but think, was not so fortunate. Her skin had resembled that of a waxwork, tinged with yellow, although her smile, when she bestowed it, had been beatific. As soon as Birgit had been able to sit up in bed, the woman had introduced herself.

"You must be feeling better!" she'd said in German that though clearly not her native language was more than adequate. "I am so glad. I knew you would recover. You're young, you have so much to live for." She'd smiled, her elderly face shining with kindness, while Birgit had stared at her blankly. "My name is Betsie," she'd told her. "Betsie ten Boom. My sister Corrie has visited me once—you have a sister, as well?"

"Yes, but how do you know?"

"You spoke her name in your sleep. I thought it must be a sister. Lotte? I am sure she's all right."

Birgit had not known how to reply; Betsie ten Boom had spoken with the serene certainty of a prophetess. It had made Birgit feel alarmed, and yet she'd believed her.

"How long have you been here?" she'd asked after a moment.

"In the infirmary? Only since yesterday. It's a miracle I was allowed in. God is so good, isn't He?"

Birgit had simply stared. How could this wasted woman say such a thing, when she was in a concentration camp, most likely for no good reason at all, and looked two-thirds of the way to death's own door? She'd sounded like Lotte, but Birgit had thought she should have been older and wiser than that.

"You know I have a dream," Betsie had said after a moment, a complete change of subject that had made Birgit stare some more. "Although it's not really a dream, it's more of a certainty. My sister and I are going to have a house when the war ends, a beautiful house." Betsie had settled back against the thin pillow, a dreamy smile softening her lined features. "The most beautiful house—bigger than the Beje, that was our house back in Haarlem—with floors of inlaid wood, and statues set in the walls, and a sweeping staircase. I can see it all so perfectly."

"It sounds lovely," Birgit had replied rather dutifully, although it had seemed strange to her that a woman like Betsie, clearly so elevated and spiritual, would delight in such materialistic aspirations.

"It is lovely," she'd enthused, her whole face alight. "I know it is. And it will be for all the people who have been so damaged by this war, by this life." She'd nodded to those around them, and it had taken Birgit a stunned second to realize that Betsie ten Boom did not mean the poor, wasted creatures occupying the other beds on the ward, many of whom would most likely be dead in a few days, but the nurses tending to them, the guards outside. Their persecutors and tormentors.

"What are you saying?" Birgit had demanded, appalled, and Betsie had given her a smile full of compassion and understanding.

"They need to be shown that love is greater, don't you see? Can you even imagine what harm doing such things causes a soul? They are broken people, far more broken than you or I. It is only love that will put them together again and make them whole."

Birgit's mouth had dropped open and a sudden, icy rage flooded through her. "They're *evil.* You're condoning evil."

"Oh, no!" Betsie had smiled, but Birgit saw that she looked alarmed at the prospect of her thinking such a thing. "No, no, it is because they have done so much evil that they need help. One cannot do such things and not be scarred. I believe in forgiveness. I believe in healing, by God's grace. That is what our house will be about. For everyone." She had settled once more against the pillow. "A place for people to come together, to heal. There will be flowers, so many flowers. Imagine the good it will do them, to tend a garden…" As Betsie's voice had trailed off, Birgit realized she was falling asleep.

Birgit had turned her head away, a burning still in her gut. A house for concentration camp guards, so they could tend flowers? She'd see them rot in hell first. She'd hoped she would.

"Hatred in your heart is like a poison you drink," Betsie had murmured then, her eyes fluttering closed. "And yet you expect someone else to die from it."

As she'd fallen asleep, Birgit had stared at her, stricken, knowing it was true.

*

A few days later, Betsie had gone from the infirmary, and Birgit wondered if she would ever see her again. Would she find her house, in the end? She had not known if she wanted her to or not. Forgiveness for people who had done so much wrong, caused so much pain? It seemed so unfair, and yet she could not deny the truth of Betsie's words. In the end, her bitterness would hurt herself most of all.

A few days after Betsie had gone, Birgit had stirred from sleep to see Lotte sitting next to her bed.

"Lotte!" She'd struggled to sit up, overcome with fatigue even after a week in the infirmary. "What are you doing here? I thought there were no visitors allowed."

"There aren't, but the nurse was kind." Lotte had put her hand over hers. "I'm so glad to see you, Birgit."

As Birgit had blinked the sleep out of her eyes, she'd seen that Lotte had a black eye and livid red scratch marks down one cheek, marring her loveliness. It had looked so strange, so *wrong*, that she hadn't been able to keep from gasping out loud. "Lotte, what happened to you?"

Her sister had shaken her head, a quick, dismissive movement, her gaze lowered, pale lashes fanning her paler cheeks. "It doesn't matter."

"Was it a guard? Were you beaten?" Lotte had not replied and Birgit had stared at the scratches—fingernail marks, she'd realized, a woman's, and hardly the kind of beating one received from a guard, even one of the *Aufseherinnen*. "It was another prisoner, wasn't it?" she'd said slowly, and still Lotte would not answer.

Why on earth would a prisoner fly at Lotte—*Lotte,* who was always so gentle and kind, who prayed with the women no one else would speak to—the Russian peasants, the feebleminded, the prostitutes and the abortionists? There was a pecking order in every barracks, revealing the depravity in every human soul, and yet somehow Lotte had risen above it all. But here she was, her face bloody and bruised.

"Lotte—"

"It doesn't matter." Lotte had squeezed her hand. "The important thing is, you're safe and getting well. And when you are released from here, you will go to the knitting brigade! We both will. Isn't that wonderful?"

Birgit had simply stared, realization seeping slowly through her. A prisoner didn't get seconded to the so-called knitting brigade without reason.

"How has all this happened?" she'd asked. "The infirmary for over a week! And medicine." Suddenly she'd felt as if she could choke. "And now the knitting." It was too much kindness. "Lotte… *Lotte*… what have you done?" Birgit had stared at her despairingly, until Lotte had looked away.

"I'd do it again, and gladly," she had said quietly. Birgit had shaken her head as a tear slipped down her cheek, and Lotte had put her arms around her. "It's fine," she'd whispered as she'd pressed her cheek against hers. "It's fine, I promise. Don't think about it for a moment, Birgit, please. The war is almost over."

And yet Birgit had not been able to think about much else, knowing what her sister had sacrificed for her, and willingly. Not just the act itself, but also the shame and scorn that accompanied it. She'd received more than one black eye, especially after the other prisoners saw that both she and Birgit had been moved to the knitting brigade. One woman in their barracks in particular—Marta, a woman from Dresden who had been sent to Ravensbrück for theft—seemed to take every opportunity to harass Lotte, to trip her up or give her a push. It was like being in a schoolyard, only so much worse.

Somehow still Lotte had retained her sense of cheer, her gentleness. She took the harassment and even the beatings as her due, never fighting back, until, dissatisfied, the women, even Marta, subsided. She was adept at knitting, and when she'd finished her daily quota of socks she'd help any other woman who was struggling, smiling and chatting easily as her fingers flew with the needles. The guards rarely came into the room, and so she was free to move about, chatting and praying as she could, always smiling.

Birgit had been surprised to see someone else she knew in that room—Betsie ten Boom. Of course, she realized, Betsie was far too weak to do anything else, and she knitted as cheerfully as Lotte, and continued to tell Birgit about the house she'd have after the war.

"And you still want to fill it with guards?" Birgit had asked with more incredulity than cynicism, and Betsie had laughed.

"With everyone who has been damaged. We have to learn to live again, Birgit, to love again. People are capable of terrible things, but they are also capable of wonderful things. I don't believe there is a soul alive who cannot learn to love, if given the opportunity and encouragement."

"Even Hitler?" Birgit had said, disbelief warring with curiosity, and Betsie had put down her knitting and looked at her seriously, her normally joyful expression suddenly turning somber. Birgit had realized she was thinking about the question seriously, giving it a weight that Birgit never would have been able to. Of course you couldn't forgive *Hitler*.

"Yes," Betsie had said quietly, "even him." And then she'd gone on knitting.

As the weather grew colder, the mood in the camp had become even more tense and expectant. The ground was as hard as iron, with a brittle dusting of snow. Women who had become ill were turned away from the infirmary, and Birgit had seen the sick and frail from the beds she and Betsie had recently occupied being loaded on to a truck. She had known where they were going, and she'd felt sickened. *How long would this go on? Dear God, how long?*

*

In the middle of December, Betsie did not appear in the knitting room. Birgit had asked about her, but no one knew where she had gone. Absence was never a good sign of anything, and Birgit had felt far more anxious than she'd expected to.

"Her cough was getting bad again… her sister was worried for her," one woman had finally admitted. "Hopefully she's been taken to the infirmary."

The infirmary, Birgit had thought with a lurch of fear, was now nothing more than a place where people were taken to die and then be disposed of. That evening she'd slipped out of the barracks and had run all the way through the lightly falling snow, only to be sent away, as she'd known she would. Still, she'd persisted, sneaking around the back and climbing through a window into a stinking lavatory with overflowing toilets. When she'd come to the door, she'd seen a pile of bodies stacked against the wall like lumber, and her stomach had roiled.

But she'd found Betsie—Betsie lying in a bed just as she'd been before, her skin as yellow as parchment, her eyes closed forever. Birgit had backed away, one fist to her mouth. She hadn't been surprised, not really, not at all, and yet. *And yet…*

What about their house, the lovely house she and her sister were going to have after the war, with the banister and the statues and the flowers? She'd realized, in that moment, that she'd believed in it almost as much as Betsie had. She'd *needed* to believe in it, and now, like so much else, it was gone.

*

December gave way to January and then to February, and something shifted in Birgit that she hadn't expected to. The burning resentment and hatred she felt for the guards, the anger that had felt like her only strength, burned out, leaving nothing but ash.

It was strange not to feel it, like an emptiness inside her. She watched the *Aufseherinnen* screaming at them in the morning, spittle flying from their mouths, eyes bulging with fury, and thought, quite suddenly, *I pity you.*

How utterly novel, how completely odd, to feel this way, after being bitter for so long, after letting anger be the fuel that fired her soul. And yet how freeing. It was as if a weight Birgit hadn't even realized she'd been carrying fell away completely; as if the blindfold she hadn't known she'd been wearing had disappeared, and she could see the world through an entirely different lens.

She looked at the guards who patrolled the camps, who hefted their rifles and stood in their watchtowers, and thought, *you are doing such evil, and that will leave scars far greater than the ones my own body bears.*

She thought of Betsie's house, and she wished once again that she'd lived to inhabit it, make her dream a reality. Perhaps her sister Corrie still would.

In February whispers started round the camp that some of the other camps in the east had already been liberated; there were rumors of marches being made, hundreds of kilometers through the snow, in order to flee the oncoming Soviets. Most of the prisoners had died along the way.

"Is that what will happen to us?" Birgit wondered aloud one evening, as she and Lotte sat together.

"Only God knows," Lotte replied. "And I am content to leave it to Him."

"Perhaps your guard will save you," Birgit said, with hope rather than accusation. She knew Lotte was still making visits to the guard who had, in his selfish way, saved both of their lives.

She also knew her sister had no real choice in the matter. She only hoped Lotte was not being too damaged by it.

"I don't think so," Lotte replied, her gaze downcast.

"Do you..." Birgit hesitated. "Do you care for him, Lotte?"

Lotte had looked up quickly, her expression wary before she realized Birgit meant the question honestly. Some women had become attached to their SS lovers, in spite of everything. She wouldn't blame Lotte if she had. Perhaps he was kind to her, or at least kinder than some.

"I care for him as I care for any human being," Lotte replied slowly. "And I pity him, as one who is so broken and desperate."

"But no more?"

"I do not love him the way a woman might love a man," Lotte had said, and there was a flatness to her voice that Birgit had not heard before. "No, not that." She paused to draw a breath. "But neither do I despise him. There is no room in my heart for anger any more."

"You sound just like Betsie," Birgit said, experiencing a pang of grief that still took her by surprise. She'd barely known the woman, and yet she'd made such a difference.

Lotte had smiled, for she'd come to know Betsie through the knitting brigade. "I'm glad of that," she said simply, and they both smiled.

In retrospect, Birgit thought she should have realized sooner. She spent her day next to Lotte knitting, her evenings pressed up next to her for warmth, huddled under a couple of thin blankets. Of course she should have realized, all things considered; other women in their barracks had probably realized before she had, because she simply hadn't wanted to.

It was one afternoon when they had finished their quota of socks—socks Birgit wondered if soldiers would ever even wear, considering the state of the war—that the realization came so suddenly and certainly upon her.

Lotte had taken some scraps of wool and fashioned a little knitted edelweiss for each of them—khaki green for the stem, and white and mustard yellow for the flowers. The colors were slightly off, but Birgit recognized it all the same.

"Do you remember?" Lotte asked with a faint smile as she twirled one of the little flowers between her fingers.

"Of course I do."

"The Edelweiss Sisters. It seems such an age ago." She rested one hand on her middle for a moment, and that was when Birgit noticed the swelling bump outlined by the coarse fabric of her dress that she should have seen long ago. Lotte was so painfully thin that it was glaringly obvious, and yet the baggy shapelessness of her dress had disguised it, at least a little. Birgit's willful blindness had done the rest.

"*Lotte…*" Something in her voice made her sister straighten and drop her hand. She'd given Birgit a small, sad smile before she looked away. "Does he know?" Birgit asked, still reeling.

"No, although if he looked at me properly, I suppose he would be able to tell." She spoke quietly, a simple, bleak statement of fact.

"Mother of God." Birgit shook her head slowly, dropping her voice to a whisper. "What will you… how can you…" A few women had had babies while in the camp, and they were always taken away from them immediately after birth. Some—usually the children of Jews or gypsies—were drowned in a barrel of water right outside the barracks; others, if blond and Aryan enough, were allowed to live, taken away to be adopted by "racially pure" couples.

"I don't know," Lotte said simply. "I leave it to God." She paused, giving Birgit a beseeching look. "This child is innocent, Birgit. Don't blame him—or her—for anything."

"I don't," Birgit replied truthfully, and yet she was terrified for her sister. The war was nearly over, but the future remained so very uncertain. How could Lotte possibly give birth, have a *baby,* in a place like this? Would they even let her keep it? Or would they toss it aside like so much rubbish, because everyone was in a panic about the way the war would end? "How… how far along—"

"I don't know. My monthly courses had already stopped." She let out a little laugh, the sound sorrowful. "It is a miracle that I was able to get in this state at all. But I've been able to feel her kick for a while now." She gave Birgit an almost defiant look. "I know it's a girl."

"Lotte, you must tell him," Birgit urged, leaning forward as she spoke in a whisper. She still didn't know the name of Lotte's guard, had never wanted to know. "He may be able to help you, help the child. You must tell him, for your own life, for hers—"

"And what if he doesn't want to know?" Lotte countered. "What if he doesn't want to help? It might make him angry." She put a hand on her middle again, the gesture protective. "I won't risk my child's life, Birgit, not for my own comfort."

"But what about hers—"

Lotte simply shook her head, and Birgit sat back, defeated and still incredulous. *Oh God,* she thought, *why now? Why this?* "You won't be able to hide it from him for much longer," she warned her. "I'm amazed he hasn't already realized, considering—"

Lotte shook her head again. "Sometimes I think he doesn't see me at all. I'm just… a *cipher* to him. And, God willing, it won't be much longer before the war ends, and then I won't see him."

Yes, Birgit thought with growing despair, *but what will happen then?*

CHAPTER THIRTY-ONE

LOTTE

April 1945

The world was on fire. Lotte had thought that before—when Kristallnacht had burned her city, when Hitler had declared war on Poland, when she'd been bundled in the back of a truck to be taken to God only knew where, but now it really felt true; she could see—and feel—the flames.

The world was on fire, and much of it was already crumbling to ash all around her. She felt as if she were in a burning building, the timbers cracking and falling around her, everything smoke and flame, and she had no way out.

The guards of Ravensbrück were in a complete and violent panic. As she'd gone about the camp, trying to stay out of the way, she'd seen them running here and there, burying evidence, burning files, faces full of fear and fury. The Soviets were coming, and they were trying to hide the evidence of their evil, but there was too much, and it was too late.

They'd also begun transporting prisoners; every day numbers were called out, and women clambered on to trucks. No one knew where they went, what happened to them.

"Most likely to other camps," Birgit had said. "Although who knows? Maybe they just shoot them in a field."

The world was on fire, and no one knew what to do but let it burn.

"What will you do, when the war is over?" Oskar asked her one evening in early April. It was still frigid out, but a hint of spring taunted the air, the breath of a world to come, a warmth Lotte could not yet trust.

Oskar had started talking to her more, after those first few hurried and awful encounters, when he'd flung her away from him as if disgusted. Lotte suspected he was—but with himself. He couldn't bear his own actions, or the reminder she was of them. It made her pity him all the more, even as her body ached and throbbed from his treatment of it.

Now he sat sideways on the bed, his back propped against the wall, studying the cigarette he smoked rather than her.

Lotte pulled down her dress—he never asked her to take it off any more—to hide her shape. She had to be at least six months gone, although the baby seemed small. It amazed her that he hadn't realized, when Birgit and so many others had. The women in her barracks had been, in turns, condemning and compassionate. Lotte recalled the times she'd been beaten without any real resentment; she understood their anger, the tangled mix of envy and derision.

The first time had been after her third summons, and she'd returned to the barracks, exhausted, aching, only to have Marta, a woman from Dresden who had been sent to Ravensbrück for stealing ration cards, pounce on her.

"You filthy slut! You lying whore!" she'd screamed as she'd gone at Lotte with her fists and nails. Lotte hadn't even shielded herself; she'd been too tired, and she'd felt there was some weight to Marta's accusations. Not every woman in the camp agreed to sleep with a guard, even those who had been propositioned. Did she think it was somehow nobler, that she did it for Birgit?

Eventually the other women had pulled Marta off, and Lotte had lain on the floor, bleeding and bruised, while the *Aufseherin* had looked on, indifferent, even amused.

"Never mind her," Magda had whispered, as she'd used what she could to bandage Lotte's cuts. "She's just jealous."

"Jealous!" Lotte had shaken her head in disbelief at such a notion.

"Don't you think she'd sleep with a guard if one wanted her? Too bad she's got a face like a prune." Magda had smiled, but Lotte hadn't been able to smile back. She'd felt sorry for Marta, just as she did for every other miserable unfortunate there.

"If we fight each other, we'll never survive," she'd said wearily, and Magda nodded in understanding.

"It's not long now. We have to keep strong."

"Yes." Although Lotte had been hearing that it wouldn't be long for months already. *How long would it really be?*

Now, as she regarded Oskar warily, she knew those words for truth. It wouldn't be long at all; days, maybe weeks, and yet she still couldn't imagine life after Ravensbrück, after war. "I don't know what I will do after the war," she answered him cautiously. "I suppose I can't think that far ahead. I cannot imagine it."

"It won't be long now, you know."

Lotte remained silent, knowing anything she said could make him angry. His emotions were like fireworks; the sudden explosion causing her to recoil in shock and pain.

"I'll most likely be arrested, you know. Maybe even killed. If the Soviets…" He let out a shuddering breath. "We were the heroes, at the start of this. Everyone cheered for us." He shook his head in memory.

"You were never heroes," Lotte replied quietly, because she could not keep herself from it, and he looked up at her, his eyes blazing for one furious second. He raised his hand, and she braced herself for him to strike her, but then he dropped it suddenly and shook his head.

"No, we weren't," he admitted on a sigh of defeat, and Lotte exhaled. He drew deeply on his cigarette. "I told you I was a bookkeeper before, didn't I?"

"Yes."

"I was going to train as an accountant. I joined the SS to organize their damned *files*. I wasn't transferred here until '43."

Around the same time she'd come, then. Lotte said nothing.

"This isn't who I am," he said, looking up at her, his tone almost pleading, as if seeking some sort of absolution, and while Lotte knew she was willing to give it, she also knew it was not her forgiveness he needed. "When I first saw the gas chamber, I told my superior it wasn't right," he continued, his tone turning strident, almost petulant. "I told them if you're going to do the thing, at least do it *humanely*." He let out a sound like a groan. "I *tried*…" Still Lotte didn't speak. There was nothing she could say to absolve his actions. If he wanted absolution, it had to come with true repentance.

He ground out his cigarette. "What was I supposed to do?" he demanded, angry now, the shifts in mood like streaks of lightning. "Once you're part of it, what do you *do*? You're trapped. I didn't know what they were capable of till I came here. I had no idea! No one did. Who could have imagined…?" He shook his head. "I was just a cog, a useless cog, no one told me *anything*. And when I discovered—tell me, what I should have done." He glared at her in challenge, and Lotte gazed back evenly.

"You tell me," she said at last, and Oskar let out another groan as he dropped his head into his hands.

"I don't know, I don't know," he half moaned. "I admit, I never cared much about the Jews—greedy bastards, the lot of them—but I didn't expect *this*." He looked up at her through his fingers, his face stricken. "They'll paint me as evil. Someone sadistic, someone who enjoyed this, who plotted it, but I *wasn't.*"

Still she said nothing. As far as guards went, he certainly wasn't the worst. Did that absolve him? Forgiveness came freely with repentance, but there were still consequences on this earth. She did not know what his would be.

He reached for another cigarette, his fingers trembling as he lit it. "Never mind," he said as he drew deeply on it. "I suppose I deserve everything I'll get." He glanced at her now almost indifferently, the desperate anguish he'd felt before already hardening into something weary and resigned. "They are going to evacuate the camp soon, perhaps in another week or two. Only the ill ones will be left. The rest will march toward Mecklenburg."

Lotte was silent, absorbing the information. It really was almost over, then. "Mecklenburg," she repeated slowly. She did not know where it was.

"Away from Berlin and the Soviets. It's about a hundred kilometers northwest of here."

"But no one will be able to walk that far. We're all so weak."

He shrugged. "It's either that or be left to your fate with the Soviets. Have you heard about what they've done in East Prussia? The women will never be the same." He shook his head, his mouth twisting in condemnation of his enemy.

The irony of this man talking to her of the horror of Soviets raping women was not lost on Lotte, yet it hardly mattered now. She hesitated, knowing she was balancing on a precipice, the abyss yawning far below her. She had no idea how Oskar would react to the most innocuous statements, never mind something of true import. And yet Birgit was right. For the sake of her child, she had to take the risk.

"What will you do?" she asked after a moment.

He shrugged again. "Get out. Go west. I'd rather surrender to the Americans than the Soviets, that much I know."

Save himself, then. She was not surprised, of course she wasn't, yet she still felt strangely hurt, a disappointment that felt stupidly personal. "I'm pregnant," she stated, feeling lightheaded with the risk of the admission.

Oskar's gaze narrowed, his cigarette clamped between two fingers. "You aren't."

In answer Lotte stood up, smoothing the dress over her now-sizeable bump. The fact that he hadn't noticed was, she knew, a sign of his utter and callous disregard for her, nothing else. *Why* had she told him? Yet she knew she'd had to take the chance.

He was silent for a long moment, his face dangerously expressionless, and after a few seconds Lotte sat down again, perched on the edge of a chair, faint with trepidation.

"What do you want me to do?" he finally asked, and he sounded only weary.

"Help me somehow," Lotte answered honestly. "For the sake of your child."

He was silent for a long moment, staring at his cigarette once more. "You said you were a nun, before," he remarked finally. "Where?"

"Salzburg, in Austria. Nonnberg Abbey."

"And your family?"

"My father was a clockmaker. He had a shop on Getreidegasse." Not that he would know the place, but just saying the words out loud made longing ripple through her for the home and family she'd once known, the easy simplicity of the life she'd once had. It was all gone. Even if everyone in her family survived the war, it would never be the same.

"My father was a day laborer from Breslau." Oskar looked up with the glimmer of a wry smile, although his tone was strangely regretful. "If we'd met before the war, you would have been too good for me."

Lotte had nothing to say to that. She could not imagine meeting him in any other circumstances than they had. *What had he been like before the war, before the atrocities here had twisted and corrupted him?* The question alone saddened her. Perhaps, without the war, he would have been a decent man, a clerk for some innocuous firm. He would have married a local girl, had children, gone to the cinema, taken them for walks. For a few seconds she could imagine it all—a simple life, never lived.

"I'll do what I can," he said at last, but she knew such a careless sentiment wasn't enough.

"There is my sister, too," she told him. "The one you helped. We must stay together. We can't lose each other now—"

Irritation crossed his features, and he drew on his cigarette. "I told you, I'll do what I can."

Lotte found out what that meant a week later, when, early one morning, the prisoners were called out, barracks by barracks, and told to form a single column heading towards the gates of the camp.

"They're making us leave," Magda had whispered, her eyes wide with both terror and excitement. In the last week the sense of expectation in the camp had ratcheted up, become almost unbearable. To die now, when freedom was so close…! And yet the guards were twitchier than ever, punishments meted out for the smallest imagined offense. Only yesterday a woman had been shot for stumbling on her way to roll call. "The Soviets must be close." She nodded toward the guards. "Do you think they'll let us go?"

"When do they ever let us go?" a woman behind them interjected bitterly.

"Why bother with us, then? Why line us up like this?" Magda had demanded, clinging stubbornly to hope. "We're so close now, so close!"

And yet so very far. Lotte knew they were headed to Mecklenburg, just as she knew most of the women in that raggedy column would not survive such a journey, without food, water, or shelter. They were leaving the camp, but it was not to freedom. Glancing at her sister's resigned face, she suspected Birgit knew it, as well.

Then Lotte heard her number being called out, along with several others. She glanced at Birgit, who looked troubled, her gaze narrowed as she observed the women stepping out of the line.

"They're all Germans, I think," she whispered. "Aryan looking, too. It must mean something good." She hugged Lotte briefly, her arms tight around her. "Go," she said. "Perhaps your guard has helped you, after all."

"I won't leave you—"

"You must." Birgit grasped her hand. "This is your chance, Lotte, I'm sure of it. You must take it, for the child's sake as much as yours."

"Birgit—" Lotte realized she was crying, tears streaking down her face, her mind blind with panic. She could not leave her sister. She *wouldn't.*

"Go. And Godspeed. We'll see each other again, Lotte, either on Getreidegasse or in heaven." Birgit embraced her again and then gave her a little push, her lips trembling as she tried to smile.

Lotte stumbled towards the women huddled in an uncertain group; there were at least a few hundred of them. What if they'd been singled out for something worse?

They remained there, waiting and wary, as the long, tattered column of prisoners headed out of the camp. It looked so strange, so very bizarre, to see them all marching away from the death and destruction they'd been living with for so long—but to what? *Dear God, to what?*

When they'd finally disappeared towards the lake, a guard came up towards the remaining women. Lotte felt the tension that rippled through the group, uncertainty and hope mingled together, brought to a fearful, frenzied pitch.

"You're free to go," he shouted, gesturing at them as if they were a flock of sheep he had to herd. "Leave the camp. Head west. The Soviets will be here by the end of the day." He turned away, already finished with them, while everyone stared.

Go? Just… go?

Lotte glanced at the gates, flung open. The watchtowers were abandoned, and in the distance she could see a guard hurling bags into a Jeep. Everyone was desperate to leave, and yet still not one woman started toward those gates, toward freedom. *What if it was a trick?* Such ghastly games been played before, guards hinting at freedom only to shoot prisoners for "attempted escape."

The minutes ticked on, the sun now high above them. It had taken hours for the prisoners to assemble and leave the camp; the Soviets might be less than a mile away. Lotte imagined she could already hear the growl of their Jeeps and tanks, rolling ever onward. Would the soldiers treat them kindly, as the victims they so clearly were, or would they see them only as German women, the enemy they were intent on vanquishing? Lotte had no idea. She did not want to find out.

She rested one hand on her bump and then she started walking towards the gates. The space between her shoulder blades prickled as she walked. She imagined the rifle being hoisted, the imperious *Halt!* before the shot was fired.

None came.

She walked through the gates and she stood on the other side, blinking in the sunshine, dazed by her journey of just a few meters. She was free. *Free.* Yet what on earth could she do with such freedom?

She didn't even know where she was, not really. She'd come here by train; she'd never even been to the village of Ravensbrück, a short distance away. The guard had told her to head west, but what was west? *A town, a mountain, a road?*

More women had begun to walk through the gates, all of them milling around, unsure where to go, what to do. Then a straggling gaggle of women struck out west, down a rutted track, and many followed, creating their own column, and perhaps their own death march.

They walked all afternoon, thirsty, hungry, dazed, weak. Some fell behind, others dropped off to hide in the forest that fringed the dirt track they'd taken, too tired to keep going. Still Lotte put one foot in front of the other, willing herself on. She had the instinctive feeling that to stop anywhere would be dangerous, perhaps deadly. When they paused by a stream to drink some water, she heard a distant rumble.

"Tanks," someone said succinctly.

So close, Lotte thought with a thrill of both wonder and terror, the emotions seeming strangely distant from herself, from this spring afternoon by a clear, burbling stream, the sun high above.

"We must keep going," someone else said, staggering up from the stream.

"Maybe they'll be kind to us," another suggested, and someone else gave a hard huff of incredulous laughter.

"You think? A German woman alone, starving or not? I don't think so. I certainly don't want to wait and see."

Still in a ragged column, the women left the stream and continued down the road, step by painstaking step. The tanks, Lotte knew, would be faster than they were, but perhaps the Soviets would stop at the camp. Or would they search for stragglers? Would they be liberators, or just another round of persecutors?

They'd all been told by the guards the horror stories of the women of East Prussia who had been raped repeatedly by Soviet soldiers, seen only as enemies and aggressors. Why should it be any different for them? They were all blond, blue-eyed, German, never mind the prison garb they wore.

By nightfall Lotte knew she would not be able to keep going. For the last few hours pain had banded her middle and her legs trembled with every step. Her head swam and she'd started to stumble, once falling to her knees before she'd managed to hoist herself up. She had not eaten since last night.

When they caught sight of a farm along the side of a road, she fell to her knees again, pain jolting through her, along with relief at having finally stopped. She could lie down right here in the road, and she wouldn't mind…

Then she felt someone's arm around her, urging her up although everything in her protested. "You mustn't stop, not here. We must keep going."

A gasp escaped her and she doubled over, pulling away from the helping hand. "I can't."

She fell back down onto the dirt, curling up, everything a haze. She heard her companion ask grimly, "How long have you been having the pains?"

Lotte looked up, blinking the world back into focus, jolted to see who had helped her—Marta, her erstwhile attacker. "A few hours," she said.

"The baby could be here soon, then."

"What?" Lotte stared at her blankly. "No, it's far too early. They're just pains—"

"I had three children," Marta replied. "I know." She urged Lotte upward, and somehow she staggered back to her feet. "We can shelter in that barn."

"But the Soviets—"

"I doubt even the Soviets will rape a woman who is giving birth," Marta stated dryly. "And God willing they won't find us. Come."

Lotte let herself be led away from the line of women stumbling onward to the dim interior of a small, weathered barn, too dazed by shock and pain to be aware of her surroundings. Marta eased her onto the ground and she felt something both soft and prickly underneath her, smelling sweet and musty. A bed of straw.

"It's not the best place to give birth, God knows, but it will do."

"If it was good enough for our Savior…" Lotte began, and Marta let out a dry huff of laughter.

"Holding on to your faith, even now? God knows you'll need it."

A pain ripped through Lotte and she gasped out loud, the sound torn from her. Her baby really was coming—here, in this moldy old barn, with Soviets marching closer! How on earth would she manage, without food, water, clothing, even? Everything felt impossible. She scrabbled at Marta's sleeve.

"Thank you," she managed between gasps of pain, "for staying—"

"I couldn't leave you alone." Marta looked away. "I shouldn't have struck you that time, I know. You were only doing what you could, for the sake of your sister. God knows I understand that." She turned back to Lotte, her expression both bleak and resolute. "I stole those ration cards because my children were starving. The youngest one died, from rickets. All he needed was good fresh milk."

"Oh, Marta—"

"But enough about me." She gave herself a shake, her expression clearing, becoming determined, almost cheerful. "Your child will live. He must, to have survived this far, with you nothing but skin and bone!"

Marta smiled, and Lotte tried to smile back, through the haze of her pain. "It's a girl," she said, panting through the contractions, and Marta laughed.

"Is it, now? Well, girls are stronger, especially at the start. If it's early, better to be a girl."

The next few hours passed in a red-tinged blur of pain. At some point in the night they heard the rumble of cars, the slamming of doors, a scream.

Marta heaped the straw over them and put a hand on Lotte's mouth. "For God's sake, be quiet," she hissed. Lotte couldn't have made noise if she'd wanted to; her body felt as if it were separating from her mind, as if her soul was hovering above, just as it had once before. Oh bliss, to be away from all this suffering and striving. To let it all go, a sweet surrender at last, nothing but comfort and peace, no worry or fear…

She must have passed out, for when she came to they had moved deeper into the barn, half hidden by a pile of hay and a jumble of old tools. Marta's face, hovering above her, was grim.

"The Soviets came. They took turns with the farmer's wife. They've gone now, thank God." She crossed herself. "And God help that poor woman. I suppose it could have been worse."

Lotte couldn't reply; when she tried to cross herself for the sake of the farmer and his wife, her arm merely flopped to her side. Marta looked down at her, her hands on Lotte's belly as she palpated the taut flesh.

"The baby's not coming down," she told her in a low voice. "I think it must be stuck. It happens sometimes." She paused, gazing down into Lotte's dazed face, a bleak look entering her eyes. "I can try to move it, but…" Marta hesitated, and in that second's pause Lotte understood. She would not survive this birth. She realized she was not even surprised. In her emaciated state, to give birth in a barn, without adequate food or water or medicine or even a blanket… It had been difficult to begin with, never mind this new complication. It had been impossible.

All things are possible with God…

A sudden, sweet peace flooded through her, an acceptance that felt like a laying down, a coming home. *At last.* She felt nothing but certainty as she grabbed Marta's arm. "Do…" she gasped out. "Whatever you have to do… for my child."

Lotte could not remember the next few hours except for the pain, dazzling and sharp, like a diamond piercing through her, obliterating fear and thought. At times she passed out; when she swam back to consciousness, Marta was still poised above her, her hands on her belly, and there was a pain in her middle that felt as if she were being rent apart.

She felt a wetness between her thighs, on the straw beneath her, and she knew it was blood. Too much blood.

"Lotte, *push—*"

She didn't so much push as surrender to her body's insistent will, possessing a strength that did not come from her mind or her determination, but something more elemental, as if a giant hand had flipped her inside out. The world grew hazy at the edges, and still her body convulsed, expelling new life even as she felt it draining from her, into the straw.

Lotte grabbed again at Marta's sleeve, realizing how little time she had left. "There's a clockmaker on Getreidegasse in Salzburg—"

"No…" Marta looked panicked, but Lotte persevered. "A sprig of edelweiss on the sign… here…" She scrabbled again, reaching for the knitted edelweiss she'd worn tucked into her sleeve since she'd made it several months ago. "Take this, please. If there is no one at the clockmaker's, go to the abbey. They're kind there—"

"*Lotte—*"

"Please. Promise me." She stared up into Marta's face, a sudden, surprising strength seizing her as she grabbed her by the shoulders. "Please, for the sake of my child."

"Yes." Marta looked shaken but resolute. "Yes, I will."

Lotte fell back as her blood soaked the straw and a cry came into the world.

Marta let out a choked sob. "It *is* a girl!"

Lotte's eyes fluttered closed as a smile curved her lips. Already she could see that glimmering light, a beacon in the distance, as that burbling stream, placid and golden, carried her away on its sweet, silken tide. She felt Marta place a warm weight on her chest, and with the last of her strength she clasped her arms around the child she'd never know. A greater peace was beckoning, her own Father's arms opening wide and welcoming, ushering her into His embrace, where every tear would be wiped away. *At last… at last.*

Another cry split the air, weak and mewling and *right,* and Lotte smiled as her eyes closed for the last time.

CHAPTER THIRTY-TWO

Salzburg, May 1945

The house on Getreidegasse was silent, the windows holding only jagged teeth of broken glass, everything inside covered in a thick shroud of dust. Johanna picked her way among the broken glass and shattered clocks as the May sunshine poured through the empty windows. The war had ended three days ago.

Johanna had spent the last few months at 22 Traunstrasse, not daring to visit her parents, although she'd longed to. She hadn't known if they were being watched; she hadn't wanted to put them in any danger.

Georg Haas had done his best to gain information, going out into the streets, asking careful questions. From him Johanna had learned that Ingrid had been captured and killed, back in February. The small resistance group she'd been a part of had no doubt disintegrated.

In March Werner's father had seen someone he thought might be her mother leave the house on Getreidegasse to do her shopping, looking old and haggard, but alive. Johanna had let that be enough. She could wait. She would have to.

Now, as she picked her way through the ruins, she marveled at how much had changed. There was the cuckoo clock made by Johann Baptist Beha that had chimed every quarter hour throughout her childhood, discarded on the floor amidst the detritus and ruin. There was the bench where Franz had once sat, now kicked over onto its side. Johanna let out a little cry, but it sounded more like a sigh. She felt too battle-weary and scarred to make space for grief, at least not yet. She had not let herself think too much about Franz.

He is most likely dead. You know that. Of course you know that.

She'd repeated this litany to herself every day for the last few months, yet she knew it wasn't enough to snuff out the spark of hope that continued to kindle her soul, no matter how resigned she'd made herself become.

Slowly she turned to the stairs. As she climbed them, she had no idea what to expect. More abandoned, dust-filled rooms, an emptiness that echoed on forever? Her parents had surely long gone, God willing to somewhere safer. In the last few months nearly half of Salzburg had been destroyed by bombs, although the old town had been thankfully spared.

As Johanna came to the top of the stairs and then into the kitchen, she stopped suddenly, reaching out to steady herself on the doorframe, for there was her mother, standing at the table, her head bent as she peeled potatoes, the *scritch scritch* of her knife the only sound in the room.

It was as if the war had not happened at all, as if time had reeled backwards, and Johanna had just shut the door on Janos Panov. She felt the flicker of that old, petty irritation, like the remnant of a dream. *How could this be?* She opened her mouth, closed it. Her mother looked up.

"Johanna…" Hedwig's voice was a hoarse whisper. She flung the knife away with a clatter and staggered towards her daughter, her arms held out. Johanna fell into them.

"I didn't think you were here." She managed to get the words out through gasps and sobs; after feeling so hardened, so weary, the force of her emotion slammed into her and then overflowed.

"We stayed. Where else could we go? And we hoped—dear God above, we hoped at least one of our daughters would come back to us."

"Mama… oh, Mama." Johanna's eyes closed as she hugged her mother tightly. She was thinner now, harder, older, yet she was still so wonderfully the same. *Peeling potatoes…!* She almost wanted to laugh. Finally, after several moments where they simply embraced silently, she pulled away, a question in her eyes. "Papa?"

Her mother's face fell, pulled down by weight and care. "He's lying in bed," she told her after a second's pause. "He collapsed a few months ago. A stroke, the doctor said."

"A *stroke*—"

"He's alive, but…" Hedwig spread her hands. "I've done my best by him these last months. God knows I've tried, but nothing seems to…." She drew a shuddering breath. "He knows how much I love him, how much I've always loved him. I have to believe that."

"Of course he does, Mama." Johanna squeezed her mother's hand before slowly walking into her parents' bedroom, with its heavy, dark furniture, the curtains drawn against the day. Her father lay in bed, a pale, diminished figure, barely a bump under the covers.

"Hello, Papa," she whispered. He stirred, opening his eyes, but there was no recognition there, no spark of life or remembrance. No wry glint, no rueful smile. Johanna sank onto the side of the bed, her head bowed as she clasped his thin, withered hand.

Later, she and her mother drank bitter chicory coffee as they sat in the kitchen. The silence was unnerving—no planes, no bombs, no shouting, no more fear. Salzburg's old town may have escaped the worst of the bombing, but much of the outskirts was nothing but a ruin, just like the rest of the country, the whole Reich. Millions of people were without food or homes, wandering about with dazed expressions on their faces. The war was finally over, but no one knew yet what, if anything, would take its place, or what to do now that it was.

"You have no news of Birgit or Lotte?" Johanna asked. Her mother shook her head.

"There has been nothing, all these years."

"And nothing of Franz or Werner." Johanna choked down a swallow of the bitter coffee. "There's no use hoping, I suppose."

"Nonsense, Johanna." Her mother's voice sounded strong. "Hope is all we have now. Hope and faith."

Johanna shook her head, fighting a weary despair that threatened to descend on her like a fog. "Can you really have faith, Mama? After all this?"

"Of course." Although her mother was old and haggard, her hair entirely gray, her face scored with lines, a strength shone out of her eyes. "There is nothing else. Surely this wretched war has shown us that."

"And if no one else comes back alive?"

"So be it." Hedwig squared her shoulders. "That does not change anything, in my mind."

"But…" Johanna let the word trail away like a breath. Perhaps her mother was right. Perhaps faith was what they needed, amidst all this brokenness. *But Franz, oh Franz, and Lotte and Birgit and even Werner…*

What had happened to them all?

Every day for the next few weeks Johanna went out looking for answers. The city was in tatters, everything confusion and chaos, but in the midst of it order was slowly, painstakingly being restored. Offices were set up to deal with accommodation, with displaced persons, with all that had been lost and needed to be found. But no matter which weary bureaucrat Johanna turned to, American or German, no one had any information about the people she loved. She put names on lists and looked at other ones—lists of those who had died, who were missing, who had been imprisoned, but she never came across the names of those she loved. *Where were they?*

By early June she was feeling despondent. Her father continued to lie in bed as still as a corpse, and her mother continued to peel potatoes and cook with whatever meager ingredients she had, as if life could march on regardless, housework taking precedence. Together they'd tidied up the shop, boarded the windows as there was no glass to be had. And silently hoped.

As much as Johanna told herself, with a harsh resolve, that Franz, Birgit, Lotte, and Werner were surely all dead, she still wanted answers. Proof. Perhaps then she could put her frail, determined hopes to rest.

And then, in early June, a knock sounded at the side door. Johanna went downstairs, thinking it must be another beggar—there were so many these days—when she opened the door to a woman she recognized—but only just.

"*Birgit!*"

A smile split her skeletal face. "Yes, it's me."

Her sister swayed on her feet as Johanna clasped her in her arms. She wore a motley mismatch of shabby clothes, a pair of men's shoes, one sole flapping free. Her hair stuck out around her face in a ragged, tangled halo. Gently Johanna held her, gazing down into her face.

"Lotte?" she asked, her voice breaking, and Birgit shook her head.

"I don't know. We were separated, right at the end. I had to march to Mecklenburg, and she was set free."

"Why?"

"It doesn't matter. When peace was declared, I was put into a camp for displaced persons. More camps! You'd think someone would realize that was the last thing we wanted." Birgit let out a weary laugh. "Eventually I was able to speak to someone who gave me permission to return here. Everywhere I go I have always asked about Lotte, but everything is chaos. I've never heard a word."

"Perhaps, like you, she was put in one of these camps." Now that Birgit was here, right in her arms, hope flared high and hot inside her. *If Birgit, why not Lotte? Why not Franz and Werner, as well?* She felt generous now, wanting everyone to survive. To live.

"Johanna," Birgit said quietly, stepping away from her embrace, "Lotte… she was expecting. She might have had the baby by now."

"*Expecting*?" Johanna drew back, shocked into silence, while Birgit explained how it had come to pass. Afterward, Johanna could only shake her head.

"Poor, poor Lotte."

"She was so strong the whole time, Johanna." Tears clung to Birgit's lashes as she blinked them back. "Her faith was so strong. Have you asked up at the abbey about her?"

"No, I didn't even think to." The abbey, on its lofty perch above the city, had not entered Johanna's consciousness, strangely enough. Perhaps she had chosen not to think of it, the place that had, in its own way, taken the people she'd loved and offered them up like sacrifices. "What would they know?"

"Who knows? We can hope it is something."

Slowly Johanna nodded. "I shall go there," she promised, "but first you must see Mama."

Birgit's face tensed. "And Papa?"

"He's… he's still alive," Johanna said, and her sister's face fell.

"Still?"

"Come upstairs," she urged. "You can see him as well as Mama. She will be so happy to see you."

*

Johanna didn't manage to visit the abbey until the following week, in part because she doubted they would know anything. *How could they?* Besides, if Lotte were alive, she would come to Getreidegasse, or, if for some reason she didn't or couldn't, the abbey would send word, surely.

In any case, there had been so much else to do—forms to be filled in, administrators to see, rations to queue for. Life was slowly stumbling back to at least a shadow of what it once had been, although Austria was as good as divided into two, with the Red Army having taken control of Vienna, and the British and American Allies controlling the western part of the country.

A week after Birgit had knocked on the door of the house on Getreidegasse, she and Johanna walked up the Nonnbergstiege toward the abbey. It was a beautiful summer's day, the sky a bright blue studded with fleecy clouds like cotton wool, the air warm and drowsy. A day, Johanna thought, for wandering along the Salzach or sipping a mélange coffee at a sidewalk café, soaking up the sunshine. Yet here they were, knocking on the old, weathered door of the abbey, searching yet again for news.

Neither of them recognized the young, smiling nun who greeted them, and then left them to wait by the porter's lodge.

"The Mother Abbess will see you," she said upon her return, and filled with a sudden trepidation, the sisters exchanged glances before they followed the young nun to the Mother Abbess's study.

She rose as they came into the room, her expression grave even though she smiled. She looked the same—a bit older, perhaps, but still serene.

"I have no news of Sister Maria Josef," she said without preamble. "That is, your sister, Lotte Eder. But—" She paused, and Birgit took a step forward, eager, urgent.

"Yes? What is it?"

"A few weeks ago a child was left on our doorstep. A baby girl, only a few weeks old, by my reckoning, although I am not well versed in infants." She smiled, although sorrow darkened her eyes. "She had nothing but a blanket to cover her, laid in a wooden crate. But someone had tucked a sprig of edelweiss, knit from wool, inside the blanket." Birgit let out a small cry as the Mother Abbess opened a drawer and took out the knitted sprig. "Do you recognize this?"

"Lotte knitted it," Birgit said. Her voice sounded strangely distant as she stared at the frayed and stained wool in disbelief. "At Ravensbrück. And she was… she was expecting a child. It wasn't her fault—"

The Mother Abbess held up one hand. "I am not here to blame. You believe this child to be your sister's?"

"It… it must be… but why… why didn't she come to Getreidegasse?" A silence followed as they all acknowledged the truth. "She must be dead," Birgit stated hollowly. "And someone else brought the baby here. She must have told them. Asked them to."

"May we see the child?" Johanna asked, her tone assiduously formal to hide her grief. She felt it like an incoming tide, stormy and wild, threatening to overwhelm her. *Lotte, gone. And yet, her child.* The Mother Abbess nodded and rang a bell.

A few minutes later the young nun who had greeted them at the door entered the room, carrying a blanketed bundle. Johanna stared at it dumbly but Birgit ran to the nun and snatched the baby from her.

"*Johanna…* Johanna, look, she's just like Lotte!"

Still dumbfounded, Johanna gazed down at the tiny, wizened face with the rosebud lips of her sister and the dark eyes of a stranger.

"We should have taken her to the orphanage right away," the Mother Abbess said. "But I was hoping someone might claim her."

"You thought she might be Lotte's?" Johanna demanded, anger taking the place of the grief she was afraid to feel. "Why didn't you write to us? Tell us—"

"It was a suspicion only. And, in truth, there have been many other pressing needs to deal with." The Mother Abbess gave the bundled baby in Birgit's arms a tender, careworn smile. "If you are willing to take and care for her, then I am more than glad."

"Of course we will," Birgit said fiercely, even as Johanna wondered how they would manage to care for a baby. They had nothing prepared, hardly any money, barely any food. And yet, of course there was no question of doing otherwise.

"We have a few clothes and things we were able to provide for her," the Mother Abbess said. "Sister Theresa will gather them together."

The next few weeks were ones of both joy and grief, as they made space in the house on Getreidegasse for its newest member. Hedwig was thrilled by the presence of her granddaughter, even as she accepted, with her usual stoic silence, the fact of her youngest daughter's death. They named the baby Charlotte Maria, after Lotte, but somehow, after only a few days, they started calling her Mimi. It felt right, especially when she gave them her first gummy smile.

As the weeks passed, fear coalesced into certainty. Franz had to be dead, and Werner, as well. Johanna had told Birgit about seeing Werner at Mauthausen, and she had wept, smiling through her tears.

"I always knew he was a good man."

As the summer drew to a close, reality set in, new and strange as it was. They needed jobs; Johanna had started looking for a secretarial position, and was soon hired by the occupying American forces to type letters for the endless bureaucracy that now ruled the war-torn world.

Then, in September, Birgit surprised them all by announcing she was traveling all the way to the Netherlands, to work with a woman she'd known through Ravensbrück, Corrie ten Boom. Both Hedwig and Johanna had stared at her in shock, while Birgit had smiled a bit apologetically, although her expression remained resolute.

"I know it is a surprise, but her sister Betsie was kind to me at Ravensbrück, and the truth is she… she changed me. Corrie ten Boom is setting up a rehabilitation centre for survivors—not just prisoners, but guards, as well, and those who have been named as collaborators. So many people have been damaged by this war. I want to help." Her expression firmed. "I'm going to help."

"But all that way—" Hedwig said faintly.

"The center is in Bloemendaal. It won't be forever. Betsie had a dream about a house where people could grow flowers—I know it sounds silly, but her sister Corrie has found the house, right down to the statues in the walls and the staircase! A miracle, truly. I've written her, and she's written back. It is all arranged." She laid a hand on top of her mother's. "It won't be forever, but this is what I need to do now. I want to help heal… everyone. Knit this country and this world back together, through love."

"What about Werner?" Johanna asked shakily. "If he comes back—"

"He won't come back," Birgit stated quietly. She touched her chest. "I feel it in here. I know."

"Don't say that." If Werner wasn't coming back, there surely wasn't any hope for Franz, as a Jew. And yet still, despite everything, despite telling herself so many times he had to be dead, Johanna knew she still hoped. She had to.

*

A week later Johanna accompanied Birgit to the train station. Hedwig had stayed home with Manfred and Mimi, but they'd said their farewells already, embracing tightly.

"I'll be back, Mama, I promise."

"And so you'd better," Hedwig answered with an attempt at a smile.

As Johanna waved her sister off onto the train, a fresh sorrow twisted inside her. Birgit had something to look forward to, to live for, but what about her? As thankful as she was for little Mimi's presence in their lives, everything else felt like an ending. Her father's health was continuing to fail, and her mother, despite her stolid strength, was, in some ways, a broken woman. Johanna's job working for the occupying forces wouldn't last forever, and what then? How would this world go on, change and grow and strengthen? What future could she look forward to, or offer to Mimi?

These questions were still circling Johanna's mind as she walked slowly back towards home, her steps slowing as she walked down Getreidegasse, as familiar as ever, devoid of the swastika banners that had bedecked it for seven years. She had taken the afternoon off from work to say goodbye to Birgit, but right then she almost wanted the busyness of typing and filing to distract her from this new, unwelcome grief and uncertainty. What could the future hold for any of them now? She had to believe something could be built out of the ruin, but she did not know what it was.

Then, a voice, both ragged and sure.

"Johanna."

She stilled, the hope that had continued to smolder like an ember in the ashes of her heart flaring suddenly and hotly to life. *It couldn't be… she was dreaming, fantasizing, and yet… It had to be…*

She looked up, and there he was, standing by the shopfront, under the warped and weathered sign that proclaimed *Eder Clockmaking*, with its sprig of white-and-yellow edelweiss.

He was as tall and rangy as ever, although painfully thin. His hair was so short, little more than a stubbly scrub, and now held far more gray than brown. He wore ill-fitting clothes—a ragged peasant's blouse and loose-fitting trousers tied with a bit of rope—and the gauntness of his face made her want to cry, even as her heart filled with joy.

Franz.

Slowly, each step like a dream, she walked towards him. "I thought… I thought you were dead—"

"Sometimes I felt as if I was."

"But it's been months! Where have you been?" Not that it mattered now, but Johanna's mind was spinning. She could barely take the sight of him in, the actual reality of his being. *He was alive. He was actually alive.*

"I was left in the camp when it was liberated," Franz explained with a crooked smile she remembered so well. "I was ill… so ill. I couldn't even walk… I barely knew my own name." He shook his head, that old wryness glinting in his eyes. "When I was released from hospital, they put me in one of the camps for displaced persons. I'd told them I was from Vienna, but there has been no reliable communication from there, what with the Red Army. Eventually they discovered my family…" He shook his head slowly. "They're all dead, even my cousins, aunts and uncle. Everyone. In Auschwitz."

"Oh, Franz…" She knew there was nothing more she could say.

He nodded, accepting, stoic in the face of yet more grief. "It took months for them to process the paperwork, and then allow me to leave the camp so I could come here. And so here I am." He spread his hands wide and with a trembling laugh Johanna rushed into his arms.

"I can't believe it…" She felt too dazed either to weep or laugh. Franz's arms closed around her, sharp and thin and wonderful.

"I'm not the same," he said quietly, like a warning, and Johanna pulled back to look fiercely up into his face.

"Don't you dare, Franz Weber! Don't you *dare.* I won't listen to any excuses now. I've waited and waited for you, and I'm practically an old woman!"

Franz gave her a small smile, although there was a hauntedness to his gaunt features that she longed to wipe away. Perhaps time could. "You're only thirty—"

"Thirty-*one.* You will marry me as soon as possible," she informed him with mock sternness, her voice trembling with emotion, "or else!"

He laughed then, a rusty sound, and gathered her up into his arms. Johanna pressed against him, wrapping her arms even more tightly around him. "If you really do still want me?"

"Of course I do! What a foolish question to ask."

"There are other questions I should have asked before," Franz said soberly. "What of Birgit? Lotte?"

Johanna shook her head, and then told him what she knew—Birgit, Lotte, Mimi.

"A baby," he marveled. "Something new and good out of all this."

"You don't mind?" Johanna asked. "What with Birgit in Bloemendaal… I thought I—we, now—could raise her as our own."

"I'd be honored to."

She put her arms around him again, her heart so very full. "A family," she said softly. Franz nodded, holding her tightly. "And what of Werner?" she asked after a moment, although somehow, like Birgit, she already knew.

"Shot by a guard in the last days. He was trying to help some of us who were destined for the gas chamber to escape. He gave his life, Johanna. He was a much better and braver man than I ever realized."

"God rest his soul." Johanna rested her cheek against Franz's bony shoulder. She could hardly believe he was here; she felt the need to squeeze him, to make sure he was actually in her arms, alive and whole. He wouldn't disappear like the dream he still seemed. "I'm so happy," she said after a moment, her tone wondering. "I've forgotten what that feels like."

"God willing you'll have many opportunities to feel it again." Franz hugged her to him. "I will make sure of it, starting with Paris."

"*Paris*—" Johanna laughed and shook her head.

"One day, I will take you," Franz promised her.

"I know you will." She believed it then, just as she believed in their own future, could see it shimmering in front of them, finally in reach. "And I know I will be happy," she stated with firm decision. Happiness was a precious treasure, but it was also a choice, one she would make every day—for Lotte's sake, for Werner's, for Ingrid's and Kunigunde's and everyone who had laid down their lives so that they in turn could live—and love. "I will," she said again, and taking Franz's hand, she led him into the house on Getreidegasse, and up the stairs to home.

A LETTER FROM KATE

Dear reader,

I want to say a huge thank you for choosing to read *The Edelweiss Sisters*. If you did enjoy it, and want to keep up to date with all my latest releases, just sign up at the following link. Your email address will never be shared and you can unsubscribe at any time.

www.bookouture.com/kate-hewitt

I have my lovely editor Isobel to thank for suggesting I write a story of three sisters in Salzburg. All I knew of Salzburg was from *The Sound of Music* and a brief trip there in my teens, so it was fascinating to delve into the research and discover how different Austria was to Germany in many ways.

While the Eder sisters are fictional, there are some real-life characters in the book—namely Maria von Trapp, Virgilia Lutz, the Mother Abbess of Nonnberg, and Corrie and Betsie ten Boom. The von Trapps' first public concert was indeed at the Elektrischer Aufzug in 1934, and Betsie ten Boom did spend some time in the infirmary at Ravensbrück, where she shared her dream of a house where all those damaged by the war could recover and heal. The accounts of Ravensbrück are inspired by Corrie ten Boom's memoirs, including the wonderful *The Hiding Place*. There is no evidence that Nonnberg Abbey was involved in any resistance activities (despite the scene at the end of *The Sound of Music*, where the nuns assist the von Trapps!) but knowing what I have learned about Virgilia Lutz, I like to think the nuns there were involved.

I hope you loved *The Edelweiss Sisters* and if you did I would be very grateful if you could write a review. I'd love to hear what you think, and it makes such a difference helping new readers to discover one of my books for the first time.

I love hearing from my readers—you can get in touch on my Facebook page, through Twitter, Goodreads or my website.

Thanks,
Kate

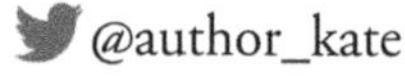

ACKNOWLEDGMENTS

First and foremost I must thank my editor Isobel, who gave me the germ of the idea for *The Edelweiss Sisters*, and set fire to my imagination! This book would have never come into being without her. Thank you, Isobel, for entrusting me with your idea. I'd also like to thank everyone at Bookouture who helps to bring my books out into the world—Peta, Kim and Sarah in publicity, Alex and Hannah in digital marketing, Radhika and Alex in editorial, Alba in audio, and Therese, Saidah, and Laura who have kept me up to date on the business side of things.

Thanks also must go to my friend Jenna, who always listens to me ruminate and asks if I've made my word count, and to all the lovely Bookouture authors in the Lounge who are so supportive.

Finally I'd like to thank my family—Cliff, Caroline, Ellen, Teddy, Anna and Charlotte. We've spent a lot of time together in lockdown, played a lot of Mario Kart and cards and gone on a lot of dog walks. I love you all, and am very grateful for all the time we've had, even if it sometimes drove us all just a little bit crazy. Love you!

CPSIA information can be obtained
at www.ICGtesting.com
Printed in the USA
LVHW091300040222
710271LV00012B/86